Thomas Carlyle, Charles Eliot Norton

Early Letters of Thomas Carlyle

1814-1826

Thomas Carlyle, Charles Eliot Norton

Early Letters of Thomas Carlyle
1814-1826

ISBN/EAN: 9783744764346

Printed in Europe, USA, Canada, Australia, Japan

Cover: Foto ©Andreas Hilbeck / pixelio.de

More available books at **www.hansebooks.com**

LETTERS

OF

THOMAS CARLYLE

Mrs Carlyle.

OF

THOMAS CARLYLE

EDITED BY

CHARLES ELIOT NORTON

1814—1826

London

MACMILLAN AND CO.

AND NEW YORK

1886

PREFACE

Mr. Carlyle was for many years, especially during his early manhood, an industrious letter-writer. A great many of his letters have been preserved and are in the possession of his niece, Mrs. Alexander Carlyle. It is at her desire that I have undertaken to edit a selection of them.

" Express biography of me I had really rather that there should be none," said Carlyle in his Will, and a biography of him, correct at least if meagre, might perhaps have been gathered from his letters, his *Reminiscences*,[1] and the *Memorials of Jane Welsh Carlyle*.[2] Mr. Froude, however, thought otherwise, and has given to the public an "express biography" of him. The view of Mr. Carlyle's character presented in this biography has not approved itself to many of those who knew Carlyle best. It may be a striking picture, but it is not a good portrait.

For the present, at least, it appears impracticable to prepare another formal biography. The peculiar style of Mr. Froude's performance, already in possession of the field, might perhaps put a portrait of Carlyle drawn by a hand more faithful to nature, and less skilled in fine artifices than his own, at a temporary disadvantage with the bulk of readers. But it has seemed right to print some of Carlyle's letters in suchwise that with his *Reminiscences* they might serve as a partial autobiography, and illustrate his character

---

[1] *Reminiscences, etc.*, edited by J. A. Froude, 2 vols. London, 1881.

[2] *Letters and Memorials of Jane Welsh Carlyle.* London, 1883.

by unquestionable evidence. They do not indeed afford a complete portrait; but so far as they go the lines will be correct.

The earliest letters of Carlyle that are known to exist are those which he wrote in 1814 and the three or four following years, while he was at Annan, Edinburgh, and Kirkcaldy. He seldom let a week pass without sending a letter home; not infrequently he wrote three or even four to different members of his family on the same day. I have printed a large number of these letters in spite of the sameness in their tone and topics, because of the light they throw upon Carlyle's character during an important period in his intellectual growth, and also because they are of more than personal interest from the striking illustration they afford of the simpler side of Scottish life.

Carlyle's chief correspondents, outside his own family, during the first years after his leaving the University, were three college friends, James Johnstone, Robert Mitchell, and Thomas Murray.

Carlyle, in his later years, writing of Johnstone, says, " He was six or seven years my elder, but very fond of discoursing with me, and much my companion while we were in Annandale together within reach. A poor and not a very gifted man, but a faithful, diligent, and accurate; of quietly pious, candid, pure character,—and very much attached to me. In return I liked him honestly well; learnt something from him (the always diligently *exact* in book-matters); perhaps ultimately taught him something; and had great satisfaction in his company (in the years 1814-16, and occasionally afterwards)." Mainly through the efforts of Miss Welsh (made for Carlyle's sake), he was in 1826 appointed Parish Schoolmaster at Haddington, where, towards the end of 1837, he died.

Mitchell was an Annandale man, who upon leaving college had looked forward to becoming a minister in the Scotch Kirk; but, like Carlyle, he soon gave up this outlook, and he became and remained a schoolmaster. He was for some years tutor in the family of the Rev. Henry Duncan, of Ruthwell, Dumfriesshire, was afterwards Rector of the Grammar School at Kirkcudbright, and latterly one of the masters of the Edinburgh Academy. Carlyle notes in his journal, 1st August 1836 : " Poor R. Mitchell dead, and buried with public funeral, Calton Hill, Edinburgh ; many sad thoughts I had sent towards him, but in silence."

Thomas Murray was a cheery, kindly youth. He became a minister, wrote a respectable literary history of Galloway, his native county, was for a time editor of the *Edinburgh Weekly Chronicle*, and lived to a good old age.

Still more interesting than these letters would have been Carlyle's letters to Edward Irving, but it is believed that they were destroyed after Irving's death.

As to what use I might be justified in making of another series of letters at my disposal, those from Carlyle to Miss Welsh from their first acquaintance in 1821 until their marriage in 1826, I have felt grave doubts. The letters of lovers are sacred confidences, whose sanctity none ought to violate. Mr. Froude's use of these letters seems to me, on general grounds, unjustifiable, and the motives he alleges for it inadequate. But Carlyle himself had strictly forbidden their printing. When he was editing the *Letters and Memorials of Jane Welsh Carlyle*, of her letters to him, and of his to her, which were written before their marriage, only one short note from Miss Welsh, dated 3d September 1825, printed by Mr. Froude (*Life*,[1] i. 308, 309), could be found ; the rest were missing. To the copy of this short note Carlyle appends the words, " In pencil all but the address. Original strangely saved ; and found accidentally in one of the presses to-day. HER note, when put down by the coach, on that visit to us at Hoddam Hill in September 1825 ! How mournful now,

---

[1] *Thomas Carlyle : A History of the First Forty Years of his Life*, by J. A. Froude. London, 1882.

how beautiful and strange !   A relic to me priceless (T. C.,
12th March 1868)."   As to the then missing Letters
written before their marriage, his and Miss Welsh's,
Carlyle, in the original manuscript from which the copy
given to Mr. Froude was made, says, " My strict command
now is, ' Burn them, if ever found.   Let no third party
read them ; let no *printing* of them, or of any part of
them, be ever thought of by those who love me !' "

I decided not to open the parcels containing these
letters.   But I was gradually led by many facts to the
conviction that Mr. Froude had distorted their significance,
and had given a view of the relations between Carlyle and
his future wife, in essential respects incorrect and injurious
to their memory.   I therefore felt obliged to read these
letters, which I have done with extreme reluctance, and
with reverential respect for the sacredness of their contents.
The conviction which determined me to read them was
confirmed by the perusal.   The question then arose whether
further publication of them was justifiable for the sake of
correcting the view presented by Mr. Froude.   The answer
seemed plain, that only such of these letters, or such
portions of them, as had not any specifically private character could rightly be printed.   I have therefore printed
comparatively few of Carlyle's letters to Miss Welsh, while,
in an Appendix, I have tried to set right some of the
facts misrepresented by Mr. Froude, and to show his
method of dealing with his materials.

CHARLES ELIOT NORTON.

CAMBRIDGE, MASSACHUSETTS,
    July 1886.

MEMBERS OF CARLYLE'S FAMILY.

JAMES CARLYLE (born at Brownknowe, near Ecclefechan, August
1758 ; died at Scotsbrig, 22d January 1832) married, 5th March
1795, MARGARET AITKEN (born at Whitestanes, Kirkmahoe,
Dumfriesshire, 30th September 1771 ; died at Scotsbrig, 25th
December 1853).

The following is a List of their Children :—

THOMAS, born 4th December 1795 ; died at Chelsea 5th February 1881.
ALEXANDER, born 4th August 1797 ; died in Canada 30th March 1876.
JANET, born 2d September 1799 ; died 8th February 1801.
JOHN AITKEN, born 7th July 1801 ; died at Dumfries 15th September 1879.
MARGARET, born 20th September 1803; died 22d June 1830.
JAMES, born 12th November 1805.
MARY, born 2d February 1808.
JANE, born 2d September 1810.
JANET, born 18th July 1813.

These still survive (July 1886).

LETTERS OF THOMAS CARLYLE

I.—To Mr. Thomas Carlyle, Edinburgh.

From his Father.[1]

Ecclefechan, *27th April* 1814.

Dear Sir—I received yours yesterday, and was very glad to hear that you were well and was teaching, for we did not know what to do, whether you were coming home or going to stop at Edinburgh; the reason of me not writing last time the Carrier came out—Sandy[2] was summoned about Dr. Thom's Mob; he was libelled with thirteen pages of paper written about the business. Dr. Henderson and Tom Minto were likewise summoned, and Peggy Kerr; there being no proof against Sandy he of course was discharged from the Bar. Dr. Henderson was fined £20 and one month's imprisonment; Minto, £10 and two weeks' imprisonment; Peggy Kerr, £5. We were all in confusion on Saturday getting witnesses to prove Sandy not guilty, and after all our labour the witnesses would not do without your Mother was there also; then she had to get ready for setting off on Monday, which she did with great difficulty, having to take Jenny and Peggy with her. You may think whether that would put us past writing or not. The Carrier is for coming off on Monday; but I thought that would not do for you [which] caused me to write this in the meantime and enclose this, and I

---

[1] This letter is apparently the earliest that has been preserved of the long correspondence between Carlyle and his family. [My Father] "wrote to me duly and affectionately while I was at college. Nothing that was good for me did he fail with his best ability to provide."—*Reminiscences*, i. 58.

[2] Carlyle's next younger brother. What "Dr. Thom's Mob" was, and what share, if any, the boy Sandy had in it, there is now no telling.

B

will send your things with the Carrier.   In the meantime
I think these two guineas will clear you.   As I am in
haste I will add no more at present.   Mention in your
next if you got the Single Note with the Box, etc.

JAS. CARLYLE.

II.—To Mr. ROBERT MITCHELL, Linlithgow.

EDINBURGH, 30th April 1814.

DEAR MITCHELL—You are perhaps thinking by this
time that I am slow in answering your long-solicited letter;
and before going further, I must beg pardon, and plead the
trite excuses of business, indolence, etc. etc.—and let me
tell you, you have been such a notorious offender in that
way yourself, you can't have the impudence to make any
complaints.

Were I disposed to moralise, there is before me the
finest field that ever opened to the eye of mortal man.
Nap the mighty, who, but a few months ago, made the
sovereigns of Europe tremble at his nod ; who has trampled
on thrones and sceptres, and kings and priests, and princi-
palities and powers, and carried ruin and havoc and blood
and fire from Gibraltar to Archangel—*Nap the mighty* is
—GONE TO POT ! ! !

" I will plant my eagles on the towers of Lisbon.   I will
conquer Europe and crush Great Britain to the centre of
the terraqueous globe."   I will go to Elba *and be coop'd up*
in Limbo ! ! !   But yesterday, and *Boney* might have stood
against the world ; now " none so poor to do him rev'rence."
" Strange," says Sancho Panza, " very strange things happen
in the boiling of an egg."   All those fine things, however,
and twenty thousand others have been thought and said
by everybody who thinks or speaks upon the subject—
and so I leave them.

Having got out of this rhapsody, I now proceed to consider the contents of your letter.   It gives me the sincerest
sorrow, that you *did not* accomplish that redoubtable undertaking in which you were engaged.[1]   There is a real

---

[1] Mitchell, in his letter (from Linlithgow, 9th April) to which this is an
answer, had written as follows.   The passage is characteristic, and shows
his liveliness of spirit and his studious bent : " For three or four days I was

pleasure attends those same castles which all of us so often build, and though, "like the baseless fabric of a vision," they must "all dissolve and leave not a rack behind," still there is enjoyment while the illusion lasts. The trisection of an angle by simple geometry is a complete *wild-goose chase*, at any rate, and in it disappointments must be *relied on*. Still your achievement (even had it come that length) was but like the drop in the bucket to some of *my projected* exploits. 'Twas but the other day, for instance, that I had got into a sure and expeditious way of boring a hole, right, slap, souse down through the centre of the earth we inhabit, and receiving point blank the productions of New Zealand and the South Sea!!!!

As I will be in Edinburgh at least *part* of the summer, I cannot but highly approve of the plan you proposed of sending our essays to be remarked on by each other. It is impossible that it *could* do any *harm :* and since it would afford a very useful exercise *at least*, it would, I am convinced, be a very profitable way of carrying on our correspondence. I shall expect, therefore, in a few days to receive, per Carrier, a paper of yours to peruse, and directions how to proceed, with regard to time, etc. etc. Don't be particular as to the choice of a subject—*any* will do. It is very likely that I may send you some Mathematical thing or other, seeing I have got Bossut's *History of Mathematics* at this time, where perhaps there may be something new to you ;—and again, I stumbled the other night upon a kind of a new demonstration of Pythagoras' *square of the hypotenuse ;* and if you don't find it yourself (most likely you will), I will send you it too. We need be at no loss for subjects, literary, metaphysical, mathematical, and physical are all

idle ; but idleness is the inlet to every mischief. The wildest notion that ever entered into mortal man's brain took such possession of my poor cranium that I believe it was as effectually deranged by Leslie's *Geometry* as ever the valiant Knight of La Mancha's by Amadis de Gaul. In short, I believed it was destined for me to solve the problem of the trisection of an angle. I'll not tell you how many solar revolutions were performed whilst I was possessed with this Mathematical frenzy. Need I tell you how long after midnight I watched my armour of scale and compasses,—how often I believed that I had wrought the doughty deed, and secured to myself the applause of a wondering world? Truly I might be denominated the Knight of the Rueful Countenance, when I returned to curse the hour in which I undertook the desperate enterprise. I am now content to read Sharp's *Sermons*, the *Border Minstrel*, and even the *Confession of Faith !*"

before us. I am sure this would be a very good way of spending part of the summer ; and you who are the *projector* will surely never draw back from what you yourself proposed, and therefore *will not fail* to send me your production the very next opportunity.

Firmly had I resolved, on the faith of your recommendation, to read *Thaddeus*,[1] and you may believe me, when I declare that it was not for want of exertion on my part that I have not seen it yet. The truth is, I am acquainted only in one circulating library, and there *Thaddeus* has always been "out." Getting a book from a strange library is a little troublesome, and thus expecting every day to get it from that where I am known, I made no effort elsewhere. However, I *will* have it read, *if possible*, before I address you again—which, if you stick to promises, will not be long.

By the way, you have heard of Dr. John Leyden,[2] the unfortunate author of *Scenes of Infancy*, etc. from (I believe) Roxburghshire, who went to India and met an untimely end.

> Leyden, a shepherd wails thy fate,
> And Scotland knows her loss too late.—HOGG.

Well, if I am not much deceived, you will thank me for transcribing the following poem of his, composed on (Wellington, then) Wellesley's victory at Assaye, while Leyden was in India. I met with it in *The Spy*, a kind of periodical thing published the other year in Edinburgh.

> Shout, Britons, for the battle of Assaye ;
>   For that was a day,
>   When we stood in our array,
>   Like the Lion's might at bay ;
> And our battle-word was Conquer or Die.
>
> Rouse, rouse the cruel leopard from his lair,
>   With his yell the mountain rings ;
>   And his red eye round he flings,
>   As arrow-like he springs,
> And spreads his clutching paw to rend and tear.

---

[1] Miss Jane Porter's high-flown romance of *Thaddeus of Warsaw*, published in 1803, but still, in 1814, much admired by young people.

[2] Leyden died in 1811 ; his memory is kept alive by Scott's sympathetic biography of him—one of those biographical sketches which give a high impression alike of its subject and its author.

> Then first array'd in battle front we saw,
>   Far as the eye could glance,
>   The Mahratta banners dance,
>   O'er the desolate expanse,
> And their standard was the leopard of Malwa.
>
> But when we first encountered man to man,
>   Such odds came never on
>   Against Greece at Marathon
>   When they shook the Persian throne,
> 'Mid the old barbaric pomp of Ispahan.
>
> No number'd might of living men could tame
>   Our gallant band that broke
>   Through the bursting clouds of smoke,
>   When the vollied thunder spoke,
> From a thousand mouldering mouths of lurid flame.
>
>   .   .   .   .
>
> Shout, Britons, for the battle of Assaye ;
>   Ye who perished in your prime,
>   Your hallowed names sublime,
>   Shall live to ceaseless time,
> Your heroic worth and fame shall never die.

Can anything be grander? what *fire !* what *energy !* If there is anything in existence that surpasses this, it must be Hohenlinden—but what is like Hohenlinden? Tell me in your next what you think of this piece. Is not, think you, "From a thousand *mouldering* mouths of lurid flame" misprinted somehow? Would "smouldering" do any better? . . .

Do not neglect to write to me *immediately*, and send me your essay—no matter what about. Tell me too, how you come on in your sermon ; mine ("good easy man") is not *begun*, and I don't know when it will—but I have a long year before me, till it be required.

I have thus, my dear Bob, sent you a sheet filled with very close and small letters, as you desired, and whether there be anything in it or no, still it is full. Pay me *directly*, I repeat it. Meantime I am, till I hear from you, my dear sir, yours truly,   THOMAS CARLYLE.

Have you read Shakespear? If you have not, then I desire you, read it directly, and tell me what you think of him—which is his masterpiece. He is always excellent.

The following passage from Carlyle's *Reminiscences*, vol.

i. p. 89, illustrates the preceding letter and those which immediately follow :—

"It was now the winter of 1815. I had myself been in Edinburgh College ; and above a year ago had duly quitted it ; had got (by competition at Dumfries, summer 1814) to be 'Mathematical Master' in Annan Academy, with some potential outlook on Divinity as ultimatum (a rural 'Divinity Student' visiting Edinburgh for a few days each year, and 'delivering' certain 'discourses'). Six years of that would bring you to the church-*gate*, as four years of continuous 'Divinity Hall' would ; unlucky only that, in my case, I had never had the least enthusiasm for the business (and there were even grave prohibitive doubts more and more rising ahead) : both branches of my situation flatly contradictory to all ideals or wishes of mine ; especially the Annan one, as the closely actual and the daily and hourly pressing on me, while the other lay theoretic, still well ahead, and perhaps avoidable. One attraction, one only, there was in my Annan business. I was supporting myself (even saving some few pounds of my poor £60 or £70 annually, against a rainy day), and not a burden to my ever-generous father any more ; but in all other points of view I was abundantly lonesome, uncomfortable, and out of place there ; . . . in short, thoroughly detested my function and position, though understood to be honestly doing the duties of it ; and held for solacement and company to the few books I could command, and an accidental friend or two I had in the neighbourhood (Mr. Church and his wife, of Hitchill ; Rev. Henry Duncan, of Ruthwell, and ditto ; these were the two bright and brightest houses for me. My thanks to them, now and always!) As to my schoolmaster function, it was never said that I *misdid* it much ('a clear and correct' expositor and enforcer) ; but from the first, especially with such adjuncts, I disliked it, and by swift degrees grew to hate it more and more. Some four years in all I had of it ; two in Annan, two in Kirkcaldy (under much improved social accompaniments) ; and at the end, my solitary desperate conclusion was fixed, That I, for my own part, would prefer to perish in the ditch, if necessary, rather than continue living by such a trade :—and peremptorily gave it up accordingly."

III.—To Mr. Robert Mitchell, Linlithgow.

Mount Annan, 18*th October* 1814.

My dear Mitchell.—When I look at the date of your last elegant and endearing letter, I feel a throb of something approaching to *remorse* for the suspicion of ingratitude and inconstancy which you (if you thought of me at all) must have entertained of me, for my apparently unaccountable neglect of a correspondence which I had been the first to solicit, and the most eager to cultivate. I hope, however, that when you shall have heard "the story of my woes"—that is, my history for the last four months, you will be ready to grant me your forgiveness, and to receive me once more into your good graces.

Some three or four days after I received your lucubrations, an advertisement appeared in the newspapers for a Mathematical Teacher in the Annan Academy;—the place is worth about £70 a year—and is respectable enough; my friends, therefore, were anxious for my becoming a candidate. Having been favoured with a letter of recommendation from Mr. Leslie,[1] I *did* apply, and was informed that the candidates must undergo a comparative trial at Dumfries in the course of a few days, and that, in course, I must repair thither. Not to detain you with all the tribulations and heart-burnings I went through, it will be sufficient to inform you that I and another man having been examined by Mr. White,[2] I was preferred, and told I must enter on my office *next day*. This, you see, was quick work—but you have not heard all. General Dirom came to reside at Mount Annan towards the end of June, and two of his boys, learning Greek, Latin, and Mathematics, were consigned to my care. You can conceive the hurry and trepidation attendant upon obtaining and entering upon a new situation. You can conceive me just thinking of a subject for a *reverie* for *your* perusal, and a new engagement knocking all my *reveries* on the head, and telling me that for four months I must lead the life of a *Mill-horse*—you can conceive all this, and can you help pardoning me? The truth is, scarcely a day these three months has passed over my head, but I have reproached myself for ingratitude to my friend, to the companion of my studies, my speculations and *perpendings* (sweet *bygane times!*); and, strange as it may seem, every day I have again *put off*. "Procrastination is the thief of time," and I am persuaded that nothing but the fear of your quitting my correspondence in disgust could have *aroused me*. I have at length *determined*, "though it were when I should

---

[1] The eminent John Leslie, Professor of Mathematics in the University of Edinburgh.

[2] Thomas White, Rector of the Academy at Dumfries, an excellent mathematician.

sleep," to write you—and here am I scribbling away at midnight your most humble servant.

My dear Mitchell, I entreat you to *sustain* this excuse, for indeed none of the circumstances are exaggerated,— and to rest assured that the friendship of a son of genius, of similar pursuits, of kindred sentiments, and congenial spirit with myself, is too highly prized to be even apparently neglected, except upon the most imperious necessity. Believe me I shall be most unhappy if this excuse don't satisfy you, and will come under any terms rather than forfeit my right to a letter *directly*. After this long preamble you are not to expect that I, all *jaded* as I am, can even attempt to *amuse* you this bout, but, my dear Boy, send me a letter informing me that you are reconciled, and I'll warrant you receive a letter full of *quirk* and *oddity*, covered thick and threefold with mirth—*humour*—WIT, and the several other appendages requisite for forming an unexceptionable *morçeau d'eloquence et d'esprit :* but at present 'tis out of the question to expect anything more spirited than a *last will*, or more witty than a *Methodist tract.*   But let me get forward as I may.

In seriousness your Mathematical investigations are excellent.   Your demonstration of the property of the circle is really neat (I at least should think so, for on reading your enunciation I set to work and brought out a demonstration of the property, which I was both disappointed and pleased to find the SAME AS YOURS) : but it is the trisection of the arc that I *admire ;* it is indeed *acutely* and *beautifully* handled. " But thereby hangs a tale."   I did not tell you that when I left Edinburgh for Dumfries I put your paper in my pocket—and whilst my right worthy *compagnons de voyage* (for I came in the Maii from Moffat) were sunk in politics, post-horses, farming, etc., I took out my friend's theorem, and leaving the base clod-hoppers to welter on among drains and dunghills and bullocks and balances of power, I entered Dumfries *wholly disengaged from sublunary things ;* and well-nigh persuaded that an angle *might* be trisected.   I went next morning to breakfast with Mr. White, and in the course of our conversation, happening to mention the trisection of an angle, " I have in my pocket," said I, " the result of an ingenious young friend and fellow-student's attempts on that subject. 'Tis here." Mr. W. had no sooner cast his eye upon your diagram than, starting up and uttering a wildly-accented "aye!!" he left the room. He soon dissipated the mystery by returning with an armful of dun aged manuscripts; he desired me to look at one of them, and I *was* surprised to see *the same property*. He complained bitterly that *Mr. Leslie had showed it you* and never mentioned *his* name! I assured him that it was an original on your part; but in vain. "'Tis *impossible!*" was his reply: I could not but feel rather vain, that I had a friend who had found out properties of which a veteran like White was proud.

By the way, could not we, think you, contrive to continue this mode of interchanging our lucubrations? 'Tis a project I like vastly, and from which I had promised myself much instruction, as well as entertainment. I have on hand (I should rather say *in head*) an explanation of the *rainbow*, together with some other *bagatelles* which I could send you—if I could think of any mode of conveyance. Could you devise no plan of regular communication? In Winter, at least, they could be conveyed to and from Edinburgh, *free of expense*, in some honest student's box. Let me have your ideas on the subject. Our college comrades, honest *Davie*, and the *son of cat-gut*—where are they? I had a hint, and only a hint, that Davie had beaten his *forceps* into *pitch-forks*,—and his *scalpels* into *pruning-hooks*—that is to say—had commenced plough-man. Pray tell me is it true? And has Andrew quitted Corstorphine?

.   .   .   .   .   .

What Books have you been perusing? and how did you like Shakespeare? Since I saw you I have toiled through many a thick octavo—many of them to little purpose. Byron's and Scott's *Poems* [I have read] and must admire, —though you recollect, *we* used to give Campbell a decided preference, and I still think, with justice. Have you ever seen Hoole's *Tasso?* I have among many others read, *it*, *Leonidas*, the *Epigoniad*,[1] *Oberon*,[2] Savage's *Poems*, etc.

[1] A happily-forgotten Epic by a Scotchman, Dr. William Wilkie. Hume professed great admiration for it, and Carlyle may have read it as a patriotic duty.   [2] Doubtless Sotheby's version of Wieland's *Oberon*.

Miss Porter's *Scottish Chiefs* and *Waverley* have been the principal of my Novels. With regard to *Waverley*[1] I cannot help remarking that in my opinion it is the best novel that has been published these thirty years. The characters of Ebenezer Cruickshanks mine host of the Garter,[2] the Reverend Mr. Goukthrapple and Squire Bradwardine display a Cervantic vein of humour which has seldom been surpassed—whilst the descriptions of the gloomy caverns of the Highlands, and the delineations of the apathic Callum Beg and enterprising Vich Ian Vohr, show a richness of Scottean colouring which few have equalled. Give me your opinion of it if you have read it;—and if not— endeavour by all means to procure it.

My sermon *is* pretty much in the same style as yours *was* at the date of your last letter—with this difference— I don't know quite so well in what part of the Bible it is. My sentiments on the Clerical profession are like yours, mostly of the unfavourable kind. Where would be the harm, should we both stop? "The best concerted schemes o' mice an' men gang aft aglee!" I intended to have said something of the bigoted scepticism of Hume—but as I am convinced you see through his specious sophisms and detect his blind *prejudice* in *favour* of infidelity, I shall defer it. At any rate I have not room, and therefore *must* wait.

Now, my dear Bob, let me see you behave as you ought, and send me a long letter, and I promise it *shall* be answered punctually if I keep my health. In sooth, I shall expect an answer to this *Chaos* of a letter (which hurry, etc., and your good-nature will excuse) within fourteen days from the date hereof; so be punctual.

Pray do write me directly an account of all your transactions, adventures, misfortunes, loves, and hates. I am close upon the bottom of my sheet, otherwise I would say some *fine thing* on the "Charms of Friendship;" but I trust, my dear Mitchell, *we can both feel* the joys arising from the commerce of kindred sentiments and congenial minds.

---

[1] *Waverley* was published in 1814.

[2] Not of the "Garter," but of the "Seven-Branched Golden Candlestick."

Direct to me at Annan Academy—*quick.*

Need I add how sincerely I am, my dear Mit., yours,

THOMAS CARLYLE.

IV.—To Mr. ROBERT MITCHELL, Ruthwell Manse.

MOUNT ANNAN, *24th October* 1814.

MY DEAR MITCHELL — Nothing could exceed my pleasure at receiving your obliging and entertaining, though laconic epistle. I hope, however, I need not tell you that the *foolishness* of your letter was not the cause of my long silence. You should know enough of me by this time, to be aware that your letter was altogether according to my heart and fancy,—and accordingly I had, the other day, written a right dolorous and woe-be-gone memorial, in which I humbly showed, that I had been over head and ears in business—that adventures and misventures and trials and tribulations had so crowded upon me that my sap and substance was evaporated ; I represented—but what matters what I represented—since with all its stains and blotches on it you will assuredly see it—after it shall have performed *the tour of Scotland,* for (O luckless man !) it was sent off to Linlithgow last Wednesday, exactly the day before I heard from Little Johnson (Corrie) that you had come to Ruthwell! "Say shall thine anger then abate, upon consideration of egregious ink-shed?" . . .

So Andrew is still at Gogar. I join right heartily in your short but fervent petition for his consolation. Davie and I, after convoying [you] that day on your way to Lithgow—struck across the fields and paid him a visit, and after considerable trouble were admitted into his *grotto* or *cavern* or CRUI.[1] The most considerable of his movables were a chair wanting a back, a joint-stool, eight potatoes, and *a pot of brimstone :* but to give you any idea of the situation and contours of this den,—to represent to you the stern and doughty appearance of its innocent inhabitant, —much more to make you *sensible* of the "*rancorous* compound of villainous smells" that on all sides "offended nostril," is impossible. The *tout-ensemble* was dank and dreary, and

[1] Sty, hog-pen.

> Dark as was Chaos e're the infant Sun was roll'd together,
> Or had tried his beams athwart the gloom profound.

And yet Andrew, good easy man! shrugging up his shoulders, told us "*he was living like the ancients.*" With all his oddity he is a good, honest lad. And Davie too! Well, peace be with ye, good kind-hearted souls!

Clint, poor man, hath taken unto himself a wife, and at this time sojourneth in the ancient burgh of Lochmaben. Hill is at Middlebie, *in statu quo;* and James Johnstone is lately returned from the Selkirk hall. Alas! poor creatures, we are all dispersing towards the four winds of heaven—and embarking on life's wide ocean—and how shall we each steer his little bark through all the shoals and hurricanes that lie before us, where so many stately Gallies have foundered on the passage! 'Tis a bleak look-out, my dear Mit.—but though the greasy *sons of pudding* may pass us by with all the *conscious dignity* of beings of a higher and a *fatter* order, yet however humble be our lot, 'tis comfortable to think that—

> Justum et tenacem propositi virum,
> Non civium ardor prava jubentium,
> Non vultus instantis tyranni
> Mente quatit solida . . .
> Si fractus illabatur orbis
> Impavidum ferient ruinæ.

But truce! whither am I running? let us quit moralising.

If ever you receive that 'foresaid stray-epistle you will see that even while I thought you at Linlithgow, I had not quitted the plan of interchanging the results of our speculations,—and you may easily imagine, I will not relinquish my expectations of your concurrence with my proposals now that you are within seven miles of me. In truth, I think it could not fail of being advantageous and entertaining to us both. What do *you* think of it? Have you any articles of the *spin-brain* manufacture by you at present? For *me*, poor soul, I have been kept like unto a cock-on-a-spit these four months, with hardly time to breathe, much less to *think*. Take an instance,—I am at this present—cold stormy midnight—*scratching* and writing what I at times think *you* will consider a letter—with a *nose*, saving the mark, I daresay as blue as indigo, and I *do* say as cold as an icicle,—with the consoling reflection, however, that when I *do* get to bed I shall not be disturbed till six in the morning. How can I *think?* But let not this interrupt *your* communications; General Dirom will be away in the course of four weeks or so, and then I shall have more time.

Mr. Duncan left Mount Annan this morning; and having invited me to Ruthwell Manse—you may expect to see me in the course of a week or two some Saturday afternoon, when, my dear Bob, we shall talk over our *bygane days o' auld lang syne*, and perhaps have another bout at PER-PENDING. Tuesday must bring me a letter brimful of all things—or else—for now *you* are in *my* debt. Let me have all your theories and trials and temptations and hypotheses. Are you disengaged on Saturdays? for if I should come out and find you—But lo! I am at the bottom of my paper—and right fortunate is it for both—for in sooth so cold and *kiestless*[1] am I,—in a short time I should have been absolutely preaching. I will not ask your pardon for this motley farrago,—rejoice it is not worse. Write me as punctually at the day appointed, as punctually as it is in human nature to write—pass not sentence of excommunication on me—and be assured, I remain, my dear old Mit., your sincere friend (and semi-frozen servant),

THOMAS CARLYLE.

.   .   .   .   .   .

V.—To Mr. R. MITCHELL, Ruthwell Manse.

ANNAN, 11*th January* 1815.

MY DEAR MITCHELL—I must send a cover to a long farrago of stuff, and in order to save appearances, and to avert the dire threats of bonds and imprisonment which you so liberally deal out in your last letter,—I have sat down to give you an account of my life and conversation since I saw you last. Nothing material happened to me in town after your parting from me,—and except purchasing Campbell's *Poems* and transacting *quelques petites affaires* which it is needless to trouble you with, and getting my lungs well-nigh suffocated with the *foul air*, and the *tym-*

---

[1] Spiritless, inert.

panum of my ears nearly torn to pieces with the war-whoops of the Edinburgh *Hogmanay*[1]-night, I might have been said to be stationary. On Sunday morning I left Edinburgh on the outside of the coach, like you, in the gayest humour in the world, but before riding half a dozen miles the "biting breezes" of the East began to disturb me, and notwithstanding the consolation I derived from a shaggy greatcoat, and from comparing the *dread-nought* appearance of our guard (who to a natural obesity of body altogether hyperbolical, had added the adventitious aids of 2738·5 cubic inches of solid cloth and leather in the form of a tremendous impenetrable roquelaure, and surmounted the whole of this terror-striking apparatus with an awful broad-brimmed hat :—displacing as he stood not less than twelve solid feet of air) with the pitiful woe-worn visages of two fellow-travellers, whose livid noses and rattling teeth proclaimed (one would have thought) that the hour of their dissolution was at hand,—notwithstanding all this, by the time we reached Hair-stanes, I was right thankful to get inside of the "leathern-conveniency,"—where I continued all the way to Moffat. I made shift to fall into a kind of *torpor* whilst travelling down the Tweed—at least to shut my eyes upon the bleak and barren uniformity of its ash-grey hills, till on our vehicle's suddenly stopping, I thrust out my head, and descried *Tweed Shaws*. Recollecting your and my horrid circumstances a few days before, I could not help silently ejaculating a fervent prayer that I might *never* again be under the necessity of passing a night in the residence of the men of Tinwald, nor of ever passing another instant of my existence with the RED CUDDY[1] of Moffat. But my paper is almost done, and only half my journey completed. "Brief therefore will I be." I left Moffat at midnight in the Glasgow mail—and having arrived at home at about four o'clock—proceeded to Annan on Tuesday morning—safe and sound after all my perils and tribulations. If you can draw any "*soul-comforting reflections* from this, much good may they do you—and meantime I remain, your (servant to command),

THOMAS CARLYLE.

2 o'clock Thursday morning.

---

[1] The last day of the year.   [2] *Cuddy*, diminutive of Cuthbert = jackass.

VI.—To Mr. R. MITCHELL, Ruthwell Manse.

ANNAN, 25th March 1815.

MY DEAR BOB—At sundry times, and in divers ways, I have pondered upon a project I had formed of sending you a letter to arouse you, if possible, from the state of torpor in which, of late, to my unspeakable regret your faculties were benumbed. You are obliged to me for my intentions, and though tribulations of various sorts have prevented me from putting them in execution, you are not the less obliged on that account. You are a happy fellow, Mit., to be allowed to sit under your vine and under your fig-tree, quietly ruminating on your thirty-nine articles, with none to make you afraid. And how could you be so cruel as to mention those heart-breaking discourses? How, or when, or wherewithal are they to be made! In sobriety, that *putting off*, and that *dissipation of studies* is a serious evil. A thousand times have I lamented that hop-skip-and-jump disposition of mine which is perpetually prompting me to fly off at a tangent from whatever I am engaged in. Your "auricular confession" owns the same propensity; and I begin to think it is a fault of *every* mind—which effort alone can cure. I could be *metaphysical* perhaps, but you will be better satisfied with an example: It was but yesternight that I, your most obedient servant, became all at once sensible of *the importance of present time*, and having brought out my *accoutrements*, set right doughtily to the composition of my *Exegesis*. I began with alacrity of soul, and had finished the fourth line when I made a —dead halt! One cannot long be idle—you will not wonder that I took up the first book that came in my way—and though it was the dullest of all dull books, yet by a fatality attendant on those things, I could not give it up. It purported to be a "history of a lover," showing how Cecilia (somebody), being poor but honest, went to Paris with some Brandy Irish Dowager (of Tipperary), and was much astounded at their goings on, yet very much liked by the *beaux*. Showing how after divers trials and temptations she married with a lord (something) who had been a very great rascal in his early days, but was now become a most delectable personage; how they lived in great harmony of souls, till the honest man riding one day on some wold, and happening to fall from his beast in presence of this notable lady, she fell into hysterics or convulsions, and was taken home in a woeful plight, where she loitered on till she was "brought to bed," when she took her leave of the good-man and all the world. Would you believe me, I read and read this horrid story, and might have been reading yet had not a most dolorous ode to Matrimonial—no "Monody on the death of a beloved, etc." compelled me to throw past the book, and set to writing you a letter. Tell *me* not again of "Jacks-of-all-trades," you are a King of a student compared with me.

You are charitable enough to suppose that my head is full of ideas; your good-nature misleads you. I have indeed had ideas, and strange ones too, since I wrote you; but like many other remarkable ideas, they have had the fortune to evaporate as soon as produced. Mathematics I have absolutely never thought on, excepting some trifles from the *Ladies' and Gentlemen's Diary*, which I shall have conscience enough not to trouble you with at present. Great and manifold are the books I have read since I saw you. You recommended *Thaddeus of Warsaw* long ago, you may remember,—and the work in my judgment fully deserves it. Miss Porter has no wit, she invariably bungles a picture of the conversation of ordinary persons whenever she attempts it. Why does she delight in unfolding the forward weaknesses of the *female* heart, and making even Mary Beaufort love first? Yet with all her deficiencies she is interesting: never failing to excite our sympathy, though she cannot rank with our Fieldings or Smolletts. She infinitely surpasses the insipid froth of

> "The mob of Gentlemen, who write with ease."

As an extraordinary instance of perseverance, I must mention my having read *Cicero de Officiis*.[1] You must read it too,

---

[1] Carlyle seems to have been reading a good deal in Cicero about this time. In a letter written in April of this year to his friend Thomas Murray, he says: "But the book I am most pleased with is Cicero, *de Finibus;* not that there is much new discussion in it, but his manner is so easy and elegant; and besides, there is such a charm connected with attending to the feelings and principles of a man over whom 'the tide of years has rolled.' We are entertained even with a common sentiment; and when

Bob; you will get through it in a week, and cannot think your time misspent. It consists of letters addressed to his son, and if we compare the steady, affectionate, unbending precepts of the venerable Roman with the only work of a similar kind in our own times, *Chesterfield's Advice*, we shall blush for the eighteenth century !

But the most extraordinary production of any I have seen these many days, is *La Pucelle d'Orléans*, an Epic by Voltaire. This Mock-Heroic illustrates several things. First, that the French held Voltaire a sort of demigod; secondly (and consequently), that they were wrong in so doing; and thirdly, that the said Voltaire is the most impudent, blaspheming, libidinous blackguard that ever lived. As proof of the first take the following specimen of French ingenuousness, from the preface by the Editor. After affirming that the poem is Voltaire's, he observes that " Personne n'a été la dupe du desaveu qu'il a fait de ce poëme, dans une lettre à Messieurs de l'Académie Française. Sa véracité est connue depuis longtemps. Tout le monde sçait, qu'affirmer ou nier, selon les temps, les lieux, les convenances fut toujours une de ses maximes favorites; et en vérité, un homme aussi extraordinaire, doit bien avoir des principes qui lui soient propres." Happy great man ! Peace be to him and his "principes qui lui soient propres !" An epigrammatist sagely remarks—

> " C'est du Voltaire—et tout est beau,
>   Tout plait chez lui, jusqu'au *blasphème*."

To illustrate the third proposition—take any part of the poem—it is infinitely inferior in point of wit to *Hudibras*— yet were we not continually shocked with some indecent, vicious, or profane allusion, it would not be unentertaining. There is a description of the Temple of Fame, something in the spirit of Swift, which I would send had I room. The following [is a] new representation of the miseries of the builders of Babel—

> " Sitôt qu'un d'eux à boire demandait,
>   *Plâtre* ou *mortier* d'abord on lui donnait."

Add that it is professedly intended "pour les jeunes

we meet with a truth which we ourselves had previously discovered, we are delighted with the idea that *our* minds are similar to that of the venerable Roman."

demoiselles." I most heartily "wish them luck o' the prize, man !" I have also read—but hold thy hand thou wayward mortal ! consign not to the flames this ill-fated scrawl !—it is egotistical, it is nonsensical—and I speak it with a sigh—it is dull ! Yet burn it not—if a condition bordering on coma, if an endless series of misfortunes and south-west winds which have almost obliterated my spirit, cannot excuse me, think for thine own sake—is there not many a dulcet precept still slumbering at the bottom of my inkhorn, which it will do thy heart good to receive ? Think and read !—Which of ye, ye long-headed ones of the earth, ever dreamt that little *Nap*, tired of fretting out his heart in Elba, would rise Phœnix-like, disdaining "the limits of his little reign," and once more front the world—determined to die "with harness on his back !" Your calculations are ruined, for *Nap* is on the field ! And now poor d——l, when so many men that wield sceptres and paving-shovels—when so many people that have diadems and gridirons are combined against thee—why should *I* be thine enemy ? No ! fight thine own battle, and come what speed thou mayest for me. And yet I fear, my little fellow, thou art upon slippery ice, still thou hast many a trick, and with more truth than it was ever said of another, may it be said of thee,

> "Ton âme impie, inflexible, implacable,
> Dans les enfers vaudra braver le Diable !"
>
> VOLTAIRE.[1]

But I must finish this *badinage*—and assure you, my dear Mit., that I never was more serious than when I add that I am yours most sincerely,

THOMAS CARLYLE.

If you don't write, sir, instantaneously—it is almost two o'clock, and I writing the most confounded nonsense merely to provoke an answer—if you fail, I can't tell what to do with you.

Direct to me at James Gass', Cabinet maker, Edmond St. For among my other adventures it was destined that I

---

[1] "In the name of wonder," wrote Mitchell in his reply to this letter, "why did you fill your letter with such blads [*Anglice*, big pieces] of French ? Besides the enormous difficulty of translation, it keeps out some of your own *jeux d'esprit*, which are much more palatable to my taste than any from the philosopher of Ferney."

should quarrel with a Lancashire Jackall, which Mr. Kennedy keeps by way of house-keeper, and consequently shift my lodgings. Adieu, my dear Mit. Write immediately.

VII.—To Mr. R. MITCHELL, Ruthwell Manse.

ANNAN, *24th May* 1815.

MY DEAR MITCHELL—You ought to thank me for not writing you sooner. Buffeted as I have been, without ceasing, since I saw you, by innumerable squadrons of blue demons, my imaginations have been only the decoctions of ill-humour, and my letter must have been either a hyper-batavian tissue of dulness, or a string of complaints and imprecations unfit for the perusal of any person, more at ease in body than a gouty valetudinarian, or in mind than a *great man* on his way to Botany Bay. Not that the case is mended. Winds and rains, and crosses and losses have reduced a temper, naturally warm, to a state of caustic irritability, that renders me unfit for anything. "How weary, flat, stale, and unprofitable, seem to me all the uses of this world!" For, what are its inhabitants? Its great men and its little—its fat ones and its lean? From the courtier to the clodhopper—from the emperor to the dust-man—what are they all? Pitiful automatons—despicable Yahoos—yea, they are altogether an unsufferable thing. "O for a lodge in some vast wilderness, some boundless contiguity of shade, where" the scowl of the purse-proud Nabob, the sneer and strut of the coxcomb, the bray of the ninny and the clodpole, "might never reach me more!" But truce to this philippic,—vexations like these affect only the poor, misguided, wandering misanthrope; and (bless thy stars, my good Mitchell) thou art not of them.

The first article in the last *Quarterly Review* is on Stewart's second volume.[1] The wise men of London are earnest in their censures of "the metaphysical heresies" of their northern neighbours; and notwithstanding the high admiration they pay to Stewart's talents, they differ from him in almost all his results, because they disbelieve his principles—the "first principles" of Dr. Reid. Their opinion (and they give no reasons), on a point of this

---

[1] Dugald Stewart's *Elements of the Philosophy of the Human Mind.*

nature, is of little consequence. All the prejudices natural
to Englishmen they entertain in their full extent, and always
modify their decisions accordingly. For my part, though
far be it from me to attempt to disparage or vilipend this
great man, I cannot help thinking that the perusal of his
book has done me hurt. Perpetually talking about analys-
ing perceptions, and retiring within one's self, and mighty
improvements that we are to make—no one knows how,—
I believe he will generally leave the mind of his reader
crowded with disjointed notions and nondescript ideas—
which the sooner he gets rid of, the better! I know you
think differently; but *de gustibus non est disputandum;* and
very probably, the fault is not with our Author, but his
subject. . . . *Guy Mannering* is reviewed in the same
number. Though we have still more reason to question
their competency here, you will probably admit that "the
Dutch boors of Mannering though never so well painted,
must cause a class of sensations different from those excited
by the Salvator banditti of *Waverley*." Yet the only extract
they give (the departure of the gypsies and Meg Merrilies'
address to Ellangowan) is very much in the Salvator style.

I am glad you saw Lara, and am indebted for your
account of it. I read the review of it in the *Quarterly
Review* some time ago. Lara, it seems, is the identical
Conrad, and Kaled no other than that same "dark-eyed
slave," Gulnare, of whom such frequent mention is made
in "The Corsair." The story appears to want *éclaircissement.*
What could become of the madcap Knight? And what
was the meaning of that carcase in the river? Why did
did he raise the war-whoop in the lobby? Your solution
of the last difficulty is too general; besides, had he really
been *an-hungered,* the natural remedy was to visit the
pantry.

I am highly indebted to you for Hume. I like his
Essays better than anything I have read these many days.
He has prejudices, he does maintain errors,—but he defends
his positions with so much ingenuity, that one would be
almost sorry to see him dislodged. His essays on "Super-
stition and Enthusiasm," on "The Dignity and Meanness
of Human Nature," and several others, are in my opinion
admirable both in matter and manner, particularly the first,

where his conclusions might be verified by instances with which we are all acquainted. The manner, indeed, of all is excellent ; the highest and most difficult effect of art— the appearance of its absence—appears throughout. But many of his opinions are not to be adopted. How odd does it look, for instance, to refer *all* the modifications of "national character" to the influence of moral causes. Might it not be asserted with some plausibility, that, even those which he denominates moral causes, originate from physical circumstances ? Whence but from the perpetual contemplation of his dreary glaciers and rugged glens, from his dismal broodings in his long and almost solitary nights, has the Scandinavian conceived his ferocious Odin, and his horrid "spectres of the deep"? Compare this with the copper-castle and celestial gardens of the Arabians— and we must admit that physical causes *have* an influence on man. I read *The Epicurean, The Stoic, The Platonist*, and *The Sceptic* under some disadvantage. They are perhaps rather clumsily executed—and the idea of David Hume declaiming, nay of David Hume *making love*, appears not less grotesque than would that of [*seal covers*] or [*seal covers*] dancing a French cotillon. As a whole, however, I am delighted with the book, and if you can want it, I shall moreover give it a second perusal. I have got to the end of this rambling letter, and I think in rather better spirits than I commenced. Why did you not write me again ere this? You knew my woful plight, and ought to have had compassion on my infirmities. To make amends, I allow you a week, and within that time you are to send me a most spirit-stirring epistle. Abuse me, if you will, for my vagaries, only be pithy, and be speedy too.

I am confidently informed that the man of music, Andrew, is still bent upon exploring the new world. Nay, it is stated by his intended comrade (who has now wisely preferred making wheel-barrows at Castle-Milk, and living as his fathers did, to going to labour he knows not where, and feed upon he knows not what) that Andrew's accoutre-ments—his box—was on its way to Greenock a fortnight ago ! The Yankees are long-headed personages, and Andrew is a simple man. But he can fiddle, he can dig, and to beg he is not ashamed. You know what *you must do*, Bob, before Thursday first—*be pithy*—nothing but pepper and salt will suit me in my present humour.—My dear Mit., ever yours,

THOMAS CARLYLE.

VIII.—To Mr. ROBERT MITCHELL, Ruthwell Manse.

ANNAN, *14th June* 1815.

MY DEAR BOB—Your letter of the 31st May gave me a great deal of pleasure. I had heard a sort of vague account that you were sick ; and I had formed the project of coming up to condole with you, when (it seems) you had so much need of condolence, buffeted as you have been by "ennui, torpor and hepatitis." It made me happy to learn that you had come to a "quietus"—and the only remark I shall make on the subject is—*be thankful* that such moderate allowances of "Leech's bolus" were able to produce the effect—for there are froward creatures in the world, to make whose "quietus" defies the power of anything less efficacious than "a bare bodkin."

You take it upon you to scold me for not calling as I went to Dumfries. But hear my story, Mit. I was proceeding quietly from Ecclefechan to Annan, without the smallest intention of going on any such expedition, when I met with Johnstone, and he advised me to accompany him. We were obliged to use all possible despatch for fear of being too late ; and (before we got Jeffrey accoutred at Flosh, etc. etc.) it being about eleven o'clock, I had absolutely no time to see you, though I certainly intended it when I left Annan. Indeed, I did see from the road, a tall lank figure performing its gyrations round Ruthwell Church with much solemnity : but whether it was Mitchell, I know not. It was near two when we got to Dumfries—and being consequently prevented from getting within half a league of St. Michael's—we saw the ceremony of laying the stone,[1] exactly as well as if we had been in the grand square of Timbuctoo. Yet notwithstanding this—notwithstanding that all the scullions in Dumfriesshire were "let slip," notwithstanding the cantering and parading of the Ettrick Yeomen, notwithstanding the paper caps, the figured

---

[1] The foundation stone of the monument to Burns.

roquelaures, the magic-lanterns of free masonry, it was a striking scene. Scotland paying the tribute of well-earned honour to one of the noblest of her sons. It is a great pity that the monument will not be over his grave; many inconveniences ought to have been submitted to in order to gain this point. When I passed Ruthwell again, it was after midnight, so that you have nothing to blame me for on that score.

I could not send you the *Review*, for the man of whom I had borrowed it had got it again, and lent it to another. If I can get it again at any time, I will send it you. Have you seen the last *Edinburgh Review*? There are several promising articles in it—Scott's "Lord of the Isles," "Standard Novels," "Lewis' and Clarke's Travels up the Missouri" (of which a most delectable account is given in the *Quarterly*), "Joanna Southcott," etc. etc. I have been revising Akenside since I saw you. He possesses a warm imagination and great strength and beauty of diction. His poem, you know, does not, like Campbell's "Hope," consist of a number of little incidents told in an interesting manner, and selected to illustrate his positions,—it is little else than a moral declamation. Nevertheless I like it. Akenside was an enthusiastic admirer of the ancient republics and of the ancient philosophers. He thought highly of Lord Shaftesbury's principles, and had a bad opinion of Scotsmen. For this last peculiarity he has been severely caricatured by Smollett in his *Peregrine Pickle*, under the character of the fantastic English doctor in France. When we mention Shaftesbury, is his book in your possession, and can you let me have a reading of it? I am inclined to suppose that the prevalence of infidelity is on the decline. Pride will often overturn what reason had attempted in vain, and when the carrion and offal of human nature begin to adopt the tenets of our sages, we look for something new. What leads me to say this is that I have heard lately that there are in Middlebie sundry cunning workmen, some skilled in the intricacies of the loom, some acquainted with the operations of the lapstone, who are *notable deists*—nay, several aspire to taste the sublime delights of *Atheism!* Now, when creatures superior in so few respects (inferior in so many) to the cow that browses on their hills, begin to tread upon the heels of the wise ones of the earth, the hue and cry about freedom from popular errors, defiance of vulgar prejudices, glory of daring to follow truth, though alone, etc. etc. etc., is annihilated, and "all the rest is leather and prunella." But we will talk on those subjects afterwards.

Give my best respects to Mr. and Mrs. Duncan, and mention that I intend to have the pleasure of seeing them in a short time. I cannot come first Saturday for many reasons. I cannot come the next Saturday, for then is Mr. Glen's [1] sacrament, and I believe I shall be constrained to go to sermon. There is nothing that I know of to hinder me the week after that, and if all things answer I shall likely see you then. Though I began this letter last night, I have been obliged to write the greatest part of it since twelve o'clock to-day. It is within three minutes of one— and I have no more time. Write me immediately and I will be punctual in answering. Your Irish play is an *unique* in its kind. I shall be obliged to you for your *pun*. I have never heard it. Keep Blair till I come and seek him—and believe me to be—my dear Mitchell, yours sincerely,

THOMAS CARLYLE.

IX.—To Mr. MITCHELL, Ruthwell Manse.

ANNAN, *11th December* 1815.

MY DEAR MITCHELL—I opened your last letter with fear and trembling. I expected nothing but reproaches— when lo! my sins are laid upon the back of the unoffending Post-John, and I am never blamed. Indeed, Mitchell, you have been too good : and I look for nothing but that you will be ready to slay me when you come to know that I have never written you at all. I beseech you let not your wrath be kindled. Stay till you have heard my piteous circumstances—and I am persuaded you will pardon me. I might justly preface my account with an *infandum regina*, but to proceed without ornament. "Ye probably

---

[1] In the *Reminiscences*, i. 107, is an account of Mr. Glen, "Burgher minister at Annan, with whom I had latterly boarded there, and been domestically very happy in comparison."

may not know those lines of *Scaliger* (applied to dictionary-makers, and *mutatis mutandis* to dictionary-users)—

> Si quem dura manet sententia judicis olim
>
> .   .   .   .   .   .
>
> Lexica contexat, nam cætera, quid moror ? omnes
> Pœnarum facies hic labor unus habet."

You certainly imagine I am got terribly learned since I saw you. But fair and softly—I know nothing at all about honest Scaliger ; and "those lines" of his are, I believe, none of the most honestly come by. I conveyed them (*convey* the wise it call) from Morell's preface to Ainsworth's Dictionary, —a preface, I may observe, the most strongly impregnated with pedantry of any I ever read. But once more let me proceed—"those lines of Scaliger " and many other "lines," are applicable to me—as you shall presently hear. After parting from you at Ruthwell I consumed the remainder of our vacation in sundry idle projects : one of which was —going to Dumfries, and suffering "the pain of three intolerable deaths " for the purpose of hearing certain wise and faithful counsellors display their eloquence at the circuit trials. When I returned to Annan, it occurred to me that it would be proper to see what had become of my Hall discourses. It occurred to me, much about the same time, that it would be proper to study Rumford's *Essays*, Mackenzie's *Travels*, Humboldt's *New Spain*, Berkeley's *Principles of Knowledge*, Stewart's *Essays*, Simson's *Fluxions*, etc. etc. etc. It was some great man's advice to every person in a hurry—never to do more than one thing at a time. Judge what progress I must have made when I engaged in half a dozen. Manufacturing *theses*—wrestling with lexicons, chemical experiments, Scotch philosophy and Berkeleian Metaphysics—I have scarcely sufficient strength left to write you even now. Upon consideration, therefore, of these egregious labours—I hope, you cannot refuse to forgive me.

I am anxious to consult you about going to Edinburgh this winter. I have already partly told you that I have been making my *Exegesis*. It is now nearly finished ;— and truly a most delectable production it is—but of this some other time. I wrote to Murray in great haste, to commission me a day, and it seems, I am engaged to read

on Friday the 22d current.   So that you see my time of
setting out is decided upon.   You will ask me, why, since
I have almost come to a determination about my fitness for
the study of Divinity, why all this mighty stir—why this
ado—about "delivering" a thesis—that in the mind's eye
seems vile, and in the nostril smells horrible?   It is not
because I have altered my sentiments about the study of
Theology : but principally because it came into my head
to try what sort of an essay upon natural religion I could
make.   I have tried, and find accordingly that I can make
one perfectly—"weary, flat, stale, and unprofitable,"—but
I am engaged, and must read it now.   I do not expect yet
that you will be able to tell me "whether the Sabbath is of
divine institution "—but I do hope you have determined to
go to Edinburgh this winter along with me.   If you have
not I must not try to persuade you.   You would suspect
that my arguments arose from selfish motives,—and you
would not be far from right ; for if you do not go, I shall
be the most melancholy person imaginable.   But I cannot
help bringing to your recollection the possibility that you
may change your opinion about becoming a clergyman, in
which case your annual visit to Edinburgh will be of
essential service.   It does good, at any rate, by preventing
that pity which certain people of grave minds are so
disposed to bestow on every one that has not a fixed
prospect in life ; and, over and above, it is pleasant to revisit one's *alma mater*.   For these reasons, and for one (I
confess it) as strong as any—that I shall be uncomfortable
if you refuse—I earnestly wish you to determine upon this
journey.

       .   .   .   .   .   .

You would have Landalls preaching last Saturday.
How *does* he seem to do?   "Doctrinal discourses "—true
blue—I suppose.   I have heard of a criticism passed by the
late Dr. Finlay of Glasgow upon some eminent probationer ;
I know not whether it will apply.   Upon being asked his
opinion concerning the gentleman's oratorical powers, he
made answer—"He hath a comely appearance, and hath
attracted the notice of divers young men—and also of
some young women."   Have you heard that the very
learned and very orthodox divine of Ochiltree is preparing

to apply his polyglot stores to translating the New Testament—*Bonum, faustum, felix et fortunatum sit;* I am only sorry that I was obliged to become a subscriber—it is one pound four—if you take a thought of buying it, apply to me, and you shall have it for the odd silver.

I am obliged to you for your account of your Swiss visitants. With all imaginable deference to those who practise the sublime virtue of charity—I cannot altogether see what concern the peaceable inhabitants of Dumfriesshire have with the management of the convents situated among the glaciers of the Alps. Had the task of repairing their breaches been consigned to the *virtuosi* and the *cognoscenti* that frequent those regions, it might have been more befitting. But "all for the honour of England!"

Can you tell me whether Davie Graham is continuing to practise physic? He is a good honest lad;—I am only afraid that the aphorisms of Celsus will not answer [for] the men of Tundergarth.[1] And Andrew!—alas! the green ocean is betwixt us! *Illi robur et aes triplex circa pectus erat.*

The fate of poor Andrew disposes one to be melancholy. What is to become of us, Mitchell? The period of our boyhood is past: and in a little while, if we live, behold we shall be bearded men! from whom wisdom and gravity will be required. It is now a year since we last visited Edinburgh. For my part, though I have laboured as I could in my vocation, can I say that I am either wiser or better in any perceptible degree? Out upon it! This is a miserable world.

But let us quit moralising, and bethink us of our journey. You must write me on Thursday, that you will be ready at the time. I cannot think of any excuse you can plead with any chance of success. Are you afraid lest it hurt your health? Wrap yourself up in your roquelaure, and you can take no harm. You have been curling; and I am happy to believe, you have got round again. You certainly will come. I know not whether you will have heard that I am living with Mr. Glen since I came to Annan last. He is a real good man, as far as I can see; and Mrs. Glen is a fine cheerful woman,—so that upon the

---

[1] A parish in Dumfriesshire.

whole, I am not uncomfortable in my present circumstances. Most of the ministers that come here (no great number, let me be thankful) are curious bodies;—but I will speak of this elsewhere. In the meantime I must again repeat my petition—and hope that in a short time we shall be in Edinburgh together.—I am ever yours, my good Robin,

THOMAS CARLYLE.

"About Christmas time (1815)," writes Carlyle in his *Reminiscences* (i. 92), "I had gone with great pleasure to see Edinburgh again, and read in Divinity Hall a Latin discourse—'*Exegesis*' they call it there —on the question '*Num detur religio naturalis?*' It was the second, and proved to be the last of my performances on that theatre. My first, an English sermon on the words, 'Before I was afflicted I went astray, but now,' etc. etc., a very weak and flowery sentimental piece, had been achieved in 1814, prior to or few months after my leaving for Annan. Piece second, too, I suppose, was weak enough, but I still remember the kind of innocent satisfaction I had in turning it into Latin in my solitude, and my slight and momentary (by no means deep or sincere) sense of pleasure in the bits of 'compliments' and flimsy 'approbations' from comrades and Professors on both these occasions. Before Christmas Day I had got rid of my Exegesis, and had still a week of holiday ahead, for old acquaintances and Edinburgh things, which was the real charm of my official errand thither."

X.—To Mr. ROBERT MITCHELL, Ruthwell Manse.

ANNAN, 15*th February* 1816.

MY DEAR MITCHELL—I know I should have written you a month ago, and I am not going to take up your time with excuses. I have indeed no excuse, except the perpetually forthcoming one—no time and no subject; and it would be but aggravating my misconduct to harangue you upon a topic that has been so fully discussed by every writer of letters in every age of the world. The truth is— I have been a very torpid person of late. After undergoing the fatigues of a most uncomfortable journey to Edinburgh, I returned with renewed keenness to my old habits of seclusion and repose; to reading when I was able, and when I was not, to the forming of vain hopes and silly projects, at which I have a peculiar knack. But though I have not written to you, I have had you often in my mind. Many a time during my dreary pilgrimage to Edinburgh did I solace myself with the hope of making you merry with the recital of my adventures : a hope which (as you are just going to see) has, like many other hopes, proved utterly fallacious.

I left Ecclefechan on the evening of Tuesday the 19th December on the top of the Glasgow mail. Little occurred worthy of notice, till on my arrival at Moffat I discovered among my fellow travellers, along with three Lancashire cotton men, a fine species of the *popinjay*—of whom, all that I can now say is, that he was much shocked at seeing '*roos-beef fo suppa*,' and expressed his grief and surprise by several nondescript interjections; that he was unable to determine whether the fowl on the table was a tame duck or wild, and thereupon "did patiently incline" to the reasonings of an ancient Scottish *gourmand* who at length succeeded in settling his mind upon this important subject; and that upon my inquiring after the news of the paper which he was reading, he informed me that the *Aachdoocs* had returned to England, and that (this he preluded by three nods of satisfaction) the Prince Regent was gone to Brighton.

The next day I had different objects to speculate upon. I was mounted on the roof of the coach in one of the most dismal days I ever saw. It snowed heavily ; on our arrival at Erickstane particularly, the roaring of the wind and the ocean of drift carried with it, together with the bellowings of the distracted coachmen, and the outlandish warwhoops of two Irish doctors, who, along with myself, had dismounted till we should ascend the hill, formed a scene sufficiently wild. Of this I intended, for your benefit, a very pathetic description,—as well as of the desolation of the Broughton Inn, where after a day of violent struggling we finally stopped. The kitchen, I remember, when I entered it, was filled with shepherds and carriers, and in the midst, like a breathing iceberg, stood our guard, describing with much emphasis the hardships of the day. Two female passengers had taken possession of another quarter of the house, and left the two Hibernians and me to pass the evening as we best were able. I did not by any means like my comrades. One of them (according to my conceptions)—but that he from time to time uttered certain acute sounds, and had a pair of little fiery eyes,—pretty much resembled an

Egyptian mummy—a little meagre thing—skin apparently
of the nature of parchment, and a complexion that seemed
to have been produced by repeated immersion in strong
decoctions of logwood.   The other had a Kilmarnock
bonnet.   Both seemingly exceeding vain as well as stupid.
I spent an unhappy evening.   The mummy blew upon a
German flute, and both talked of Antrim and Drogheda,
till I had come to a resolution of leaving them next morning at all hazards.   I must not neglect to tell you of our
dormitory;—finding there was only one bed allotted to us
all, and wisely judging it prudent to make the best of a
bad bargain, the mummy took possession of the middle.
There is no happiness, it is said, without alloy,—at least it
proved so in this case ; for although by this manœuvre the
mummy received a comfortable proportion of warmth, yet
the pressure of the Kilmarnock-bonnet-man upon his fragile
sides seemed considerably to damp his enjoyment.   It
became at length so intolerable, indeed, as to compel him
(after a desperate and ineffectual effort at release) to exclaim
" *Marciful* Heaven preserve my *sowl*—what will become
of me now ?"   The bitter whine in which this sentiment
was uttered, and the sudden nature of such a preparation
for dissolution (which, I might have inferred from the
words, he expected forthwith) would in any other circumstances have overcome my gravity.

I left them next morning and set out on my forlorn
expedition at four o'clock.   It was truly an Icelandic scene.
The wind had subsided during the night—all was silent—
and the moon disclosed the dreary expanse of snow, which
in many places was drifted into heaps of several feet in
depth.   I made but indifferent progress,—for after infinite
flounderings (at one time literally up to the chin in snow)
the sun rose upon me in the wolds of Linton.   The track
was entirely obliterated—and I suppose I was beginning
to look silly enough, when I luckily descried a benevolent
herdsman, who pointed out to me the road for Noblehouse,
—from which I had deviated at the suggestion of a road-
man, at whose cottage I had called, and who thought the
higher road would be the clearer.   I was glad to meet, at
Noblehouse, with a Thomas Clark, Divinity student, whom
I had known in Edinburgh.   He was preparing to mount

on horseback, and in the meantime introduced me to a
tall thin man, who, he said, intended to walk to Edinburgh,
having been long disappointed of a passage in the coach.
There was a stagnant placidity in this person's countenance,
which inclined me to believe that he would prove a sufficiently inoffensive companion. He did turn out a very
shallow man. He questioned the workmen whom we
passed, with much minuteness, concerning the state of the
rods that were before us ; and conversed with me upon no
subject but that of the effects of snow upon human bodies,
—seeming particularly anxious about the fate of his own
vile carrion. He tired ; and I left him at Pennycuick sitting
with a kindred spirit, to all appearance a Peebles weaver.
I pursued my journey with unabating velocity, and arrived
at John Forrest's at last about nine o'clock. I never was
more happy at seeing Edinburgh.

I gave in my Discourse next day along with Samuel
Caven and another whom I did not know. It was sustained
without difficulty. Caven's was a precious morsel. Its
author, it seems, is in some family in the East Country.
He is a jumbling person to speak with ; he says "an infinite
deal of nothing ; his reasons are as two grains of wheat
hidden in two bushels of chaff ; you shall seek all day ere
you find them, and when you have them, they are not
worth the search." But enough of him. Our old college
cronies have left Edinburgh nearly to a man. Waugh still
continues there teaching and learning with all his might.
I think he was not quite so full of *calculi* as usual. When
we speak of *calculi*, I brought home [some] mathematical
books, which I must tell you of. Bossut's *History of
Mathematics*, Wood's *Optics*, and Cunn's *Euclid* and Newton's *Principia* constitute my stock of this sort. I got
Lucan's *Pharsalia* also, and some little extracts of Fenelon's
Dialogues des Morts. If there are any of these (except
Newton, for which you would be obliged to wait awhile)
that you wish to see—they are ready for you. I had read
Bossut before—and have not done much at him of late.
Neither have I read any quantity of Wood yet, having been
nibbling at the *Principia* (which with all my struggling, I
come but ill at understanding—indeed in some places I
don't understand it at all) ever since I came home. Of

Lucan I have not read above seven lines. I saw Scott's *Waterloo* and *Guy Mannering* when I was in Edinburgh. The former has been so dreadfully abused already, that I have nothing to add to the newspaper puns, etc., with which it has been assailed. There are (as Gray said of *The Castle of Indolence*) some good lines in it. I have far too little room for speaking of Mannering's beauties and defects at present. I will discuss it next time I write, if I can find nothing better.

But I must close this long letter. I have, as you see, devoted the night to writing my adventures. You asked for *Cuddies* [1] and truly I think I have driven you in an abundant herd. There is still another person whom (if he continues thus) you may think it reasonable to add to the list. I beseech you give him quarter.

Notwithstanding my misdeeds, I will ask you for a letter—and a pretty early one too. You used yourself to be a sad correspondent you know, and ought therefore to have some conscience. I saw Landalls to-night—he says you have been unwell. I do hope, my good Mit., you are recovered. Tell me soon—and believe me ever, my dear Robin, yours sincerely,

THOS. CARLYLE.

XI.—To Mr. R. MITCHELL, Ruthwell Manse.

19th April 1816.

MY GOOD LAD—You must be aware that I have a right to rate you with considerable acrimony. Last time I saw you, you promised to send me a letter in a few days, yet several weeks have elapsed, and no letter has appeared. This is very blameworthy, but I need not scold you, for, in all probability, by the time you have studied the following disquisition—you will think yourself punished to the full. It is one of the theorems we were speaking of. I found it out some months ago ; and an odd fancy struck me of turning the demonstration into the Latin tongue. My dialect of that language is, I doubt not, somewhat peculiar

---

[1] "You must write me on your return from Edinburgh, conveying the Doctor's criticism, and your adventures with all the red *Cuddies* you may meet with."—Mitchell to Carlyle, 15th December 1815.

—and you may chance to find some difficulty in interpreting it. [Here followed the theorem in Latin.]

Such is the result of this investigation. Your theorem about the heptagon does not answer exactly: it is only a good approximation, as I perceive, and as you may perceive also, by consulting a table of sines and tangents,—I have forgot West's theorem about the circle and curves of the second order. It is no great matter surely, since I should not be able to demonstrate it, though I had it. I wish you would send it me notwithstanding.

I hope you have sustained no injury from your excursion to Edinburgh. I hope, too, that you spoke to Mr. Leslie concerning the books. If you have not procured [me] one, I must request you to lend me yours immediately for a short time, if you can do without it: for one of the boys has begun conics and I have lent him my book—and should like to have another copy of it by me, to consult at home. You must send me the theorem and book by Mr. Johnstone of Hitchill—who I understand is to be at Ruthwell to-day and who can easily bring them to Annan. A letter I am expecting with impatience. Yours ever,

Thomas Carlyle.

. . . . . .

XII.—To Mr. R. Mitchell, Ruthwell Manse.

Annan, 15th July 1816.

My dear Friend—I am greatly obliged to you for your letter. At present I had no great reason to expect it. Yet you must not suppose that I have wilfully neglected to write. It is two months since I set resolutely to work, determined to send you a very handsome letter without loss of time. And I had assuredly done so, had I not clearly perceived that it was not in my power to send you anything that could at all have interested you. Since that time I have been continually loading myself with unavailing reproaches; and I have begun to write at last, solely, lest by my silence I should offend you without remedy. You are therefore to expect nothing but a very useless letter from me; and dull as may be.

I am very sorry that you are so unhappy—it is my own

case also, for I have been extremely melancholy during the last six weeks, upon many accounts. It is about ten days since I got rid of a severe inflammation of the throat, which confined me to the house for two weeks. During two or three days I was not able to speak plainly, and you will easily conceive that I passed my time very heavily. I endeavoured to read several things : I tried a book of modern Biography, *The British Plutarch ;* but soon finding it to be a very miserable book, I shut it for good and all. I next opened the *Spectator*—and though his jaunty manner but ill accorded with my sulky humours, I toiled through a volume and a half with exemplary patience. Lastly, I had recourse to Lord Chesterfield's advice to his son ; and I think I never before so distinctly saw the pitiful disposition of this Lord. His directions concerning washing the face and paring the nails are indeed very praiseworthy : and I should be content to see them printed in a large type, and placed in frames above the chimney-pieces of boarding schools, for the purpose of enforcing the duties of cleanliness upon the rising generation. But the flattery, the dissimulation and paltry cunning that he is perpetually recommending, leave one little room to regret that Chesterfield was not his father. Such was the result of my studies, in my sickness ;—a result highly unfavourable to those feelings of prostration before high birth and weight of purse, which (many tell us) it is so eminently the duty of all men to cultivate. Indeed this is not the first time that I have noticed in my mind a considerable tendency to undervalue the great ones of this world. Conscious that this sentiment proceeds in a considerable degree from my situation in life, I sometimes endeavour to check it : but after all, it requires little observation to teach us that the Noble of Political society and the Noble of Nature are different persons, in nine cases out of ten. I am also aware that Flaccus has said that " *Principibus placuisse viris, non ultima laus est;* " but with great deference, I would submit to Flaccus, that the justness of his aphorism must depend upon the character of these same " Principes viri ; " otherwise—it is easy to conceive a state of society, in which this *non ultima laus* of his must be very liberally shared with sycophants and pandars. But, I daresay, you have enough of these reflections. Turn we to something else :—I daresay I know as little of Navigation as you ; and yet I do not feel great difficulty in explaining how Hamilton Moore [1] "resolves triangles on the surface of a Sphere into plane triangles." Hamilton Moore, honest man, gives himself no uneasiness about resolving his triangles—he takes them as he finds them—and considering them as plane triangles—solves his problems very comfortably. (I believe Leslie has a note in his *Trigonometry*, explaining the method of reducing the angles of a spherical triangle to the plane triangle formed by its chords.) I readily agree with you that Moore's rules are very defective :—his remarks are often quite stupid—for instance, his statement (noticed by Humboldt) that the attraction of a boat to a ship, or a ship to a rock, is caused by *gravitation*. A similar phenomenon may be witnessed by causing two pieces of wood to float on a bowl of water —and all men know that it is caused by capillary attraction. I have never seen Keith's *Trigonometry*, and therefore cannot tell you anything about it. I am glad to hear that you are getting forward so well with Homer—I know almost nothing about him—having never read anything but Pope's translation, and not above a single book of the original, and that several years ago. Indeed, I know very little of the Greek at any rate. I have several times begun to read Xenophon's *Anabasis* completely ; but always gave it up in favour of something else. You complain that nothing that you do leaves a vestige behind it ;—what do you make of Homer? For my part—I cannot well say what I have been about since I wrote to you last. Out of a considerable quantity of garbage which I have allowed myself, at different intervals, to devour, I have only to mention Crabbe's Poems as worthy of being read. In addition to great powers of correct description, he possesses all the sagacity of an anatomist in searching into the stormy passions of the human heart—and all the apathy of an anatomist in describing them. For the rest—I continued reading Newton's *Principia* with considerable perseverance and little success,—till on arriving a short way into the third book—I discovered that I had too little knowledge

---

[1] The nineteenth edition of John Hamilton Moore's *Practical Navigator* was published in London in 1814.

of astronomy to understand his reasoning rightly.   And I
forthwith sent to Edinburgh for Delambre's *Abrégé d' Astronomie*, and in the meantime betook myself to reading
Wood's *Optics*.   I cannot say much about this book.   Its
author intermeddles not with the abstruse parts of the
science,—such as the causes of reflection and refraction,—
the reason why transparent bodies at given angles of
incidence reflect their light almost entirely (concerning
which I meet with many learned details in the *Encyclopædia
Britannica*), but contents himself with demonstrating, in a
plain enough manner, the ordinary effects of plane and
spherical mirrors,—and of lenses of various kinds,—applying his doctrines to the explanation of various optical
instruments and remarkable phenomena.   But in truth, I
know little about it ; I read it with too great velocity.   I
also read Keill's [1] *Introductio ad veram Physicam;* but I
shall let it pass till next time I write.   In fine, Delambre
arrived ; and I have read into his fourth *Leçon*—and like
it greatly.   I intended to have told you some of his
observations—but I would not overwhelm you with ennui
all at once—and therefore I shall be silent at present.   *Ne
quid nimis*, as the proverb saith.

On Friday we enjoyed the society of Brother Saffery of
Salisbury—a solicitor (of money) for the benefit of the
Baptist Mission.   I was rather disappointed in the appearance of this person.   The name of a missionary suggests
the idea of a lean and mortified ascetic—travelling with his
staff and scrip—and with pious avarice, hoarding, for the
behoof of his brethren, the scanty donations of a precarious
charity.   Brother Saffery was the reverse of all this ; He
arrived in a post chaise, and was a tall man of a florid
complexion, and very great diameter.   Nevertheless it was
easy to see that his was no common character.   His brow
was knit together very gloomily—and his voice (naturally a
deep-toned bass) was compressed into an inharmonious
whine,—all denoting profound humility and passive obe-
dience.   He spoke of the designs of Providence and the
projects of the Devil with great *sang-froid;* and quoted
largely from the Scripture, backing his quotations with

---

[1] John Keill was Savilian Professor at Oxford from 1709 to 1721.   He
was a voluminous writer, and his works had value.

Wiltshire proverbs—and other baser stuff of his own composition. His conversation, you will easily believe then, was very oppressive. Indeed, so strongly did it savour of stupidity, if not of something worse, that I could not perceive it to be at all a pressing duty to put money into the hands of persons like him, for any purpose whatever. However, Brother Saffery had no great room for misguiding the talent committed to his care by the people of Annan ;—inasmuch as said talent amounted only to two pounds four shillings and sixpence—a sum which, considering the trouble he put himself to, was trifling enough. It is pity that the missionaries cant so violently. There is no doubt that many of them are serious, well-meaning men— yet it would be too much to expect that, in such a number, there should not be several with whom the propagation of Christianity is far from being the primary object ; and of the best it is to be regretted that their zeal is not tempered by a little more prudence.

I had several other matters to write about ; but my paper draws to a close. Yet I cannot forbear noticing that strange project of going to France, which you talk of. Possibly it might be extremely pleasant,—but there are many perplexing questions to be answered before it can be put in execution. First, how are we to get to France ; second, how are we to live in France ; and third, what good will living in France do to us ? " Chill penury," my dear Mitchell, here as in other cases, represses our " noble rage " of visiting this country, and, may be, it is no great matter. For it may be doubted, one would think, whether a country inhabited by fierce revolutionists, and rascally marauders, and flimsy aristocrats—all sweating under a foreign and arbitrary yoke—would be a fit place for an honest man to dwell in—if he could help it. At any rate, it seems I am to stay nearer home for a while. For, you must know, I have received two letters from Professor Christison concerning the situation of Teacher to the Parish School of Kirkcaldy—or rather, I believe, assistant to the present teacher, who (being a very useless man) has agreed to resign upon consideration of being allowed to retain his salary—retaining also the name without any of the power of Parish Schoolmaster. I cannot say that I am violently taken with this offer. The emolument is rated about a hundred-a-year, but there appear to be some ambiguities about it which I do not understand; and I have written to them, that if they should like to wait, I could come to Edinburgh in Autumn, and talk with them about the place —and if they should not like to wait, that there would be an end of the matter. And there it stands. I wish you would send me as long a letter as this by this day week—I wish also that you would come down and see me—say on a Saturday when the tide is about mid-day, and then we might cross the water to Skinburness. Write soon—send me West's *Exercise*, that I mentioned last time—and believe me, dear Mitchell, yours ever,

THOMAS CARLYLE.

The project referred to in the preceding letter of leaving Annan and becoming master of the school at Kirkcaldy took effect. Carlyle in his *Reminiscences*, i. 98 *sqq.*, gives an account of the circumstances of this change. Its first great result was the making friendship with Edward Irving. " Blessed conquest of a Friend in this world ! That was mainly all the wealth I had for five or six years coming, and it made my life in Kirkcaldy (*i.e.* till near 1819, I think) a happy season in comparison, and a genially useful. Youth itself—healthy, well-intending youth—is so full of opulences ! I always rather like Kirkcaldy to this day. Annan the reverse rather still when its *gueuseries* come into my head, and my solitary quasi-enchanted position among them,— unpermitted to kick them into the sea."

XIII.—To Mr. ROBERT MITCHELL, Ruthwell Manse.

ANNAN, 3*d August* 1816.

MY DEAR LAD—You will easily guess, by the speediness with which I have answered your letter, that I am anxious to be reinstated in your favour. We have indeed written to one another much too seldom of late. I suppose a good part of the blame is my own—but I will not take it all. Let us try to be more regular in future. I was at a loss what to make of the first part of your letter. I could have laughed at the causes which your sagacity has pointed out for the mistake, had I not been grieved at the mistake itself. You expect my explanation, but in truth I am unable to give any explanation of the matter. I am altogether unconscious of having mentioned any particular Saturday for our excursion ; and had I done so, I cannot conceive how I should have hit on that day you speak of, for I must have known that the tide would not serve. If you have not destroyed that letter, I think you will find in it that I wished you to come on the first Saturday that would suit our purpose. But in reality it was late at night, or rather early in the morning, before I finished that immense epistle,—and I dare say I was half asleep over the latter part of it; and so I cannot vouch for its contents. But let us be of comfort. I have looked into the *Belfast Town and Country Almanack*—and consulted several cunning men on the subject,—and from all quarters I collect that the moon will be full about one of the clock on the morning of Thursday the 8th inst.—so that in all human probability—the time of full sea, next Saturday after that, will be between 1 and 2 o'clock;—a time that will answer our purpose very well. Now, if notwithstanding your late disappointment you could be induced to come to Annan about twelve o'clock that day—we could eat a morsel of dinner together—and forthwith embark for Cumberland. I am anxious that you should come—for I wish to see you; and this will be a pleasant enough way of spending the time; and besides it will do no harm to you— it may happen to be of service. Write on Tuesday if you can; and at any rate on Thursday, and let me know if you can come. . . .

I am very glad that you have met with a book of Natural Philosophy that you like. Send me your demonstration (or bring it) of the accelerated motion. I return always to the study of Physics with more pleasure after trying the "Philosophy of Mind!" It is delightful, after wandering in the thick darkness of metaphysics, to behold again the fair face of truth. When *will* there arise a man who will do for the science of Mind what Newton did for that of Matter—establish its fundamental laws on the firm basis of induction—and discard for ever those absurd theories that so many dreamers have devised? I believe this is a foolish question,—for its answer is—never. I am led to talk in this manner by having lately read Stewart's *History of Philosophy* in the Supplement to the *Encyclopædia Britannica*. I doubt I am going to displease you—but I must say—that I do not recollect of ever having bestowed as much attention with so little effect upon any author as upon Professor Stewart. Let me study his writings as I like, my mind seems only to turn on its axis,—but without progressive or retrograde motion at all. During these eighteen months, for example, have I been at times labouring to comprehend the difference between the *primary and secondary qualities* of bodies, and my labour has always been in vain. Can you resolve me this difficulty? I can easily see that *heat* (a secondary quality) has two meanings,—either it means the sensation in our mind—or it means the disposition of the particles of the body that causes this sensation : but is not hardness (and the other primary qualities) in the same predicament?

I designed to say many other things—but Post-John is about to set out—and I must hold my hand. Write me at the time I mentioned—and see if you can come at the time specified. I have many things to show you and tell you—and ask you. I remain, in the meantime (in great haste), my dear friend, yours truly,

THOMAS CARLYLE.

XIV.—To Mr. R. MITCHELL, Ruthwell Manse.

MAINHILL,[1] 13*th November* 1816.

MY DEAR MITCHELL—I shall set out for Edinburgh to-morrow morning ; and before going, I have begun (as in duty bound) to give you an account of my procedure. I have done nothing at all since I saw you, but put off my time. I was sick two or three days ; and went over to Allonby to recreate myself. I returned from Allonby in three days, and remained mostly at home, waiting with patience for the day of my departure, which at length is near at hand.

---

[1] "He" [my Father] "became Farmer (of a wet clayey spot called Mainhill) in 1815, that so 'he might keep all his family about him,' struggled with his old valour, and here too prevailed."—*Reminiscences*, i. 61. "About two miles distant" from Ecclefechan, "on the left hand side as you go towards Lockerby, there stands, about three hundred yards in from the road, a solitary low whitewashed cottage, with a few poor outbuildings attached to it. This is Mainhill, which was now for many years to be Carlyle's *home*. . . . The situation is high, utterly bleak, and swept by all the winds. . . . The view alone redeems the dreariness of the situation."—Froude, *Life*, i. p. 35.

I am glad you got on so well with your mathematics. Your demonstration of that theorem of West—about the triangle—which you sent me, is very simple and neat, much better than mine, as far as I can recollect. . . . I have got nothing to send you—of any use—unless you think of inserting[1] the following problem; which notwithstanding the technical jargon with which it is enveloped, is after all a silly enough piece of work. You will perceive that it is a general solution of the problem, concerning a particular case, of which Mr. White was so facetious above two years ago. It is almost the only thing I have done since I saw you : and as I now write it out for the first time, I am not without apprehensions of errors in the computation, though sure enough of the principle. But if you propose it, I shall have time enough to give it a revisal before a solution is required. . . .

But here is Johnstone with intelligence that my intended *compagnon de voyage* cannot go to-morrow ; and I must off in the coach to-night at six o'clock. " Night thickens, and the crow makes wing to the rooky wood." I have not a moment to lose. Good-bye, my dear Mitchell. You shall hear of me ere long.—Yours ever,

THOMAS CARLYLE.

XV.—To Mr. ROBERT MITCHELL, Ruthwell Manse.

KIRKCALDY, 12*th February* 1817.

MY DEAR SIR—I yesterday received a letter from our friend Johnstone, who tells me that you are greatly astonished at my long silence. And in truth you have some reason, but you are wide of the mark in the hypothesis which you have formed to account for the phenomenon. I am certainly much dissatisfied with your conduct ; but this could only have induced me to write with greater vehemence and celerity. The truth is, I began you a letter about three weeks after my arrival in this place, and had proceeded a great way—when some stupid business or other interrupted me ; and the paper was thrown by for ten days. I began another with renovated zeal, and had actually got to the last page, when your letter from Edinburgh arrived—and

---

[1] *Viz.*, in the *Dumfries Courier*, Mr. Duncan's newspaper.

struck me dumb with grief and surprise. I was in a sad taking. To think that my very last employment before leaving home was writing to you—that I had calculated the weeks and days that must elapse before the month of March could bring us together to hold a solemn conference touching all that should concern us ; and then to hear in the midst of my calculations, that though during a fortnight you were within ten miles of me—that though in two hours from any given point of time you might have been transported to my habitation—you came not near me ! It was a dog's trick, Mitchell. Little prevented me from throwing down my implements and crossing the salt sea to seek you,—had I known to what quarter of the great city my search must be directed. All that remained for me then, was, by writing a most abusive letter, to show you how much "the galled jade will wince." But alas ! no sooner had I collected my energies for this enterprise, than a sore throat seized me—and (after a protracted struggle on my part) confined me nearly a whole week to my room. My heart died within me at the sight of the gargles and boluses and blisters with which I was assailed : and till two days ago, I was able to think of nothing but the sickness and sorrow to which mortal man is subject in this miserable planet. This is the reason of my silence. You will perceive that the blame rests with you and fortune. I am faultless—or nearly so. Still I am in a very considerable rage against you. Whether "mine anger shall abate" upon consideration of a long letter speedily sent me, I know not—but I wish you would make the experiment. Johnstone will have told you all about my condition and operations in this long and dirty town ; and it would but fatigue you to repeat the statement. I am sufficiently comfortable ; and feel considerably less spleen and ennui than I used to do at Annan. My habits have been so much deranged by change of place, that I have not yet got rightly settled to my studies.

I have read little since I saw you ; and of that little I doubt I have not made the best use. Have you seen Playfair's Introductory Essay in the *Encyclopædia ?* I am sure you will like it. It is distinguished for its elegance and perspicuity. I perused it some weeks ago, and thought it greatly preferable to Stewart's. Indeed, I have often told you that I am somewhat displeased with myself because I cannot admire this great philospher half as much as many critics do. He is so very stately—so transcendental, and withal so unintelligible, that I cannot look upon him with the needful veneration. I was reading the second volume of his *Philosophy of the Human Mind* lately. It is principally devoted to the consideration of Reason. The greater part of the book is taken up with statements of the opinions of others; and it often required all my penetration to discover what the Author's own views of the matter were. He talks much about Analysis and Mathematics, and disports him very pleasantly upon geometrical reasoning; but leaves what is to me the principal difficulty untouched. Tell me if you have read it. You have no doubt seen the *Tales of my Landlord.* Certainly, *Waverley* and *Mannering* and the *Black Dwarf* were never written by the same person. If I mistake not, Dr. M'Crie's strictures are a little too severe on some occasions,—and his love of the Cameronians too violent. The worthy Doctor's humour is as heavy as lead. I am afraid you are tired of this.

Is is very comfortable that you and Samuel Cowan go on so lovingly together. I am unacquainted with your lucubrations; for I have not seen a *Courier* since I left Dumfriesshire. Long ago, when I was in Edinburgh, I had demonstrated a theorem for your behoof—but I have nearly forgot it now. I think it may be enunciated thus: " If the diameter of a circle be divided internally and externally in the same ratio, the straight lines drawn from one of the points of section to the extremities of the chord passing through the other, will make equal angles with that diameter." It bears some analogy to one of Matthew Stewart's. You will get the demonstration well enough. Johnstone tells me that Mr. Duncan has engaged a certain Mr. M'Diarmid to assist him in conducting the paper. I think I have heard of this person's speeches in the forum —and also that his wit was very great. I hope in his hand the torch of eloquence will burn bright—and shed a strong ray of intellectual light over the whole district.

I have not been in Edinburgh since you left it; and therefore I can give little news from that quarter. Your countryman Frank Dixon came into the town a few days ago; and I believe he intends to remain, if he can obtain employment.[1] He was in this place last week, visiting Edward Irving. He is a fellow of infinite jest, and spares no pains to keep his company in convulsions. A variety of works have been begun about the new year (as is the fashion) in the "periodical line." A weekly newspaper, the *Scotsman*, has reached the third number. I have seen them all—a little violent in their Whiggism; but well enough written in some places. Pillans and Jeffrey and Moncrieff and many others have been respectively named as the Editor. There is also a weekly essay, *The Sale Room*, begun about six weeks ago—by whom, I know not. The writers are not without abilities; but the last numbers seem to indicate that the work was about to give up the ghost. I understand you had the famous Dr. Spurzheim[2] among you lately, examining the head of George Ross. What said the sage cranioscopist about this wonderful being? And what do you think of his doctrine of skulls? For myself—having never been within the sphere of his influence, there is little merit in being sceptical. I own his system seems to me to be a mass of crude hypotheses with a vile show of induction about it—calculated to impose only upon the lazy and wonder-loving. I say *show* of induction, for it seems from the nature of the case to require a number of experiments almost immense to establish any one of its positions. There are, it seems, three-and-thirty bumps upon the human headpiece, which the Doctor says are faculties. Now, any peculiar character may have originated from one of these, or from two or more of them, or from the whole together. Calculate the combinations that can be made of thirty-three bumps, and allow for the original constitution of the mind, and you

---

[1] The readers of Carlyle's *Reminiscences* will recall the figure of this "Annandale Rabelais," "a notable kind of man, and one of the memorabilities;" "a most quizzing, merry, entertaining, guileless, and unmalicious man; with very considerable logic, reading, contemptuous observation, and intelligence, much real tenderness too," etc. etc.—i. 145.

[2] Spurzheim, originally a disciple of Gall, had come to England in 1813, when he was thirty-seven years old, full of enthusiasm to propagate his new doctrine of phrenology. He was received with especial favour in Scotland, and gained a large following there—among those whose heads were not as hard as Carlyle's.

will require, I believe, millions of instances to prove the title of one single bump to the name of organ. Tell me what you think of this.

I am very much afraid that you will think this letter dull—I think it so myself—but what can I help it? Be as content with it as you can. I am longing greatly to hear from you. Let me know all that you are reading and saying and thinking. Stand not upon ceremony, but send me a very long close-written letter, with all the speed imaginable. Remember me kindly to Mr. and Mrs. Duncan, and to all about the Manse that care for me. Write soon. Good-night, my old friend; I am in a hurry, for the post hour is nearly come.

THOMAS CARLYLE.

XVI.—To Mr. ROBERT MITCHELL, Ruthwell Manse.

KIRKCALDY, 31*st March* 1817.

MY DEAR MITCHELL.—Certainly your letter ought to have been answered before this. But it seems to be the fate of all my lucubrations to be behind their time. I have no excuse to offer, except, of course, no time and no subject,—and I need not aggravate my offence by taking up your time longer with discussing it. If you shall be graciously pleased to pardon me, I promise to behave in future as becometh me. I have nothing surprising to tell you. I myself am leading a quiet and peaceable life; and my neighbours, like every other person's neighbours, are exclaiming against the hardness of the times, and praising or blaming the proceedings of the Government, according as the late "strengthening of the hands of the Executive" happens to strike their mental optics. We had two lectures upon the pathognomy of Drs. Gall and Spurzheim lately. The cranioscopist was a Mr. Allen, a Yorkshire man, who has been expounding the doctrines of "chemical philosophy" amongst us for the last three months. He seems to possess talents,—but to be very much addicted to building hypotheses. On this occasion he had the honour of addressing all that was rich and fair and learned in the burgh. After considerable flourishing, he ventured to produce this child of the Doctor's brain—and truly it seemed a very Sooterkin.[1]   I have since looked into the Doctor's book, and if possible the case is worse.   Certainly it is not true that our intellectual and moral and physical powers are jumbled in such huge disorder; surely it will be marvellous if these powers can be defined and estimated with such mathematical precision from the size and figure of the skull.   It is very silly to say that Spurzheim has *demonstrated* all this; Spurzheim has demonstrated nothing.   For anything he knows to the contrary, the faculties of the soul are to be ascertained by the figure and size of the abdomen—if the venerable science of Palmistry is not to be revived.   It is in vain to rail against the opposition shown to novelties; the doctrine is not to be rejected for its novelty, but for its want of truth.   Neither does it serve any purpose to tell us of the many ingenious persons who support it.   A century has not elapsed since Dr. Berkeley wrote a book on the virtues of Tar-water, and the learned in Europe were loud in its praise: yet now tar-water is accounted vile.   So it may fare with Spurzheim.   Nevertheless Allen has converted the lieges of Kirkcaldy.   So strong is the desire which we all feel of knowing the character, talents, and disposition of our neighbour, and so deep is the regret that

> "Nature has made his breast no windores
> To publish what he does within doors, etc.,"

that (to say nothing of other inducements) craniology, if urged with a proper quantity of dogmatism, will find many believers.   And why not?   *Si populus vult decipi, decipiatur.*

I was in Edinburgh two weeks ago; but there was nothing worthy of notice taking place.   I heard Leslie give a lecture on Heat: it displayed great ingenuity, but his experiments did not succeed.   His Geometry is to be out in a few days.   I intended to have enrolled in the Divinity Hall; but their Doctor was too busily engaged otherwise to attend to me.[2]   He had been quarrelling with

[1] "It is reported of the Dutch women that making so great a use of stoves, and often putting them under their petticoats, they engender a kind of ugly monster which is called a *sooterkin*."—Note to *Hudibras*, part iii, canto ii, 146.—T. C.

[2] "Irving's visits and mine to Edinburgh were mostly together, and had always their attraction for us in the meeting with old acquaintances and objects of interest, but except from the books procured could not be

his students about the management of the library ; and the committee, which has been appointed to draw up regulations for the management of it, had that very day submitted them to the Doctor and his students assembled in the Hall. They gave much dissatisfaction to the Doctor, and immediately (as I was told—for I was not there) there was great confusion, and several speeches, vituperative and objurgatory, passed among them ; till at last the mutineers, to the number of fifty, adjourned to a neighbouring school-room, *con strepitu*, and valiantly drew up twelve resolutions proclaiming their grievances, and their determination to apply to the Presbytery for advice. The Senatus Academicus has since taken up the case ; and, as the committee appointed to decide on it consists of Meiklejohn, Ritchie and Brunton, it is easy to see how the affair will end. Your picture of this Hall, and the dudgeon it seems to have excited in you, gave me great amusement. I have not been within its walls for many months—and I know not whether I shall ever return, but all accounts agree in representing it as one of the most melancholy and unprofitable corporations that has appeared in these parts for a great while. If we are to judge of the kind of Professors we should get from the Edinburgh Kirk by the sample we already possess, it is devoutly to be wished that their visits may be short and far between. It may safely be asserted that though the Doctors Ritchie, junior and senior, with Dr. Meiklejohn, Dr. Brunton, and Dr. Brown, were to continue in their chairs, dozing, in their present fashion, for a century, all the knowledge which they could discover would be an imperceptible quantity—if indeed its sign were not negative. We ought to be somewhat sorry for the Divinity Hall ; but our grief need not stop here. If we follow its members into the world, and observe their destination, we shall find it very pitiful. With the exception of the few whom superior talents or better stars exempt from the common fortune, every Scotch Licentiate must adopt one of two alternatives. If he is made of pliant stuff he selects

accounted of importance. . . . On one of those visits my last feeble tatter of connection with Divinity Hall affairs or clerical outlooks was allowed to snap itself and fall definitely to the ground. Old Dr. Ritchie 'not at home' when I called to enter myself. 'Good,' answered I ; 'let the omen be fulfilled.'"—*Reminiscences*, i. 115.

some one having authority, before whom he bows with unabating alacrity for (say) half a score of years, and thereby obtains a Kirk, whereupon he betakes him to collect his stipend, and (unless he think of persecuting the Schoolmaster) generally in a few months falls into a state of torpor, from which he rises no more. If, on the other hand, the soul of the Licentiate is stubborn, and delights not to honour the Esquires of the district ;—heartless and hopeless he must drag out his life—without aim or object —vexed at every step to see surplices alighting on the backs of many who surpass him in nothing but their *love for gravy*.[1] This is the result of patronage, and this is one of the stages through which every Established Church must pass, in its road to dissolution. No government ever fostered a Church unless for its value as a State-engine, and none was ever ignorant of the insecurity of this engine till it is placed upon the rock of patronage. But it ends not here. Though all "constituted authorities" are ready to admit that Truth is great and will prevail—none have ventured to let their "true religion" descend unsupported into the arena, and try its hand at mauling the heresies which oppose it. On the contrary, every "true religion" is propped and bolstered, and the hands of its rivals tied up ; till by nursing and fattening it has become a bloated monster that human nature can no longer look upon—and men rise up and knock its brains out. Then there is great joy for a season, and forthwith a successor is elected, which undergoes the same treatment—and in process of time meets with a similar fate. Such is the destiny of Churches by law established. Let every one of us be as contented with it as possible—and gird up his loins to attain unto a share of the plate, whilst the game is good.

I am glad that you like Adam Smith. I agree with you very cordially, and regard him as one of the most honest and ingenious men of his age, or indeed of any other. He is one of the very few writers who have not gone delirious when they came to treat of Metaphysics. He wrote his *Wealth of Nations* in a room not a hundred yards from the

---

[1] "I would advise every young man" (says Dr. Goldsmith), "at his entrance into the world, *to like gravy:* I was once disinherited by an old Uncle for not liking gravy" (from memory).—T. C.

place where I am sitting—and the men of Kirkcaldy are with reason proud to remember him. You view Lord Bacon with a different eye ; and, without doubt, you have some reason to be scandalised at the admiration with which he is treated. It looks as if philosophers could not do without some one to worship. It is not long since they tumbled poor Aristotle from his temple—and it rests not with Playfair and Stewart, or Bacon would soon be exalted in his stead. I have read little of any consequence since I wrote to you. You will have seen the last numbers of the *Edinburgh* and *Quarterly Reviews*. In the latter, among a great deal of foul and nauseating stuff, I was happy to see that due credit is at last given to Mr. Duncan for his valuable institution.[1] I was reading Pascal's *Lettres Provinciales*. None can help admiring his wit and probity. He sustains excellently the character of *naiveté* which he has assumed—and with infinite dexterity hunts the Jesuits through all their doublings and subterfuges, till he has triumphantly exposed the wretched baseness of their conduct. It is pity that the Salvation of Europe required the re-establishment of this vile order of men. Last week I perused Von Buch's *Travels in Norway and Lapland*. Much of his attention is devoted to Mineralogy, of which I am very ignorant, and his movements are sometimes not a little mysterious, from the want of a proper map of the country. Nevertheless he communicates some valuable information respecting the natural productions and the wandering inhabitants of those dreary regions. His manner is as clumsy and ponderous as that of German philosophers generally is, and nowhere is this more apparent than when he attempts to be striking, or tries his powers in the pathetic line. I took Bailly's *Histoire de l'Astronomie* out of the College library last time I was over the Firth. [He seems] to write with great eloquence and perspicuity ; but I have read little of him. We get a *Dumfries Courier* here amongst us. Our third number reached us a few days

---

[1] Mr. Henry Duncan, the minister of Ruthwell, near Dumfries (born 1774, died 1846), to whose sons Mitchell was tutor, was a man of good sense and public spirit. He had established at Ruthwell "a Parish Bank for the Savings of the Industrious" (the parent of all modern Savings Banks) ; and he had lately published an account of it, which was noticed with warm praise in the *Quarterly Review* for January 1817.

ago. It seems M'Diarmid is become sole Editor—it is not the opinion of the readers here that the paper has been a gainer by the change. The Ranger seems (under favour) to be but a silly kind of person—and his friend Mr Bright is a very vapid gentleman. It is a pity that Spondastes[1] his labours have been curtailed before he has completed his investigations. But we must make a shift to live without knowing who wrote *Mary's Dream.* I expected to have seen Samuel Cowan's investigation last week—but it did not appear. If you have given over your Mathematics, well and good ; but if you have not, you may throw the following exercises into your storeroom, if you like. [Here followed mathematical propositions.]

And now, my beloved Mitchell, what more can I do for thee ? My sheet is full—and if thou speak of *pica*[2]—this is dense enough in all conscience. I do hope and trust I shall hear from thee very soon. I know I have been to blame—but that is past and gone. Therefore let us forget and forgive—and believe me, my dear Robin, yours faith-fully,   THOMAS CARLYLE.

XVII —To Mr. R. MITCHELL, Ruthwell Manse.

KIRKCALDY, *5th July* 1817.

MY DEAR ROBIN—After waiting very impatiently for such a long period, I received with great satisfaction the short but savoury morsel which thou hast at length been pleased to despatch me. It does not by any means quell my appetite ; but you assure me it is only a precursor, and what can I do but be " propitiated." I turned pale when I noticed your charge of " palming." The proposition about the harmonic section was, as I said before, included in one of Matthew Stewart's problems,—the source, I suppose, from which Leslie himself obtained it. No doubt

---

[1] " Little Murray," wrote Mitchell, 23d February 1817, meaning their common friend Thomas Murray, " has been writing in the *Courier* under the name of Spondastes. He gave an account of all the learned Gallovidians from the Creation of the World to the present day ; and had not sheer modesty prevented him, himself would have been among the number."

[2] In the letter to which this is an answer Mitchell had written : " I have selected the largest sheet of paper I have in the world ; my ' page ' is sufficiently ' dense,' and my type a perfect *pica*,—all this that ' thine anger may abate.' What can I do more ? "

it was stupid enough not to know that it was deducible from Prop. 22, iii. of the *Analysis*, or still more directly from prop. 9, vi. *Elements*—and therein lies my error. The problem concerning the minimum was proposed last winter in Leslie's class; and I know not when or where or in what manner you and Waugh had discussed it. That " to find the locus of the vertex of a triangle given in species whose base is one of the sides of a given angle standing on a given straight line," was also derived from one of Leslie's. It seems to have no affinity with prop. 4, iii. *Analysis*. I suppose it has been wrongly enunciated to you. So that you see the quantity of palming has in this case been very inconsiderable. The same day on which I received your letter, I perused Alpha's Newspaper-solution. Edward Irving thinks it a learned investigation. I think so likewise. The very same result (for I tried it) is obtained, and by a nearly similar process, from the 32d prop. of Newton : but I do not understand your integral calculus. It would be a more difficult business to find the time of descent to the centre of the earth. I wish you would try this and send me your result. I am afraid I cannot do it.

Three weeks ago I finished M. Bailly's *Histoire de l'Astronomie Moderne.* His acquaintance with the science seems to have been more extensive than profound ; his style is elegant—perhaps too florid, and interspersed with metaphors which an English critic might be tempted sometimes to call conceited. I wish I were an Astronomer. Is it not an interesting reflection to consider, that a little creature such as man—though his eye can see the heaven but as it were for a moment—is able to delineate the aspect which it presented long ages before he came into being—and to predict the aspects which it *will* present when ages shall have gone by? The past, the present, and the future are before him. Assuredly the human species never performed a more honourable achievement. " The boast of heraldry, the pomp of power," must disappear like those that delighted in them ; but when the hand that wrote the *Principia* is reduced to a little black earth, and the spirit that dictated it is gone no one knows whither— the work itself remains in undecaying majesty to all generations. But Dr. Chalmers, it would seem, is fearful lest these speculations lead us away from Christianity, and has written a volume of *Discourses* to prove that the insignificance of our planet in the Universe is no argument against the truth of religion. Orthodox men declare, of course, that he has completely discomfited his opponents. I read it some time ago. It abounds in that fiery, thoroughgoing style of writing for which the Author is so remarkable; nevertheless his best argument seems to be, that as it is in the Scriptures, we have no business to think about it at all—an argument which was well enough known to be a panacea in cases of that nature before his volume saw the light. One is a little surprised to see the Doctor so vehement in his praise of Newton for what certainly was very laudable—his rejecting all manner of probabilities, and refusing to admit any hypothesis till it was supported by direct and uncontrovertible proof. Without doubt this answers exactly in the present instance, but if carried to its full extent on the other side, it will lead to alarming results. Christianity itself is only supported by probabilities; very strong ones certainly, but still only probabilities. But here, we are informed, it is necessary "to sit down with the docility of little children" and believe everything that is told us; which is a very comfortable way of reasoning. It is perhaps not surprising that the Author should be dogmatical; but it seems strange, when his own side of the question is so very evident, that he should deal so largely in denunciations against his adversaries. It is very certain that the unhappy sceptic cannot believe one jot the better, though he were brayed in a mortar. Yet almost all the writers on the evidences of Christianity that I have seen (excepting Paley) have treated him in this manner. These reflections occur naturally enough in perusing this book (which after all is no ordinary production, though better books have not always passed through six editions in so short a space); but I have not stated them often. When a poor creature's sentiments, in such cases, happen to be contrary to those of his neighbours, the less he says of them the better. This same Doctor, as you will know, writes the first article in the late *Edinburgh Review*—on the "Causes and Cure of Mendicity." After expatiating at considerable length upon the evils of pauperism, he proposes, as a remedy, to increase the number of clergymen. They who know the general habits of Scottish ministers will easily see how sovereign a specific this is. The remainder of the *Review* is good reading; but as you will have seen it before this time, I will not trouble you further on the matter. I have seen the last number of the *Quarterly Review*. It seems to be getting into a very rotten frothy vein. Mr. Southey is a most unblushing character; and his political lucubrations are very notable. He has been sorely galled by the Caledonian oracle, poor man. I know nothing about Mr. Duncan's controversy except through the *Scotsman ;* and they assign him the victory. I received about a month ago the Rev. William Thomson of Ochiltree's new translation of the Testament. Of course I am no judge of his " new renderings ;" but the style, both of writing and thinking, displayed in those parts which I have looked at, is dull and sluggish as the clay itself. He brags of having altered the expressions of the old translation—everybody, I suppose, will readily admit this, and be ready to wish him joy of all the honours that can arise from such alterations. I might say more of books, but this will abundantly satisfy you for one course.

I have heard nothing of Johnstone yet. Truly, I think, never any poor wight had two such lazy correspondents as I am yoked withal. Much might be said on this subject —but it is needless to punish you before the time. In four or five weeks I hope to be with you, and you shall hear your evil deeds [proclaimed] with energy enough. As I may reach Annandale by various routes, it will be an object of great importance to fix upon the best. Sometimes I am for proceeding through Peebles and the wolds of Selkirk by Polmoodie and Ettrick Pen. This track is almost as the crow flies. At other times I think of Tweedsmuir and Moffat; and at present Irving and a Mr. Pears (schoolmaster in this neighbourhood) are persuading me to accompany them by Stirling and the Trossachs to Glasgow.[1] They tell me we shall see Loch Katrine and climb Ben Lomond and do many other exploits ;—but we have not yet counted the cost—and notwithstanding all that has

---

[1] Of this journey there is a lively account in the *Reminiscences,* i. 122-134.

been said about the sturdy independent feelings of a
pedestrian, I am inclined to think that in my case they are
greatly overbalanced by the more vulgar consideration of
stiffened joints and blistered feet. Upon the whole it is
not unlikely that I must again penetrate the moors of
Tweeddale—a district which I never crossed except in the
most woful plight both of body and mind—and which
therefore I hate very cordially. At all events, I am to be
three or four weeks beside you. I wish you would contrive
some excursion for our mutual benefit. What say you of
a sail to Liverpool? The expense would not be great—
and it might tend to dissipate that headache which, I am
sorry to find, still infests you. We could embark at
Dumfries or Annan, and we could not fail to find a ship
bound to some Scottish port whenever it should please us
to return. We could go to the Isle of Man or to Wigtown
or anywhither. If Johnstone would go with us, we should
be three merry souls—wind and weather permitting. Write
me your opinion of this project immediately—I had other
things to tell you of—but daylight and paper are both
failing me,—and this half-hour I have been driving my pen
as fast as ever Jehu, the son of Nimshi, drove his chariot,
to be in time for the mail,—and, after all, I am afraid that
I am out. One thing I must mention. Write soon ; call
to mind thy engagements, and, to make the matter definite,
I hereby give you notice that unless I receive a letter from
thee within fourteen days from the date hereof (allowing
three days of grace) thou shalt be punished as a *crack tryst*[1]
and a breaker of promise, without benefit of clergy—so
look to it. Thine old and faithful friend,

THOMAS CARLYLE.

XVIII.—To Mr. JAMES JOHNSTONE, Hitchill,[2] Annan.

KIRKCALDY, 25th September 1817.

MY DEAR JOHNSTONE—I fear you are already fretting
at my silence ; and, as I have no satisfactory apology to

---

[1] One who does not fulfil his engagement.

[2] Hitchill, a substantial farmhouse, built by Carlyle's father, stands
about midway between Ruthwell and Annan. Johnstone was tutor to Mr.
Church's sons there.

offer, it would but augment your dudgeon to attempt one.
Therefore, without preface, I desire you to be content, and
you shall hear all things in their order. To begin at the
beginning—the day after my parting with you and Mitchell
was rainy, and I spent it at home in a state of torpid and
unprofitable dreaming. But next morning being dry, I
resolved to commence my journey. Sandy accompanied
me to Moffat; and during my ride my mind was occupied
with all the cheering reflections which a passage through
Tweedsmuir, the recommencement of Paedagogy, and the
jolting of a strong cart-horse naturally inspired. About
two o'clock I was on the summit of Ericstane. I looked
down through the long deep vale of the Annan, remembered my friends upon the dim horizon, and half-uttering
the wish that rose within me for their welfare, I turned me
round and pursued the tenor of my way. In a short time
I overtook two fellow travellers. One of them was a
peasant of those parts: the other a stout square-made
[man] of thirty in sailor's clothes, without shoes or shirt,
with a countenance that seemed tanned by wind and
weather, and expressive at once of energy and harmlessness.
Upon investigation, I found that this unlucky person was
one Thomas Cuvallo, a native of Constantinople, whose
father had gone from the neighbourhood of Corinth—that
he had served two years on board the Achilles English
ship of war—was discharged in 1814—had afterwards
been twice at India, whence he had returned last spring—
and that travelling from one harbour to another in the vain
hope of finding a vessel to carry him to his own country,
he had expended all his money, and was now, as a last
resort, making his way to Leith to try to procure either a
passage to the Continent, or work to keep him from
starving till times should mend. This Thomas Cuvallo,
cast thus forlornly upon the wolds of Tweeddale, seemed
to view his condition with an indifference that Zeno himself
might have envied. The present of a piece of bread and
cheese, which Mrs. Johnston had stowed into my pocket
at Moffat, secured me his favour, and rendered him very
communicative—though his stock of English vocables was
far from extensive. After repeating me the Greek alphabet,
he gave me the names of several objects in Romaic—most

of which bore a striking resemblance to the Hellenic; and when I inquired the signification of *Zoë mou sas agapo*, he replied with a grin of intelligence—"My life, I love thee." Then he proceeded to unfold to me the various grievances and molestations to which he (being a Djour) was exposed in Istambol—interspersing some account of his adventures in the Levant, together with notices of Mullahs, Jemams, and spinning Dervishes. Insensibly he digressed into the subject of magic and divination—and then set about revealing to me his ideas touching miracles and spectres. He said there were ten kinds of spectres. Under the head of miracles, he told me of certain pictures in St. Sophia's Church which no efforts of the Turks can efface, though they scrape and whitewash never so manfully. In the same church, it seems, there is a pulpit into which these unhappy Mussulmans can never gain admittance— axes and crows avail them nothing: but every Easter-eve there appears in it the figure of a man reading in a book, which when he shall have finished, the Mohammedan empire shall pass away for ever. He told me likewise of a well in Constantinople which contains a fish whose history is very remarkable. It happened to be frying in a pan in the palace at the time the Turks were about to enter the city; when the incredulous and phlegmatic sovereign declared to the General who came to ask his advice, that he would as soon believe that this fish would jump from his frying-pan and live, as that the Turks were within many leagues of him. Whereupon the fish sprang out with great agility, and at this hour, he said, is living in its well—one side roasted and the other raw—and intends to do so till Greece shall be finally delivered from bondage. He never saw it, but his mother did. On our arrival at the Bield, I presented this unfortunate Argive with a draught of porter; and leaving him—with a shilling, half a foot of tobacco, and my best wishes—to exert his begging powers in the neighbourhood, I advanced to Broughton in the midst of rain, and reached it at nightfall. In about half an hour there came a *return chaise*, into which I mounted: and after being dosed by the quaverings of a foolish Grocer who frequently attempted to sing, and sometimes amused by the proofs which our driver (a kind of Cuddie Headrigg fellow) produced of the insanity of Kennedy and his fair wife—both of renowned memory in your country, I came to Noblehouse at ten o'clock. Next day at noon I was in Edinburgh ; met with Irving at Leith in the evening, and finally without loss or detriment I reached my habitation in time for tea.

Thus you see, after all the pains and pleasures, and triumphs and discomfitures, and perils by land and water, which a month spent in journeying upon the face of this fair earth has caused me to experience, I find myself once more seated in my little chamber, in this ancient burgh of Kirkcaldy—all my labours (like those of many wiser persons) having brought me only to the place from whence I started. Now that I have shaken hands with my honest neighbours, and resumed my occupations, I find that the remembrance of the wild and wondrous features of the Highlands assorts but awkwardly with the vulgar feelings to which the duties of a school give rise. Nevertheless I am peaceful and contented, and my days pass on pleasantly enough. What I deplore is that laziness and dissipation of mind to which I am still subject. At present I am quieting my conscience with the thought that I shall study very diligently this winter. Heaven grant it be so ! for without increasing in knowledge what profits it to live ? Yet the commencement has been inauspicious. Three weeks ago I began to read Wallace's *Fluxions* in the *Encyclopædia*, and had proceeded a little way, when the *Quarterly Review*, some problems in a very silly *Literary and Statistical Magazine* of which the Schoolmasters are supporters, Madam de Staël's *Germany*, etc. etc., have suspended my operations these ten days. After all I am afraid that this winter will pass as others have done before it—unmarked by improvement ; and what is to hinder the next, and its followers till the end of the short season allotted me, to do so likewise ? Pitiful destiny ! my friend —yet how to be avoided ? Lately I was renewing my old project of going to the French University. I have flattered myself with the thought that the collision with so many foreign minds, all toiling with might and main after the same object, would excite in me a permanent enthusiasm sufficient to carry me as far as my powers would go— straight forward—and not in the zig-zag directions—now

flying, now creeping, which I at present pursue.   Once I
had almost determined next time I went to Edinburgh to
inquire whether it would be possible to put this scheme in
execution.   But I suppose it will shortly dissipate—like
other schemes of a similar nature, and leave me to form
resolutions, and lament their failure as before.   You will
think me very weak and silly : I think so myself (*hinc illae
lacrymae*), and know not whether I shall ever mend.   I
hope you order these matters better at Hitchill.

I told you I had seen the *Quarterly Review.*   You
would notice its contents in the newspaper.   It is a long
time since I ceased to be one of its admirers.   The writers
possess no inconsiderable share of dogmatism ; and their
learning, which they are, to an unpleasant degree, fond of
displaying, is of that minute scholastic nature which is
eminently distinguished from knowledge.   Moreover their
zeal for the " Social Order " seems to eat them up, and
their horror of revolution is violent as a hydrophobia.
These qualities are prominent in the last number—and
accordingly it contains much disgusting matter ; but I like
it better (as a whole) than some of its predecessors.   There
is in it a distant and respectful but severe criticism on
Dugald Stewart's writings, which comes much nearer my
views of his character than any of the panegyrics which the
Edinburgh Reviewers have so lavishly bestowed upon him.
The other night I sat up till four o'clock reading Matthew
Lewis's *Monk.*   It is the most stupid and villainous novel
that I have read for a great while.   Considerable portions
of it are grossly indecent, not to say brutish : one does not
care a straw about one of the characters—and though
" little Mat " has legions of ghosts and devils at his bidding,
one views their movements with profound indifference.   I
have seen the first number of *Constable's Magazine*—it
seems scarcely equal to *Blackwood's*—the last number of
which has appeared.   B. advertises a new one with a slight
variation in the title.   There is also another periodical
publication published once a fortnight (I forget its name),
begun under the auspices of Peter Hill.   I perused only
one article and can give no account of it.   I cannot pretend
to say what this influx of magazines indicates or portends.

Tell Mr. Church that the harvest began here about a

week after my arrival. Barley seems to be the principal crop in this neighbourhood—and all hands are now busily engaged in cutting it. It has been sadly tossed and broken by the wind and rain, but as the last fortnight has been excellent weather—the people have great hopes of it yet. What the price of the grain is I know not—new oatmeal was $19\frac{1}{2}$d. the peck—but two days of soft weather have raised it a penny. Make my best compliments to Mrs. Church and Miss Harper. I hope you are happy with them. I long to hear what you are all doing. Write me, I pray you, a full and particular account of all your transactions. Pardon my delays—and let me tell you even now I have been obliged to write this letter most doggedly, and as it were by main force, so great was my desire to keep you in peace. Can you tell me what that knave Mitchell is doing? He should have sent me a letter two weeks ago. Remember me at Bogside. Do write very soon, and believe me, dear Johnstone, yours faithfully,

Thomas Carlyle.

P.S.—I am just going down to Irving's to get the newspaper and concert measures for an expedition to Edinburgh, which we are meditating to accomplish to-morrow evening. I shall put this into the office by the way—so good-night once more.

XIX.—To Mr. R. Mitchell, Ruthwell Manse.

Kirkcaldy, 19*th November* 1817.

It is a great while, my dear Mitchell, since I wrote you a letter that did not require an apology for its lateness. You too are chargeable with similar practices; and could I with any conscience, I would rate you very severely. It is certainly a deplorable way of proceeding. If it be true in your case, as it is in mine, that the letters which pass between us occasion some of the happiest feelings that diversify this languid scene—it is pity that they are, on both sides, so sparingly supplied. I am no stranger to the dreary sense of vacuity that occupies the soul of him who sits down to fill a fair unblotted sheet of paper—when fit materials are wanting. But we are too fastidious in our choice of subjects; and, above all, we ought to exert ourselves. It cannot be expected, that leading this un-varied life, which Providence has allotted us, we should have any wonderful tidings to communicate. We have nothing to say about the musical glasses, or *bon-ton*, nor can we pretend to speak of moving incidents by flood and field, of Cannibals that each other eat—the Anthropophagi —or aught of that nature. Yet are we not destitute of topics. The feelings and adventures of each of us (though of no moment to nearly all the world beside) may be interesting to the other, and by mutually communicating the progress of our studies, and the ideas (if any) that at times penetrate these benighted minds of ours—we may be encouraged to proceed on our way; rejoicing together, without flattery or jealousy or any such thing. I desire you to ponder upon this subject with due attention. Let us both write oftener—no matter how dull the letters be. When men cannot be social, they are content to be gregarious—and, though it be in a state of silence and torpor, experience some gratification from mere juxtaposi-tion; so with regard to letters, it may safely be affirmed, that the shortest and meagrest is preferable to none at all. I am writing to you at present from a conviction of the truth and utility of this proposition. Since my departure from your country, nothing at all worth relating has hap-pened to me. I have gone the round of my duties with all the regularity and *sang-froid* of a mill-horse. My mind has on the whole been placid—sometimes almost stagnant. And if it be true, as Flaccus hath it, that

> " Nil admirari prope res est una,
>   Solaque, quae possit facere et servare beatum,"

I am in a fair way of obtaining and preserving a considerable share of felicity. But I am much inclined to doubt Flaccus. The history of my studies exhibits the same stupid picture of impotent resolutions and unavailing regrets as heretofore. I may lay aside my French project when I please. What, as you say, should take me to Paris?[1] If they could pluck

---

[1] " What wild-goose scheme is this of yours of going to France? Do you not know that the Polytechnic School is knocked on the head? The rest are not worth the naming. I say, ' Laddie Dinwoodie o' the Garden-holm, compose yourself to your potatoes there.'" From letter of Mitchell, 4th October 1817.

from my brain this rooted indolence, it might be worth thinking of. Soon after my arrival I fell to Wallace's *Fluxions*[1] with might and main. I would study, I thought, with great vehemence, every night—and the two hours at noon which I have to dispose of, I would devote to the reading of history and other lighter matters. But alas! two hours I found to be insufficient—by degrees poor Wallace was encroached upon—and is now all but finally discarded. His introduction, it must be confessed, is ponderous and repulsive. His horror of the binomial theorem leads him into strange bye-paths. But he demonstrates with great vigour. The worst of it is, we are led to his conclusion, as it were through a narrow lane —often, by its windings shutting from our view the object of our search, and never affording us a glimpse of the surrounding country. I wish I had it in my head. But, unless I quit my historical pursuits, it may be doubted whether this will ever happen. I have read through that clear and candid but cold-hearted narration of David Hume, —and now seven of Toby Smollett's eight chaotic volumes are before me. To say nothing of Gibbon (of whom I have only read a volume), nor of the Watsons, the Russells, the Voltaires, etc. etc., known to me only by name. Alas! thou seest how I am beset. It would be of little avail to criticise Bacon's *Essays*. It is enough to say, that Stewart's opinion of them is higher than I can attain. For style, they are rich and venerable—for thinking, incorrect and fanciful. Some time ago I bought me a copy of La Rochefoucault. It has been said that the basis of his system is the supposition of self-love being the motive of all our actions. It rather seems as if he had laid down no system at all. Regarding man as a wretched, mischievous thing, little better than a kind of vermin, he represents him as the sport of his passions, above all of vanity, and exposes the secret springs of his conduct always with some wit, and ('bating the usual sacrifices of accuracy to smartness), in general, with great truth and sagacity.

I perused your theorems with some attention. They are well worthy of a place in the *Courier*—though not for the purpose you mention. Mr. Johnston, if I mistake not,

---

[1] Wallace was Professor of Mathematics in the University of Edinburgh.

is a small gentleman, whom it would be no honour to demolish. I have scarcely done a problem since I saw you. There is one—" to find the locus of the vertex of a triangle, whose base is given, the one angle at the base being double of the other "—which I was trying some time ago. You will easily see that the locus is a hyperbola. The solution of problems, I begin to think, depends very much upon a certain sleight of hand, that can be acquired without great difficulty by frequent practice. I am not so sure as I used to be that it is the best way of employing oneself. Without doubt it concentrates our Mathematical ideas—and exercises the head; but little knowledge is gained by the process. If I am wrong—put me right when you send me a letter.

It is long since I was at Edinburgh, and when I was there nothing of importance was a-doing. I heard Alison[1] preach. His elocution is clear—his style elegant—his ideas distinct rather than profound. Some person contrasting him and Chalmers, observed that the Prebendary of Sarum is like a glass of spruce beer—pure, refreshing, and unsubstantial—the minister of the Tron Kirk, like a draught of Johnnie Dowie's ale,—muddy, thick, and spirit-stirring.

Ivory[2] the celebrated analyst has quitted his situation at the College of (I forget its name). Wallace has succeeded him—and has left his own place to his brother. They were saying that Ivory had it in his mind to come to Edinburgh, and become a Teacher of Mathematics. Leslie has published an arithmetic—similar I suppose to that treatise contained in the supplement of the *Encyclopedia*. He is to have a third class this winter. Playfair, I believe, is returned—and is to teach his class himself. Some time since, all the world was astonished at the 2nd number of *Blackwood's* (formerly the *Edinburgh*) *Magazine*. The

---

[1] The Rev. Archibald Alison, " alors célébre" as a preacher for the elegance of his style, and as a writer of an " Essay on Taste," which was thought to "deserve a conspicuous place in every well-chosen library." He was a marked figure in the society of Edinburgh.

[2] Professor Ivory, born 1765, later Sir James Ivory, gave up in 1819 the chair of Mathematics at the Royal Military College at Sandhurst, which he had held for fifteen years. He succeeded Leslie in the chair of Mathematics in Edinburgh.

greater part of it is full of gall: but the most venomous article is the "Translation of a Chaldee Manuscript," said to be found in the Library of Paris. It is written in the phrase of the Scriptures, and [gives] an allegorical account of the origin and end of the late *Edinburgh Magazine*—greatly to the disparagement of Constable and the Editors. Most of the Authors of Edinburgh are characterised with great acrimony—under the likeness of birds and beasts and creeping things. Blackwood is like to be beleaguered with prosecutions for it—two are already raised against him. Replies in the shape of "explanations," "letters to Drs. M'Crie and Thomson," have been put forth—more are promised, and, doubtless, rejoinders are in a state of preparation. Whatever may become of Blackwood or his antagonists—the "reading" or rather the talking "public" is greatly beholden to the Author. He has kept its jaws moving these four weeks—and the sport is not finished yet.[1]

As I have nothing more to say, I believe it will be as well to conclude here, by desiring thee to commend me to all my friends in thy neighbourhood—and to write immediately if thou hast any love for—Thine old and trusty friend,

THOMAS CARLYLE.

XX.—To Mr. JAMES JOHNSTONE.

KIRKCALDY, 20th November 1817.

O thou Turk in grain!—Did not I send thee long ago a letter of three dense pages? Have not I any afternoon these three months turned my eye to the mantelpiece, upon my return from school, to see if peradventure the postman had brought me no word from Hitchill? And did he ever bring me any? Have not I—but what availeth it to talk? In sobriety I am dreadfully enraged. Write me a letter, I say, without further parley, or I will roar (as

---

[1] This "Chaldee Manuscript" was mainly the work of Hogg, the "Ettrick Shepherd;" he was assisted by Wilson and Lockhart. It is reprinted in the collected edition of Professor Wilson's works, with notes by his son-in-law, Professor Ferrier. The notoriety it had is due more to the character of the persons referred to in it, and the scandal occasioned by its ill-mannered satire, than to any genuine wit or humour.

Bottom saith), so that it shall do any man's heart good to hear me. It is vain to tell me that you have no subject. Send me the meditations of your own heart—send me a register of your domestic occurrences—in short anything— an account of the prices of grain and black cattle rather than nothing at all.

My history since I wrote last to you contains no particular worth relating : I continue to follow my vocation with a peaceful and quiet heart, and might live under my vine and fig-tree, in case I had one, with none to make me afraid. I will not detain you long with my studies. I have been reading little except Coxe's travels in Switzerland, Poland, Russia, etc., Hume's history, together with part of Smollett, Gibbon, etc. Coxe is an intelligent man, and communicates in a very popular way considerable information concerning the countries through which he passed. Hume you know to be distinct and impartial : but he has less sympathy than might be expected with the heroic patriots—the Hampdens and the Sidneys, that glorify the pages of English history. I fear Smollett is going to be a confused creature. I have read but a volume of Gibbon—and I do not like him : his style is flowery ; his sarcasms wicked ; his notes oppressive, often beastly. They that cultivate literary small-talk have been greatly attracted for some time by the late number of *Blackwood's* (formerly the *Edinburgh*) *Magazine*. It contains many slanderous insinuations against the publisher's rivals — particularly a paper entitled " Translation of a Chaldee Manuscript "—concerning the author and date of which it is gravely asserted the celebrated Sylvester de Sacy is writing a dissertation. The piece is divided into chapters and verses, and written in the Scripture language. It relates, in an emblematical manner, the rise, progress, decline and fall of the late *Edinburgh Magazine*. Constable and the Editor, as well as most of the Edinburgh Authors, are bitterly lampooned—under the similitudes of magicians, enchanters, spirits, birds, and four-footed beasts. The writer displays some talent—but his malice and profanity are as conspicuous as his wit. Three prosecutions have been raised against Blackwood on account of it—and the press is groaning with animadversions and replies. It

is curious to observe the importance which the writings of
Walter Scott have conferred on everything pertaining to
the Border. These manufacturers deal largely in that
article. Not a beldame, in the Merse,[1] can plant her
cabbages—nor a tinker solder his kettle, but it must be
forthwith communicated to the public in *Blackwood's* or
the *Scots Magazine.* As if the Public had anything to do
with the matter. I marvel that they have not some correspondent in the West Marches, to transmit them intelligence about the Spoon-men of Hightae, and the visions
of Madam Peel. The dead-lights *"gaun luntin by"*[2] would
be a rare morsel for them.

Little occurs in this neighbourhood to disturb our tran-
quillity—and still less that you would care for hearing. I
attended the examination of Irving's Academy lately. He
acquitted himself dexterously and seemed to give general
satisfaction. His assistant is gone to Edinburgh—and he
now manages the school himself—more comfortably, I
hear, than formerly. A month ago that same Allen, whom
I once mentioned before, gave us a concluding lecture on
the applications of Spurzheim's theory of Cranioscopy. It
was greatly past comprehension. He seemed to have
taken the fly-wheels from his brain, and said to it—brain,
be at thy speed—produce me stuff—no matter of what
colour, shape or texture:—and truly it was a frantic,
incoherent story as heart could wish. It appears to have
knocked the bottom out of Spurzheim's doctrine in these
parts. Next came sundry players and other migratory
animals of that sort. Last week we had a reciting man,
Mr. Hamilton from Glasgow. Perhaps Miss Harper may
have seen him. He understands his trade well; but he is
a drinking dog. The other day, there arrived from Edinburgh a large shoal of preachers—Dixon, Nichol, Bullock,
etc.—they preached all along this coast of ours. I heard
Dixon—on Death;—somewhat in King Cambyses' vein.
He is a witcracker by profession — otherwise a good
fellow enough. Between ourselves, our own minister here

---

[1] The Merse or March, one of the divisions of Berwickshire extending
from the Lammermoor Hills to the Tweed.

[2] Hightae was the headquarters of the tinkers and spoonmakers in
Dumfriesshire. "Madam Peel" of Ecclefechan had a dream, in which
she saw the death-lights going fuming by.

is the veriest drug that ever hapless audience yawned under.   He has ingine [1] too—but as much laziness along with it as might suffice for a Presbytery.   I protest if he become no better, I shall be compelled to abandon him in a great measure.   Yesterday all the world was in mourning—and hearing sermons for the Princess Charlotte. I was much struck with the fate of that exalted person. Her age was within a month of my own.   A few days ago she was

> "As full of spirit as the month of May ;
> And gorgeous as the sun at Midsummer "—

and now !   Truly pale Death overturns, with impartial foot, the hut of the poor man and the palace of the King.

It is past midnight—so I shall have done.   Greet Mrs. Church and Miss Harper in my name.   Mr. Church will prefer an account of the harvest to compliments.   Therefore let him know that the state of Agricultural affairs in this district is very pitiful : the crops are backward to a degree that is quite unaccountable—and not paralleled by any season within the memory of man.   Part of the oats is uncut ; and the whole country hereabout and westward, as I learn, is covered with shocks.   The weather is moist too —so that altogether the Husbandman has an afflicting prospect. . . .

To-morrow I go to Edinburgh with Irving.   If we get safe over, you will find it noted in the vacant space. Meantime I'll to my truckle-bed.   I have nothing more to tell you, but that I am as heretofore, yours truly,

THOMAS CARLYLE.

XXI.—To Mr. R. MITCHELL, Ruthwell Manse.

KIRKCALDY, 16*th February* 1818.

After an arduous struggle with sundry historians of great and small renown, I sit down to answer the much-valued epistle of my friend.   Doubtless you are disposed to grumble that I have been so long in doing so ; but I have an argument in store for you.   To state the pro-position logically—this letter, I conceive, must either amuse you or not.   If it amuse you—then certainly you cannot

---

[1] Scotch for "genius" or "mind" in general.

be so unreasonable as to cavil at a little harmless delay : and if it do not—you will rather rejoice that your punishment has not been sooner inflicted. Having thus briefly fixed you between the horns of my dilemma—from which, I flatter myself, no skill will suffice to extricate you—I proceed with a peaceful and fearless mind.

My way of life is still after the former fashion. I continue to teach (that I may subsist thereby), with about as much satisfaction as I should beat hemp, if such were my vocation. Excepting one or two individuals, I have little society that I value very highly, but books are a ready and effectual resource. May blessings be upon the head of Cadmus or the Phœnicians, or whoever invented books ! I may not detain you with the praises of an art that carries the voice of man to the extremities of the earth, and to the latest generations, but it is lawful for the solitary wight to express the love he feels for those companions so stedfast and unpresuming—that go or come without reluctance, and that, when his fellow animals are proud or stupid or peevish, are ever ready to cheer the languor of his soul, and gild the barrenness of life with the treasures of bygone times. Now and then I cross the Firth : but these expeditions are not attended with much enjoyment. The time has been when I would have stood a-tiptoe at the name of Edinburgh, but all that is altered now. The men with whom I meet are mostly preachers or students in divinity. These persons desire, not to understand Newton's philosophy, but to obtain a well 'plenished manse. Their ideas, which are uttered with much vain jangling, and generally couched in a recurring series of quips and most slender puns, are nearly confined to the church or rather kirk-session politics of the place, the secret habits, freaks, and adventures of the clergy or professors, the vacant parishes and their presentees, with patrons, tutors, and all other appurtenances of the tythe-pig-tail. Such talk is very edifying certainly : but I take little delight in it. My Theological propensities may be enclosed within very small compass—and with regard to witlings, jibers or such small deer—the less one knows of them, it is not the worse. Yet there are some honest persons with whom I spend sometimes an afternoon comfortably enough. Before leaving this subject I wish to ask how *your* theological studies are advancing—and chiefly when you are to be at Kirkcaldy? I doubt my career "in the above line" has come to a close. Perhaps I have already told you that there are a thousand preachers on the field at present. Now from calculations founded on *data* furnished me by persons well versed in these matters—and managed by the rules laid down in Dilworth—I find that the last draught of these expectants, supposing *no new* ones to appear in the interim, will at their settlement be upon the verge of their grand climacteric. After which, the "prospects of being useful" cannot, one would think, be very bright.

I am sorry that Mathematics cause *hepatitis* in you. The pursuit of truth is certainly the most pleasing and harmless object that can engage the mind of man in this troublous world : and where shall we find her in her native purity, if not in the science of quantity and number? I counsel you to resume your operations as soon as your cranium will permit—which I trust will happen without loss of time. You will thank me, no doubt, for this sage advice ; but if you knew the need I have of it myself, you would be the more disposed to admire my generosity. It is long since I told you I had begun Wallace, and that foreign studies had cast him into the shade. The same causes still obstruct my progress. You will perhaps be surprised that I am even now no farther advanced than "the circle of curvature." I have found his demonstrations circuitous but generally rigorous. Yet I must except the proof of Maclaurin's theorem in page 414—which, if I were not a little man and Wallace a great, I should have small hesitation to pronounce unsatisfactory, not to say absurd. I suppose I had read Hume's *England* when I wrote last ; and I need not repeat my opinion of it. My perusal of the continuation—eight volumes, of history, as it is called, by Tobias Smollett, M.D., and others, was a much harder and more unprofitable task. Next I read Gibbon's *Decline and Fall of the Roman Empire*—a work of immense research and splendid execution. Embracing almost all the civilised world, and extending from the time of Trajan to the taking of Constantinople by Mahomet II. in 1453, it connects the events of ancient with those of modern history.   Alternately delighted and offended by the gorgeous colouring with which his fancy invests the rude and scanty materials of his narrative; sometimes fatigued by the learning of his notes, occasionally amused by their liveliness, frequently disgusted by their obscenity, and admiring or deploring the bitterness of his skilful irony —I toiled through his massy tomes with exemplary patience. His style is exuberant, sonorous, and epigrammatic to a degree that is often displeasing. He yields to Hume in elegance and distinctness—to Robertson in talents for general disquisition—but he excels them both in a species of brief and shrewd remark for which he seems to have taken Tacitus as a model, more than any other that I know of.[1]   The whole historical triumvirate are abundantly destitute of virtuous feeling—or indeed of any feeling at all.   I wonder what benefit is derived from reading all this stuff.   What business of mine is it though Timur Beg erected a pyramid of eighty thousand human skulls in the valley of Bagdad, and made an iron cage for Bajazet? And what have I to do with the savage cold-blooded policy of Charles, and the desolating progress of either Zinghis or Napoleon?   It is in vain to tell us that our knowledge of human nature is increased by the operation.   *Useful* knowledge of that sort is acquired not by reading but experience.   And with regard to political advantages—the

[1] "Irving's Library was of great use to me," writes Carlyle, "Gibbon, Hume, etc. etc.   I think I must have read it almost through; —inconceivable to me now with what ardour, with what greedy velocity, literally above ten times the speed I can now make with any book.   Gibbon, in particular, I recollect to have read at the rate of a volume a day (twelve volumes in all); and I have still a fair recollection of it, though seldom looking into it since.   It was of all the books, perhaps, the most impressive on me in my then stage of investigation and state of mind.   I by no means completely admired Gibbon, perhaps not more than I now do, but his winged sarcasms, so quiet and yet so conclusively transpiercing and killing dead, were often admirable, potent, and illuminative to me.   Nor did I fail to recognise his great power of investigating, ascertaining, of grouping and narrating; though the latter had always, then as now, something of a Drury Lane character, the colours strong but coarse, and set off by lights from the side scenes.   We had books from Edinburgh College Library, too.   (I remember Bailly's *Histoire de l'Astronomie*, ancient and also modern, which considerably disappointed me.)   On Irving's shelves were the small Didot French classics in quantity.   With my appetite sharp, I must have read of French and English (for I don't recollect much classicality, only something of mathematics in intermittent spasms) a great deal during those years."—*Reminiscences*, i. 102.

less one knows of them, the greater will be his delight in the principles of my Lords Castlereagh and Sidmouth, with their circulars, suspensions, holy leagues, and salvation of Europe. Yet if not profit there is some *pleasure* in history at all events. I believe we must not apply the *cui bono* too rigorously. It may be enough to sanction any pursuit, that it gratifies an innocent and still more an honourable propensity of the human mind. When I look back upon this paragraph, I cannot but admit that reviewing is a very beneficial art. If a dull man take it into his head to write either for the press or the post office, without materials— at a dead lift, it never fails to extricate him. But too much of one thing—as it is in the adage. Therefore I reserve the account of Hume's *Essays* till another opportunity. At any rate the second volume is not finished yet —and I do not like what I have read of it anything [like] so well as I did the first. Neither would it be profitable to tell you the faults of *Godwin's* powerful but unnatural and bombastic novel[1]—or to sing the praises of *Rob Roy*— which you have no doubt read and admired sufficiently already. Nor will I say one word about the swarms of magazines, pamphlets and observations, which, like the snow that falls in the river, are one moment white, then lost for ever. Here ends my chapter of reviewing.

Though possessing a sufficient confidence in the efficacy of my dilemma, I dare hardly venture to *demand* a speedy answer to this letter. But I do entreat you to overcome the *vis inertiæ* which adheres to mind as well as matter— and send me some account of yourself with all the velocity imaginable. You will be through Russell before now. I long to hear your estimate of his merits[2] before I try him. I am thankful for your remarks upon Hunt and Hazlitt. Except through the medium of newspapers and reviews, I have no acquaintance with them. Hazlitt is somewhat celebrated for his essay on " Fine Arts " in the supplement to the *Encyclopædia Britannica;* and for his critique on " Standard Novels " in the *Edinburgh Review.* I know not whether you have heard anything of Playfair's new demon-

---

[1] Godwin's now hardly remembered novel, *Mandeville*, was published in 1817.

[2] Russell's *History of Modern Europe.*

stration (for such he protests it is) of the composition of forces—I have no room for it now. But if you like you shall have it next time—together with the wonderful *slide* upon mount Pilatus in the canton of Lucerne for conveying timber to the lake—which he examined whilst travelling in foreign parts—and described when I was in his class, with great complacency. Do you ever see that sluggish person Johnstone of Hitchill? I protest—but there is not space for protesting. Tell him simply to write instanter if he wish his head to continue above his *hass-bone*.[1]—I remain, my dear Mitchell, yours faithfully,

THOMAS CARLYLE.

(Send a letter quickly, an thou love me.)

XXII.—To Mr. R. MITCHELL, Ruthwell Manse.

KIRKCALDY, 25*th May* 1818.

MY DEAR FRIEND—After parting with you on the quay of Burntisland, I proceeded slowly to the eastward ; and seating myself upon the brow of that crag from which the poor King Alexander *brak's neck-bane*,[2] I watched your fleet-sailing skiff till it vanished in the mists of the Forth. So Mitchell is gone ! thought I, we shall have no more chat together for many a day ; but he will write me a letter in a week at any rate : and with that consolatory expectation, I pensively returned to Kirkcaldy. If excessive studiousness has frustrated this hope, then it is well, and I shall wait contentedly till some hour of relaxation occur, when you may sport upon paper for my benefit—without detriment to your graver pursuits. But if sheer indolence possesses you, it were proper to cast off the noxious spell, as soon as possible. From the fact of my writing at present, you may conjecture (and rightly) that my own avocations are slackly pursued. My conduct, I fear, is absurd. I believe it to be

---

[1] Neck.

[2] "As he [Alexander III.] was riding in the dusk of the evening along the sea-coast of Fife, betwixt Burntisland and Kinghorn, he approached too near the brink of the precipice, and his horse starting or stumbling, he was thrown over the rock and killed on the spot. It is now no less than five hundred and forty-two years since Alexander's death [in 1285], yet the people of the country still point out the very spot where it happened, and which is called the King's Crag."—*Tales of a Grandfather*, ch. vi.

a truth (and though no creature believed it, it would continue to be a truth) that a man's dignity in the great system of which he forms a part is exactly proportional to his moral and intellectual acquirements : and I find more-over, that when I am assaulted by those feelings of discontent and ferocity which solitude at all times tends to produce, and by that host of miserable little passions which are ever and anon attempting to disturb one's repose, there is no method of defeating them so effectual as to take them in flank by a zealous course of study. I *believe* all this— but my practice clashes with my creed. I had read some little of Laplace when I saw you ; and I continue to advance with a diminishing velocity. I turned aside into Leslie's *Conics*—and went through it, in search of two propositions, which, when in your geometrical vein, you will find little difficulty in demonstrating. Take them if you will. [Propositions omitted.] . . .

I likewise also turned aside into Charles Bossut's *Mécanique*—to study his demonstration of pendulums, and his doctrine of forces. The text is often tediously explanatory—and in the notes it is but a dim hallucination of the truth that I can obtain through the medium of integrals and differentials by which he communicates it. However, I am now pretty well convinced that a body projected from the earth with a velocity of 39,000 feet per second will never return. I got Lagrange's *Mécanique Analytique* also, but to me it is nearly a sealed book. After all these divarications, and more which I shall mention afterwards, you must pardon me if I am not above half through the *Exposition du système du monde.* The first volume is beautiful, and can be understood ; great part of the second is demonstrated, he says, in the *Mécanique celeste,* and I am obliged to be content with ignorantly admiring these sublime mysteries which I am assured are *de hautes connaissances, les delices des êtres pensans.* Surely it *is* a powerful instrument which enables the mind of a man to grasp the universe and to elicit from it and demonstrate such laws—as that, whatever be the actions of the planets on each other, the mean distances of each from the sun and its mean motion can *never* change : and that, *every* variation in *any* of their elements must be periodical. To see these truths, my good Robert—to *feel*

them as one does the proportions of the sphere and
cylinder !   'Tis a consummation devoutly to be wished—but
not very likely ever to arrive.   Sometimes, indeed, on a fine
evening, and when I have quenched my thirst with large
potations of Souchong, I say to myself—away with despondency—hast thou not a soul and a kind of understanding in
it ?   And what more has any analyst of them all ?   But
next morning, alas, when I consider my understanding—
how coarse yet feeble it is, and how much of it must be
devoted to supply the vulgar wants of life, or to master the
paltry but never-ending vexations with which all creatures
are beleaguered—I ask how is it possible not to despond ?
Especially, when, as old Chaucer said of the *Astrolaby*,[1]
"the conclusions that have been founden or ells possiblye
might be founde in so noble an instrument, ben unknowen
perfitely to any mortal man in this region, as I suppose."
But I fear you are tired of these prosings—you must bear
with them.   Excepting the few friends whom Providence
has given me, and whose kindness I wish never to forfeit, I
have and am likely to have little else but these pursuits to
derive enjoyment from ; and there is none but you to talk
it over with.   They are all preaching here, and care not a
straw for Laplace and his calculus both.   You will be
preaching one of these days too—and perhaps—but it is
needless to anticipate—you must not leave off Mathematics.

Moore's *Lalla Rookh* and Byron's *Childe Harold* (canto
fourth) formed an odd mixture with these speculations.   It
was foolish, you may think, to exchange the truths of
philosophy for the airy nothings of these sweet singers : but
I could not help it.   Do not fear that I will spend time in
criticising the *tulip cheek*.   Moore is but a sort of refined
Mahometan, and (with immense deference) I think that his
character in a late *Edinburgh Review*[2] is somewhat too high.
His imagination seldom quits material, even sexual objects
—he describes them admirably,—and intermingles here and
there some beautiful traits of natural pathos ; but he seems
to have failed (excepting partially in the Fire-Worshippers)
in his attempts to portray the fierce or lofty features of

---

[1] *Vide* his treatise of the Astrolaby, "compowned for oure orizont after
the latitude of Oxenforde," to instruct "lytel Lowis my sonne."—T. C.

[2] In an article on *Lalla Rookh*, by Jeffrey, November 1817.

human character. Mokannah in particular, insensible to pain or pity or any earthly feeling, might as well, at least for all practical purposes, have been made of clockwork as of flesh and blood. I grieve to say that the catastrophe excited laughter rather than horror. The poisoned believers sitting round the table, with their black swollen jobber-nowls reclining on their breasts, and saucer-eyes fixed upon the ill-favoured prophet—appeared so like the concluding scene of an election-dinner, when all are dead-drunk but the Provost, a man of five bottles, with a carbuncled face and an amorphous nose, that I was forced to exclaim, *Du sublime au ridicule il n'y a qu'un pas*. Moore is universally said to be the author of *Letters from the Fudge Family*—a work, if I may judge by copious extracts, of extraordinary humour. Phil Fudge seems to mean poor Southey. I perceive, Mitchell, that I cannot finish this letter in time for the post as I intended, and since there is still a streak of radiance on the horizon's brim, I may as well go forth to enjoy it. Therefore good-bye, my old friend, for a short season. $8\frac{1}{2}$ o'clock P.M.—11 o'clock—I return from a saunter with Pears, and an unprofitable inspection of his chaotic library, to conclude my task. *Pennam* amens capio; nec sat rationis in *penna*. Be easy in your mind; I am going to *write*, not *fly*. That dissertation upon the Eastern Romance is so long-winded that I cannot in conscience afflict you with any remarks upon the deep-toned but [word illegible] poetry of Lord Byron. What think you of his address to Alphonso duke of Ferrara, the persecutor of Tasso?

> " *Thou !* formed to eat, and be despised and die,
> Even as the beasts that perish, save that thou
> Hadst a more splendid trough and wider sty :
> *He !* etc."

This is emphatic enough. I need not speak of Dr Chalmers's boisterous treatise upon the causes and cure of pauperism in the last *Edinburgh Review*. His reasoning (so they call it) is disjointed or absurd—and his language a barbarous jargon—agreeable neither to Gods nor men. And what avail the Church politics of the General Assembly—the performances of the fire-proof signora (Geraldini ?)—or the flagellations of Bill Blackwood, and the as paltry antagonist of Bill Blackwood ? But let me repress these effusions of vanity;—pleasant they may be to myself—yet unbecoming— till I turn a renowned man—which unless things be miserably conducted—will certainly (one would think) come to pass one way or another. What is the matter with Johnstone? He is becoming very unguidable—and declines apparently either to *hop or win*—in the way of writing letters. If you will not write to me yourself, Mr. Robert, I cannot help it, but must continue though "*without the least prefarment,*" to subscribe myself your faithful but disconsolate friend,

THOMAS CARLYLE.

XXIII.—To Mr. JAMES JOHNSTONE.

KIRKCALDY, 26*th June* 1818.

DEAR JOHNSTONE—It is about three weeks since, after entering my chamber on a Sunday evening, wearied with the toil, and sick with the inanity of an excursion to Edinburgh, my eyes were rejoiced with a sight of your letter. I must not exchange the sentiments with which you commence ; the partiality of friendship, and the modesty of him who feels it, may become excessive without ceasing to be amiable. I have little genius for the complimentary, and, therefore, shall not say in what esteem I hold your communications,—let it be sufficient to observe that the emotions they awaken are among the happiest of my life, and that you write so seldom is the very subject of complaint.

My journey to Edinburgh, you have learned, was productive of little enjoyment. How should it indeed? Most of my acquaintances are looking out for kirks ; some by diligent pedagogy, accompanied by a firm belief in the excellence of certain country gentlemen, and others by assiduously dancing attendance upon the leading clergymen of our venerable Establishment. This is as it should be ; but I have no part or lot in the matter. The rest speak of the St. Ann-street-buildings, the *Brownie of Bodsbeck*, with other tales by James Hogg, and things of that stamp. Now, the St. Ann-street-buildings concern only some feuars of the extended royalty ; and as for the *Brownie of Bodsbeck*, with other tales by James Hogg, they seem to have been written under the influence of a liquor more potent than that of the Pierian spring. So there needs not be much said about them. If I go to the bookseller's shop I find polemical Sciolists and pathetic *beaux-esprits*. And when I walk along the streets I see fair women, whom it were a folly to think of for a moment, and fops (dandies as they are called in current slang), shaped like an hour-glass— creatures whose life and death, as Crispin pithily observes, " I esteem of like importance, and decline to speak of either." It would be ridiculous to fret at this. Being a person of habits—I fear somewhat anomalous—belonging to no profession, and waiting, therefore, on no idol of the tribe, or rather fashionable one, to bow down before, it is but little sympathy I can look for.

I am far from laughing at your agricultural studies, nor is it wonderful that you dislike teaching—a lover of it is rare. No trade—but why do I talk ? Discontent is the most vulgar of all feelings. It is utterly useless, moreover, more than useless. Let us cultivate our minds, and await the issue calmly, whatever it may be. The honest Hibernian had nothing to support himself, his wife, and children, nothing but these four bones. Yet he did not mourn nor despair.

Your project of a tour to the Cumberland Lakes meets my mind exactly. Get matters arranged, and I shall gladly accompany you to Keswick or Ulleswater, or wheresoever you please. . . . You must endeavour to have the route marked out before this night five weeks. On Saturday, the 1st of August, if all goes well, I hope to see you at Main- hill. You must be there any way if it be in your power.

The last book worth mentioning which I have perused was Stewart's *Preliminary Dissertation*, for the second time. The longer I study the works of this philosopher, the more I become convinced of two things—first, that in perspicacity and comprehension of understanding he yields to several ; but, secondly, that in taste, variety of acquirements, and what is of more importance, in moral dignity of mind, he has no rival that I know of. Every liberal opinion has at all times found in him a zealous advocate. When he has come before the public he has borne himself with a carriage so meek, yet so commanding, and now, when, with unabat- ing ardour, he is retired to devote the last remnant of his well-spent life to the great cause of human improvement, his attitude is so pensively sublime, I regard him with a reverence which I scarcely feel for any other living person. He is a man, take him for all in all, we shall not look upon his like again. There is something melancholy in the thought that the world cannot long enjoy the light of such a mind. But the cup goes round, and who so artful as to put it by. Poor Donaldson, you see, is cut off in the prime of his days. Poor fellow, few summers have passed since he was my companion, as careless, good-natured a being as ever breathed the air of this world. And to think that he is gone excites many painful reflections upon the obvious but solemn truth that the place which now knows us will ere long know us no more at all, for ever. It is foolish, we are told, to shrink from or repine at the unalterable fate to which this earth and those that it inherit have been doomed. It is unspeakably ungrateful, too, for who would wish to live thus for ever? And one year or a thousand centuries are the same fleeting instant in the everlasting sweep of ages that have been and are to come.

"Ex Asia rediens (says Servius Sulpicius in his far-famed letter to Tully) cum ab Aegina Megaram versus navigarem, cœpi regiones circumcirca prospicere. Post nos erat Aegina, ante Megara, dextrâ Piræeus, sinistrâ Corinthus ; quæ oppida quodam tempore florentissima fuerunt, nunc prostrata ac diruta ante oculos jacent. Cœpi egomet mecum sic cogitare : Hem ! nos homunculi indignamur, si quis nostrûm interiit aut occisus est quorum vita brevior esse debet, cum uno loco tot oppidorum cadavera projecta jacent ! Visne tu te, Servi, cohibere, et meminisse, hominem te esse natum ?"

All this may be true philosophy, yet still some internal tears will fall on the graves of those whom we have loved, and who are departed to that land of darkness, and of the shadow of death, about which so much is hoped or feared and so little understood. Those are mournful thoughts. They come across my mind at times in the stillness of the solitary night, and plunge me into an ocean of fearful conjectures. "My God," exclaims the melancholy and high-minded Pascal, "enlighten my soul or take from it this reasoning curiosity." Montaigne tells us that he "reposed upon the pillow of doubt." And there is a day coming—it is even now not far distant—when all mine shall be explained or need no explanation. I will pursue these reflections no further. One thing, let us never cease to believe whatever be our destiny—an upright mind is the greatest blessing we can obtain or imagine.—Believe me to be, yours faithfully,

THOMAS CARLYLE.

XXIV.—To Mr. THOMAS MURRAY, Manse of Sorbie, by Wigtown, Galloway.

KIRKCALDY, 28th July 1818.

MY DEAR SIR—Whilst arranging some scattered papers previously to my departure from this place, which I am to leave to-morrow for Dumfriesshire, I happened to alight upon your letter. The recollection that it was unanswered awakened a feeling of remorse in my mind; and though it is near midnight, I have determined to employ the passing hour by writing you a few lines by way of a return for your affectionate farewell. If I have not done so sooner, impute it, I beseech you, to want of ability rather than of inclination. Be assured, I have not forgotten the many joyful days which long ago we spent together—sweet days of ignorance and airy hope! They had their troubles too: but to bear them, there was a light-heartedness and buoyancy of soul, which the sterner qualities of manhood, and the harsher buffetings that require them, have for ever forbidden to return.

I forbear to say much of the pursuits which have engaged me. They would little interest you, I fear. With most young men, I have had dreams of intellectual greatness, and of making me a name upon the earth. They were little else but dreams. To gain renown is what I do not hope, and hardly care for, in the present state of my feelings. The improvement of one's mind, indeed, is the noblest object which can occupy any reasonable creature: but the attainment of it requires a concurrence of circumstances over which one has little control. I now perceive more clearly than ever, that any man's opinions depend not on himself so much as on the age he lives in, or even the persons with whom he associates. If his mind at all surpass their habits, his aspirings are quickly quenched in the narcotic atmosphere that surrounds him. He forfeits sympathy, and procures hatred if he excel but a little the dull standard of his neighbours. Difficulties multiply as he proceeds; and none but chosen souls can rise to any height above the level of the swinish herd. Upon this principle, I could tell you why Socrates sacrificed at his death to Esculapius—why Kepler wrote his *Cosmographic Harmony*, and why Sir Thomas More believed the Pope to be infallible. Nevertheless one should do what he can.

I need not trouble you with the particulars of my situation. My prospects are not extremely brilliant at present. I have quitted all thoughts of the church, for many reasons, which it would be tedious, perhaps displeasing, to enumerate. I feel no love (I should wish to see the human creature that feels any love) for the paltry trade I follow; and there is before me a chequered and fluctuating scene, where I see nothing clearly, but that a little time will finish it. Yet wherefore should we murmur? A share of evil greater or less (the difference of shares is not worth mentioning) is the unalterable doom of mortals: and the mind may be taught to abide it in peace. Complaint is generally despicable, always worse than unavailing. It is an instructive thing, I think, to observe Lord Byron surrounded with the voluptuousness of an Italian Seraglio, chaunting a mournful strain over the wretchedness of human life; and then to contemplate the poor but loftyminded Epictetus—the slave—of a cruel master too—and to hear him lifting up his voice to far distant generations, in these unforgotten words: Ἀπαιδεύτου ἔργον, τὸ ἄλλοις ἐγκαλεῖν, ἐφ' οἷς αὐτὸς πράσσει κακῶς · ἠργμένου παιδεύεσθαι, τὸ ἑαυτῷ · πεπαιδευμένου, τὸ μήτ' ἄλλῳ, μήθ' ἑαυτῶ.[1] But truce to moralising—suffice it, with our Stoic to say, ἀνέχου και ἀπέχου, which, being interpreted, is *suffer and abstain*.

I heard with pleasure that you had got *licence*, and had preached with success. May you soon obtain a settlement, and feel happy in it. A Scottish clergyman, when he does his duty faithfully, is both a useful and honourable member

---

[1] "It is the way of an uninstructed man to blame others for what falls out ill for him; of one beginning to be instructed to blame himself, but of one well-instructed to blame neither another nor himself."—*Encheiridion*, c. v.

of society.   When he neglects his office, and has subscribed his creed "with a sigh or a smile" (as Gibbon spitefully remarks)—the less one says of him the better.   But I hope other things of you.

Three weeks ago I had a visit from the forlorn Poet Stewart Lewis.   He came into the school one morning, and stood plumb up without speaking a word.   I was touched to see the gray veteran, in tattered clothes, and with a pensive air, waging against necessity the same unprosperous battle which, any time these forty years, has been his constant occupation.   His wife died many months ago; and since that event he has been protracting a miserable, useless existence (he called it) by selling small poems of his own composing.   I understand he got rid of some part of his cargo here;—and of all his sorrows, by a copious potation of *usquebaugh.*   He spoke to me with much gratitude of a certain young lady in Wigton, who for your sake (I think of that Master Brook) had sought out his lodgings and replenished his purse.   He has many faults, and the crowning one of drunkenness—but some genius likewise, and a degree of taste, which, considering his habits and situation, is altogether surprising.   Moreover he is old, and poor, and not unthankful for any kindness shown him.   I pity the man and would not wish to see him die a mendicant.[1]

Perhaps you are aquainted with the tragic end of poor William Irving whom you once knew.   Though auguring little good of him, I never feared that he would do that deed, which renders his name a thing which sober people may not mention.   But now that it has happened, suicide

---

[1] Mitchell, writing to Carlyle on the 12th of October, says, "You would probably see by the Newspapers the death of poor Stewart Lewis. He had been somewhere about Maxwelltown tasting a little of his dear *usquebaugh.* He fancied his face dirty (I have this account from his son), and, with laudable desire to get it cleaned, went to the Nithside, where, stooping too low, he toppled headlong, and with difficulty regained the side. Though his clothes were hung before a fire during the night, they were still wet next day; an inflammatory fever ensued, and Lewis ended his changeful life in a low lodging-house in the village of Ruthwell. The least thing that I could do was to attend the funeral of him who had dedicated his poems to the Students of his native Annandale. He was decently interred in this churchyard, where a stone with a suitable inscription, as is customary in cases of this kind, is about to be erected to his memory."

seems a not unsuitable conclusion to his frantic and miserable way of life. I bewail his mournful destiny. Had the talents which he certainly did possess been cultivated with judgment, and directed by principle of any kind—he might have been a credit to his country.

If you write to me before September, let your letter be directed to Mainhill near Ecclefechan—after that period, to Mrs. Skeens, Kirkwynd, Kirkcaldy. Are you to leave Sorbie? I must hear of your destination. During the vacation I intend to visit the Cumberland Lakes; and I should like to see Galloway also, but I cannot make it out this Summer. Will you be in Edinburgh any time soon? When or where shall I see you? Write me a letter at least when you can find leisure, and believe me to be, my dear Murray, yours faithfully,

THOMAS CARLYLE.

XXV.—To his FATHER.

KIRKCALDY, *2d September* 1818.

MY DEAR FATHER—Having arrived in safety at this place, I sit down to give you an account of my adventures by the way—and my proceedings since I left the Mainhill. After shaking hands with Sandy I winded down the Baileyhill, easily forded the Black Esk, and proceeded along the banks of its sister stream to Eskdalemoor-manse, which I reached about seven o'clock. I cast many an anxious thought after Sandy and the horses which he was conducting: but I hope they arrived in safety after all. The minister is a kind, hospitable man. Saturday morning was wet, and he would fain have persuaded me to stay all day with him, but when he could not succeed he spread before me a large map of Dumfriesshire, pointed out the best road, and gave me a line to one Anderson (a cousin of his wife), from whom I was to get some meat as I passed Lyart upon Meggat water. After my departure the rain slackened a little, but the hilltops were covered with a dark mist which the wind tossed about briskly. I proceeded up the Esk, which originates about six miles above the manse in the junction of two streams, the Tomleuchar and the Glenderg—of which the latter rises near the eastern edge of Ettrick Pen, the former a few miles eastward. Ascending Glenderg I came into Ettrick water, which I crossed at a place called Cosser's hill, where a hospitable but sluttish and inquisitive old woman gave me some potatoes, etc., with directions for finding Kiskenhope—the head of the two Lochs (St. Mary's and the Lowes) upon Yarrow water, distant about four miles. I was upon the brow of a solitary ridge of moorland hills when I saw the two clear blue lakes, and in about half an hour I had crossed the stream which unites them, and was upon the road up Meggat, a brook which rises a little to the north of Whitecomb, and joins the eastermost lake (St. Mary's) after a course of about six miles. When I got to Anderson's at Lyart it was almost seven o'clock, and his sister pressed me much to stay all night, the man (an arrant miser as I found afterwards) did not press me so keenly. As it was raining a little, and Peebles fourteen miles distant, I thought of accepting their invitation, and having got some tea was endeavouring to enter into some conversation with this rich old farmer. But when he perceived that I was going to continue with him all night he became so churlish in his replies that I could think of it no longer, and taking my hat and stick I thanked him for his entertainment, and crossed the water of Meggat, leaving this Nabal of Yarrow with his sister in utter amazement at my departure, for it was now near eight, and the night was rainy. But in half an hour I came into road which I had travelled over before (as I came down), and though the rain continued, I reached the house of a kind herdsman upon Manor water (which comes into the Tweed near Peebles), and met with a warm reception from him, after nine o'clock. Next morning was dry, and the day became windy : so I arrived at Edinburgh that same afternoon about five—and staid all night with Donaldson—formerly Irving's assistant at Kirkcaldy. Next day I saw Mr. Leslie, who was very kind, and got me a book that I was wanting from the library, and talked with me about two hours very frankly. I also purchased for my kind Mother a black bonnet with ribands and other equipments, which the people engaged to put into a box and send by Gavin Johnston the Annan carrier. I hope she will accept of it for my sake, who owe her so much.

It is directed to the care of Robert Brand, Lockerbie. I enclose you a draught for £15, which you will know how to dispose of. It is not likely that I shall feel any want of it at present, and no one can have a better right to it than you.

My prospects in this place are far from brilliant at present. About a month before I went away, a body had established himself in my neighbourhood, and taken up a school, but could make next to nothing of it. During the vacation, however, he seems to have succeeded in getting most of my scholars—and to-day I mustered only twelve. This will never do. The people's rage for novelty is the cause of it, I suppose, for the poor creature is very ignorant, and very much given to drink. I make no doubt I could re-establish the school, but the fact is I am very much tired of the trade, and very anxious to find some other way of making my bread, and this is as good a time for trying it as any other. Irving is going away too, and I shall have no associate in the place at all. I think I could find private teaching perhaps about Edinburgh to support me till I could fall into some other way of doing. At any rate, I have more than seventy pounds (besides what I send you) of ready money, and that might keep me for a season. In short, I only wait for your advice, till I give in my resignation against the beginning of December. I have thought of trying the law, and several other things, but I have not yet got correct information about any of them. Give my kindest love to all my brothers and sisters. I expect a letter very soon, for I shall be unhappy till I resolve upon something. In the meantime, however, I remain, my dear Father, yours affectionately,

THOMAS CARLYLE.

I have not yet seen much of the country, but the crops seem more backward than in Dumfriesshire. They are busy exporting potatoes from this place to England—what part I know not—so the article will probably be dear.

XXVI.—From his MOTHER.

MAINHILL, 31st *October* 1818.

DEAR TOM—You will by this time be thinking that I

have forgot you quite, but far from that you are little out of my mind.   I have sent your socks; they are not so fine as I could have wished, not having as much [wool] as could be done on the mill, but I hope they will do for the winter. I received the bonnet; it is a very good one.   I doubt it would be very high.   I can only thank you at this time. I have been rather uneasy about your settlement, but seek direction alway from Him who can give it aright, and may He be thy guide, Tom.   I have been very uneasy about your things being so long in going off, but one disappointment after another it is so.   Tell me if anything else is wanting that is in my power and I will get it you.   I have reason to be thankful I am still in good health and spirits, yet I would be gratified much to hear of you comfortably settled nevertheless.   Let us learn to submit, and take it as God is pleased to send it.   It is a world of trouble at the best. Write me soon, Tom, do, and tell me all your news, good and bad.   We have got all our crop in; it looks very well. I daresay you will have heard of Mrs. Calvert's death.   She died soon after you went away, rather hastily.   But I daresay I have as much written as you will be able to read well. Send me a long letter.   Tell me honestly if thou reads a Chapter every day, and may the Lord bless and keep thee. I add no more, but remain your loving mother and sincere friend,

MARGARET CARLYLE.

XXVII.—To Mr. R. MITCHELL, Ruthwell Manse.

KIRKCALDY, 6th November 1818.

MY DEAR MITCHELL—About a week ago I received a letter from the Magistrates of this burgh (which letter I even now use as a blot sheet) accepting my "resignation of the Teacher of the Grammar school," as their phrase goes: and in a fortnight I shall quit my present situation.   Although I relate this event so abruptly, my part in it has not been performed without profound deliberation.   You shall hear it all.   The miseries of school teaching were known long before the second Dionysius, who opened shop, in the city of Corinth, about the middle of the fourth century before Christ.   Lucian (the Voltaire of antiquity) has left his opinion, in writing, that when the Gods have determined to render a man ridiculously miserable, they make a schoolmaster of him ; and an experience of more than four years does not, in my own case, authorise me to contradict this assertion. But of late, the loss of my companions (Irving, who left us last Saturday, and Pears, who will depart in ten days), together with some convincing proofs of unpopularity, have given to my reflections on this subject a complexion more serious than ordinary.[1] I have thought much and long of the irksome drudgery—the solitude—the gloom of my condition. I reasoned thus : These things may be endured, if not with a peaceful heart, at least with a serene countenance ; but it is worth while to inquire whether the profit will repay the pain of enduring them. A scanty and precarious livelihood constitutes the profit; you know me, and can form some judgment of the pain. But there is loss as well as pain. I speak not of the loss of health : but the destruction of benevolent feeling, that searing of the heart, which misery, especially of a petty kind, sooner or later, will never fail to effect—is a more frightful thing. The desire, which, in common with all men, I feel for conversation and social intercourse, is, I find, enveloped in a dense repulsive atmosphere—not of vulgar *mauvaise honte*, though such it is generally esteemed—but of deeper feelings, which I partly inherit from nature, and which are mostly due to the undefined station I have hitherto occupied in society. If I continue a schoolmaster, I fear there is little

[1] "In the space of two years," writes Carlyle in his *Reminiscences* (i. 140), "or rather more, we had all got tired of schoolmastering and its mean contradictions and poor results : Irving and I quite resolute to give it up for good ; the headlong Piers [*sic*] disinclined for it on the then terms longer, and in the end of 1819 (or '18? at this hour I know not which, and the old *Letters* which would show are too deep hidden), we all three went away ; Irving and I to Edinburgh, Piers to his own 'East Country' —whom I never saw again with eyes, poor good rattling soul. Irving's outlooks in Edinburgh were not of the best, considerably checkered with dubiety, opposition, or even flat disfavour in some quarters ; but at least they were far superior to mine, and indeed I was beginning my four or five most miserable, dark, sick, and heavy-laden years ; Irving, after some staggerings aback, his seven or eight healthiest and brightest. He had, I should guess, as one item several good hundreds of money to wait upon. My *peculium* I don't recollect, but it could not have exceeded £100. I was without friends, experience, or connection in the sphere of human business, was of shy humour, proud enough and to spare, and had begun my long curriculum of dyspepsia, which has never ended since !"

reason to doubt that these feelings will increase, and at last drive me entirely from the kindly sympathies of life, to brood in silence over the bitterness into which my friendly propensities must be changed. Where *then* would be my comfort? Had I lived at Athens, in the plastic days of that brilliant commonwealth, I might have purchased "a narrow paltry tub," and pleased myself with uttering gall among them of Cynosarges.[1] But in these times—when political institutions and increased civilisation have fixed the texture of society—when Religion has the privilege of prescribing principles of conduct, from which it is a crime to dissent—when, therefore, the aberrations of philosophical enthusiasm are regarded not with admiration but contempt—when Plato would be dissected in the *Edinburgh Review*, and Diogenes laid hold of by "a Society for the Suppression of Beggars" —in these times—it may not be. But this cure, or any other that I know of, not being applicable, it were better to avoid the disease. *Therefore I must cease to be a pedagogue.* The question is now reduced within a narrower compass. It remains only to inquire at what time I can quit this employment, with the greatest chance of finding another. But how, except by some brisk sally, am I likely ever to emerge from my thraldom? Scantily supplied with books, without a rival or a comrade in the pursuit of anything scientific, little can be achieved in that direction. With none here even to *show* me the various ways of living in the world, much less to help me into any of them—reduced to contemplate the busy scene of life, through the narrow aperture of printed books, Damoetas being judge, I have a right, metaphorically speaking, to be his great Apollo; inasmuch as I have found and occupied that station where the space of heaven extends not more than three ells.[2] The brightest of my days too are flying fast over my head; and the sooner I resolve, the better. Besides at this time (that of Irving's departure) I give my employers the fittest opportunity to erect an institution for education, that may end their woes on that head—which, for the last six years, have

---

[1] The gymnasium outside Athens where Antisthenes taught, whence the Cynics, some say, derived their name.

[2] " Die, quibus in terris,—et eris mihi magnus Apollo—
Tris pateat coeli spatium non amplius ulnas."
Virgil, *Ecloga* iii. 104, 105.

been neither few nor small.   In short the present is the time.
And I wrote my demission on the 23d October accordingly.
After receiving the answer above alluded to, the business
seemed to be done ; when on Monday last, a certain very
kind and worthy banker, Mr. Swan, attended by another
person, came to ask me, whether if they could offer me a
salary between £120 and £150, for teaching, in a private
capacity, some thirty scholars, I would not be induced to
remain another year among them.   Upon my signifying an
assent, they left me : to procure subscribers, I suppose ; and
I have heard no more of their proceedings.   But for this
proposal, the probable success of which I cannot estimate,
and do not rate highly—Edinburgh is certainly my destination for the winter.

I have calculated that, with economy, I can live there
for two years ; independently of private teaching, which
however I should not refuse, if, as is not likely, it should
offer itself.   During that period, if I do not study, I deserve
to continue ignorant.   Mineralogy is to be my winter's
work.   I have thought of writing for booksellers.   *Risum
teneas;* for *at times* I am serious in this matter.   In fine
weather it does strike me that there are in this head some
ideas, a few *disjecta membra*, which might find admittance
into some one of the many publications of the day.   To
live by Authorship was never my intention.   It is said not
to be common at present ; and happily so : for if we may
credit biographers, the least miserable day of an author's
life is generally the last.

> " . . . Sad cure ! for who would lose,
> Though full of pain, this intellectual being,
> Those thoughts that wander through eternity,
> To perish rather, swallow'd up and lost
> In the wide womb of uncreated night,
> Devoid of sense and motion ?"

I have meditated an attempt upon the profession of a
lawyer, or of a civil engineer ; though what person would
afford me any assistance in executing either of these
projects, I cannot say.   It is doubtful if I can even learn
the nature of the obstacles to be overcome, and the recompense of success.   This is the most provoking thing of all :
yet how to remedy it ?   I have thought of asking Mr.

Duncan for an introduction to some of his friends in Edinburgh, who might *inform* me at least upon these points, help me to get books, and show me countenance in other ways that might not interfere with their own convenience. Tell me what you think of this. But do not mention it to Mr. D.; he might regard it as an opening of the first parallel and *that* would be a mistake. When (if ever) I shall have convinced myself that it is right to overcome the scruples which one naturally feels against asking such a favour, for the first time in one's life I shall wish to execute the task, without any unnecessary meanness. The minister here is a worthy, kind man: but he has been beset with similar applications; and I cannot trouble him. Last time I was in Edinburgh, I called at Professor Christison's, with full purpose of talking with him upon this subject: but the good man was already environed with a crowd of hungry schoolmasters. I felt for myself—and made my exit in half an hour; though not till he had expounded the views of Messieurs Dufief and Sabatier, and discussed the merits of Sir James Mackintosh, the King, the late Lord Hopetoun, Dr. Parr, the Calton-hill observatory, with twenty other things, in a way, which (no offence to the General) I could not think very edifying. Mr. Leslie has already befriended me; I must allow him to " pursue the labyrinths of Physical research," without molestation. Yet without some such interference, I must be contented with *angels' visits* to the College library, and my society must consist of private teachers and probationers—a class of creatures (I speak it with a sigh) not the least despicable in Edinburgh. Their ideas are silly and grovelling, their minds unvisited by any generous sentiments; I love them not; and of course, the feeling will be mutual.

You see, my boy, that my prospects are not the brightest in nature. Yet what shall we say? Contentment, that little practised virtue, has been inculcated by saint, by savage, and by sage—and by each from a different principle. Do not fear that I shall read you a homily on that hackneyed theme. Simply I wish to tell you, that in days of darkness —for there *are* days when my support (pride or whatever it is) has enough to do—I find it useful to remember that Cleanthes, whose ὕμνος εἰς τὸν Θεόν may last yet another two thousand years, never murmured, when he laboured by night as a street porter, that he might hear the lectures of Zeno by day; and that Epictetus, the ill-used slave of a cruel tyrant's as wretched minion, wrote that Enchiridion which may fortify the soul of the latest inhabitant of Earth. Besides, though neither of these men had adorned their species, it is morally certain that our earthly joys or griefs can last but for a few brief years; and, though the latter were eternal, complaint and despondency could neither mitigate their intensity nor shorten their duration. Therefore my duty, and that of every man, on this point, is clear as light itself.

Excuse, my dear Mitchell, the egotism of this almost interminable letter. I have few other friends before whom I can unfold my secret soul. Do not say, with the French wit, *on aime mieux dire du mal de soi-même, que de n'en point parler.* Regard this rather as an *auricular confession,* intended to answer, with other purposes, that of marshalling my own reasons for my conduct—that I may be the better able to meet the result, whatever it be, with a resolute spirit. I have left myself no room for criticism (falsely so called), or remarks upon your interesting letter. How fully I participate in your feelings with regard to the men of Cambridge will appear from the foregoing pages. Yet never despair. Remember Jeremiah Horrox, John Kepler, Samuel Johnson, and a cloud of other witnesses. Have you advanced far in Gibbon? You would not, or will not, fail to admire the characters of Stilicho, of Aetius, of Boniface, of Belisarius—whilst the threefold coffin of Attila the Hun, with the barbaric splendour of his life and funeral, no less than the boisterous spirit of Alaric the Goth, whose bones *yet* repose beneath the waves of the Cosenza, might inflame your fancy with martial pomp and circumstance. What think you of Gibbon's views of the habits and opinions of those ages—his understanding—his style? I will not speak of Watson's history of the two Philips—an interesting, clear, well-arranged and rather feeble-minded work; any more than of the *Harrington and Ormond* of Edgeworth, or the chaotic jumble of Analytical institutions, Poems, Encyclopædias, Reviews, which of late I have grappled withal. I am glad to find you pleased with your Newton —the carriage was 1s. 8d., the residue I keep for you. Of

course you will write to me before I leave this place—I
say of course.   I was going to ask whether our friend
Johnstone was in the body—when lo! a letter from him
reached me;—it shall be answered, tell him, in due time.
I mourn for poor Lewis.   Where is his son?   Sir Samuel
Romilly too!   His peer is not within the empire.   But I
have done.   Write (*obsecro*) in less than a week, to, my
dear Mitchell, your faithful friend,

THOMAS CARLYLE.

XXVIII.—To Mr. R. MITCHELL, Ruthwell Manse.

EDINBURGH, *27th November* 1818.

MY DEAR MITCHELL—Those who have never known
what it is to buffet with Fortune, and to hear the voice of
a friend encouraging them in the strife, cannot understand
the pleasure which I felt from reading your letter.   It found
me on the eve of my departure from Kirkcaldy.   The plan
of a subscription-school was, according to my expectation,
given up for want of subscribers.   I was packing my clothes
and books, writing directions, settling accounts—weighing
anchor, in short, to venture once again with little ballast,
provision or experience, upon the stormy ocean of life;
when your admonitions came to shed a gleam of light
athwart my rough and doubtful course.   I thank you for
them, with all my soul.   If I have not done it sooner, or
if I do it now in a clumsy way—I desire you to consider
the trouble and vexation which a change of place and
habits produces : and if this excuse will not satisfy you, add
to it, that for some days I have enjoyed very poor health,
which two ounces of sulphate of magnesia which I swallowed
two hours ago, have not *yet* tended to diminish.

It would be ridiculous to affect displeasure at your kind
violation of my prohibition.   You have acted towards me
as became a friend.   To Mr. Duncan, who possesses the
rare talent of conferring obligations without wounding the
vanity of him who receives them,—and the still rarer disposition to exercise that talent—all gratitude is due on my
part.   It is needless to say more about my feelings upon
this head.   With regard to the abilities which you are kind
enough to suppose that I possess for writing in Reviews

and Encyclopædias—I have much doubt: I have very little respecting the alacrity with which I should engage in these enterprises. At all events, I am highly indebted for all that has already been done in that matter; and shall receive with great thankfulness the introductory letters which you mention. The countenance and conversation of such a man as Dr. Brewster [1] cannot fail to be both gratifying and instructive to one in my circumstances. If I mistake not, I have seen Mr. Henderson at Ruthwell Manse. His manners seemed to be such as become a gentleman. The information which might be derived from him, concerning the profession of law, is what I earnestly desire.

Perhaps you are curious to know the state of my feelings at this crisis of my affairs. I need not use many words to describe them. Conceive to yourself a person of my stamp (about which you should know something before this time) loosened from all his engagements with mankind, seated in a small room in S. Richmond Street, revolving in his altered soul the various turns of fate below—whilst every time that the remembrance of his forlorn condition comes across his brain, he silently exclaimes, " Why then the world's mine oyster; which I (not with *sword*, as Ancient Pistol) will open "—as best I may: and you will have some idea of my situation. I am not unhappy :—for why? I have got Saussure's *Voyages dans les Alpes;* and it is my intention to accompany him, before much time shall elapse, to the summit of the *Dôle* as well as to the *Col du Géant.* Besides, I have Irving to talk with about chemistry, or the moral sublime—Frances Dixon also, and Waugh, to spout poetry, not by weight and measure,—but in a plenteous way. There are others too—a numerous and nameless throng. I saw that admirable creature, Mr. Esbie, some weeks ago at Kirkcaldy. He came in company with one Galloway, a small dogmatical teacher of Mathematics—a wrangler of the first order—of brutal manners, and a terror to those embryo philosophers which (or rather who) frequent the backshop of David Brown. The contrast between this hirsute person and the double-refined travelling tutor was what Mr. E. himself would

---

[1] Sir David Brewster.

have called *magnifique*.   I thought of the little lap-dog, the dog of knowledge, which I had seen dancing in a ring with the rugged Russian bear.   Esbie seems to have some good nature, and as his vanity, which is very considerable, lies quite in a different direction from one's own vanity (which in most cases is also considerable), he is, I should think, rather amusing than otherwise.   To-day I saw him enter the College-yard—"and surely there never lighted upon this earth, which he scarcely seemed to touch, a more beauteous vision."   I then thought (to continue in the words of Burke) that "ten thousand swords (fists rather) would have leapt from their scabbards to avenge even a look that threatened him with insult."   But alas! poor Esbie must be content, he thinks, "*with some devil of a curacy*" as he calls it; though his acquaintance with "the first houses in England" is of the most intimate nature.

I have heard Professor Jameson deliver two lectures. I am doubtful whether I ought to attend his class after all. He is one of those persons whose understanding is over-burthened by their memory.   Destitute of accurate science, without comprehension of mind,—he details a chaos of facts, which he accounts for in a manner as slovenly as he selects and arranges them.   Yesterday he explained the colour of the atmosphere,—upon principles which argued a total ignorance of dioptrics.   A knowledge of the external character of minerals is all I can hope to obtain from him.[1]

You will readily believe that I have not read much since I wrote to you.   Roscoe's *Life of Lorenzo de' Medici*— a work concerning which I shall only observe, in the words of the Auctioneer, that it is "well worth any gentleman's perusal"—is the only thing almost that I recollect aught about.   I was grieved to read your brief notice of your ill-health.   I do hope it is re-established.   What says Newton?

---

[1] Professor Jameson's reputation was very high at this time in Edinburgh.   One may learn what was thought of him from Lockhart's account in *Peter's Letters to his Kinsfolk* (i. 250), which were published in 1819. These Letters give an entertaining picture of the Edinburgh of these years, well worth comparing with Carlyle's incidental sketches.   Chalmers, Jeffrey, Playfair, Spurzheim, Leslie, Brewster,—all the Edinburgh nota-bilities—appear in the lively and flippant pages of the brilliant and success-ful man of the world in different lights and colours from those in which they were seen by the serious, lonely, struggling student.

and Gibbon? Have you given up *all* thoughts of the Divinity Hall? Though there are few persons on earth I desire as much to see, I do not advise you to prosecute it. From the conversation which we had in the inn at Bassenthwaite Halls, and elsewhere, I judge that you are as unfit as myself for the study of Theology, as they arrogantly name it. Whatever becomes of us, let us never cease to behave like honest men.

When did you see Johnstone? I hope you often meet to point out, when other topics fail, the contour of that Alpine range in whose unforgotten bosom we spent some days in so happy a manner. Certainly he will soon hear from me. I intended to have written him long ago.

I must have a letter from you as soon as your good nature will afford me that pleasure. Excuse the dulness of this epistle and its brevity (a most uncommon fault), both of which you will charitably impute to the proper cause. I will try to do better another time. Believe me to be, my dear friend, yours faithfully,

THOMAS CARLYLE.

.   .   .   .   .   .

XXIX.—To his MOTHER, Mainhill.

EDINBURGH, *Thursday*, 17th December 1818.[1]

MY DEAR MOTHER—I expected that the Carrier would have been here before this time, and that consequently I should have had it in my power to give you notice of my condition, without putting you to the expense of postage. But as there is now little probability of his arriving this week, I can no longer delay to answer the letter which I received from my Father a considerable time ago. Few things in the world could give me greater pleasure than to learn that you are all in good health, and that your affairs are in a somewhat prosperous condition. I trust they still continue so. The boys deserve my thanks for the alacrity with which they explored the condition of that same unfortunate box. I call it unfortunate, for upon calling at the person Kay's in the Grassmarket here, I found it ill-

---

[1] A few sentences from this letter are printed in Froude's *Life of Carlyle*.

used in every particular. In the first place, though the carriage, as appeared by the marks upon the lid, had been paid—the poor dog Beck had contrived to make Kay (as a Porter testified) pay it again, inadvertently—and *he* stoutly refused to part with it, unless he were reimbursed. This, by the way, was the reason why it had never come to Kirkcaldy; all the carriers refusing to take it, because they must first pay the carriage to Edinburgh, which was marked as paid already. So the poor box was left standing for six weeks, in a damp cellar, without any one to claim it. I was forced to comply with Signor Kay's requisition—and upon paying him the 2s. 1od., had my articles brought home at last. The socks fit me well, and altogether are admirable things. The butter also was there undamaged : but the shirts—which your kindness had incited you to make for me—those shirts I was enraged to find all spotted and sprinkled with a black colour—which the body Davie here says is *mellemdew*—and which will never come out, according to the same authority. I have had them washed ; but the blackness remains. Much of it is about the breast, and if it be true that it cannot be erased, I must make night-shirts of them. This cannot be remedied, and therefore ought not to be regretted ; but the creature Smith should refund his carriage-money at the least. I find living here very high. An hour ago, I paid my week's bill, which, though 15s. 2d., was the smallest of the three which I have yet discharged. This is an unreasonable sum when I consider the slender accommodation, and the paltry ill-cooked morsel which is my daily pittance. There is also a schoolmaster right over my head, whose noisy brats give me at times no small annoyance. On a given night of the week, he also assembles a select number of vocal performers, whose *music* (as they charitably name it) is now and then so clamorous, that (when studying a Mathematical theorem) I almost wished the throats of these sweet singers full of molten lead, or any other substance which might stop their braying, for the time. Yet neither can this be avoided. I was through about fifty rooms the other day—only *one* was offered cheaper and that greatly inferior—so I shall be content till the spring. There is nothing very tragical in all this : yet it is the worst side of the picture. I ought not to forget that I am more healthy than I have been this twelvemonth. I have plenty of time to read, and am not destitute of good society—that of Irving—James Brown, a truly good lad, who was at Mainhill once—Francis Dixon, etc. Also I have *three hours* of private teaching—at two guineas a month for each hour. The first two hours I got three weeks ago. A young man had been directed to Irving to get lessons in Astronomy—Irving not finding it convenient to supply him, sent him to me : and I engaged immediately. His name is Robertson—he is an officer in the East India Company, and I find him a pleasant youth. I am only sorry that he must leave this place, in a short time, and thus cut off my salary. The other hour, which I undertook ten days ago, is devoted to teach Geometry to an old English (or Jersey) gentleman, called Saumarez, who asked Irving one day in the Natural History class, which I also attend, if he could recommend a mathematical teacher—and was immediately introduced to me. He is a most amusing creature, and the space between 8 and 9 o'clock which I daily spend with him—no less than the arguments we have together in the class, about Newton and natural philosophy—is often the most diverting of the day. He lives at the north end of the New Town, above a mile from this place ; and this walk for me, before breakfast (which is of porridge), is another advantage. Robertson lives with his mother, much in the same quarter. I go thither between ten and twelve o'clock. Then comes a walk with Brown or Dixon—or else a bout at reading till two ; next the Natural History class till three ; then dinner of fish or mutton and roots ;—and reading till midnight. This is a picture of my life ; and notwithstanding a fair proportion of anticipations and forebodings, I am not at all uncomfortable.

I saw Professor Leslie twice or thrice since I wrote to you. He requested me to attempt a most difficult problem which he was going to put into a book that he is publishing. He had not time for it himself. I wrought at it for a week ; and, notwithstanding several advances, could not do it. The day before yesterday, he advised me to let it alone a while—which I was willing to do ; and then to try it again, which I also intend to do. "Upon the whole,"

said this curious philosopher, "I see nothing so eligible
for you as to learn the engineer business; and then go *to
America*.   Great business there—Swiss gentleman went
lately—making a large fortune—many bridges and canals
—I must have you introduced to Jardine."   This Jardine
is an engineer of this city; and came from Millhousebridge
near Lochmaben—report says he is a conceited disagreeable
person.   You will start, my dear Mother, at the sound of
America.   I too had much rather live in my own country;
and lay my bones in the soil which covers those of my
Fathers.   Nor do I despair of getting a comfortable situation for the exercise of my talents somewhere within this
sea-girt isle.   On Monday I received a letter from Mr.
Duncan of Ruthwell containing three notes of introduction
—one to a certain Bailie Waugh, a bookseller of this place
who wishes to employ me as a writer in some *Review* which
he is about to commence.   I had half an hour's pleasant
chat with this Bailie, left my address with him, and went
on my way.   What the upshot may be I cannot guess.
A second letter I delivered to Dr. Brewster, Editor of the
Edinburgh Encyclopædia.[1]   He received me kindly—took
my address—talked with me a while on several subjects
—and let me go.   The kind minister of Ruthwell had,
I understand, written about getting me to write in the
Encyclopædia—the Doctor said nothing on that head.   No
matter.   The third letter is to J. A. Henderson, Esq.,
Advocate, which I have not yet delivered.   Perhaps he
will inform me about the lawyer business.   This law, I
sometimes think, is what I was intended for naturally.   I
am afraid it takes several hundreds to become an Advocate.
But for *this*, I should commence the study of it with great
hopes of success.   We shall see whether it is possible.
One of the first advocates of the day, Forsyth, raised himself from being a disconsolate Preacher to his present
eminence.   Therefore I entreat you, my Mother, not to
be any way uneasy about me.   I see none of my fellows
with whom I am very anxious to change places.   They are
mostly older than I by several years, and have as dim prospects generally as need be.   Tell the boys to *read*, and

---

[1] Brewster had undertaken the editorship of the *Edinburgh Encyclopædia* in 1808; the work was not completed till 1830.

not to let their hearts be troubled for me. Tell them, I am a stubborn dog—and evil fortune shall not break my heart, or bend it *either*, as I hope. I must write to them and to my Father before long.

I know not how to speak about the washing which you offer so kindly. Surely you thought, five years ago, that *this* troublesome washing and baking was all over ; and *now* to recommence ! I can scarcely think of troubling you. Yet the clothes are ill-washed here, and if the box be going and coming anyway—perhaps you could manage it.

But my paper is done. I add only, that with a heartfelt wish for the happiness of you all, I remain, my dear Mother, your affectionate *bairn*,

THOMAS CARLYLE.

P.S.—I know not whether I mentioned that Mr. Martin,[1] the minister of Kirkcaldy, of his own accord, gave me at my departure a most consolatory certificate—full of encomiums upon talents, morals, etc., which gratified me not a little. He was always kind to me. The favourable opinion of such a man is worth the adverse votes of many ignorant persons. The poor people of Kirkcaldy are *ill off*, I hear, for a dominie. Charles Melville was here upon the scent lately. There are many good men amongst them. I wish they had a right school.

XXX.—To Mr. JAMES JOHNSTONE.

EDINBURGH, *8th January* 1819.

MY DEAR JOHNSTONE—. . . I am grieved to see your embryo resolution of going to America. It is always a mournful thing to leave our country ; to a man of sensibility and reflection it is dreadful. I speak not of that feeling which must freeze the soul of an emigrant, when landing on the quay of Boston or New York, he reflects that the wide Atlantic is roaring between him and every heart that cares for his fate. But to snap asunder, *for ever*, the

---

[1] The Rev. Mr. Martin's house had been hospitably open to Irving and Carlyle while they were living at Kirkcaldy, and Irving afterward married his eldest daughter. The minister was "a clear-minded, brotherly, well-intentioned man."—*Reminiscences*, i. 117.

associations that bind us to our native soil ; to forget the Hampdens, the Sydneys, the Lockes, the Stewarts, the Burnses,—or to remember them only as men of a foreign land ; to change our ideas of human excellence ; to have our principles, our prejudices supplanted ; to endure the rubs which hard unkindness will have in store for us ; to throw aside old friendships, and with a seared heart to seek for new ones—all this is terrible. And after all what would you *do* there ? To teach is misery in the old world or the new : and perhaps (if it *must* be so) England is as fair a field for it as the Union. I entreat you, my dear friend, to lay aside this enterprise—at least for the present. I look upon emigration as a fearful destiny—Not more fearful, I grant, than others that might be imagined ; than such failure, for instance, as might call forth the pity of those who love us (I was about to add—and the triumph of those who hate us : but it is a paltry sentiment to care for *that ;*—if it exists within me I would wish to hide it both from you and myself) ; but thank Heaven things are not yet come to this. Consider the talents you possess—the classical, scientific, historical, above all, the agricultural knowledge, which you have acquired ; look around you ; continue to improve your mind in patience, and do not *yet* imagine that, in our own country the gates of preferment are shut against you. It will give satisfaction to me, and perhaps some relief to your own mind, to have your situation and views distinctly explained in your next letter. Write to me without reserve—as to one who can be indifferent to nothing which concerns you.

It is superfluous to say that I have bid farewell to Fife. My resolution was taken without advice, because none was to be had ; but not without long and serious meditation. I could not leave Kirkcaldy but with regret. There are in it many persons of a respectable—several of an exemplary character ; and had the tie which united us been of a less irritating nature, my time might have been spent very happily among them. At present my prospects are as dim, and my feelings of course nearly as uncomfortable as they have been at any period of my life. About the end of 1816, I remember informing you, that, in the space of two years, my views of human life had considerably altered. A similar period has again elapsed and brought with it a change less marked indeed, but not less real. Till not very long ago, I imagined my whole duty to consist in thinking and endeavouring. It now appears that I ought not only to suffer but to act. Connected with mankind by sympathies and wants which experience never ceases to reveal, I now begin to perceive that it is impossible to attain the solitary happiness of the Stoic—and hurtful if it were possible.[1] How far the creed of Epictetus may require to be modified, it is not easy to determine ; that it is defective seems pretty evident. I quit the stubborn dogma, with a regret heightened almost to remorse ; and feel it to be a desire rather than a duty to mingle in the busy current which is flowing past me, and to act my part before the not distant day arrive, when they who seek me shall not find me. *What* part I shall act is still a mystery. . . . Your faithful friend,

THOMAS CARLYLE.

P.S.—I forgot to say (what was indeed of no consequence) that I spent, along with Irving, the Christmas holidays in Fife. They were the happiest, for many reasons which I cannot at this time explain, that for a long space have marked the tenor of my life.

XXXI.—To Mr. R. MITCHELL, Ruthwell Manse.

EDINBURGH, 15*th February* 1819.

MY DEAR FRIEND—Although well aware of the propensity which exists in men to speak more about themselves than others care for hearing, yet, as you have hitherto been the participator of all my schemes, I venture to solicit your forbearance and advice, at a time when I need them as much perhaps as I have ever done.

My situation may be briefly explained. All the plans that I have formed for succeeding in any profession have involved the idea of subsisting in the interim by writing ; and every project of this kind which I have devised, up to the present date, has been frustrated by my inability to

---

[1] *Rien ne doit tant diminuer la satisfaction que nous avons de nous-mêmes, que de voir que nous désapprouvons dans un temps ce que nous approuvions dans un autre*, is the unpleasant but faithful observation of La Rochefoucault.—T. C.

procure books either for criticising or consulting.   I have,
it is true, the privilege of appearing on the floor of the
College library, to *ask* for any book,—to wait about an hour
and then to find it—not in.   But this is of small advantage.   My private teaching came to an end about a month
ago : and at this time, except a small degree of attention
which I pay to the shadow rather than to the substance of
Mineralogy—for which science it is perhaps less surprising
than unlucky that my unsettled condition and my indifferent
state of health have left me little enthusiasm ; excepting
also a slight tincture of the German language which I am
receiving from one Robt. Jardine of Göttingen (or rather
Applegarth), in return for an equally slight tincture of the
French which I communicate,—there is no stated duty
whatever for me to perform.   The source of that considerable quantity of comfort, which I enjoy, in these circumstances, is twofold.   First, there is the hope of better days,
which I am not yet old and worn enough to have quite laid
aside.   This cheerful feeling is combined with a portion of the
universal quality which we ourselves name firmness, others
obstinacy ; the quality which I suppose to be the fulcrum of
all Stoical philosophy ; and which, when the charmer Hope
has utterly forsaken us, may afford a grim support in the
extreme of wretchedness.   But there are other emotions
which, at times, arise ; when, in my solitary walks round the
Meadows or Calton Hill my mind escapes from the smoke
and tarnish of those unfortunate persons, with whom it is
too much my fortune to associate,—emotions which if less
fleeting, might constitute a principle of action at once
rational and powerful.   It is difficult to speak upon these
subjects without being ridiculous if not hypocritical.
Besides, the principles to which I allude, being little else
than a more intense perception of certain truths universally
acknowledged, to translate them into language would
degrade them to the rank of truisms.   Therefore unwill-
ingly I leave you to conjecture.   It is probable, however,
that your good-natured imagination might lead you to over-
rate my resources if I neglected to inform you that, on the
whole, my mind is far from philosophical composure.   The
vicissitudes of our opinions do not happen with the celerity
or distinctness of an astronomical phenomenon : but it is

evident that my mind, at the present, is undergoing sundry alterations. When I review my past conduct it seems to have been guided by narrow and defective views, and (worst of all) by lurking, deeply-lurking affectation. I could have defended these views by the most paramount logic : but what logic can withstand Experience ? This is not the first, and, if I live long, it will not be the last of my revolutions. Thus—*velut unda supervenit undam*—error succeeds to error ; and thus while I seek a rule of life— life itself is fast flying away. At the last, perhaps my creed may be found to resemble too nearly the memorable Tristrapedia of Walter Shandy, of which the minute and indubitable directions for Tristram's baby-clothes were finished when Tristram was in breeches.

But I forget the aphorism with which I began my letter. Here, at least, let me conclude this long-winded account of my affairs ; and request from you as particular an account of your own. We cannot help one another, my friend, but mutual advice and encouragement may easily be given and thankfully received. Will you go to Liverpool or Bristol or anywhither, and institute a "classico-mathematical Academy"? or what say you to that asylum or rather hiding-place for poverty and discontent, America? To be fabricating lock No. 8, among the passes of the Alleghany !

Some nights ago, by the kindness of Dr. Brewster, I was present at a meeting of the Royal Society. It is pleasant to see persons met together—when their object even *professes* to be the pursuit of knowledge. But if any one should expect to find, in George Street, an image of the first Royal Society,—when Newton was in the chair, and Halley at the table,—he cannot (unless his fancy be the stronger) fail of disappointment. He will find indeed a number of clean, well-dressed (some of them able-bodied) men : but in place of witnessing the invention of fluxions or the discovery of gravitation, he may chance to learn the dimensions of a fossil stick, or hear it decided that a certain little crumb of stone is neither to be called *mesotype* nor *stilbite*. This (a critic would say) has very much the look of drivelling. But *pauca verba.*—Dr. B. is said to be almost the only efficient member of this philosophical guild. I may mention (though this has nothing earthly to do with it) that I have seen the Doctor twice since my first visit; that I have met with a kind reception, and found instruction as well as entertainment in his conversation.

In conformity with ancient custom, I ought now to transmit you some of my studies. But I have too much conscience to dilate upon this subject. Besides, it is not so easy to criticise the brilliant work of Madame de Staël —*Considerations sur quelques Événemens de la Révolution*— as to tell you, what I learnt from a small Genevese attending Jameson's class, that she was very ugly and very immoral —yet had fine eyes, and was very kind to the poor people of Coppet and the environs. But she is gone; and with all her faults she possessed the loftiest soul of any female of her time. Upon the same authority, I inform you that Horace Benedict Saussure (whose beautiful *Voyages dans les Alpes* I have not yet finished) died twenty years ago; but Theodore, his son, is still living. Moreover Sismondi (another member of the Geneva Academy) is *un petit homme, vieux, mais vif, très vif.* I read Bailly's *Mémoires d'un Témoin de la Révolution*, with little comfort. The book is not ill-written: but it grieved me to see the august historian of astronomy, the intimate of Kepler, Galileo, and Newton, "thrown into tumult, raptured, or alarmed," at the approbation or the blame of Parisian tradesmen—not to speak of the "*pauvres ouvriers,*" as he fondly names the dogs *du faubourg St. Antoine.* With regard to Mineralogy—the maxim of Corporal Nym is again applicable. Peace be to Brochant, Brongniart, and "the illustrious Werner!" It is a mournful study—and the Teacher, "a cold long-winded native of the deep." Do you wish to know the important fact, that the stone which I brought from Helvellyn is feldspar-porphyry? Skiddaw is of *Thonschiefer* (clay-schistus); and I firmly believe that the other rocks of that wild country have names equally beautiful and descriptive. Of their *properties* I am forbid to know anything. *En-veut-on la cause?* The "external characters" are reckoned enough in the school of Freyberg.

Upon a cool comparison of dates, I find that if I carry this letter to the post-office to-night, you may have it on Monday. The thing is then resolved upon. But it verges upon midnight; and it is high time to conclude the useless

labours of the day—on which I have walked to Dalkeith
for the purpose of exercise,—heard a heart-rending sermon
—and have *not* studied the moon's erection in *Lalande*.
When am I to hope for an answer? It may be short or
long—it will not fail to comfort the soul of, my dear
Mitchell, your faithful friend,

THOMAS CARLYLE.

XXXII.—From his FATHER.

MAINHILL, *20th February* 1819.

DEAR SON—We received the box with your letters in
it, which we were very glad to see, and you said it was a
long time since you had a letter from your Mother or me,
as Sandy has been much engaged this week and the waffler[1]
did not get his cart home till Monday, and Sandy set out
for Dumfries Fair on Tuesday morning, and did not come
home till Thursday night, and on Friday night he was at
the library, as their Books was come home, and he got
Guy Mannering for the first, and we think in time there will
be a good library; however that may be, I thought I
would send you a scrawl. I have nothing to write you
worth reading, but I thought you would be disappointed if
you got the box and no letter in it, but I can say we are
all in good health at present. Your Mother is hearty, and
baking you two or three cakes and sorting your shirts and
stockings, and in short we are very comfortable, having
plenty of meal and potatoes. We have a good deal of
corn this year, more than we had last year, and I think we
will can pay the Rent this year at any time we think proper.
We are well forward with ploughing, as there has been
very little frost to stop the Ploughs this winter. . . . I
must have done, but not without telling you that the little
Lassies are all running about, and Jamie and John are a
good deal bigger since you saw them, and Sandy and
your Mother agree very well now, though we have many
arguments about Religion, but none in ill-nature ; but I
add no more, but all the family's kind respects to you, and
I remain, dear Son, your affectionate and loving Father,

JAS. CARLYLE.

---

[1] The carrier's nickname, whiffler, loiterer.

XXXIII.—To Alexander Carlyle, Mainhill.

EDINBURGH, 23*d February* 1819.[1]
(Mrs. Scott's, 15 Carnegie Street.)

MY DEAR BROTHER—I sit down to write a letter to you, at this late hour of the night, in order to inform you of some steps which I have taken since you last heard from me. The uncomfortableness of the person Davie's lodging has been frequently alluded to in our correspondence. Vermin of various sorts, which haunted the beds of that unfortunate woman, together with sluttishness and a lying, thievish, disposition with which she was afflicted—at length became intolerable ; and on Wednesday, I told the creature that her "ticket-board" (fatal signal !) must once more be hoisted—in plain words, that I was about to forsake her house entirely. She received the news with considerable dudgeon ; but as my words to her were calm and few as well as emphatic, she made no remonstrance. To secure another room was my next care. John Forrest's place, which has few recommendations except the excellent demeanour of Mrs. F., was engaged, I found, till the beginning of April. Of the other places at which I called, some were dirty, others dear, others had a suspicious look ; none were suitable. In short, not to trouble you with the detail of these pitiful affairs, I saw no better plan than to propose a junction with one Hill (a Nephew of Mrs. Irving's—Bogside —from Panteth Hill, Mouswald), who is here studying law. He is a harmless kind of youth—and had a clean landlady, who kept two rooms with a bed in each, which we could get for 8s. per week. My proposal was immediately accepted of : and I removed hither yesterday (Monday) evening. This comradeship is not altogether to my liking, as I fear it may encumber my researches ; but when I consider the saving of 3s. 6d. per week (not to speak of that which arises from *two* eating together)—as well as the neatness and comfort which seems to pervade this place, I am induced to put up with the other inconveniences till April, when I may take Forrest's room, or have a choice of others. Besides, we stipulated to have a fire in each room when we liked at night, so that I can retire to this

---

[1] A brief extract from this letter is given by Mr. Froude in his *Life*.

small chamber whenever I have anything particular to investigate. The chamber, to say truth, is not many square feet in extent, yet it will do excellently well for the short season during which I shall occupy it. *Flitting* is an operation which has, of late years, become very irksome to me; so you are not to expect that, in this letter, I can give you any very interesting remarks: forasmuch as I have even now scarcely ended the arrangement of my goods. I write principally to send you my address, and to request an answer from some of you.

I know it will please you all to hear that my health is good. Whenever the morning is fair, I walk before breakfast; and after finishing the German at eleven o'clock, I generally stroll for an hour or so about the environs of this city—a practice which, I know well, is the only plan for securing vigorous health. There is a young man, Ferguson (a cousin of the Celt Maclaren, whom you dined with at Dysart),[1] formerly Irving's assistant at Kirkcaldy—who, being disengaged at that hour, is as glad as I to escape from the sin and sea-coal of Edinburgh, and often accompanies me. He is a sensible, pleasant man, three or four years older than myself. On Tuesday last, when he and I were returning into the town from our excursion, we met Dr. Brewster, in company with two men of note. The Doctor stopped to tell me that he had got a paper on Chemistry written (in French) by Berzelius, professor of that science at ·Stockholm—which was to be published in April:—would I translate it? I answered in the affirmative; and next day went over to get the paper in question. It consists of six long sheets, written in a cramp hand, and in a very diffuse style. I have it more than half-done. The labour of writing it down is the principal one. In other respects there is no difficulty. I do not expect great remuneration for this thing; but as I am anxious to do it pretty well, it interrupts my other pursuits a little. Before I began it, I was busied in preparing to write about some other thing; but what will be the upshot of it I cannot say. I tell you all these things, because I know that nothing which concerns me is matter of indifference to you.

---

[1] A village near Kirkcaldy, now almost joined to it.

About a week ago, I very briefly discussed an *hour* of private teaching.   A man in the New Town applied to one Nicol, public teacher of Mathematics here, for a person to give instruction in Arithmetic or something of that sort. Nicol spoke of me, and I was in consequence directed to call upon the man next morning.   I went at the appointed hour, and after waiting a few minutes, was met by a stout impudent-looking man—with red whiskers—having very much the air of an attorney, or some creature of that sort. As our conversation may give you some insight into these matters, I report the substance of it.   " I am here," I said after making a slight bow, which was just perceptibly returned, " by the request of Mr. Nicol to speak with you, sir, about a mathematical teacher whom he tells me you want."   " Aye.   What are your terms?"   " Two guineas a month, for each hour."   " *Two guineas ! !* for private *teaching*—that is perfectly extravagant !"   " I *believe* it to be the rate at which every teacher of respectability in Edinburgh officiates ; and I *know* it to be the rate below which *I* never officiate."   " *That* won't *do* for *my* friend." " I am sorry that nothing less will do for *me*.   Good morning."   And I retired with considerable deliberation. The time has been when I should have vapoured not a little, at being so cavalierly treated by a wretched person of this description.   But it is altered now.   I reflected only that this man wanted (and that was natural) to have his business done cheap ; and that his ill-breeding was. his misfortune perhaps as much as crime.   A day may come when I shall look back upon these things with a smile,—if that day should never come, the maxim of the poet is not more trite than true—

> " Honour and shame from no condition rise ;
> Act *well your part : there* all the honour lies."

This world, my boy, is but a fight at best ; and though the battle go against us, yet he who quits him like a man is an object upon which (as an old philosopher has written) superior natures delight to look.

Last week I received an umbrella which I had left in Fife, and a kind letter from Mr. Swan.   If ever I come to anything, *that* is one person whom I shall remember.

.   .   .   .   .   .

Tell me how Father, Mother, and all the rest of you are doing. Give my kindest love to all about the house, and believe me to be, my dear Brother, yours faithfully,

THOMAS CARLYLE.

XXXIV.—From his MOTHER and his Sister MARGARET.

MAINHILL, 25*th March* 1819.

DEAR TOM—It is a long time since I wrote you a single line, and I am blundering already, as I am very desirous to know how you are coming on. Tell me all about it. Do you sit late? Do you read a Chapter or two every night? I hope you do, and pray for a blessing on all your undertakings. O seek while you have time to know Him whom to know is life eternal; our time is short and also uncertain. I am sorry to inform you that my sister Mary died last Sabbath night. We must all follow in a little, and O that we were wise to think on our latter end. I beg, Tom, you do not sit late to injure your health; but I will say no more, but hope you will excuse this scrawl, and I am, your affectionate Mother,   PEGGY C.

MY DEAR BROTHER—We received your letter, and we were very happy to hear that you were in good health. There is nothing that is worth telling you about. I have read *Guy Mannering*, and I liked it very well. I have read the *Indian Cottage*, and I liked it very much. I am reading the *History of England*, and I have got to the reign of George III. I will have done, as Sandy has to go to the clachan[1] this night. I add no more, but that I remain your   MARGARET CARLYLE.

XXXV.—To ALEXANDER CARLYLE, Mainhill.

EDINBURGH, 29*th March* 1819.

MY DEAR BROTHER—I snatch a hurried hour from the German lesson, to answer your kind and entertaining epistle, which reached me this forenoon. I need not say how pleasing it is to me to learn that you are all in good bodily health and comfortable spirits. The most important part

[1] Village.

of my task will be accomplished, when I have assured you that the same is the case with me. I still walk out before breakfast—and for an hour or two after; of which practice I find the beneficial effects in an increased appetite for *victual*, and a general vigour of body. I have no doubt that two or three months of summer exercise will completely restore this my *digestive apparatus* (as our Professor calls it) to that state of activity which a person at my age, not addicted to excesses of any kind, and gifted with a sound constitution, ought naturally to expect. . . .

I am glad to understand that the library is in a prosperous state. It is to be hoped that our native village will no longer be the scorn of neighbouring districts, for its deficiency in this particular.

You are very right in stating that the Abbé Raynal is rash in some of his conjectures. He was a jesuit priest in his time; but afterwards quarrelled with them—renounced their society, and with it, all moderation in treating of their religion. He was obliged to leave France for his opinions, and resided for a time in England, and lastly in the Netherlands. The man seems to have had a fiery temper; and it is only for the *facts* that his books contain, that any one can respect them. There is no wonder that you feel it impossible to find much time for reading in the present season. Keep doing a little at your hours of relaxation—both in writing and reading; and you will never repent it. In reading Raynal, you will, of course, attend to the Geography of the countries.

What ails that indolent young person, Doil, or more properly speaking, Jack, that he will not write? If I had any time, I would send him a letter this very night.

With respect to my occupations at this period; they are not of the most important nature. Berzelius' paper is printed. I was this day correcting the proof-sheet. The translation looks not very ill in print. I wish I had plenty more of a similar kind to translate : and good pay for doing it. Let us wait a while. I am still at the German, as I hinted above. My teacher is not a man (any more than he was a boy) of brilliant parts ; but we go on in a loving way together—and he gives me the *pronunciation* correctly, I suppose ; I am able to read books, now, with a dictionary.

At present I am reading a stupid play of Kotzebue's—but to-night I am to have the history of Frederick the Great from Irving. I will make an *awfu' struggle* to read a good deal of it and of the Italian in summer—when at home. . . .

There is nothing new here that I wot of—fierce sort of weather, which I daresay is no stranger to you. How do the farming operations proceed? I hope to help you at the haytime. But time is our tedious scroll should now have ending. I am always, my dear Boy, yours faithfully,

THOMAS CARLYLE.

XXXVI.—To his MOTHER, Mainhill.

EDINBURGH, Monday (29th March), 1819.[1]

MY DEAR MOTHER—I am so much obliged to you for the affectionate concern which you express for me in that brief letter—that I cannot delay to send you a few words by way of reply.[2] I need not repeat what I have already told to Sandy, who will be glad to communicate it, that I am in good health. If I continue to walk, I shall become very strong shortly. I was affected by the short notice you give me of Aunt Mary's death, and the short reflection with which you close it. It is true, my dear Mother, that "we must all soon follow her"—such is the unalterable and not unpleasing doom of men—then it is well for those who, at that awful moment which is before every one, shall be able to look back with calmness, and forward with hope. But I need not dwell upon this solemn subject—it is familiar to the thoughts of every one who has any thought.

I am rather afraid that I have not been quite regular in reading that best of books which you recommended to me. However, last night I was reading upon my favourite Job; and I hope to do better in time to come. I entreat you to believe that I am sincerely desirous of being a good man; and though we may differ in some few unimportant particulars, yet I firmly trust that the same Power which created us with imperfect faculties will pardon the errors of every

---

[1] The larger part of this interesting letter is given by Mr. Froude, *Life*, i. 62.

[2] Mr. Froude prints this sentence as follows: "I am so much obliged to you for the affectionate concern which you express for me in that long letter, that I cannot delay to send you a few brief words by way of reply."

one (and none are without them) who seeks truth and righteousness with a simple heart.

You need not fear my studying too much. In fact, my prospects are so unsettled that I do not often sit down to books with all the zeal that I am capable of. You are not to think I am fretful. I have long accustomed my mind to look upon the future with a sedate aspect ; and, at any rate, my hopes have never yet failed me. A French author (D'Alembert, one of the few persons who deserve the honourable epithet of honest man) whom I was lately reading, remarks that one who devotes his life to learning ought to carry for his motto *Liberty, Truth, Poverty ;* for he that fears the latter can never have the former. This should not prevent one from using every honest effort to attain a comfortable situation in life ; it says only that the best is dearly bought by base conduct, and the worst is not worth mourning over. But I tire you, I doubt. We shall speak about all these matters more fully in summer. For I am meditating just now to come down to stay awhile with you, accompanied with a cargo of books—Italian, German, and others. You will give me yonder little room—and you will 'waken me every morning about 5 or 6 o'clock—then *such* study. I shall delve in the yard too ; and in a word become not only the wisest but the strongest man in those regions. This is all *claver*, but it pleases one. The young man Murray (with whom I used to correspond) informs me that he thinks of going to teach and preach in the island of Man : and invites me to spend a month or two with [him]. Perhaps it would be well to go. But we shall talk about all this afterwards.

If the carrier do not come before a fortnight, you may direct the box to me at Forrest's. I long to have some cakes. The last, I think, were the best I ever ate. The butter you will be astonished to learn is nearly done. I have no doubt that it has been filched : and besides Hill has eaten of it since I came, having given me meal in return. If you send any, let it be a pound or so. I am reduced to this part of the sheet [the first page, above the date] to subscribe myself, my dear Mother, yours most affectionately,

THOMAS CARLYLE.

XXXVII.—From his MOTHER.[1]

MAINHILL, 10th April 1819.

DEAR SON—I received your letter gladly, and was happy to hear of your welfare. We are all about our ordinary way, thank God !

Oh, my dear, dear son, I would pray for a blessing on your learning. I beg you with all the feeling of an affectionate mother you would study the Word of God, which He has graciously put in our hands. Oh, that it may powerfully reach our hearts, that we may discern it in its true light. God made man after His own image, therefore he behoved to be without any imperfect faculties. Beware, my dear son, of such thoughts ; let them not dwell on your mind. God forbid ! But I daresay you will not can read this scrawl. I have sent you a few cakes and a little butter. I will send you more next time. Send the box back with the carrier. I would advise you to come home early in season. I know it would be for your health, and it is surely very necessary. Do send me a long letter and tell me when you will be home, and all your news. I am in a hurry, as you may see by blunders I have [made]. I hope you will overlook them, and I am [your] affectionate mother,

MARGARET CARLYLE.

P.S.—Do make religion your great study, Tom ; if you repent it, I will bear the blame for ever.

XXXVIII.—To Mr. R. MITCHELL, Ruthwell Manse.

MAINHILL, 31st May 1819.

MY DEAR FRIEND—In compliance with your request, I transmit to you, by the medium of our dearly beloved Johnstone, the information which I have gleaned respecting your Brother at St. John's,—and the plan of our correspondence during the summer. It is the rainy evening of a dull day, which I have spent in reading a little of Klopstock's *Messias* (for the man Jardine, who broke his engagement) ;

<hr>

[1] Printed in part, and with errors, in *Life*, i. 63

and in looking over the inflated work of Squire Bristed on *America and her Resources*.[1] "Vivacity," therefore, on my part, is quite out of the question. But without further preface. . . .

I have done, as usual, almost nothing since we parted. Some one asked me with a smile, of which I knew not the meaning, if I would read *that* book, putting into my hands a volume of Rousseau's *Confessions*. It is perhaps the most remarkable tome I have ever read. Except for its occasional obscenity, I might wish to see the remainder of the book ; to try, if possible, to connect the character of Jean Jacques with my previous ideas of human nature. To say he was mad were to cut the knot without loosing it. At any rate, what could have induced any mortal, mad or wise, to recollect and delineate such a tissue of vulgar debauchery, false-heartedness and misery, is quite beyond my comprehension. If we regret our exclusion from that Gallic constellation, which has set, and found no successor to its brilliancy—the *Memoirs of Marmontel* or Rousseau's *Confessions* should teach a virtuous Briton to be content with the dull sobriety of his native country. I will not speak of the Abbé Raynal : of others I have nothing to say.

It is late ; the husbandmen of this rustic mansion are all sunk in profound repose : why should *I* longer wake ? A slender steed is to be saddled for me to-morrow by six o'clock—whereupon I design to ride with this sheet to Johnstone at Bogside—an important errand, you will say. Meanwhile, Good-night. Ever yours,

THOMAS CARLYLE.

.   .   .   .   .   .

XXXIX.—To Mr. R. Mitchell, Ruthwell Manse.

MAINHILL, 14*th July* 1819.

I have not taken up the pen, my dear Mitchell, because of being smit with the love of sacred letter-writing ; but simply to acquit me of a debt, which for some time has lain rather heavy on my conscience. An ancient sage philosopher has said that nothing should be done *invita*

---

[1] This book, which made some noise at the time, was by the Rev. John Bristed, a clergyman of the Church of England, who settled in America.

Minerva; my respect for antiquity is very considerable; but without infringing such precepts, which laziness also raises her amiable voice to applaud, my terrestrial exploits would quickly have a close. After all, this communication by letter gives occasion to many squabbles between the moral and the active powers: I wish from my soul some less laborious mode of friendly intercourse could be devised. Much may be done in the flight of ages. I despair of steam indeed; notwithstanding its felicitous application to so many useful purposes: but who can limit the undiscovered agents with which Knowledge is yet to enrich Philanthropy? Charming prospect for the dull, above all, the solitary dull of future times! Small comfort for us, however, who in no great fraction of one age shall need to care nothing about the matter. But wherefore whine? Employing rather our own very limited gifts, *agamus pingui Minervâ, ut aiunt*—since we can have no other. The best quality which I can communicate to my narrative of my journey to Cumberland is extreme brevity. In fact, however strongly a love of the sublime might tempt me to renew the kind anxiety you felt on our account, the love of truth, which is or ought to be more powerful, compels me to declare that nothing dangerous or wonderful occurred. Maugre the predictions of your light-bodied grocer, the Skinburness wherry buffeted the billows of the Solway, as proudly as ever the Bucentaur did those of the unquiet Adriatic. We had not even the dubious pleasure of being frightened. A poor Cumbrian statesman, however, enjoyed a more spirit-stirring fortune. Unused to his situation, he cast a penetrating glance upon "the secrets of the hoary deep;" his visage became pallid and elongated; and when, turning round, he noticed the entrance of a spoonful of spray—"*Lock*," he exclaimed in a sepulchral tone, "*Lock prasarve us! see as it's coomin' jain' in theare!*"[1] But the lapse of two hours delivered him from all his terrors. On arriving at Workington next morning, the *Severn*, we were told, was not to proceed on her voyage for a week. Though wishing to enjoy the melancholy satisfaction of seeing Johnstone fairly under way;[2] yet.

---

[1] See how it is coming rushing in there.

[2] Mr. Johnstone was about to sail for Nova Scotia, where, at Annapolis

when Friday came, and (Harrington, Whitehaven, Cocker-mouth, Crummock Water, etc., being visited) his day of sailing was still at a considerable distance—the opportunity of a Dumfries sloop induced me to take farewell of our friendly emigrant. What my feelings were that afternoon, I need not describe. To some days of mournful excitement, a sort of stupor had succeeded, which the noise of two half-civilised shipmen and the task of *guessing* at some stanzas of Tasso were little calculated to dispel. By this time, poor James is most probably inspecting the rugged shores of Fundy Bay. Let us hope that his talents, and those virtues which are their modest adornment, will secure, from the Acadians, that affection and esteem which all who know him have never failed to pay. I do not wish you to convince me that we three shall never meet again under more benign auspices.

Since my return, except one journey to Dumfries, which I undertook for the purpose of engaging a supply of poetry, reviews, and such small gear, during my continuance in these parts,—I have not been four miles from home. Jardine gives me a solitary lesson each week in German, which I repay by one in French. Of Italian nothing should be said: and with respect to Lesage's *Theory of Attraction*,[1] my efforts are feeble and far between. I know not if there be a Goddess of Sloth—though considering that this of all our passions is the least turbulent and most victorious, it could not without partiality be left destitute. But if there be, she certainly looks on with an approving smile—when in a supine posture I lie for hours with my eyes fixed upon the pages of Lady Morgan's *France* or the travels of Faujas de Saint-Fond [2]—my mind seldom taking the pains even to execrate the imbecile materialism, the tawdry gossiping of the former, or to pity the infirm speculations and the already antiquated Mineralogy of the

Royal, he was to be tutor in the family of a Mr. Ritchie. Mitchell, in a letter of 23d April 1819 says, "Johnstone would rival Moses if he were living, being by far the meekest man in these times. Like Kilmeny, he is as pure as pure can be; like Nicodemus [sic], he is one in whom there is no guile."

[1] Lesage's *Traité de Physique Mécanique* was published in 1818.

[2] Probably *Voyage en Angleterre, en Écosse et aux iles Hébrides*, par Faujas de Saint-Fond, Paris, 1797.

latter. What shall I say to the woebegone Roderick, last of the Goths; and others of a similar stamp? They go through my brain as light goes through an achromatic telescope. When even this task becomes tiresome; or when the need of exercise (which I never neglect for a day with impunity) induces me to take the fields; I saunter about, building deceitful hopes; or when otherwise disposed, indulging an obdured recklessness, which I am apt enough to dignify with the name of patience. Do you know of a more edifying life? Seriously it becomes you, as my Father Confessor, to administer an appropriate rebuke.

I am glad to hear of your innocent enjoyments. Malcolm Laing produced in me, some years since, an opinion of Ossian similar to yours;[1] from which indeed I do not recollect of hearing any but one person dissent. The exception in question was an Aboriginal from the edge of Mid-Lorn, whom I met with last Winter. Some two hundred Latin vocables, which he had picked up at St. Andrews, seemed only to have strengthened his conviction of the Gael's infinite superiority in every department of Nature and Art. The mention of the sledge-cars, the itch, the ignorance of his Celtic kinsmen was a piercing thrust, which could not be parried by the barrenness and altitude of the highland hills, since Switzerland was ready with her Alps to oppose his Grampians, and with her Zwingles, her Gessners, her Hallers, Eulers, Bernouillis, to eclipse his solitary Fergusson and Maclaurin. Poor Pseudo-Ossian was silenced as easily by the intrepid Orkney man; and this fervid patriot, after an hour of torture, uttered a keen vituperation on Malcolm and me for being "Mongrels of the plain," which shut the scene. "The schoolmaster of Badenoch," like every dog, has had his day.

You speak very much at your ease about visiting me

<hr>

[1] "I have just been reading," Mitchell had written in his last letter, "Malcolm Laing's dissertation on the authenticity of Ossian's Poems, which seems to prove beyond the possibility of a doubt that these productions existed nowhere but in the brain of the Schoolmaster of Badenoch, M'Pherson's life in his Son-in-law's [Dr. Brewster's] *Encyclopædia* gives us to understand nearly the same thing, and I confess to you that I feel a sort of secret pleasure in beholding lying vanities like these exposed to public indignation and contempt. I would be glad to know your opinion on this subject."

in—a few weeks! I should lose patience, but there is one sad and sole relief—if the mountain will not come to Mahomet, Mahomet knows what course to take. I was going to say one of these Saturdays, but, since I began to write, a letter from Dr. Brewster has arrived, which will very possibly bring me over on Saturday first. It is about that calculating Geo. Ross; and I must see Mr. Duncan. The letter has already spent a week upon the road, and there is no time to lose. Expect me therefore, unless "Diana in the shape of rain"[1] prevent me and my poor shelty from travelling. O that I saw the "imp of fame" wherewith poor Murray is in travail! "The Stewartry."[2] But I have done.—Yours, my dear Mitchell, in all sincerity of heart,

THOMAS CARLYLE.

XL.—To John A. Carlyle, Mainhill.

EDINBURGH, 11*th November* 1819.

MY DEAR BROTHER—At length I have leisure to devote a few minutes to the duty of detailing the particulars of my history, since our parting on the summit of Ericstane. . . .

I am seated in the back-room of a Mrs. Thomson (wife of a Tailor), which I rent at the rate of 6s. per week, fire included. This person seems to have a good character in the neighbourhood; and from the few symptoms I have yet been able to observe, it appears likely that I shall be very snug here. The room is not large, but it is clean,—

---

[1] The allusion to "Diana" as an obstruction in one shape or another, was one that Carlyle made more than once in later years. See his letter to Emerson of 13th May 1835, and his letter to me in 1874, cited in a note to the letter to Emerson in the published Correspondence of Carlyle and Emerson, i. 69. But his memory, usually of extraordinary accuracy, had in this, through all his life, played him false. The allusion was derived from *Hudibras*. But in *Hudibras* it is "Pallas," not "Diana," who intervenes to hinder the intent of the knight.

> "But Pallas came in shape of rust,
> And 'twixt the spring and hammer thrust
> Her Gorgon shield, which made the cock
> Stand stiff, as 'twere transform'd to stock."
>
> *Hudibras*, Part i. Canto ii. 781-784.

[2] The Stewartry of Kirkcudbright. This, in reference to Murray's *Literary History of Galloway*, published in 1822; "valuable but undeservedly neglected," Lowndes calls it.

and the neat little landlady says it is perfectly free of smoke and of most detested *bugs.*

Thus, my dear Jack, have I written for thy friendly perusal a full account of my transactions up to this date. The Waffler (well he deserves that *nom de guerre !*) is not yet come to town ; so that being unable to transact any business, I have full leisure to reflect upon every part of my condition. Pretty strong in body, and capable, as I know, of vigorous effort, I am far from despairing. However, as I have nothing new to tell you upon this subject, I forbear to discuss it further for the present. Let us be contented, my bonny boy, prudent, active, resolute in improving *every* advantage which our situation affords—and moderate success is hardly doubtful.

9 o'clock P.M.—After an interval of five hours, spent in reading the *Edinburgh Review*, and executing various commissions, I resume my lucubrations. The unhappy carrier is not come. What can it be that keeps him ? Is his steed foundered—or himself overpowered with liquor ? Alas ! poor Rose !

At this time, I guess, Alick and the rest of you are seated around the *room*-fire—each pursuing his respective study. Good luck to you all ! Be diligent and you will not miss your reward. Tell the small *childer* that I expect copies from them all, next box,—letters from all that have *any* powers of diction, and have advanced beyond the *strokes* in the art of writing.

Having scarcely spoken to any one once since my arrival, I have none of that much-coveted commodity, news, to send you. The burghers of this city are, for most part, minding their private affairs ; and the few of them who take any share in public transactions, are occupied, as elsewhere, in talking about the massacre of Manchester, and the foolish Carlile's conduct at his trial. The distress under which the universal kingdom suffers seems not to be felt in Edinburgh—to the extent that it is likely ere long to reach. Already, however, there is much poverty among the lowest orders ; and the issue of this crisis seems anxiously antici- pated by all. For the rest, *dandies* and cattle of that stamp are still in considerable force ; but you and I have other things to do than take up our time with them.

Have you got Hume yet? Does Geo. Johnston come to get his French lesson from you? Try the Latin, if he come: you are sure to make progress in it; most probably it will turn to good account for you, and any way, it is a wholesome adage that says: Can do is easily carried about with one. Again let me renew my often repeated desire that you will punctually attend to your writing. I must send you *lines*—unless I forget—as I did to give you the money last Tuesday 'till I was several miles from you, when it was utterly useless to deplore my negligence. Send me your copy to inspect any way. I finish, my dear Jack, with subscribing myself, thy affectionate brother,

THOMAS CARLYLE.

XLI.—To Mr. R. MITCHELL, Ruthwell Manse.

EDINBURGH, 18*th November* 1819.

MY DEAR MITCHELL.—Without reluctance, I push aside the massy quarto of Millar on the English government,[1] to perform the more pleasing duty of writing a few lines to you, by the conveyance of Mr. Duncan. No material event has been added to my history since the day when I parted with you at the avenue of Cummertrees: but by scribbling upon some portion of this sheet, I expect to secure the advantage of hearing from you in return; and independently of this, if my labour do no good, the comfort is, it can do little ill.

I reached what certain persons have been pleased to call " the intellectual city," on the afternoon of yesterday-week. The country of Tweedsmuir, you have often heard me say, is the most mournful in Europe. Rugged, without being elevated; barren, stormy, and covered, at least in winter, with an ever-brooding darkness, it seems a fit haunt for the harassed fanatics who tenanted it in the seventeenth century. I never crossed this dismal region without melancholy, bitter recollections of the good which I had left; and forebodings of the evil I was likely to meet with: in short, if Trophonius should ever think of setting up in the world again, I would have him leave far behind the

---

[1] The once noted book of Professor John Millar of Glasgow, entitled *An Historical View of the English Government*, first published in 1787.

vales of Thessaly, however tempting they may seem, and
dig his grotto in some *hope*[1] of this dark Cimmerian desert!
You may wonder why I so vehemently abuse this "excellent
sheep country:" I cannot say—unless that on Tuesday
the roads were very bad and the weather very wet; and
according to David Hume *contiguity in time or place* is a
principle of association among our ideas.

Since my arrival in Edinburgh, the employment of
waiting for carriers, travelling to Fife, etc., has consumed
most of my time. On Tuesday morning the benevolent
Mr. Duncan carried me to Bailie Waugh's. This worship-
ful magistrate seems (under the rose) to be a very flimsy
vapouring sort of character. I left him my address; and
shall probably hear no more of him. With regard to your
most kind Minister, my circumstances qualify me but poorly
for doing any justice to the feelings which his conduct is
calculated to excite. Even to you I cannot enter upon
this subject. Yester-night I enrolled in the class of Scots
law.[2] The Professor, Dr. Hume, a nephew of the philosopher already mentioned, speaks in a voice scarce audible;
and his thinking has yet to show all its points of similarity
with the penetrating genius of his Uncle. Yet I prophesy
I shall not dislike the science. If health continue, I shall
feel for it all the ardour which is naturally inspired by the
prospect (however dubious) of its affording a permanent
direction to my efforts: I shall require, moreover, to
investigate the history, antiquities, manners, etc., of our
native country—a subject for which I feel nothing like
repugnance: and for the details of the subject—six years
of solitary reading (would it had been *study !*) have given
me a most courageous indifference to the *magnitude* of any
folio capable of being lifted without the aid of the mechanical powers. · My fear at the present is even that I shall *not* be

---

[1] *Hope* = a sloping hollow between two hills.

[2] "I had thought of attempting to become an advocate. It seemed
glorious to me for its independency, and I did read some law books,
attend Hume's lectures on Scotch law, and converse with and question
various dull people of the practical sort. But it and they and the admired
lecturing Hume himself appeared to me mere denizens of the kingdom of
dulness, pointing towards nothing but money as wages for all that bogpool
of disgust. Hume's lectures once done with, I flung the thing away for
ever."—Note of Carlyle's cited by Froude in his *Life of Carlyle*, i. 64.

able to procure a copy of Erskine's *Institutes*.[1]   But next time I write you shall know more particularly about these affairs.

I have not seen Dr. Brewster, because he was not in town till this day.   His journal[2] appears to be in a sickly state.   Few speak of it ; and those few without respect.

There is little that I can tell you respecting the news civil or literary of these parts, which Mr. Duncan will not be much better qualified to lay before you.   I heard Leslie once only.   Desirous, it would appear, of beating Chalmers on his own ground, he is said to have been greatly distinguished this season for the *piety* of his opening lectures. When I was there, he spoke of many philosophers and their deeds from Hipparchus to Malus inclusive, in a pompous style—somewhat in Gibbon's vein—except that Gibbon is seldom tawdry.   Wallace,[3] whom I went this day to see, is a person about fifty years old—short, bald-headed, with a grim and intelligent countenance.   His manner is blunt ; he speaks with a Scotch accent ;—and if his unaffected and patient demeanour is accompanied with a display of philosophical reflection—which I cannot assert or deny— he ought surely to be a great favourite with the public. Leslie and he are said to be on the eve of battle,—for the Elements of Geometry and curves of the second order are to be discarded for Playfair's Euclid !   Love me, love my dog—the saw says : still more should it say, love me, love my book.   Science you see, as well as religion, is at times disturbed by the feuds of its professors.   What have we to say but wish these worthies a fair field and no favour ?

> *Non nostrum inter vos tantas componere lites :*
> *Et vitula tu dignus, et hic.*

But I must quit these lucubrations—tell me very soon what progress you make in Crombie ; give me an order to get you Lipsius, either of the Scaligers, Casaubon, or the never-dying Ernesti, and I shall obey you with immense cheerfulness.   Seriously though, I think your study of

[1] *Institutes of the Laws of Scotland*, by John Erskine, Professor of Scottish Law in the University of Edinburgh, 1773.

[2] *The Edinburgh Philosophical Journal*, the publication of which had just begun.

[3] Professor William Wallace, appointed in 1819 Professor of Mathematics in the University of Edinburgh.

classical literature likely to benefit you. It is not enough to pursue philosophy through all her intricate recesses : we must have a trade—since we have no fortune. And although we have quitted one profession, in which many lead a tranquil, and one or two a dignified life, it may be we shall both yet have our wishes gratified. Who knows indeed but you being Professor of Humanity, I a tired *causidicus*, may delight to interrupt your evenings of literary leisure—and call to mind the days of yore ? *Espérons*, say I always ; and in the meantime, I conclude this sheet—and its most hurried contents, with subscribing myself once more, your old and faithful friend,

THOMAS CARLYLE.

Lipsius is here—I mean his *Roma Antiqua.* You shall have it in summer—sooner if you like. Write immediately.

XLII.—To JOHN A. CARLYLE, Mainhill.

EDINBURGH, DUFF'S LODGINGS,
35 BRISTO STREET, *2d December* 1819.

MY DEAR JACK—I am very much satisfied, as may well be supposed, to hear that thou and the cattle got safely home—though faint, yet persevering. I have only to hope that nothing sustained any serious injury by that adventure. Most probably you are already come home from Cumberland. I trust you and our cousin (to whom give my best love) were pleased with the beautiful, though at this season prostrate, aspect of that interesting county. You have no doubt resumed your occupations ; and at this hour (six o'clock) I suppose are " forming the circle " around your cheerful fire, to teach, and to be taught. Innocent group ! peace be with you all !

    .   .   .   .   .   .

I have very little time to enter into particulars about my studies, which indeed are yet (alas !) hardly begun. I am at the Scots law class ; and the professor (a nephew of the historian Hume) is most perspicuous ; but law is to me an untrodden path, and much toil will be requisite for mastering it. Yet I fear *that* little. I have got four very ponderous quartos of notes taken from these lectures, in shorthand—they promise to be of much use to me.   I have read Millar on the English government, etc.   The notes came from Hill (my comrade for a part of last winter) : perhaps I shall send these letters in the box, which once held these *learned* papers.   But I must have done, Jack. Remember me in the most kind manner to Mag, Jemmy, Mary, Jean, and little Jenny.   Tell all of them to write me that can write.   Be *good* to them, poor things.   Send me all your copies, write copiously (in your letter to me) ; and be assured that I remain, my dear Brother, yours most faithfully,   THOMAS CARLYLE.

I have not time to send the box—7¾ o'clock.

You will send down that great ugly Italian book *Nani, Storia della Venezia*, along with the note to Annan. Geordy is to send me a book of the Scots Acts of Parliament : you will put it in the box.

XLIII.—To his MOTHER, Mainhill.

EDINBURGH, DUFF'S LODGINGS,
35 BRISTO STREET, 15th December 1819.

MY DEAR MOTHER—Nothing could give me greater pleasure than to learn that you continue in good health, and are improving even in that particular.   I entreat you, for the sake of us all, to be careful of this invaluable privilege.   It is the foundation of every earthly blessing.   With it and a clear conscience, no human creature need in general be miserable.   You will be satisfied to learn that I am very well.   By taking a proper degree of exercise my bodily frame, I find, may be made to do its duty pretty well ; and accordingly I make a point to divide the day between study and walking.   It is the more necessary, as when I neglect it, the dark side of my affairs never fails to present itself to my solitary imagination, and I am as unfit for study as for flying.   Upon the whole, however, I go courageously along ; and to beat the hoof half an hour before breakfast, and an hour before entering the law class at two or rather half-past one, is quite sufficient to keep me in good heart.   The law I find to be a most complicated subject ; yet I like it pretty well, and feel that I shall like it better as I proceed. Its great charm in my eyes, is that no mean compliances are requisite for prospering in it. I must struggle, and solace myself with the delightful hope that the day *will* yet come when I may show you all what sense I entertain of your affectionate conduct.

The cakes are excellent and most acceptable. I think you must have left out one sock : at least I can find but three in the box. You need not take all this trouble on you, about these articles. I have plenty of socks. I know not whom to thank for the ham : doubtless it will do me good service. I have not yet fairly arranged the newspaper, not having looked for the carrier so soon. I shall tell you fully about it when he returns. Write to me very copiously, whenever you can find as much time. I trust, my dear Mother, we *shall* yet agree in all things. But absolute sameness of opinion, upon any point, is not, as I have often said, to be looked for in this low erring world. Excuse my brevity ; and believe me to be, my dear Mother, ever yours most affectionately,   THOMAS CARLYLE.

My compliments to Margaret : she must write before the milking hour another time. My father, I trust, is well, though you say nothing of him.

XLIV.—To ALEXANDER CARLYLE, Mainhill.

EDINBURGH, 15*th December* 1819.

MY DEAR ALICK— . . . You will be glad to learn that I am well and comfortable. . . . I attend the law class, with some satisfaction, and read a book called Erskine's *Institutes* upon the same. This Erskine's *Institutes* would weigh about four stones avoirdupois ; and you would think the very Goddess of dulness had inspired every sentence. Yet I proceed without fainting. I go likewise occasionally to the Parliament House, and hear the pleadings. I imagine it would not be difficult to demolish certain persons whom I see gain a livelihood by pleading there. In the meantime it behoves me to live in hope, and make every effort. There is nothing new here almost. Some timorous individuals about Glasgow imagined that the Radicals (as their cant name is) intended to *rise* on

Monday last ; and accordingly on Saturday all the soldiers were sent from Edinburgh and Jock's Lodge ;[1] our volunteers took possession of the Castle ; and there was riding, running, marching, and counter-marching in every direction. I saw the yeomen set out on Sunday morning. This was very gallant ; and the five thousand soldiers that surrounded Glasgow were, I doubt not, very gallant fellows ; but the Radicals *stuck to their looms*. A mountain was once in labour, and when all men had come to see the issue—a mouse was born. So is it with the "rebellion in the west," and the five and twenty thousand men in arms that were to murder all his Majesty's lieges in Lanarkshire.[2]   I am very vexed that you see no newspaper at this most interesting period.   I must try to get a *Scotsman* some way ; for I see none myself, except when I go to the bookseller's shop, which is very unsatisfactory.   You have not sent me any copy, yet I hope you continue to write, and also to mind your spelling.   How does Hume go forward?   I expect a long account of everything from you when you write next.   I do not think of leaving Edinburgh during the vacation at Christmas.   I shall stay and read or write rather.   Believe me to be, my dear Brother, yours most faithfully,   THOMAS CARLYLE.

[1] Barracks in the neighbourhood.

[2] The misery of the Working Classes in England and Scotland at this period made a lasting impression on Carlyle.   The condition and disposition of these people already began to seem to him, as he said twenty years later in his *Chartism*, "the most ominous of all practical matters whatever."   A passage from his *Reminiscences* (i. 152) fills out the narration in this letter.   "Year 1819 comes back into my mind as the year of the Radical 'rising' in Glasgow ; and the kind of (altogether imaginary) 'fight' they attempted on Bonnymuir against the Yeomanry which had assembled from far and wide.   A time of great rages and absurd terrors and expectations, a very fierce Radical and Anti-Radical time.   Edinburgh endlessly agitated all round me by it, not to mention Glasgow in the distance ; gentry people full of zeal and foolish terror and fury, and looking disgustingly busy and important.   Courier hussars would come in from the Glasgow region covered with mud, breathless, for headquarters, as you took your walk in Princes Street ; and you would hear old powdered gentlemen in silver spectacles talking with low-toned but exultant voice about 'cordon of troops, sir,' as you went along.   The mass of the people, not the populace alone, had a quite different feeling, as if the danger from those West-country Radicals was small or imaginary, and their grievances dreadfully real ;—which was with emphasis my own poor private notion of it.   One bleared Sunday morning, perhaps seven or eight A.M., I had gone out for my walk.   At the Riding-House in Nicolson Street was

I forgot to send your money last time. I shall (unless this hurry mislead me) send you four notes this journey. I believe the debt is somewhat less, but I owe Jack something; and the remainder you can give my Mother for shirts, etc., retaining a few shillings to buy me tobacco from time to time. Keep it very wet—the tobacco I mean.

XLV.—To Alexander Carlyle, Mainhill.

EDINBURGH, 29th December 1819.

MY DEAR BROTHER—. . . I said I should stay in Edinburgh during the Christmas holidays; but happily my firmness in this determination was not put to the test. Our professor *gives no holidays;* so, at the present festive season, we are labouring with our wonted assiduity in the complex study of Law. I have not yet gained much knowledge of it : but he (Mr. Hume) is very plain hitherto, and by the help of those monstrous tomes with which I am environed, there is little doubt that I may in time acquire competent information upon all the branches of this science. I have not been so diligent of late, on account of a paper I am writing—which I have a design to offer for publication. No mortal is aware of it, so you need not mention the cir-

---

a kind of straggly group, or small crowd, with redcoats interspersed. Coming up I perceived it was the ' Lothian Yeomanry ' (Mid or East I know not), just getting under way for Glasgow to be part of ' the cordon.' I halted a moment. They took the road, very ill-ranked, not numerous or very dangerous-looking men of war ; but there rose from the little crowd, by way of farewell cheer to them, the strangest shout I have heard human throats utter ; not very loud, or loud even for the small numbers ; but it said as plain as words, and with infinitely more emphasis of sincerity, ' May the Devil go with *you*, ye peculiarly contemptible and dead to the distresses of your fellow-creatures !' Another morning, months after, spring and sun now come, and the ' cordon,' etc., all over, I met a gentleman, an advocate, slightly of my acquaintance, hurrying along, musket in hand, towards the Links, there to be drilled as an item of the ' gentlemen ' volunteers now afoot. ' You should have the like of this,' said he, cheerily patting his musket. ' Hm, yes ; but I haven't yet quite settled on which side !'—which probably he hoped was quiz, though it really expressed my feeling. Irving too, and all of us juniors, had the same feeling in different intensities, and spoken only to one another : a sense that revolt against such a load of unveracities, impostures, and quietly inane formalities would one day become indispensable ;—sense which had a kind of rash, false, and quasi-insolent joy in it ; mutiny, revolt, being a light matter to the young."

cumstance : but I can see well enough that to this point my chief efforts should be directed. In fact, unless my pen will afford me present subsistence, what hope have I in Law ? I ought to try at least,—and I shall tell you the issue of my trial when it happens. Yet if these schemes should fail I need not still despair. Teaching and preaching are the only trades that I have forsworn ; and it will be hard, very hard, if a humble man cannot earn his *bit of bread* in any other department of art or science. I will not despair nor even despond.

In the meantime it is pleasant to have these few hard-earned notes by me, to answer every exigency. Economy and diligence will go far in all cases. . . . I remain, my dear Brother, yours most faithfully,

THOMAS CARLYLE.

XLVI.—To ALEXANDER CARLYLE, Mainhill.

EDINBURGH, *26th January* 1820.

MY DEAR BROTHER—I was very happy to learn by the carrier's arrival, some hours ago, that you were all in a state of health and motion at the period of his departure. You will be satisfied, in your turn, to hear that I am still afoot, notwithstanding the late tremendous reign of frost, which seemed enough to destroy every symptom of animal or vegetable life. Of all the kinds of weather that in my lifetime have descended from the pitiless North, the tract which is just ended appears to have been the most appalling. What with ice and snow and biting breezes, Edinburgh seemed to be the capital of Greenland rather than of Caledonia. But the thaw has come at last, and I have gone through the process of freezing without any inconvenience, except a filthy, snivelling cold, which I picked up last Saturday, and which I expect to lay down to-morrow or next day. It may last a week if it will, for it gives me very small inconvenience.

Your long letter gratified me not a little. You are by far too severe a critic of your own productions. The account of your journey to Cumberland was replete with amusing notices. I can perfectly conceive the feelings excited by your situation at Workington, upon being refused admittance at Curwen's Arms. It is at such a time that the dogged stubborn sentiment of obdured patience (too nearly allied to ill-nature, in some other cases) is really valuable. One has often room to use it in the business of life. You have now partly seen Cumberland ; and though at a time of disadvantage, your journey will not be altogether fruitless : the remembrance of Skiddaw and the wild mountains that have frowned, since the creation's dawn, beside him, is a pleasing subject for the mind to rest on ; and even the sight of the rude but honest-hearted boors that inhabit those regions, and the comparison of their ways of thinking and acting with our own, is always attended with enjoyment, and might be with advantage.

I am truly glad to find that you persevere in Hume. The remarks you make upon the various characters of whom he treats seem just, as far as I can remember. Nor can I blame your enthusiasm at the name of Wallace or him of Bannockburn. Those heroes stood in the breach when their country was in peril ; that Scotland is not as Ireland [1] is perhaps owing in a great measure to their exertions. As you proceed in the narrative, the events will become more interesting ; and you will have more occasion to be on your guard against Mr. Hume's propensities to Toryism. Next time you write I shall expect to hear about Surrey and Wolsey, Elizabeth, Raleigh, Drake, etc. Before concluding, I will again take the liberty to advise you to be very careful of your writing. Your spelling is materially improved : a little further care will make it quite perfect.

Your fears about my health are very obliging ; though quite unnecessary at the present. In fact I am generally in very fair health : and I do not study at all too severely— indeed not diligently enough, I fear. For some time back I have been employed a part of each night in writing a

[1] This thought remained with Carlyle. In *Past and Present*, published in 1843, he wrote (p. 16) : " A heroic Wallace, quartered on the scaffold, cannot hinder that his Scotland become, one day, a part of England : but he does hinder that it become, on tyrannous unfair terms, a part of it. . . . If the union with England be in fact one of Scotland's chief blessings, we thank Wallace withal that it was not the chief curse. Scotland is not Ireland : no, because brave men rose there, and said, ' Behold, ye must not tread us down like slaves ; and ye shall not,—and cannot ! '"

paper for the *Edinburgh Review*. I at last gave it in last Monday—in a letter to Francis Jeffrey, Esq., desiring him to send it back if it did not suit the purpose. I have yet got no answer. Indeed, I should not be surprised if it were not accepted:[1] it was written on a very dry

[1] A fuller account of this attempt is given in the *Reminiscences* (ii. 17). " It was still some eight or ten years before any personal contact occurred between Jeffrey and me ; nor did I ever tell him what a bitter passage, known to only one party, there had been between us. It was probably in 1819 or 1820 (the coldest winter I ever knew) that I had taken a most private resolution and executed it in spite of physical and other misery, to try Jeffrey with an actual contribution to the *Edinburgh Review*. The idea seemed great and might be tried, though nearly desperate. I had got hold somewhere (for even books were all but inaccessible to me) of a foolish enough, but new French book, a mechanical *Theory of Gravitation* elaborately worked out by a late foolish M. Pictet (I think that was the name) in Geneva. This I carefully read, judged of, and elaborately dictated a candid account and condemnation of, or modestly firm contradiction of (my amanuensis, a certain feeble but enquiring quasi-disciple of mine, called George Dalgleish of Annan, from whom I kept my ulterior purpose quite secret). Well do I yet remember those dreary evenings in Bristo Street ; oh, what ghastly passages and dismal successive spasms of attempt at ' Literary Enterprise '—*Hevelii Selenographia*, with poor Horrox's *Venus in Sole visa*, intended for some ghastly *Life* of the said Horrox,—this for one other instance ! I read all Saussure's four quartos of *Travels in Switzerland* too (and still remember much of it) I know not with what object. I was banished, solitary, as if to the bottom of a cave, and blindly had to try many impossible roads out ! My *review of Pictet* all fairly written out in George Dalgleish's good clerk hand, I penned some brief polite note to the great Editor, and walked off with the small parcel one night to his address in George Street. I very well remember leaving it with his valet there, and disappearing in the night with various thoughts and doubts ! My hopes had never risen high, or in fact risen at all ; but for a fortnight or so they did not quite die out, and then it was absolute *zero ;* no answer, no return of MS., absolutely no notice taken, which was a form of catastrophe more complete than even I had anticipated ! There rose in my head a pungent little note which might be written to the great man, with neatly cutting considerations offered him from the small unknown ditto ; but I wisely judged it was still more dignified to let the matter lie as it was, and take what I had got for my own benefit only. Nor did I ever mention it to almost anybody, least of all to Jeffrey in subsequent changed times, when at any rate it was fallen extinct. It was my second, not quite my first attempt in that fashion. Above two years before, from Kirkcaldy, I had forwarded to some magazine editor in Edinburgh what, perhaps, was a likelier little article (of descriptive tourist kind after a real tour by Yarrow country into Annandale) which also vanished without sign ; not much to my regret that first one, nor indeed very much the second either (a dull affair altogether, I could not but admit), and no third adventure of the kind lay ahead for me. It must be owned my first entrances into glorious ' Literature ' were abundantly stinted and pitiful ; but a man does enter if, even with a small gift, he persist ; and perhaps it is no disadvantage if the door be several times slammed in his face, as a preliminary."

subject; and I was not at the time in my happiest mood for writing well. But if (as is very likely) it be returned upon me, I shall not take it greatly to heart. We can try again upon a more promising theme. No mortal but you knows of it; so I shall not feel abashed at the failure of an attempt which was honest in its nature, and will be unknown in its consequences—to any except friends. I shall tell you the result next letter. You do well to read the *Scotsman.* You will find in it a considerable quantity of information, and by combining it with the *Courier* (of the Manchester paper I know little), you will be able to form some idea of the state of the country, which at this time has an aspect particularly striking. In case I should forget to do it elsewhere, I must beg you to tell the Sutor that I cannot get the *Scotsman* till he send me an order in writing to that effect. I may have it next journey.—Believe me to be your affectionate Brother, THOMAS CARLYLE.

XLVII.—To JOHN A. CARLYLE, Mainhill.

EDINBURGH, 26*th January* 1820.

MY DEAR JACK—I have read over your letter with great satisfaction; and I devote the short while, which yet remains before Geordie's departure, to scribble this half-sheet by way of reply to it. I ought in the first place to ask your pardon for misdirecting you about the Latin book you were to read. The volume in question is not, I find, at Mainhill, but here: I shall send it down in the box, and if you can manage it—well; if not, send me word, and I shall not fail to get you another edition of it, with notes and a glossary, which you will find quite intelligible.

You do well to proceed with the Latin: it can in no case be quite useless to you; it may eventually be of great service. The understanding of one's own Tongue is at all times an important matter; and no way is so completely efficient for that purpose as the study of Latin, which it is mainly grounded on and derived from. But particularly attend to your penmanship; neglect no night to write a copy—longer or shorter. I approved very much of your remarks upon David Hume. Sandy tells

me that you and he are in the habit of attending chiefly
to the manners, opinions and general features of the
different periods which you read about. This is the true
way of proceeding in the study of history. It is good,
surely, because it is pleasing, to know about battles and
sieges and such matters—and these things ought carefully
to be stored up in the mind; but a person who gathers
nothing more from the annals of a nation is not much wiser
than one who should treasure up the straw of a threshing-
floor and leave the grain behind. You are right to attend
to dates; do not neglect the geography of the countries.
In a short while you will find some of your old friends
whom you met with in *Charles V.* I am very glad that
Alick and you are going fairly to get through Hume: it
is a task which very few accomplish, notwithstanding its
pleasantness and utility. No one without it can be said to
understand the first principles of the laws, church government or manners of his own country. . . .

There is nothing new here; at least nothing that
penetrates my secluded abode. The common people are
in great distress; though for several reasons that distress is
less severely felt here than in manufacturing districts. The
substantial burghers and other idle loyalists of the place are
training themselves to the use of arms for the purpose of
suppressing the imaginary revolts of the lower orders. When
I meet one of those heroic personages, with his buff-belts,
his cartouche-box and weapons of war, obstructing the progress of his Majesty's subjects along the streets, I can scarce
suppress a bitter smile at the selfishness and stupidity of men.
In fact "steel pills," though a very natural, are a very
ineffectual remedy for a decayed "constitution." . . .

You must write at great length next time: send me
all the news in any degree or even no degree interesting.
Mind your reading, that is, an account of it for my inspection.—I am, my dear Brother, yours affectionately,

THOS. CARLYLE.

XLVIII.—To his MOTHER.

EDINBURGH, *26th January* 1820.

MY DEAR MOTHER—Though you have not favoured

me with a line this great while, yet, as I have still a few minutes left, I take the opportunity thus afforded me of sending you some small account of my proceedings.

You will doubtless think me a very trustless person for taking no farther notice of the *Philanthropic Gazette*, which I promised to get for you. The truth is, the poor drivelling bookseller, about whom I spoke, hampered and hummed so piteously last time I broached the subject, that I took compassion on his indecision and left the subject at rest. I am very sorry that you should be disappointed in this matter; but after all, I do not think very highly of the gazette in question, and the *Repository* seems to be a better book in several respects. If you want any publication that I can procure, do not fail to tell me, and it shall be forthcoming. *Anything* that I can ever do to serve you must lie far behind what I have owed to you since the earliest days of my existence.

The cakes you sent came in good season, their predecessors having been concluded two or three days ago. I was also glad to see the butter; for the first excellent pot came to an end soon after Farries' last visit to this city. The stuff which they sell here under the name of butter has few titles, often, to that honourable epithet. The main ingredient is sea-salt; the rest a yellow sour-tasted substance, which, whether it ever actually existed in the shape of milk, I cannot determine. I am likewise obliged by the pieces of meat : but though I have sent home the meal-poke, its contents are not exhausted—a portion of them yet remains, in some jar or other, for future consumption.

Having now discussed these small matters, I must proceed to make some inquiries about your actual situation. And first of health. I entreat you, my dear Mother, to be careful of that greatest of blessings. Do not expose yourself on any account in this intemperate weather : you are not calculated to stand it. Indeed its effects are pernicious to any one; but much more to one in your situation. When you write, I expect to hear very minutely about every thing pertaining to you. Do you ever recollect our evening-meals in the little room, during the last, to me unusual but not unhappy summer ?

I have already told the *callants*[1] that I am in a good state of health; therefore I need not enlarge upon this point. My way of life is very simple. I see few acquaintances; those I might see are not without good qualities, but their conversation cannot benefit me greatly: so I devote my time to reading—all but two or three different portions of it which are daily spent in walking. Whether I shall succeed in this undertaking of law, must depend on several circumstances. Providence, as you have often told me, will regulate them. Meanwhile let no malignant person put you in fear about my future destiny. With health, which I hope to enjoy, and with a frugal disposition, which I am pretty sure of enjoying, there is no room to fear. You must write to me whenever you can find time. Remember me to my Father and all the rest about home. —I remain, my dear Mother, yours most affectionately,

THOS. CARLYLE.

XLIX.—To ALEXANDER CARLYLE, Mainhill.

EDINBURGH, 1*st March* 1820.

MY DEAR BROTHER—One of the first objects which saluted my eyes this morning, on sallying forth to take the usual walk, was the welcome figure of George Farries. But though this diligent wayfaring man promised to send my box to me without loss of time; and though I did actually get it, on personal applications being repeated, about eleven o'clock; yet so many small engagements have intervened, that twilight has arrived before I am able to commence my reply to your letter. . . .

I have not been altogether idle, though my efforts have been directed to trifling objects. The Life of Montesquieu[1] was delivered to Brewster Saturday gone-a-week; and one of the small engagements alluded to above, was the concluding of Lady Mary Wortley Montagu's Life, which little George Dalgleish finished copying for me, about an hour ago. The two will occupy some five or six pages. I am also to write the Life of Dr. Moore, his son Sir John Moore, Nelson, etc. etc. I do not get on very quickly in these operations; but this is like my apprenticeship as it were; in time I shall

---

[1] Boys.   [2] Job-work for the *Edinburgh Encyclopædia*.

do it far more readily. So soon as I can seize upon anything fit to be employed with—a book to translate or the like, which I am not altogether without hopes of doing—I shall hie to Annandale, to inhale my native breezes once again. Last summer's residence there did me a world of good : another summer so spent would entirely new-model me. If I come, I shall not fail to make proof of that *shallow-made, high-standing* quadruped which you have purchased : its price and your description lead me to expect a beast far preferable to poor Duncan.

As you read the *Scotsman* and *Courier* newspapers, intelligence of that plot [1] at London cannot but have reached you. It is a horrid piece of business—assassination has long been a stranger to the British soil : but whilst we deprecate such shocking attempts, some pity should be mingled with our abhorrence of the frantic conspirators. Well-founded complaints of poverty, one might almost say starvation, met with indifference or cold-blooded ridicule on the part of Governments, very naturally exasperate the ignorant minds of the governed, and impel them to enterprises of a desperate nature. If the King and his ministers do not adopt a set of measures entirely different from those which they have followed hitherto, it is greatly to be dreaded that more formidable and better concerted resistance will ensue—or what is worse, that Britain, once the mistress of the ocean, and the renowned seat of arms and arts, will sink from her lofty elevation, her rude cliffs, no longer embellished by freedom, presenting only their native barrenness and insignificance. But I hope better of Old England yet. In the meantime, what constitutes *our* wisest plan is to follow our private concerns as diligently as we may, without mingling in evil broils—unless imperious necessity call us so to do.

You are very just in supposing that the offer (poor indeed but the best the circumstances will permit) which I made you was quite serious and unfeigned. I know not whether any channel opens in which you might try your commercial skill : but if it do, I would certainly advise you to embrace

---

[1] The famous Cato Street Conspiracy,—a plot for the assassination of the Ministers on the 23d of February, which, for a while, " absorbed every other topic of public interest."

the opportunity—though it were but to instruct you with
regard to what, I suppose, will be your future occupation.
Command me, my boy, so far as the few pounds I have
are able to extend : they will increase yet, I ween, by
diligence and activity. I cannot employ them better. But
lo ! the end of my paper. Excuse my dulness—believe
that I shall do better another time ; and do not doubt that
I remain (my dear Brother) ever yours most affectionately,

THOMAS CARLYLE.

L.—To Mr. R. MITCHELL, Ruthwell Manse.

EDINBURGH, 18th March 1820.

MY DEAR MITCHELL—Ever since the month of January
last, a train of ill-health, with its usual depression, aggravated
by other privations and calamities too tedious to particularise,
has pressed heavily upon me. The victim of inquietude
and despondency, I could not resolve to afflict you with my
sorrows or my dulness ; and though conscience frequently
accused me of neglect, three months, you see, have passed
away before the simple duty of answering your letter is
performed. Though the period of my silence has been
long, the excuse which I have offered might apply still
longer ; but my friends are too few, and my opportunities
of acquiring more too slender for allowing me to stand
such hazards : I cannot afford to lose the pleasure of our
intimacy, and lest desuetude may cool (I trust it will not
extinguish) that feeling, I write although it be " in spite of
nature and my stars."

You would suspect me of a closeness, far enough from my
disposition, if I did not attempt to trace you a sketch of
the life which I have led for some time past. It must be
a brief sketch for many reasons, however ; and chiefly
because it will contain no feature calculated to interest any
one, even a second self. Zimmermann has written a book
which he calls *The Pleasures of Solitude ;* I would not have
you to believe him : solitude in truth has few pleasures,
uninterrupted solitude is full of pain. But solitude, or
company more distressing, is not the worst ingredient of
this condition. The thought that one's best days are
hurrying darkly and uselessly away is yet more grievous. It

is vain to deny it, my friend, I am altogether an unprofitable creature. Timid, yet not humble, weak, yet enthusiastic; nature and education have rendered me entirely unfit to force my way among the thick-skinned inhabitants of this planet. Law, I fear, must be renounced; it is a shapeless mass of absurdity and chicane, and the ten years, which a barrister commonly spends in painful idleness, before arriving at employment, is more than my physical or moral frame could endure. Teaching a school is but another word for sure and not very slow destruction: and as to compiling the wretched lives of Montesquieu, Montagu, Montaigne, etc., for Dr. Brewster—the remuneration will hardly sustain life. What then is to be done? This situation—but I touch a string which generally yields a tedious sound to any but the operator. I know you are not indifferent to the matter, but I would not tire you with it. The fate of one man is a mighty small concern in the grand whole of this best of all possible worlds; let us quit the subject, with just one observation more, which I throw out for your benefit should you ever come to need such an advice. It is to keep the profession you have adopted, if it be at all tolerable. A young man who goes forth into the world to seek his fortune with those lofty ideas of honour and uprightness which a studious secluded life naturally begets, will in ninety-nine cases out of the hundred, if friends and other aids are wanting, fall into the sere, the yellow leaf, and if he quit not his integrity, end a wretched though happily a short career in misery and failure. Dissipation is infinitely worse: I thank Heaven I am not a poet, I shall avoid that sad alternative.

I was glad to learn that you had finished the perusal of Homer. Certainly the blind bard is little obliged by your opinion of him: I believe, however, Candour is, and that is better. If from the admiration felt by Casaubon, Scaliger and Co., and still more by the crowds that blindly follow them, we could subtract that portion which originated in the as hollow admiration of others for the same object; and if, further, all affectation could be banished; I fear a very inconsiderable item would remain. In fact Mæonides has had his day—at least the better part of it; the noon was five and twenty centuries ago; the twilight (for he set in 1453) may last for another five and twenty centuries—but it too must terminate. Nothing that we know of can last for ever. The very mountains are silently wasting away, and long before eternity is done, Mont Blanc might cease to be the pinnacle of Europe, and Chimborazo lie under the Pacific. Philosophy and literature have a far shorter date. Error, in the first, succeeds to error, as wave to wave. Plato obscured the fame of Pythagoras, Cudworth and Kant of Plato: the Stagirite and his idle spawn have been swept away by Lord Bacon, himself to be swept away in his turn. Even in the narrow dominion of truth the continuance of renown is not more durable: each succeeding observer from a higher vantage-ground compresses the labours of his forerunner; and as the *Principia* of Newton is already swallowed up in the *Mécanique Céleste* of La Place, so likewise will it fare with this present Lord of the ascendant. Poetry, they tell us, escapes the general doom: but even without the aid of revolutions or deluges, it cannot always escape. The ideas about which it is conversant must differ in every different age and country. The Poetry of a Choctaw, I imagine, would turn chiefly on the pains of hunger, and the pleasures of catching Bears or scalping Chicasaws. In like manner, though some of the affections which Homer delineates are co-existent with the race, yet in the progress of refinement (or change) his mode of delineating them will appear trivial or disgusting—and the very twilight of his fame will have an end. Thus all things are dying, my friend,—only ourselves die faster. Man! if I had £200 a year, a beautiful little house in some laughing valley, three or four pure-spirited mortals who would love me and be loved again, together with a handsome library, and—a great genius, I would investigate the hallucinations that connect themselves with such ideas. At present I must revisit this nether sphere. . . .

I know not whether I shall see you in summer; most probably I shall leave this town—if for ever I need not greatly care: but whether or not, I need not add that I remain, my dear Mitchell, yours ever,

THOMAS CARLYLE.

EDINBURGH, *29th March* 1820.

Many thanks, my dear Alick, for your agreeable and entertaining Letter. . . .

You and my other affectionate friends at Mainhill are very kind to press me so urgently to come home. I shall not forget this speedily. The word home is sweet to a Scottish ear: and I should be the most unthankful soul on earth, if I did not gratefully reflect, that among all my wants and disappointments, I have yet Parents and brethren left with whom I can repose for a season, and forget, in the midst of sincere affection, liberty, and vernal breezes, the smoke and stir of this dull world. Of late I have often been meditating to come home; last summer was of very great importance to me, and had I some stated job of work to keep me in employment and drive away "the vultures of the mind," I could spend the approaching months among you with great advantage. I was happy at Mainhill, happier upon the whole than I have been in general since my boyhood; and though we, degenerate posterity of Adam as we are, have in our hearts a fund of *aloes* that would chequer even the felicity of Eden, I hope to be happy there again. Before writing, I expected to have it in my power to give you some satisfactory account of the chance I have to get a translation or other business of the like stamp to manage in my rustication; and when the box arrived, I was busy writing the lives of Sir J. Moore and his father Dr. Moore, in order that upon presenting them to Brewster to-morrow, I might make some inquiries as to this matter. What my success may be I shall be better able to tell you next opportunity. In the meantime I have some hope. I anticipate pleasure if I succeed;—rising early, evening *cracks*, Duncan's worthier representative (I mean the steed Duncan), and many things more, arise before the fancy: but if I should fail, as much doubt there is,—seeing "the best concerted schemes of mice and men gang aft aglee," I shall not altogether droop. With health, I can turn me many ways; and I hope completely to recover that blessing. Dr. Brewster tells me that for fifteen years he was at death's

door; and now in his forty-second year he is perfectly
well.—After these lives above referred to, I have none to
write, but those of Necker and Admiral Nelson, which will
not be needed for six months. A review for Brewster's
Philosophical Journal of a German book on Magnetism, I
must also write or say I cannot; the former alternative is
better: and then (as our man of law concludes in a few
days) I am my own master, to go whithersoever I list. I
shall make a violent effort to accomplish all these things :—
and come home with a French or Latin book under my
arm. Home any way.

I expect earnestly to see what are your opinions regarding Hume. Poor Carruthers ! The strong and the weak
alike wither at the touch of fate.—Write to me at large,
and believe me to be, my dear Brother, yours most faithfully,   THOMAS CARLYLE.

LII.—To ALEXANDER CARLYLE, Mainhill.

EDINBURGH, 19th April 1820.

MY DEAR ALICK—I received your letter about noon ;
and being this day upon the fasting list (not from religious
but medicinal motives), I have spirits to write but very
imperfectly to you and not at all to my valuable correspondent Jack, whose letter, however, I esteem very highly
on many accounts. In truth my silence is of small importance any way : I am coming home soon, and if once I
"loose my tinkler jaw" among you, you shall get enough
and to spare of it. This flitting plan is a most soul-tearing
thing at best ; and besides the unavoidable labour of packing goods and clearing scores, I have to strive with multiplied engagements relating to my summer's employment.
When I wrote last, I knew not whether I should get any
business at all to keep my hands in use ; but it now appears
that I am to write several Articles for the *Encyclopædia*
(what they are I do not know—for I have just been putting
down a pretty long list, which Dr. B. is to examine and
select from and report about on Friday morning); I have
also two pretty long articles to translate which is the easiest
job ; and lastly (which ought to have been *first*) I have to
write a kind of review of that clear-backed large book

which you will see in the box—upon Magnetism and other
points : I ought to have done it here you know ; but I felt
my poor head so embarrassed and confused with one thing
and another that it seemed upon the whole an easier plan
to take the concern home with me, and prepare it at my ease
—what ease at least I can find before the middle of May,
when it will be needed.   I have likewise some (slender)
hopes of getting a French book to translate, *Life of Madame
de Staël ;* but of this I am far from certain, having only
Dr. Brewster for my henchman on this occasion, and he
having no personal interest in the affair.   But whether his
application, which he was to make this day to one Tait a
bookseller, be successful or not, I shall have plenty to do
for one half-year : and though the money resulting from
such labour is not at all abundant, it is considerably better
than the rewards of laziness.   It will serve at least to keep
the *Evil One* out of one's pocket.

Now you will naturally be rather impatient after all this
preamble, to know *when* I am actually to be at Mainhill.
In brief then, my project is this.   I have promised to go
and see Irving at Glasgow before my return ; I design to
leave this smoky and most dusty town on Saturday next ;
the same night and next day I shall likely spend with Nicol
at Airdrie, and on Monday I shall be with Ned.   How long
I shall stay there is not so certain : it will depend upon
the state of the city, of Irving's engagements, etc.   Upon
the whole, however, it seems likely that if all go well I
shall see you about Saturday (29th), or very soon after.   It
may be before : but you are not to weary if it should be
Tuesday or Wednesday, though I think *that* unlikely.   I
trust I shall find you all in good trim. . . . Yours most
faithfully,   THOMAS CARLYLE.

The Radicals are quiet.   How many lies have been told
about them !   Poor wretches ! they are to be pitied as well
as condemned.   Cobbler Smith is in Edinburgh Castle.

LIII.—To Mr. JAMES JOHNSTONE, Annapolis, Nova Scotia.

MAINHILL, 5*th May* 1820.

MY DEAR JOHNSTONE—It is vain to apologise or dissemble.   I am one of the most careless, negligent, ungrateful dogs in existence.   I ought without doubt to have answered your long-looked-for and most valuable letter by the very first opportunity.   To have intended it, and gone directly to the Post-office for information about the Nova Scotia mails, is nothing : this long silence, the longest that has occurred in our correspondence, since we first had the happiness to know each other, gives you just ground to suspect that the lapse of a few months can obliterate all the traces of a long friendship from my mind, and render the duties of that honourable relation an empty name.   I confess you have just grounds for such thoughts : and I despair of gaining credit when I assure you that in entertaining them you would do me anything but justice.   Yet the fact is, I have not at any time forgotten you.   Strolling about these moors last summer, the sight of Bogside,[1] of the sun setting in the *West*, and twenty other objects, incessantly and painfully recalled you to my memory : and in Edinburgh the presence of silly students with whom I could have no sympathy or fellowship recalled you still more painfully. Why then did I not write ?   I know not ; I have said that there is no apology of a satisfactory kind, and I shall not attempt to offer you a frivolous one : but something like a palliation for my conduct may be found in the successive fits of activity and low spirits which occupied my time last winter, in the paucity of our opportunities to send letters to America, above all in the desultory procrastinating habits which a fluctuating being like me is sure to contract, and which steal away our minutes, we know not how, till they amount to months or years of time gone uselessly and irrecoverably by.   It seemed so easy when I had missed the January mail (a few days after your letter reached me) to be in readiness against the first Wednesday of February ; and when February and March had both passed fruitlessly away the thing became so painful to think upon, and Hill's projected voyage to New Brunswick offered such a flattering unction to my soul, that at last I gladly resolved to postpone the operation till his departure, which has been delayed several weeks longer than was expected.   I ought to say also that I tried twice to write to you : but the

<hr>

[1] Johnstone's home, near Mainhill.

demons of dulness and disquietude shed their poppies and
their gall upon me ; twice I attempted, and *bis patriæ
cecidere manus.* Upon the whole, I see well enough that I
have made out but a very lame case for myself ; therefore
after all that I can say my only resource is to throw myself
on the mercy of the judge, and to entreat him to hope that
I shall never in future behave so badly. If bulk can supply
other deficiencies you shall be satisfied ; for I design to
scribble nearly all the paper in the house.

I was going to congratulate you on the safe termination
of the voyage described so vividly by your letter, and to
express my hope that time had already moulded your way
of thinking and living into some degree of toleration for
that of Annapolis ; when I learned that your new situation
appeared likely to yield nothing but discomfort and
chagrin ; that your boys are stupid, your society brutish,
your climate disagreeable, and everything about the place
repulsive and disheartening. Alas ! my dear friend, I am
grieved to the heart for it. That by crossing the ocean you
have not escaped from care, is not surprising—she climbs
the deck along with us ; she follows us to the throne and
the temple ; the grave alone is delivered from her visits :
but that after so much exertion, danger, and vexation you
should still find so little to sweeten the cup of life is an
affliction that I did not anticipate. Yet what can I say to
comfort you ? My words cannot transform Acadia into
Tempe, its rude Planters into Roscoes, or its Trulliber into
what a clergyman ought to be. Nor am I at all prepared,
even if I were qualified, to advise you at such a juncture—
the circumstances have found me at second-hand ; I have
been but two days at Mainhill, and I have yet seen none of
your letters or correspondents. At first view, however, it
certainly strikes me that America has presented its worst
side to you. A new situation commonly resembles a new
suit of clothes : rarely does it fail to gall the wearer in
some points at the beginning ; yet a little while is generally
sufficient to put all to rights, to make the robe accommodate
itself to the man or the man to the robe. So may it fare
with your tutorship at Annapolis. I can easily conceive,
for I have often felt, the forlorn sensation that takes possession of the mind when no object is at hand to interest it,

and no other mind to communicate with : I can understand
the painfulness of teaching, the trouble of interrupted
habits, and twenty other inconveniences that your place
abounds with : yet still before determining (as I hear you
have well-nigh done) to revisit Europe, I would have you
steadily reflect upon the consequence of such a step. Can
you determine to become a schoolmaster finally, to peram-
bulate the country as a dissenting preacher, or to spend
some dozen painful years in the family of a paltry squire
with the hope of gaining an obscure footing in the Establishment ?[1] None of these plans I think would suit you
well ; yet they are almost the only avenues which the
literary profession holds out for preferment to persons in
our station. Even these poor avenues are in this country
overcrowded ; one is jostled in them at every step : other
lines of life are not less overcrowded ; and in place of times
mending, it seems clear to most unprejudiced people that
the distress, not to say starvation which at present involves
the trading part of the community, must ultimately, and that
ere long, involve all the lower classes entirely. Nothing
then to be hoped but the dubious and distant result of revolution and civil discord. This is a pale and dreary
prospect, my friend, which Great Britain holds out to one ;
I fear, however, it is too faithful. On the other hand, consider how many of the evils that now torment you, custom
will inure you to endure with indifference, perhaps with
satisfaction—consider the pleasure of an independent maintenance—consider the boundless field which the new
country opens for exertion of every sort—a field not impoverished like ours and disputed in daily strife ; but thinly
occupied and fertile though coarse. Consider all this, I
entreat you, before adopting a resolution which must now
be final. Fortune and the world conspire to chastise us
severely for inconstancy ; and at our time of life it is highly
disadvantageous to change.

In all this long discussion, I have endeavoured to speak
the cold and naked truth, as it appears to my own mind, on
considering every circumstance that has come to my knowledge on the subject. I have endeavoured to divest myself
of every partial or selfish feeling ; because I consider that

<hr>

[1] The Established Kirk.

your demeanour on this occasion may give a colour to the
rest of your life ; and whoever takes upon him to advise a
friend ought to speak with an eye to that friend's interest
alone. It has cost me an effort so to do in this case : few
persons, I suppose, have missed you more than I ; and
though you, upon maturely contemplating both sides of the
question, determine to return to Scotland, I shall be the
very first to welcome you with heart and hand to your
native shore. Perhaps you have views, which I know not of ;
perhaps your agricultural skill might be exercised in England
more advantageously than any of your other acquirements ;
I shall be most happy to find it so : but I would not advise
you to lay any stress upon the pleasure of spending another
winter in Edinburgh ; unless you have distinct prospects of
putting the knowledge you will acquire there to use, I would
not advise you to go thither even though you were in Scotland and doing nothing. Edinburgh looks beautiful in the
imagination, because the heart, when we knew it of old, was
as yet unwrung and ready to derive enjoyment from whatever came before it. Visit the *Alma Mater* now, and you
are disgusted, probably, with the most feeble drivelling of
the students—shocked at the unphilosophic spirit of the
professors—dissatisfied with the smoke and the odour and
everything else in or about the city. I certainly would not
counsel you to make any sacrifices, for what I know from
sad experience would almost without doubt disappoint you :
yet this, I think, ought hardly to weigh at all in forming
your determination. Edinburgh may have changed since
we knew it—we ourselves may have changed still more—
yet after all, there is a world even in Scotland, there is a
world elsewhere. I repeat my request (and with it conclude
this prolix dissertation) that you would steadfastly and
seriously consider the circumstances of the case—do nothing
rashly—and if you resolve to return back to Annandale, be
sure all your friends, and they are not few, will experience
the greatest satisfaction at beholding you once more.

After perusing the preceding pages, gratuitously consecrated to advice upon a subject which I know so imperfectly, you will be ready to infer that myself am placed
on some commanding eminence, above the vicissitudes of
Fortune, and qualified to cast down an experienced eye

upon the vortex of human affairs. You were never in your life more mistaken. At no period, that I recollect, have matters had a more doubtful aspect. I went to Edinburgh in winter, after a summer pleasantly but not very profitably spent at my Father's, with the view of studying Scots Law —intending, as you know, if all things prospered to make one desperate effort at obtaining an Advocate's gown ; and gaining my bread by a profession recommended to my fancy so strongly by the honourable nature of the exertions that ensure success in it. I went in moderate health, and with considerable hopes : but alas ! David Hume owns no spark of his uncle's genius ; his lectures on law are (still excepting Erskine's *Institutes*) the dullest piece of stuff I ever saw or heard of. Long-winded, dry details about points not of the slightest importance to any but an Attorney or Notary Public ; observations upon the formalities of customs which ought to be instantly and for ever abolished ; uncounted cases of blockhead A *versus* blockhead B, with what Stair thought upon them, what Bankton, what the poor *doubting* Dirleton ; and then the nature of actions of —— *O infandum !* By degrees I got disheartened ; the *science of law* seemed little calculated to yield a reward proportionate to the labour of acquiring it ; I became remiss in my efforts to follow our Lecturer through the vast and thorny desert he was traversing ; till at length I abandoned him altogether—with a resolution that if ever I became familiar with law, it must be under different guidance. Occasionaly too I tried writing, but most of my projects in that department altogether failed. The silly Lives of Montesquieu, Montaigne, etc. etc., which I wrote for Brewster's *Encyclopædia* are not worth mentioning ; the rest are yet in embyro. At length these incidents, aided powerfully by the last horrible winter, began to act upon my health : I determined to quit Edinburgh ; and on Wednesday evening I returned once more to Mainhill— wearied and faint, and though long used, not altogether reconciled to the rest which is enjoyed upon the pillow of uncertainty. I am to translate and write some trifles during Summer if my spirits serve ; what next—— I am sorry that I care so much more than I know. Upon the whole I am altering very fast. Hope will not always stay with one ; and despair is not an eligible neighbour. I do not think I am ever to have any settled way of doing. Teaching and Preaching I have forsworn ; and I believe I am too old for beginning any new profession. One leads a strange miscellaneous life at that rate : yet if it cannot be helped——

It must be owned, however, that I have no great reason to complain. On looking at the condition of many others there seems rather cause for gratulation. Never in the history of Britain did I read of such a situation. Black inquietude, misery physical and moral, from one end of the island to the other, Radical risings, and armed confederations of the higher classes, and little or no expectation of better times. This neighbourhood, I find, is suffering very slightly in comparison ; on my way from Paisley I passed several groups journeying hither in search of work and food, like the Israelites of old to Goshen in the dearth : yet none can doubt that the Agriculture [*sic*] *must* feel the pressure of those taxes which at present exclude our commerce—except at a ruinous rate—from almost all the markets in the world. I am not a croaker ; but I forecast nothing except an increase of calamity for several years to come. I suppose you have heard fully from the Newspapers of the Radical commotions, the marching, countermarching, and battles that have marked this troubled winter. The disturbances are quelled for a season ; but as an old peasant, whom I overtook on the road from Muirkirk, expressed himself, unless these times alter, folks will all be Radicals together. One of the events which have occurred in the late troubles may affect you more than many other events of greater importance. I allude to the capture of William Smith, shoemaker, Ecclefechan, who had travelled to Glasgow for the purpose of buying leather ; and falling in with sundry men of kindred sentiments, had further invested himself with the character of delegate from our poor unpolitical village, and proceeded to act forthwith in that capacity. His dignity soon withered from his brow : and scarcely had he got his sentiments disclosed, when the room in the Gallowgate which those statesmen occupied was environed by a party of soldiers, and the whole fraternity of reformers, with poor Will among them, were lodged in Glasgow jail. Poor Sutor! I know not the extent of his criminality: but from the complexion of the times, I should not be at all surprised if he were sent to botanise in New Holland. I have much to say on the present state of public affairs; and if you were beside me, you would have to hear it all: but it is a little too much to occupy our brief interview with such matters—now that you are beyond the ocean and not at all concerned by them, and that I, though on this side of the great water, am so situated as to have nothing to hope and almost nothing to fear from any political change whatever. I consign you therefore, if desirous of additional information, to two well-written Articles by Jeffrey in the last *Edinburgh Review*—and, if you know the maxim *audi alteram partem*, to sundry delirious speculations from the pen of Mr. Southey, wherein these points are handled at considerable length in the *Quarterly Review*.

I betake me to private history, in which, though with equal dulness and haste, I am sure of exciting deeper interest. . . .

And now, my friend, I must draw this wretched tissue to a close. My paper is coarse, my mind has been distracted and hurried by a thousand cross accidents since I began to write: I have written stupidly and tediously of course; nothing has been as it should be but the wish to please you, which I do most conscientiously pretend to. I am persuaded you will pardon my inconsistencies and blunders for the sake of this last circumstance; nay, further, that in spite of all my faults you will write me at immense length by the ship's return. I have said that it would not much surprise me if you returned on board of her; it will hardly please any one so highly as myself: yet if so be not, if we must not see each other for many long eventful years, I hope both of us will always retain a happy and heartfelt remembrance of the many days we have spent together; and neglect no opportunity of cultivating an intercourse so pleasant, by every means that yet remains to us. My Mother sends her most kind respects to you and best wishes for your—safe return—so she phrases it; my Father is prevented by absence from joining at the present moment in this wish, but Alick and Meg, who are beside me—and

every other heart about Mainhill—desire to be most cordially
included in it. Bogside, I suppose, has written a letter
by this conveyance—so I have not mentioned any domestic
news. Edward Irving is at Glasgow, Dr. Chalmers's Assistant ; I spent a week with him on my return from Edinburgh.
He succeeds wonderfully. But I have room for nothing
more. Write to me as fully as you possibly can ; unless
you intend to bring *yourself:* and believe me to be, with
the warmest wishes for your prosperity, my dear friend,
ever most faithfully yours,   THOMAS CARLYLE.

LIV.—To JOHN A. CARLYLE, Academy, Annan.[1]

EDINBURGH, *7th December* 1820.

MY DEAR BROTHER JACK—I had no time last night to
write a reply to your lively little note ; and besides, I
gathered from some expressions in it that you intended to
write me by the Annan carrier—Richardson as I con-
jectured ;—for which reason I was the more willing to
postpone the operation that so I might shoot two dogs
with one ball, *Anglice*, answer two letters at once. Richardson is here, and you have not written ; nor, considering
the time, am I surprised at it. You will write to me next
time, I know, at great length as to everything that concerns
you. Be free in stating all your doubts and queries and
difficulties : I shall be as free in answering them.

It is very fortunate that you have got Fergusson to hear
you a lesson ; stick to it while you have such an opportunity ;
against winter you will be ready for Edinburgh. I confess,
however, that I feel a reluctance in advising you to diligence ; because I know you are likely to be at least diligent
enough, and present appearances give me room to fear, not
that you will become a sluggard, but that you will become
a drudge—and thus being ever more enticed by the charms
of literature, and ever more repulsed by the *foreignness* of
everyday mortals, that you will play the same miserable
game that I have played, sacrificing both health and peace
of mind to the vain shadows of ambition—unattainable by
one of us, and useless though they were attainable. There-

1 John Carlyle was now at the Annan Academy, teaching and preparing
for College at Edinburgh.

fore, my good boy, let me entreat you by the warmth of brotherly affection—to beware of this, to guard against the *first* advances of debility, to enjoy yourself in society by every honest means, and to regard it as a *certain fact* that continuous study will waste away the very best constitution, the loss of which is poorly, most poorly, recompensed by all the learning and philosophy of the human race. I fear you will not listen to me: young men feel flattered when it is said they are studying themselves into ill-health; but they bitterly regret their conduct when it is too late. Believe my experience, my dear Jack; may it never become yours!

I have been led into these reflections, because I am not yet quite recovered from a wicked rebellion of the intestines—produced by the change of air, I suppose, and also by inclement circumstances in which that change was brought about. I have studied none yet, and read next to none. Indeed I must be re-established before I *can* study to any purpose. . . .

I hope you still go home on Saturdays; and "janner[1]" for an hour or two with our dearly-beloved Alick and other as dear friends. It will lighten your spirits. Be good to my Mother and Father—they have given us much, the time is coming to repay it. But I must out to walk, windy and dark though it be. Write immensely to—Your affectionate brother,

THOMAS CARLYLE.

LV.—To ALEXANDER CARLYLE, Mainhill.

EDINBURGH, 2d *January* 1821.

MY DEAR ALICK— . . . I see easily that the *Black Dwarf* and *Old Mortality* have hurried you rather, in your epistle; which, however, contains the gratifying intelligence—still eminently gratifying, though happily it is common—of your continued good health and peaceable situation. The times are hard, my man; and the hope of their improvement is still distant: but with a sound body and a free spirit, our life is not without its charms. . . .

I am got better considerably, in point of health; so be

---

[1] Janner, jawner = to talk idly.

not uneasy on that score. Health I feel to be the greatest of all earthly goods—the basis of them all ; and therefore I shall study the maintenance of it with primary care. I get low, very low in spirits, when the clay-house is out of repair ; indeed I almost think at such times that health alone would make me happy ; and in fact when strong outwardly, I seldom feel depressed within. . . . I have translated a portion of Schiller's *History of the Thirty Years' War* (it is all about Gustavus and the fellow-soldados of Dugald Dalgetty, your dearly-beloved friend) ; and sent it off, with a letter introduced by Tait the Review-book-seller, to Longmans and Co., London. Tait was to send it away very soon, in a package of newly published books, and to accompany it with a letter, setting forth that I was one of the most hopeful youths of the part, and that hence it were well for the men of Paternoster Row to secure my co-operation forthwith. The answer will come in (perhaps) three weeks. To say truth, my Brother, I am not sanguine in this matter : But now is not the time to discuss it, both because my paper is waning, and because out of fatigue from travelling I might give you too dark a picture of that and all my other schemes. . . .

Irving is a kind good fellow. He would have me come and spend some months with him, because he thought I felt uncomfortable here ; and he had all the *sappy* hospitality of Bailie Jarvie's children at command. William Graham [1] is also a friend and a deserving one : I could pass my time swimmingly among them : but I must work *with my own hands*, and work while it is called to-day. You cannot conceive what a week I have had. Fat contented merchants—shovelling their beef over by the pound, and swilling their wine without measure, declaiming on politics and religion, joking and jeering and flowing and swaggering along with all their heart. I viewed them with a curious, often with a satisfied eye. But there is a time for all. Last night, I was listening to music and the voice of song amid dandy clerks and sparkling females ; laughing at times even to soreness at the marvellous Dr. John Scott (see *Blackwood's Magazine*) ; and to-night, I am *alone* in

---

[1] Merchant in Glasgow and Laird of Burnswark in Annandale ; of whom there is a long account in the *Reminiscences*, i. 164.

this cold city—alone to cut my way into the heart of its
benefices by the weapons of my own small quiver. Yet
let us be of cheer, for *braw days are comin'* : and now, my
boy, at this noisy season accept the prayer, put up for you
and all our family, that many new years, and far happier
ones, may be in store for each of us, that we may all love
one another here, and in due time be made fit for that
better land, where the just shall flourish, where the wickedness of men and the painfulness of Nature shall be hid
from us, and peace and virtue substituted in their room :—
Ever yours,   THOMAS CARLYLE.

LVI.—To ALEXANDER CARLYLE, Mainhill.

EDINBURGH, 10th January 1821.

MY DEAR BROTHER— . . . My possessions of worldly
comfort are still mostly in *perspective.* Yet I live in hope,
and no sooner is one scheme blasted than another springs
up instead of it. Brewster is to settle with me about my
writings whenever I like to go over : and what *might* be
better he professes great readiness to furnish me with a
letter of introduction to Thomas Campbell, who has lately
been appointed Editor of a Magazine in London, the
publishers of which are said to offer about fifteen guineas a
sheet. I *must* try somewhat for Campbell. O for one
day of such vigorous health and such elastic spirits as I
have had of old ! I will try, however. Brewster came to
me on the street to-day, and talked long : he seems to feel
that I can be of some use to him, and *therefore* he treats
me gently. I was at dinner with him the other day ; and
there were Professor Wallis, Telford the engineer, Jardine,
another of the same, and one Wright, a very ugly loud-
speaking man. They are persons to hear whom would
make one admire how they have got the name and the
emolument they enjoy at present. Telford spoke of his
" friend the Duke " of this, and his " friend the Marquis " of
that—all honourable men. I left the party without regret
to sup with little Murray (you recollect about him), where
was to appear McDiarmid of Dumfries and McCulloch, the
great McCulloch, better known to you as the " Scotsman." [1]

---

[1] To become still better known as a writer on Political Economy, and
the compiler of various useful works.

McCulloch fell sick, and we had to content ourselves with one of his coadjutors—a broad-faced, jolly, speculating, muddle-headed person called Ritchie. I debated with Ritchie in a very desultory style about poetry and politics, less to his edification than surprise; and the dapper little McDiarmid sat by as umpire of the strife. McDiarmid is not "an elegant gentleman;" . . . in mental qualities he is estimable rather than otherwise—showy but unsubstantial —broad but shallow. . . .

After all, perhaps I shall fall into some agreeable society here, and finally be restored to something like steady peace and comfort. In the meantime, as you remark, I ought to be thankful that I am as I am. Witness Waugh! sad emblem of imprudence! Hunted by duns, destitute of cash, he has left his luggage to make good the payment of his lodging, and is now winding his zigzag way among the pursebearers of Annandale, to raise a little money from the wrecks of his prosperity. No one but pities Waugh, no one but blames him. . . .

[End of letter wanting.]

LVII.—To his MOTHER, Mainhill.

EDINBURGH, *Wednesday night,*
10*th January* 1821.

MY DEAR MOTHER— . . . I am afraid that you take my case too deeply to heart. It is true, I am toiling on the waves, and my vessel looks but like a light canoe; yet surely the harbour is before me, and in soberness when I compare my tackle with that of others, I cannot doubt hardly that I shall get within the pier at last. Without figure, I am not a genius, but a rather sharp youth, discontented and partly mismanaged, ready to work at aught but teaching, and to be satisfied with the ordinary recompense of every honest son of Adam, food and raiment and common respectability. Can I fail to get them if I continue steadfast? No, I cannot fail. The way, indeed, is weary; it leads through a dry parched land wherein few waters be; but how happy it is that I journey unattended by Remorse! that my conscience, though it wound, does not sting me: that my heart, when it faints, does not condemn! I ought to be grateful that it is so ; and to bear these "light afflictions" calmly—they are not sent without need.

You observe, Mother, I talk about my own affairs most fluently : yet there are other affairs about which I am any-thing rather than indifferent.   It will be changing the direction more than the nature of my thoughts (for this also is one of *my* concerns) if I inquire particularly into your situation at Mainhill.   *How* are you ?   Tell me largely when you write.   I fear your health is feeble : I conjure you be careful of it.   Do you get tea—the weary tea—*alone* now ?   By the little table *ben* the house ?   I advise you to use it frequently : it is excellent for weak stomachs.   And do not, I entreat you, let any considera-tions of thrift or such things restrain you in those cases. None of us is rich ; but we should certainly be poor indeed, if among us we could not muster enough for such a purpose. Keep yourself from cold most carefully this unhealthy season, and read the *Worthies* or anything that will satisfy that high enthusiasm of your mind, which, however you may disbelieve it, is quite of a piece with my own.   Do you still get the *Repository ?*   I observe there is to be a fresh Magazine at Glasgow, embracing the interests of the *United* Secession Church.   I wish it could be got for you.

But here I must end.   A happy new year to you, my dear Mother, and many, many of them—to be a blessing to us all !   Write to me next time in the most ample manner. My best love to all the children.—Ever your affectionate son,   THOMAS CARLYLE.

Do you care about that fish ?   One kind costs $3\frac{1}{2}$d., the other $2\frac{1}{2}$d. per pound.   Boil it, change the water, and— *beit* [1] butter.

LVIII.—To JOHN A. CARLYLE, Annan.

EDINBURGH, 10*th February* 1821.

I send you the Virgil, my dear Jack, according to pro-mise ; and I need not say how much I wish you luck in the perusal of it.   By help of the notes, and marginal interpret-ation—especially if David still continues with you—I do

---

[1] Scotch for "add."

not expect that you will find much difficulty in penetrating the meaning of this harmonious singer : and though you are not likely to reckon him " the Prince of Poets," you are still less likely to miss being struck with the high elegance and regular flowing pomp both of his thoughts and language.

I have a long sheet here before me, boy, and the consciousness that I have lately written you three or four most *leaden* letters, to inspire me with greater eagerness for amendment : but alas ! it is not to-day that I can amend. I have not been in worse trim for writing this twelvemonth. If you saw me sitting here with my lean and sallow visage, you would wonder how those long bloodless bony fingers could be made to move at all—even though the aching brain were by miracle enabled to supply them with materials in sufficient abundance. I have been sick, very sick, since Monday last—indeed I have scarcely been *one day* right, since I came back to this accursed, stinking, reeky mass of stones and lime and dung. . . . Were it by moral suffering that one sunk—by oppression, love or hatred, or the thousand ways of heartbreak—it might be tolerable, there might at least be some dignity in the fall ; but here ! —I conjure thee, Jack, to watch over thy health as the most precious of earthly things. I believe at this moment I would consent to become as ignorant as a Choctaw—so I were as sound of body.

Upon the whole it seems very cruel in me to describe my miseries in such glowing colours (does it not ?) and make you unhappy, when all that you can do for me is to *be* unhappy on my account. The thing is so, I do admit, Jack, but really I am grown a very weak creature of late. The heart longs for some kind of sympathy : and in Edinburgh I find little of it—except from the well-meant though ineffectual kindness of Geo. Johnston, who indeed watches over me very attentively. Here was the *gritstone* theologian, Crone, about half an hour ago—he had called upon me twice—not to ask for my welfare, but to glean information about a history of the West Indies, information which the dog means to utter as his own in some house where he is teaching. He said he was very sorry for me : I could have thrown him out at the window for his sorrow ; but contented myself with saying that I knew well how deeply my condition affected his most compassionate soul.

You need not tell any one of those things except Sandy —not our Mother or Father, it would but vex them ; and they are not young and strong and full of hope like you to stand vexation. Nor would I have you to trouble yourselves much on my account. I shall surely get over this yet : and if summer were come I am thinking it will be well to secure quarters about Kirkcaldy or some bathing town and transport myself thither with all my tackle, to enjoy the manifold benefits of such a station. There is a project on foot about translating one D'Aubuisson, a Frenchman's geology—a large book, for the first edition of which I am to have 60 guineas—the same sum for every succeeding edition. Brewster was *very* diligent in forwarding it ; and though I neither like the book nor the terms excessively, I feel much obliged to him for his conduct. There is also an edition of [*seal covers*] works with a Life about which I [was] speaking to Tait—and [I have] not yet been able to go and hear his answer, which, however, I do not strongly expect to be favourable. Now with some such job as one of those —with good sea-breezes, and decent people about me, I think I could get quite whole and well after all that's come and gone. This grievous state of languor and debility—the *only* thing that can break my heart—I feel inclined to hope may be but temporary, the transition from youth to hardened manhood : in a year or two it may be all gone. There is Waugh (*cy mon !* etc.) was once ill, and now never knows the name of distemper. Do not mind me, then, my boy : be diligent at your studies—yet careful of excess ; and next winter you will live with me here—and be my *comforter*, and I will be your tutor in return. Give my warmest love to all at Mainhill. Remember me to Ben Nelson if you see him.—Your affectionate brother, THOMAS CARLYLE.

John Fergusson is come in, and I have consented to crawl out with him and try the St. Bernard's *spa*—a fountain on the north of Edinburgh.

LIX.—To Alexander Carlyle, Mainhill.

KIRKCALDY, 19*th February* 1821.

. . . I know there is within me something *different* from the vulgar herd of mortals; I think it is something *superior;* and if once I had overpassed those bogs and brakes and quagmires, that lie between me and the free arena, I shall make some fellows stand to the right and left—or I mistake me greatly. . . .

I accompanied Irving over here on Saturday last, took up my abode at the Provost Swan's, and as on all hands they kindly invite me to continue, I have allowed Irving to return, and I am to continue here for a few days.

Already the sea-breezes are acting beneficially on me; and in two or three days I expect they will have set me in such a case that zealous exercise will keep me moderately well in *that* old smoky city—the smoke of which I sicken at—even while viewing it across the pure azure frith of Forth. You know this "long town," and you can easily conceive with what emotions of melancholy pleasure, of joy and sadness, I traverse all the well-known turnings of it. There is something mournful in the view of a half-forgotten scene, associated with many of our pains and pleasures, something that reflects back on us the rapid never-ceasing flight of time, and makes us solemn or pensive, even though our recollections may be mostly of sorrows that we are now escaped from. I view Kirkcaldy like an old acquaintance that is fast forgetting me, that I am fast forgetting: yet there are some people in it whom I could wish to remember and be remembered by. They are not many; they are the more valuable for that. . . .

LX.—To his Father, Mainhill.

EDINBURGH, 25*th February* 1821.

MY DEAR FATHER—You would get the letter addressed to Sandy from Kirkcaldy about Thursday morning; and I trust it would have the effect of calming your solicitude on account of my health and outward welfare, about which I have lately given you so much unprofitable anxiety. The sea-breezes of Fife, and the kind attentions of its inhabitants, produced the most salutary results on me; I grew better every day, and in the course of a few weeks I doubt not I should have been as strong as ever at any period of my life. It was with regret that I quitted them on Friday to meet Irving here, who, however, in the interim had been forced to return home. I felt in a state of decided convalescence, which I am happy to add has since continued without interruption.

    .   .   .   .   .   .

At present I look forward to a busy and therefore a contented summer, in which I shall accomplish much, and among other things the long-wished-for results of gaining for myself some permanent employment, so that I may no longer wander about the earth a moping hypochondriac, the soul eating up itself for want of something else to act upon, or a withered schoolmaster eyeing my fellow-men with a suspicion and solitary shrinking, which should be peculiar to felons and other violators of the law.

In fact, matters have a more promising appearance with me at the present date than they have had for a long season. Besides Jack's letter and some others which awaited my return from Fife, there was one which I read with indifference, abandoning the proposed undertaking of translating D'Aubuisson (for which consult Sandy); and one, which I read with considerable interest, proffering to me on the part of Bookseller Tait to *become a candidate* for the translating of a French book, *Maltebrun's Geography*, which one Adam Black, Tait's brother-in-law, is engaged with at present, and designs to put into fresh hands. Two persons (unknown to me) are to submit specimens of their work, I am to do so likewise; and Tait assures me that, if Black had known sooner, there would have been no competition in the case. So that I am not without hope of getting this job, and if the judge be a correct one, of deserving it. You may think the latter proviso is like dropping feather-beds out of a window from which one is soon to be precipitated in person: but within my own mind, I feel a kind of assurance that I can surpass my fellow-translators, unless they are far superior to the usual run of such creatures. And if I divine right, it will be very advantageous for me: a steady employment (the book extends to five or six large volumes—of which only one and a part are finished) that I can address myself to in any humour—for it requires no study; and by means of which it would not be difficult to clear the matter of £200 per annum for a considerable time. I shall hear of it by and by—like enough I may fail in those expectations; but we can do either way.

.   .   .   .   .   .

But my sheet is done and my feet are cold—good reasons both for drawing to a close. I long to hear news of you all; but I suppose Farries had stolen a march on you, or you expected me home. My love to all there.— Ever your affectionate son,   THOMAS CARLYLE.

George Johnston and I have been working all day at Maltebrun—or I would have written to Jack and Sandy. They of course will write at great length next opportunity.

LXI.—To JOHN A. CARLYLE, Annan.

EDINBURGH, *9th March* 1821.

MY DEAR JACK—I have wasted this whole blessed evening in reading poetry and stuff, while I should have been writing a substantial life of Necker, out of materials accumulated two days ago; and now that eleven o'clock is struck, I may as well devote the remaining hour to your gratification, and my own, in this new mode, which, if equally idle with the mode it succeeds, has at least the merit of amusing two at once. . . . I am considerably clearer than when I wrote to Sandy, the day before yesterday, and I should have been still more so had not this afternoon been wet, and so prevented me from breathing the air of Arthur's Seat, a mountain close beside us where the atmosphere is pure as a diamond, and the prospect grander than any you ever saw. The blue, majestic, everlasting ocean, with the Fife hills swelling gradually into the Grampians behind it on the north; rough crags and rude precipices at our feet ("where not a hillock rears its head unsung"), with Edinburgh at their base, clustering proudly over her rugged foundations, and covering with a vapoury mantle the jagged, black, venerable masses of stonework, that stretch far and wide and show like a city of fairyland. There's for you, man ! I saw it all last evening—when the sun was going down—and the moon's fine crescent (like a pretty silver creature as it is) was riding quietly above me. Such a sight does one good ; though none be there to share it, except the Jurisconsult —"poorest of the sons of earth."

But I am leading you astray after my fantasies—when I should be inditing plain prose. It is painful for me to learn that you already begin to experience the effects of too close application. Let it be a warning, my dear Jack, I solemnly charge you ; or the issue will make you repent it bitterly, when it cannot be remedied. Why do you sit so constantly poring over books? Go out, I tell you ; and talk with *any* mortal to relieve your mind rather than converse perpetually with the imagination. What would you be at, man ? Your learning is advanced most respectably ; and depend upon it there is a learning more available often than the learning of books,—the learning of the ways of men, which cannot be acquired except from conversing with them and observing them. Speak with all honest men then, enter into their views, and be one of them. I have suffered deeply from ignorance of this counsel, which I offer you with all the warmth of fraternal affection. Do not disregard it. I would advise you also to bethink you of some Profession, on which to fix your endeavours ; for it is an unlucky thing to be drifting on the waves of chance as I am now, and must long be, without companion or guide on my track, which for aught I know may lead me into whirlpools or breakers after all. What think you of the Church ? Or of Medicine ? Or *can* you teach for a livelihood ? Consider this matter, and write me about it fully.   In fact you must study to be more copious in your details henceforth. Is not paper cheap, the postage nothing ? And what need for caring *how* you write to *me.* Tell me everything—whether you are merry or sad—busy or idle—your whole *manière d'être et d'exister.* Is Waugh still with you ? Remember me to the luckless. Are you teaching Ben ? Is Davie teaching you ? How do you like Maro ? How are they at Mainhill ? etc. etc. etc. . . . .

But hark ! the lugubrious chant of our watchman—"*ha-*

alf-pa-ast twelve!" So Good-night, my boy. Go to Mainhill on Saturday, and say that my heart thanks them for all their kindness; and that if I do not get *quite* well in a week or two, I will profit by it. My love to them all *nominatim.*—I remain, your affectionate brother,

THOMAS CARLYLE.

LXII.—To Mr. R. MITCHELL, Ruthwell Manse.

EDINBURGH, 18*th March* 1821.

MY DEAR MITCHELL—I have just read over your letter, and to show you that I am not altogether extinguished in sloth, I sit down to pen an answer instantly. The colossal Wallenstein with Thekla the angelical, and Max her impetuous lofty-minded lover, are all gone to rest; I have closed Schiller for a night; and what can I do better than chat for one short hour with my old, my earliest friend? I have nothing to tell you, it is true; but the mere neighbourhood of your image brings so many pleasing though pensive recollections, so many shadows of departed years along with it, that I may well write *without* having anything to say. And do not fear, my gentle brother, that I will lead you into the mazes of Kantism; I know you have but a limited relish for such mysteries, and among my many faults, an enemy even would not reckon the inordinate desire of making proselytes. As to Kant, and Schelling and Fichte and all those worthies, I confess myself but an esoteric after all; and whoever can imagine that Stewart and Hume, with Reid and Brown to help them, have sounded all the depths of our nature, or, which is better, can contrive to overlook those mysteries entirely,—is too fortunate a gentleman for me to intermeddle with. Nor shall I trouble you with my views of men,—at least not greatly; and for a like reason. I have been a solitary dreamer all my days, wrapt up in dim imaginings, strange fantasies, and gleams of all things; so that when I give utterance to the sensations produced on me by the actual vulgar narrow stupid world of realities, you very justly think me on the verge of—*coma*. But toleration, man! toleration is all I ask, and what I am ready to give. Do you take your Lipsius, your Crombie, your Schweighäuser;

and let me be doing with Lake poets, Mystics, or any trash I can fall in with : why should we not cast an eye of cheering, give a voice of welcome, to each other as our paths become mutually visible, though they are no longer one?

I meant to give you my history for the bygone months. It is easily done. I have had the most miserable health—was in a low fever for two weeks lately, meditating to come home, and actually did elope to Fife ; and during all the winter I have had such delightful companions to interrupt my long solitudes, such intellectual, high-spirited men as you have no idea of. My progress has been proportionable. It boots not, as you say, to indulge reproachful afterthoughts. Indeed I have begun to apply the all-consuming maxim *cui bono?* to study as well as other things ; and to ask how can it serve one to be learned and refined and elevate? Is it not to imbibe a feeling of pity for the innocent dolts around one ; and of disgust (alas!) at the thistles and furze upon which they are faring sumptuously every day? The most enviable thing, I often think, in all the world, must be the soundest of the seven sleepers : for he reposes deeply in his corner ; and to him the tragi-comedy of life is as painless as it is paltry. But to return—I have tried about twenty plans this winter in the way of authorship ; they have all failed ; I have about twenty more to try : and *if* it does but please the Director of all things to continue the moderate share of health now restored to me, I will make the doors of human society fly open before me yet, notwithstanding my petards will not burst, or make only *noise* when they do : I must mix them better, plant them more judiciously ; they *shall* burst and do execution too. But all this, you say, is nothing to the point—*what* are you doing? Teaching two Dandies Mathematics ; who leave me (*Io Bacche!*) in a month ; compiling for Encyclopædias (hewing of wood and drawing of water) ; I was translating —and am soon to Review. Waugh has relented, for his book is reeling like a drunken man,—got himself *re*-introduced to me, and sent over a book lately—Joanna Baillie's *Legends*, so I beg, Sir, you will view the embryo Aristarchus with all the gravity in your power.

But to retort the question, what are *you* doing? Are such geniuses as we, think you, to live crammed up as it

were in the stocks, pinfolded thus, and shut out from all the cheerful ways of men, for ever? And what are the levers you intend to use? Tell me seriously, and think of it seriously, for it demands consideration. I think your classical teaching plan bids fair if you mature it well; and really I would not advise any one to launch, as I was forced to do, upon the roaring deep, so long as he can stay ashore. For me, the surges and the storm are round my skiff; yet I must on—on, lest biscuit fail me ere I reach the trade-wind and sail with others.

This I confess is a very pragmatical *Frank-Dixon-ish* way of talking to you; but it is too late now for mending it. I shall be less figurative next time. . . . "My address" is in your hands; see how you will use it—diligently and soon, if you care a farthing for your old friend,

THOMAS CARLYLE.

LXIII.—To his MOTHER, Mainhill.

EDINBURGH, Wednesday morning
[March 1821].

MY DEAR MOTHER—Though you have not said a word to me personally for a great while, I am well aware that there is no one in the world who has experienced more anxiety on my account of late, or will experience more satisfaction at being told that I am now relieved from my state of languor and pain, into a state of comparative strength and happiness. I know not whether I am rightly thankful to Providence for this great blessing, but certainly I am "*unco gled*"[1] as your pauper said; and I cannot resist the desire of communicating the agreeable intelligence to you myself, though very much straitened in time, and obliged, as you see, to content myself with a half-sheet, notwithstanding your well-known repugnance to such penurious doings. Another object which I have in view in writing to you is to inquire most minutely into your own state of health, which I fear is nothing so good as it should be. My dear Mother, let me counsel you to spare no trouble or care, with regard to this. Endeavour to avoid all things that will fret or discompose your mind, be as much

---

[1] Greatly pleased.

as possible in the open air, and go about to visit your friends and acquaintance in the neighbourhood, whenever you can by any means go. I am most anxious to hear a full and *faithful* account of this matter from your own hand.

.   .   .   .   .   .

You must write to me, if you can find *any* time. I am ignorant, and not patiently ignorant, of all your movements. You must send me a description of the whole. For myself, besides what I have detailed in many recent letters to my various correspondents at Mainhill, there is little that I can add at present. I write a very little, read some and walk some ; and that is almost all my history. Last Sabbath I was to hear Dr. M'Crie (Author of *Knox his Life*), who preaches to [a] few poor people within two or three hundred yards of this. He is an earnest-looking, lean, acute-minded man ; with much learning and thought, but no eloquence. It did me good to see the poor people with their clean faces, their attentive looks, and to hear our own old *St. Paul's* and *St. Peter's* (venerable tunes !) chanted with so much alacrity and apparent devoutness. It brought the little meeting-house at home, and all the innocent joyance of childhood back, to mingle strangely with the agitations of after-life. But I have done. Is there any book that I can get you, or *any* thing that I can do for you? Speak if there is ; and gratify your affectionate and thankful boy,   THOMAS CARLYLE.

LXIV.—To JOHN A. CARLYLE, Annan.

EDINBURGH, *Wednesday* [*March* 1821].

MY DEAR JACK—Twelve o'clock is past; but I confide in Garthwaite's unpunctuality a little, and send you two lines of advice about your studies merely—for about this time, I guess, you are reading the letter sent by Gavin, which will satisfy you on all other points.

You have certainly been very diligent if you can at all read Virgil and Sallust in so short a time. I really wonder at it. You must give up the Georgics, however, I think, without delay. They are the most uninteresting and by far the most difficult of all Virgil's writings. Take to the

Eneid immediately; you will like it far better. Do you mind the Grammar? and the scanning? Attend to *both* particularly. For Sallust, you cannot go wrong. Catiline is an admirable narrative; and the writer of it ever shows himself the same lynx-eyed, hard-headed, bitter little *terrier;* to whom nothing was agreeable because nothing was pure; and still more because he was not pure himself. Crispus was a *rip* of a body, in his youth. When you read the Eneid do not fail to admire the calm gracefulness, the stately and harmonious diction, the clear imagination of Maro; but do not [neglect] to have your *winnow-cloth* expanded by the grandeur and immensity of Milton, or your heart quickened by his stern and elevated strength of soul. Each after his kind. Think too that *you* (poor Jack in Bitty Geel's) do actually read the very words and admire the very thoughts that Augustus read and admired two thousand years ago, and all great men since. Let this be a spur in the head, which is better than two in the heel —than the pressure of want—that is—or the lucre of gain.

But do not, do not, I repeat it, neglect your morning and evening walks—and your talks and laughs and re-creations. It is well to read Johnson's *Lives;* though the man is prejudiced to a pitch (see Milton and Gray), he has great power of head, and his insensibility to the higher beauties of poetry does not extend to the most complicated questions of reasoning. His Rambler is very good; but not so amusing. Can you not get Shakespeare, or Byron? Goldsmith's essays are "*capital*"—in style and liveliness. Dean Swift is a merry grinning dog. Did you ever see his *Tale of a Tub?* John Johnstone (Mrs. Dr.'s) has it and will lend it. Johnson's *Journey to the Western Isles* is likewise good. And *Don Quixote*—read it, till your sides crack, which they will do, if you have risi[ble or]gans. Try if you can get Russell's *History of Modern Europe.* George Irving will procure it from the library of the burgh. Except the last, those things are principally for amusement; yet if you attend to the style—and imitate it judiciously, they will profit you not a little. At any rate they fill the head pleasantly, and therefore usefully.

We shall talk of your school when I come home, about August or so. Perhaps you may get some teaching here,

which will do better. Go on and prosper, my boy!
There is no fear. Adieu!—Your affectionate brother,

THOMAS CARLYLE.

LXV.—To Mr. R. MITCHELL, Ruthwell Manse.

EDINBURGH, *4th April* 1821.

MY DEAR MITCHELL—Your pupil George John having
it in view to proceed shortly home again to Ruthwell, you
cannot be surprised that I seize the opportunity which this
circumstance affords me to disport a little in the way of
innocent chat with you—and relieve my solitude by an
emblem of society, since I cannot get the real article to my
mind. *Le plus grand des plaisirs, c'est l'abandon de soi-même :*
in order to enjoy it, however imperfectly, I have kicked
out the frolicksome Christopher North, and the " Monthly "
—in spite of its paralytic affections,—with a host of other
écrivassiers, who have beset me all day ; and confused me
with their incessant and unmusical hubbub—driving all old
thoughts away, and putting no new one in their room.

It is natural for you to expect that, seeing I have volun-
teered a letter, I must needs have some important news to
tell you—something fresh in the literary world ; or at least
something very strange in my own poor history. Neither
of your suppositions is correct. The literary world is going
on much as it was wont : frisking Reviewers come forth
once a quarter, tipsy Magazinemen once a month ; both
as usual

> " Trip it as they go,
> On the light fantastic toe,"

and see around them a nameless throng, digging like moles
at Encyclopædias, Journals, Monthly Reviews, etc. etc.,
quite in the old style. Nor has anything particular happened to myself since I wrote last to you. I am moving
on, weary and heavy laden, with very fickle health, and
many discomforts—still looking forward to the future
(brave future !) for all the accommodations and enjoyments
that render life an object of desire. *Then* shall I no longer
play a candle-snuffer's part in the Great Drama ; or if I do,
my salary will be raised : *then* shall—— which you see is
just " use and wont."

Our old acquaintances here are many of them alive ; but few, very few of them, anything more. By "the long positive prescription" they have acquired a kind of right to live, and they exercise it quietly—travelling about the city to diffuse the knowledge of Ruddiman [1] and the *Horn Book,* consuming a stated, stinted portion of indifferent whisky punch, scenting every breeze for *dead* parsons, and trusting that Providence will not be blind to merit *always.* Such are the nascent pillars of our venerable Church. I see few of them, and desire to see still fewer. Murray is here, with *his* Galloway History. Upon the whole, Murray is among the best of them. He has an inexhaustible fund of activity—wishes greatly to be loved, and takes the proper mode of becoming so : he possesses indeed very little more than the small *peculium* of knowledge customary in such cases, but he has some warmth of heart, and is not without gleams of a generous enthusiasm to cherish thoughts a little way exalted above the mire and clay of mere physical existence. When Murray can snatch an hour from his far-extended pedagogics, he visits me now and then. . . .

They have got (*on a eu*) intelligence of Frank Dixon. He has eaten victuals with the Governor of Bermudas, drunk kill-devil (rum-toddy) with many of the planters there ; and gives high promise of being useful in illumin-ating the heads and edifying the hearts both of men and boys on that "ever-vexed" isle.[2]

I hear not a word of poor James Johnstone. *Ubi terra-rum,* where in all the world is he ? If at New York still— he might have an introduction to a first-rate man there, did I but know his address. Poor James ! I cry to think of the spoiler Time, how he dashes us unhappy worms far and wide,—now here, now there—in this noisy vortex of things. It is but few years since we three were—no matter.

My dear Mitchell, thou must write to me as soon as may be. Doubt not, I shall be more scientifical and philosophical and steady next time I reply. Really the

---

[1] Ruddiman's *Rudiments of the Latin Tongue* was for a century at least well known to every Scottish schoolboy.

[2] "Having no good prospect of Kirk promotion in Scotland, he (Dixon) had accepted some offer to be Presbyterian chaplain and preacher to the Scotch in Bermuda, and lifted anchor thither with many regrets and good wishes from us all."—*Reminiscences,* i. 147.

fiend Mephistopheles catches one at times.   Excuse his
capers and his grins, believing that in spite of all, I remain in sincerity your faithful friend,

THOMAS CARLYLE.

My kindest, most respectful compliments to Mr. Duncan
and his Lady.

LXVI.—To ALEXANDER CARLYLE, Mainhill.

EDINBURGH, 11*th April* 1821.

MY DEAR BROTHER—I had just concluded the first
meal of the day now passing over me, when a tall wench
interrupted my reflections, by lugging in that respectable
box—the sight of which never fails to inspire me with
agreeable ideas of various kinds.   It gives me promise
not only of substantial accommodations for the outward
man, but also of intelligence refreshing for the inward man,
and it holds out the prospect of an hour or two to be spent
agreeably in transmitting intelligence from myself in return.
The second gratification I have already enjoyed ; the first
is certainly in store for me ; and the last, you see, I am
purposing to make sure of without delay.

Your sheet (the first real *sheet* for a long time) is well
filled and pleasantly. . . . I daresay you are very busy at
this period,—tilling the soil for potatoes, or harrowing it
over corn, or *fallowing* it, or doing twenty things besides :
so I do not look for such minute and comprehensive
despatches yet as I shall get by and by.   Only be as liberal
as you can ; do not fail to give me *something*, and I shall
be satisfied.

There is nothing different in my condition, since I wrote
last to you. . . .

We must all fight and fight—if we would live in this
world.   I often think they are happier that fight for solid
necessary objects, than they that vex themselves in vain for
dainty cates to satisfy the boundless cravings of a spirit
left unoccupied.   To see them hunting and drinking and
debauching all ways ; dancing, dressing, strutting—not to
mention your great conquerors and projectors of various
sorts—alas ! the mind is languid and tempest-tossed and

discontented, do what one will. Your husbandman keeps hold of Health any way ; and I tell you the possession of that blessing is better than the empire of the world. If you could penetrate into the hearts of our poor shambling lairds—whether they be dandies or jolly ones, and see the yellowness and flatness of their inward landscape, you would fly with double speed back to your fresh fields and bracing air ; gladly forsaking the switch and quizzer and other *plaiks* [1] invented by French barbers and the like, for the venerable plough—invented by Father Adam himself, and dignified by the usage of patriarchs and heroes, and still better dignified intrinsically as the Upholder of the human race. But a truce with Philosophy. There is no room for her here.

Do you hear anything about Jamie Johnstone of late ? I have inquired often but without success. Tell me next time : and *collect* news for me from all parts, no matter how *empty*. I rejoice over the library, and its new chance of existence. Watch over it, in spite of all opposition. Write long, long: believing me to be always, your faithful Brother,

THOMAS CARLYLE.

What, in the name of wonder, is become of Jack ?

LXVII.—To his MOTHER, Mainhill.

EDINBURGH, *Saturday (candle-lit)*
[*June?* 1821].

MY DEAR MOTHER—I have studied it and find you must again be contented with a half-sheet : my time is short, and my task is great in proportion to it. I read over your little letter with such feelings as all your letters inspire in me, enlivened in the present case by the assurance that your health is tolerable, and your mind comfortable. My dear Mother, I trust Providence will long bountifully continue those blessings to us—for it is to us more than to yourself that they are valuable.

You need not doubt that I shall find employment for your generous anxiety to serve me : indeed you can hardly require more employment, I think, than what you find in those lots of clothes and stuff that I am ever sending home

[1] Playthings, baubles.

to busy you with.   These are *bra'* white socks, but really I needed them not.   And what shall I say of the cakes? What but that I have mumbled over fragments of them all the afternoon?   I suppose you put liberal allowances of butter in the dough—they are so much preferable, not to the last sample, but to the one before it.   As for the butter, it is most welcome. . . .   Many thanks also, my good Mother, for your bundle of camomile.   I have laid it by in my trunk, and whether it help the stomach or not, it cannot fail to help the *heart* every time I look at it. . . . But alas!   See how soon our little chit-chat is over—and I must take my leave.   We shall meet in August.   Pray that it be in peace and comfort.   Good-night, my dear Mother! —Your affectionate Son,

THOS. CARLYLE.

LXVIII.—To ALEXANDER CARLYLE, Mainhill.

EDINBURGH, *8th June* 1821.

MY DEAR ALICK—Your letter came most opportunely to relieve my anxieties on your account, and also to employ two hours of otherwise unprofitable time in answering it. . . .

I sighed to learn the fate of poor old Rose.   She was a good beast in her day; but beasts are mortal as well as men; and like Cato's son, our Rose "has done her duty." She has seen you through the seed-time;—which, if I may judge from personal experience here, must have been a task more than usually heavy.   We have had *such* weather! Ever since May began, a Whirlblast and a Drench, a Whirlblast and a Drench, have been our sad vicissitudes. Yesterday was a day of darkness; but it set the wind into the west, where I solemnly pray it may continue as long as —possible.   Those easterly breezes with their fine freights (of icy vapour, sand, straw, dung, etc., here) are certainly the most entertaining weather one can well fall in with.   If you be indigestive and nervous at the time,—it is quite surprising. . . .

Irving was with me lately, during the General Assembly time.   The man could not have been kinder to me, had he been a brother.   He would needs take me to East

Lothian with him for a day or two, to "see the world."
We went accordingly; and though that wretched stomach
was full of gall—so that I could neither sleep nor eat to
perfection—I was happy as a lark in May. We returned
last Thursday. I can say little about their husbandry—
though I often thought had *you* been there what fine
questions you would have put : but for the people—I saw
the finest sample in the world. There was Gilbert Burns,
brother of that immortal ploughman, "that walked in glory
on the mountain-side, behind his team ;" there was——
But no sheet (much less *this*) can be enough for them. I
came back so full of joy, that I have done nothing since
but dream of it.[1] To-morrow I must up and study—for
man lives not by dreaming *alone*. The poor paper you see
is over with it. . . . Hoping that our Father and Mother
and all the rest are well and happy, I remain as usual, my
dear Alick, yours truly,

T. CARLYLE.

LXIX.—To Miss WELSH, Haddington.

EDINBURGH, 28th June 1821.

MY DEAR MADAM—It would have been a pleasant
spectacle for Mephistopheles or any of his sooty brethren,
—in whose eyes, I understand, this restless life of ours
appears like a regular Farce, only somewhat dull at times,
—to have surveyed my feelings before opening your parcel
the other night, and after opening it : to have seen with
what hysterical speed I undid the gray cover ; how I turned
over the poor tomes ; how I shook them, and searched
them through and through ; and found—Miss Welsh's
"compliments" to Mr. Cars*lile*, a gentleman in whom it
required no small sagacity to detect my own representative!

---

[1] This was a memorable journey for Carlyle. He says of it in his
Reminiscences, i. 174, "It was in one of these visits by Irving himself,
without any company, that he took me out to Haddington [the county
town of East Lothian, on the banks of the Tyne], to what has since been
so momentous through all my subsequent life. We walked and talked,—
a good sixteen miles, in the sunny summer afternoon. . . . The end of
the journey, and what I saw there, will be memorable to me while life or
thought endures," for then he saw Jane Welsh for the first time. "I was
supremely dyspeptic and out of health those three or four days, and they
were the beginning of a new life to me."

Upon the whole, I suppose, you did well to treat me so. I had dreamed and hoped, indeed ; but what right had *I* to hope, or even to wish ?

Those latter volumes of the *Allemagne* will perplex you, I fear. The third in particular is very mysterious ; now and then quite absurd. Do not mind it much. Noehden [1] is not come, the London Smacks being all becalmed. I hope it will arrive in time to let us begin Lessing and Schiller and the rest, against October, without impediment. I shall send it out instantly.

I had a hundred thousand things to tell you ; but *now* I may not mention one of them. Those *compliments* have put the whole to flight almost entirely : there remains little more than, as it were, a melancholy echo of what has been,

Infantumve animae, flentes in limine primo.

Edward Irving and I go down to Annandale about the first of August ; he for two weeks, I for as many months. In the meantime, if there is any other book that I can get you, or any kind of service within the very utmost circle of my ability, that can promote your satisfaction even in the slenderest degree,—I do entreat you earnestly to let me know. This is not mere *palabra ;* it originates in a *wish* to serve you—which must remain ungratified, I presume, but is not the less heartfelt on that account. Farewell !— I am always, your affectionate friend,

THOMAS CARLYLE.

Irving's packet was duly forwarded.

LXX.—To JOHN A. CARLYLE, Annan.

EDINBURGH, 19*th July* 1821.

MY DEAR JACK— . . . I do not precisely know what week I shall be down ; but it cannot easily be beyond the third or so from this date.

. . . I am going to *ride* continually when I get home ; it is better than walking : and often as I have been baulked, I am not without hope of finding permanent benefit from the operation. At all events I must try : without some

---

[1] Noehden's *German Grammar*, which Carlyle had ordered from London for Miss Welsh.

improvement in the constitution, I am as good as dead in the eye of law already ; good for nothing but lolling about the room, reading poetry, imagining and fancying and fretting and fuming—all to no purpose earthly. I have *studied* none or written none for many days. Nevertheless I am moderately comfortable or even happy at present. My confidence in Fortune seems to increase as her offers to me diminish. I have very seldom been poorer than I am, or more feeble or more solitary (if *kindred* minds form society) ; and yet I have at no time felt less disposition to knuckle to low persons, or to abate in any way of the stubborn purposes I have formed, or to swerve from the track—thorny and desolate as it is—which I have chosen for journeying through this world. I foresee much trouble before me, but there are joys too : and, joy or not joy, I must forward now. When you launch a boat upon the falls of Niagara, it must go *down* the roaring cataract, though rocks and ruin lie within the profound abyss below : and just so if a man taste the magic cup of literature, he must drink of it for ever, though bitter ingredients enough be mixed with the liquor. . . .

Do not too proudly look down upon the society you can find in Annan. Believe my sad experience, *that* is a sad error. I know well enough your comrades are "a feeble folk ;" but still they are *a* folk ; and depend upon it, you will repent this gloomy seclusion of yourself from their accustomed haunts—how barren and beaten soever— if you persist in it. There is no real happiness, Jack, out of the common routines of life. Happy he who can walk in them daily, and yet ever be casting his eye over the sublime scenery which solicits us from the far and elevated regions of philosophy ! I have missed this rare combina- tion, you observe, and I am paying for it. Do not you do likewise ! Be social and frank and friendly with all honest persons. Practice will soon make it easy, and the reward is wholesome and abundant. Go out, I bid you, from the *camera obscura* of *Billy Geel ;* go out frequently and talk —talk even with the Jurist, Fergusson, Irving, or any of them.

When I get home, I am going to exhibit all this more at large and in more luminous order—appealing to myself, as

I may well do, for proof experimental of a theory which I can so easily demonstrate *à priori*. Muster all your counter-arguments before my appearance. And *when* will that be? So soon as I have got that beggarly article *The Netherlands* (for which I can find next to no materials) off my hands,—and I began working at it some days since. Irving and I spoke of travelling by the west somewhere: we have not arranged it yet. But this Netherlands is the main bar; I have no *pluck* in me for such things at present —yet it must be *clampered* together in some shape, and shall if I keep wagging. Tell David Fergusson that I am charmed with his manuscript; it is the prettiest ever was written for the *Encyclopædia*, and perfectly correct. I shall give you enough to write in harvest—at present I have nothing.

My love to all at Mainhill, including Nancy, our cousin, if she be with you still. Adieu!—Your affectionate Brother,

THOMAS CARLYLE.

LXXI.—To his MOTHER, Mainhill.

EDINBURGH, *Saturday evening*
[*July* 1821].

MY DEAR MOTHER—I have still a few minutes on hand before the time of delivering up my packet to the care of Garthwaite; I cannot easily employ them better than in writing a line or two for your perusal. A line or two, you see, is all that this paper will hold; and in fact I do not need much more. I am to see you very soon, when we shall meet over a savoury dish of tea *down-the-house;* and discuss in concert all that has happened to each of us since we parted. That will be a much finer method than the tardy plan of exchanging letters—which, however copious, are always a very unfaithful and inadequate emblem of the truth.

I care not how soon I were down at Mainhill: for this city is fast getting very unpleasant. The smell of it, or rather the hundred thousand smells are altogether pestilential at certain hours. And then the dust, and, more than all together, the *noise*—of many animals, and many carts, and fishwives innumerable; not to mention the men selling water (of which there is a thirst and a scarcity here), armed with long battered tin-horns, that utter forth a voice, to which the combined music of an ass, a hog, and fifty magpies all blended into one rich melody were but a fool. The man wakens me every morning about seven of the clock, with a full-flowing screech, that often makes me almost tremble.

I hope you are getting into better health now when the weather is bright and invigorating. Have you ever got down to sea-bathing this summer? You should try it *by all means*. It is quite a specific to me; if I lived by the shore, I am almost certain I should recover completely. This last winter and spring I have had more light thrown upon your various indispositions than I ever got before. I may say I never till lately knew how to pity you as I ought. These nerves when they get deranged are the most terrific thing imaginable. I do entreat you, my dear Mother, to take the most minute and scrupulous charge of your health —for the sake of us all. No one can tell what you have endured already—take care! take care!

As to news or anything of that sort, you will find all I have to say in the boys' letters. At any rate you see, the paper is finished, and I must withdraw. Give my love to my Father and all the *wee things*—not forgetting Nancy if she is still with you.—I am always (my dear Mother) your affectionate Son,

THOS. CARLYLE.

LXXII.—To ALEXANDER CARLYLE, Mainhill.

EDINBURGH, *9th August* 1821.

MY DEAR ALICK—I have merely a few minutes to write you in; and my head is turning sadly during the operation —for I have been dining and *gaffaaing* with one Nichol, a Mathematical Teacher here. But half a minute would suffice to say all my say; which is only to tell you that I design to come home forthwith, that is to say, on Monday next, the 13th of August, in the year of Grace eighteen hundred and twenty-one. I shall mount the Dumfries mail-coach about eight of the clock on that important morning : and I expect to be in Moffat (no miracle occurring to stop me) about four in the afternoon.

Therefore, my dear Alick, you will proceed instantly, on receipt of this, and attach the quadruped Dumple to the rack, giving him what corn and hay he is able to consume ; that so on Monday morning that famous charger may be strengthened to undertake the journey to Moffat, and transport my carcass down to Mainhill upon his back. . . .

Within the last three weeks, I have written almost as much as I had ever written before in the whole course of my natural life. Not only my own two stipulated Articles, but *another*, which the very shifty Editor called upon me not to write only but to *manufacture*, the proper Author, one Erskine, a Laird, having fallen sick,—or gone stupid (I should say *stupider*), and not being able to finish what he had already begun and even got printed. It was *such* a job. But I have done it all now ; and spite of that wretched *bog*, I am merry as a maltman. They are printing it even now ; and *if* you but saw my table ; how it is covered with manuscripts and first copies and proof-sheets and pens and snuffers and tumblers of water and pipes of tobacco ! But no matter.

On Monday morning then, you will start about nine o'clock and meet me pointedly. If *you* cannot come, even Jamie would do ; but you would do better. Should circumstances prevent you, however, do not mind it : I shall wait till eleven, and then ascend the Glasgow mail— appearing, in that case, at Mainhill before duck-rising.

. . . I was going to bid you call for *this* letter on Saturday ; but I am a Scot and no Irishman to produce *bulls ;* therefore I trust to Fate that you will get the news on Sunday at farthest.

Good-night, my dear Alick ! I am amazingly sleepy —but notwithstanding always, your affectionate Brother,

THOMAS CARLYLE.

LXXIII.—To Miss WELSH, Haddington.

MAINHILL, ECCLEFECHAN,
1st September 1821.

MY DEAR MADAM—On again noticing this crabbed

hand of mine, I fear you are ready to exclaim with some feelings of surprise and displeasure: Why troublest thou me? To this very natural question it were tedious and difficult to make any satisfactory reply. The causes which give motion to my pen at present are too vague and complicated for being discussed in the preface to a single letter; and hardly of importance enough to a second person for being discussed anywhere. Perhaps it is more expedient, as it is certainly easier, to throw myself on your good-nature at once; to supplicate your indulgence if I prove tiresome, your forgiveness if I be so unfortunate as to offend. You know well enough it is far from my intention to do either : and cases are every day arising in which a generous person finds it just to let the innocence of the purpose serve as an excuse for the faultiness of the deed. Upon this principle, if on no other, I entreat you, *be not* angry with me! If you saw into my views properly, I am sure you would not.

The truth is, in this remote district, where so few sensible objects occur to arrest my attention—while I am too sick and indolent to search for intellectual objects —the Imagination is the busiest faculty, and shadows of the past and the future are nearly all I have to occupy myself with. But in the multitude of anticipations and remembrances, it is quite conceivable that your image should be occasionally present with me : and all men love to talk or at least to write on subjects about which they often think. Nor is it merely as an absent friend that I contemplate you, and have a kind of claim to converse with you. It is impossible for me, without many *peculiar* emotions, to behold a being like you entering so devotedly upon the path of Letters, which I myself have found to be as full of danger as it is of beauty : and though my own progress in it bears but indifferent testimony to my qualifications as a Guide, I may be allowed to offer you the result of my experience, such as it is, and to pronounce the "Goodspeed!" which I wish you in silence so frequently and so cordially.

I am not now going to depreciate your studies, or tease you with advices to abandon them. I said enough on that side of the question when we were together last ; and stupidly—as native dulness, exaggerated by a sleepless week, and the fat contented presence of Mr. B. could make me say it: and after all I believe my habitual opinion is not of that sort. To me those pursuits have been the source of much disquiet; but also of some enviable enjoyment: if they have added a darker shade to the gloom of my obscure destiny, I ought not to forget that here and there they have chequered it with a ray of heavenly brightness, which seemed to make amends for all. The case is similar with every one that follows literature: it increases our sensibility to pleasure as well as pain; it enlarges the circle of objects capable of affecting us; and thus at once deepens and diversifies the happiness and the misery of our life. The latter in a higher ratio, I fear: yet here it is often blamed unjustly; there are perturbed souls to whose unrest it gives direction rather than existence: and though the charge were altogether just, what could be made of it? Happiness is not our final aim in this world—or poor Shandy [1] would be the finest character in the nation. It is the complete development of our faculties—the increase in capacity as sentient and thinking creatures, that constitutes the first want: and as mental excellence—to think well and feel nobly—is doubtless the highest of all attainments—so the mental nourishment which literature affords, as richly as any object of human activity, should stand among the foremost of our desires. Nourishment of any kind may, indeed, by injudicious application, be converted into poison; and mental nourishment forms no exception to the rule. But if its *abuse* may lead to isolation from our brethren, and to every species of wretchedness, its prudent *use* does not of necessity exclude from any other source of happiness. Often, it is true, the studious man wanders in solitude over rocky and tempestuous regions; but sometimes a lovely scene will strike his eye as well as that of another, and touch him more keenly than it does another:—some sweet sequestered dale, embosomed calmly among the barren mountains of life,—so verdant and smiling and balmy—so like a home and resting-place for the wearied spirit, that even the sight of it is happiness: to

[1] Miss Welsh's dog. See Carlyle's *Miscellanies* (Library Edition, v., 267, *n.*) for this Shandy's interviews with Sir Walter Scott!

reach it would be too much; would bring Eden back again into the world, and make Death to be indeed, what cowards have named him, the enemy of man. Oh that it lay with me to show you the means of securing all the benefits to be found in such pursuits, without any of the harm! But it may *not* be. The law of our existence is that good and evil are inseparable always: the heart that can taste of rapture must taste of torment also, and find the elements of both in all things it engages with. Nevertheless I counsel you to persevere. In your advantages natural and accidental, there exist the materials of a glorious life: and if in cultivating the gifts of your mind, you can but observe the *Golden mean*, which it is so easy to talk of, so difficult to find—if in striving after what is great and productive of honour, you do not *too* widely deviate from what is common and productive of comfort—the result will not still be unmixed, but I shall join with thousands in rejoicing at it. The hazard is great, the alternative appalling; but I augur *well*.

My sheet is done while my subject is scarce begun. Shall I not have another opportunity to enter on it? I still entertain a *firm trust* that you are to read Schiller and Goethe with me in October. I never yet met with any to relish their beauties; and sympathy is the very soul of life. This letter is amazingly stupid. It is enough if it recall to your memory, without displeasure, one who desires your welfare in every sense as honestly as he can desire anything.—Your sincere friend,

THOMAS CARLYLE.

LXXIV.—To Mr. R. MITCHELL (care of
Mr. T. Murray, Edinburgh).

MAINHILL, 3*d October* 1821.

MY DEAR MITCHELL—I was down at Ruthwell the other week, and got the two books which you so punctually left for me; but as the promise recorded on the slip of paper stuck into Keill[1] seems likely to be rather tardy in its fulfilment, I am going to interrupt your repose with a reason unconnected with borrowing or lending. I owe you an

---

[1] Probably *Introductio ad veram Physicam*. See Letter XII., *supra*.

apology for my unceremonious desertion of our appointment :
but I suppose you have already excused me.   Murray will
have told you the cause of my failure; how I went into
Galloway, and rode and ran in all directions there without
measure.   How could I withstand such an opportunity of
gadding ?   You cannot but forgive me.

In our perambulations through "that Attica of Scotland,"
the Historian and I did not fail to revisit the intended scene
of your didactic labours, and to muse a little on the fruits
which the Tree of Knowledge, pruned and watered by your
steady hand, is likely to produce to yourself and the youth
of Kirkcudbright.   Our augury was favourable : and I rejoiced individually in the thought that my oldest, nearly
my only, College friend had found so fair an arena for
exhibiting his talents in the way most agreeable to himself,
and acquiring some portion of those rewards which honest
industry has the best of all rights to claim.   Of the Gallo-
vidian Capital I know nothing in particular : but I can
easily predict that in commencing your functions, and
even in proceeding with them regularly, you will have much
to strive with, which your previous experience has made you
but imperfectly aware of.   Human nature is nearly the
same everywhere : and the tie by which a schoolmaster is
connected with his employers is at all times of so galling a
kind, that there is no wonder both parties should wince
under it occasionally.   Busybodies will be forward to offer
you advices, remonstrances, complaints ; the completion of
your ideal schemes will be marred in part (it is but the
continual destiny of man !) by the ungainliness of your
materials ; and at first, it is likely, you may languish under
the want of congenial society, and *such* a home as you
enjoyed at Ruthwell.   My own experience of these things
is trifling and unfavourable ; yet I do not reckon the problem
of succeeding in a school, and learning to remedy or endure
all its grievances, one of extreme difficulty.   First, as in
every undertaking, it is necessary, of course, that you *wish*
to succeed ; that you determine firmly to let nothing break
your equanimity, that you "lay aside every weight"—your
philosophical projects, your shyness of manner (if you are
cursed with that quality), your jealous sense of independence
—everything in short that circumstances may point out as

detrimental to your interest with the people; and then, being thus balanced and set in motion, your sole after duty is to "run with patience:" you will reach the goal undoubtedly. Public favour in some sense is requisite for all men; but a Teacher ought constantly to bear in mind, that it is life and breath to *him*: hence in comparsion with it nothing should be dear to him; he must be meek and kindly and soft of speech to every one, how absurd and offensive soever. To the same object he must also frequently sacrifice the real progress of his pupils, if it cannot be gained without affecting their peace of mind. The advantages of great learning are so vague and distant, the miseries of constant whining are so immediate and manifest, that not one parent in a thousand can take the former in exchange for the latter—with patience—not to speak of thankfulness. For the same reason he must (if the fashion of the place require it) go about and visit his employers; he must cook them and court them by every innocent mode which the ever-varying posture of circumstances will suggest to a mind on the outlook for them. This seems poor philosophy—but it is true. The most diligent fidelity in discharging your duties will not serve you—by itself. Never forget this—it is mathematically certain. If men were angels, or even purely intellectual beings having judgment and no vanity or other passion, it might be different; but as it is, the case becomes much more complicated—few, very few, had not rather be cheated than despised, and even in the common walks of life, probity is often left to rot without so much as being praised. It has the *alget* without the *laudatur*;[1]—which is a most sorry business doubtless.

I have written down all this, my dear Mitchell, not because I thought you *wanted* it; on the contrary, I imagine your talents and manners and temper promise you a distinguished success; but because I thought the fruit of my painful experience might be worth *something* to you, and that something, however small, I was anxious to offer you. Take it, and call it the *widow's mite*, if you like. It is from your friend,   T. CARLYLE.

Will you let me know where you are, and when you

---

[1] —— "probitas laudatur et alget."

JUVENAL, *Sat.* i. 74.

intend coming Southward? I must see you before you move westward : I know not when I shall go to Edinburgh. Its reek and stench are hateful to me.

LXXV.—To his FATHER, Mainhill.

EDINBURGH, 9 JAMAICA STREET,
17th November 1821.

MY DEAR FATHER—I was extremely glad to-day on passing along the North Bridge to see the countenance of Parliament Geordie,[1] all in the Annandale style :—not so much on his own account (for the man had little to say of importance), as because it afforded me an opportunity of writing to you, which I felt no less anxious to *do* than you to *suffer.* I could write but a very hurried and vague epistle to Sandy on the former occasion ; and I was within an inch of missing the chance of sending even that, Garthwaite being already under way, when I met him with it in my hand. So I daresay you will open this sheet with an additional portion of eagerness.

It struck me also that the Doctor might be a convenient means of enabling me to execute a small project which I have meditated for a while,—the project of sending my mother and you each a pair of spectacles.[2] You will find them wrapt up in the accompanying parcel. Yours I need not say are the silver ones. . . . This is the first thing, I believe, you ever got from me ; and though a trifle, I know it will be acceptable as coming from such a quarter. It affords a true delight to me to think, that, perhaps I may thus add a little to the comfort of one, to whom I myself owe sight and life and all that makes them worth enjoying. . . .

I have almost forgot to say that if the glasses do not suit exactly ;—observe merely whether you need to hold

[1] Dr. Little, "a clever and original" neighbour at Ecclefechan.

[2] "Through life I had given him [my Father] very little, having little to give : he needed little, and from me expected nothing. Thou who wouldst give, give quickly : in the grave thy loved one can receive no kindness. I once bought him a pair of silver spectacles ; at receipt of which and the letter that accompanied them (John told me) he was very glad, and nigh weeping. 'What I gave I have.' He read with these spectacles till his last days, and no doubt sometimes thought of me in using them."— *Reminiscences,* i. 63.

the book, or other object, *too near* or *too far* from the eye; write this down for me pointedly; and send the spectacles up to me by Garthwaite, that the fault may be remedied. They can put in a pair of new sights in five minutes, and I have bargained that it shall be no additional expense. In fact the *present sights* were put in to suit my description, and the man told me that as they grew too young, it was the custom to get them changed *regularly*. See, therefore, that you are properly fitted—since alteration can be made so easily. . . .

I designed to write Jack every night this week; but have failed. Tell him to look for a letter by the post in a day or two. Alick is in my debt: but I will have him deeper in it ere long. You must write me the very first evening you have leisure : it will be a wholesome exercise to yourself, and a grateful treat to me.—I am ever, my dear Father, your affectionate Son,

THOMAS CARLYLE.

LXXVI.—To his MOTHER.

EDINBURGH, 9 JAMAICA STREET,
Friday night [17th November 1821].

MY DEAR MOTHER—Little appointed six o'clock as the hour of taking in my letters, which is just at hand : so that I have but a very few minutes to be with you; and the first of these, I must devote to beg that you will accept the *brown* pair of spectacles which I have *waled*[1] for you, and wear them for my sake. They are not nearly so good as my father's, though of the best Ladies' kind : but I will *come again* some other time. If they help you to read your book at nights, and thereby yield you any pleasure, think that it is all returned to me fourfold. They can at once be changed if they do not fit.

I felt rather low in the humour several days after I went away. The fineness of the weather did not prevent the journey from trashing me a good deal : I felt nervous and spiritless; when I went to sleep, the picture of Mainhill and all my beloved friends there would flash across my brain so vividly and so " sicklied o'er with the pale cast of

---

[1] Chosen.

thought "—that I often started from my incipient slumber, and recollected with some painful feelings that I *had* changed my home and kindred for the habitation of a stranger.[1] But this soon went away : and by dint of the ordinary remedies, I am now as well as when I left you. Not that I am altogether settled yet ; though altogether in my usual health.   I have done no work—except reading a little : and till work fairly begins you know well there is no settlement.   The reasons of my wavering are various.   On Saturday after Johnstone departed, I set about the weary duty of seeking lodgings all round the environs of this city,—that if possible I might secure a place provided with the requisite comforts, and situated beyond the region of smoke and tumult.   After wandering little less than the shoemaker of Jerusalem did, I at length pitched upon this situation, which is a neat little room and bedroom, at the very north-west corner of the New Town, above a mile from the centre of the Old.   It is kept by a trim, little, *burring* Northumbrian, and commands a view of the Firth and the Fifeshire mountains.   Being a back-room, also, I thought it would needs be quiet as possible.   But it is scarcely so ;

[1] " Unwearied kindness," says Carlyle, recalling the summers that he, " for cheapness' sake and health's sake," spent at Mainhill, " all that tenderest anxious affection could do, was always mine from my incomparable Mother, from my dear brothers, little clever active sisters, and from every one, brave Father, in his tacit grim way, not at all excepted.   There was good talk also ; with Mother at evening tea, often on theology (where I did learn at length, by judicious endeavour, to speak piously and *agreeably* to one so pious, *without* unveracity on my part, nay, it was a kind of interesting exercise to wind softly out of those anxious affectionate cavils of her dear heart on such occasions, and get real sympathy, real assent under borrowed forms).   Oh, her patience with me ! oh, her never-tiring love !   Blessed be ' poverty ' which was never indigence in any form, and which has made all that tenfold more dear and sacred to me !   With my two eldest brothers also, Alick and John, who were full of ingenuous curiosity, and had (especially John) abundant intellect, there was nice talking as we roamed about the fields in *gloaming*-time after their work was done. . . . .   All this was something, but in all this I gave more than I got, and it left a sense of isolation, of sadness ; as the rest of my imprisoned life all with emphasis did.   I kept daily studious, reading diligently what few books I could get, learning what was possible, German, etc.   Sometimes Dr. Brewster turned me to account (on most frugal terms always) in wretched little translations, compilations, which were very welcome too, though never other than dreary.   Life was all dreary, ' *oury* ' (Scottice), tinted with the hues of imprisonment and impossibility ; hope practically not there, only obstinacy, and a grim steadfastness to strive without hope as with."—*Reminiscences*, i. 181-183.

there are about fifty masons chopping away at a new Circus on my right hand and on my left, by day ; and when their rattling has ceased, various other noises take up their nightly tale. Now the question is, Whether shall I stand all this, and get inured to it as I certainly might, or try my luck elsewhere ? Provost Swan, who greatly wishes me to be in the neighbourhood of his boy, called here the other night, and advised that I should move to Union Street or thereabouts (the North-east angle of the city), where Mrs. David Swan—a friend of his, with whom the boy is settled, —would find me out lodging by her own experience among her neighbours. This good lady undertook the task ; I am to see her this evening, when the matter will be decided ; and I shall shift—if I shift at all—to-morrow. Till to-morrow, then, I postpone the commencement of business. But *then*——*!*

I have troubled you, my dear Mother, with all this detail, both because I know you wish to hear of all these matters in my history, and because this circumstance will render it advisable *not* to send the little box along with Garthwaite till you hear further from me. I will write Sandy or some of them by the post, or else by the carrier —some day next week ; and then it will be time enough. In the meanwhile, you will be thankful with me, that I am well, and that (as Father's letter shows) I have the rational prospect of being happy and busy all winter. How many thousands would envy my lot ! I ought to be, and hope I am, contented.

The good Mrs. Swan was preaching up that doctrine to me largely yesterday, when I saw her for the second time. She seems to be a most amiable little woman, and I purpose visiting her whenever I have an opportunity. We got acquainted in about ten minutes—whenever she heard me speak about my Mother. She told me all her moving history forthwith ; how she lost the parent who had *only* nursed her ; how a stepmother used her ill, and kept her six long years by various machinations from marrying a worthy honest young man who loved her well ; how David and she were at length united, and lived five years together happy as unbroken affection could make them, and lastly. how she lost him suddenly a few months ago, and was left

behind with an embarrassed fortune, and one little boy—
for whom alone she desires to live. "But what," said the
cheery little body, "are the light afflictions of this life
which are but for a moment, if they work for us a far more
exceeding and eternal weight of glory?" I admired her
fortitude and humble patience. She said I *must* return to
the minister-office; lay aside vanities, be submissive, etc.;
all of which things I told her you had often inculcated
upon me; whereto she made answer that she wished to
join with you in so good a work. I do like to see such a
person; it is better than all the cold pitiful sages in the
universe.

But, my dear Mother, I must away. I have said nothing
in this letter, nothing at all: I will write again very soon,
and be more explicit. I cannot conclude without conjuring
you to take care of yourself, during the hard task that will
be allotted you during winter. O! take care. What is all
the world to us without you? Go down the house *every*
night, and make yourself a comfortable *dreg*.[1] You shall
never, never want anything you need— if it please *Him*,
who cares for us all.—Good-night, my dear Mother! I am
ever yours,   THOMAS CARLYLE.

My kindest affection to all about home: to Mag and
James and Mary and Jane and Jenny. *All* of them that
can write a stroke must write to me. Sandy will write by
Garthwaite—directed to Mrs. Robertson's—who knows
where I am. Farewell. I will send you more news soon.

LXXVII.—To his MOTHER, Mainhill.

EDINBURGH, *Wednesday evening*
[*December* 1821].

MY DEAR MOTHER—I have but a few minutes to give
you at present; but here is a little sovereign, which I got
a while ago, and must write three words along with, ere I
send it you. It is to keep the Fiend out of your Housewife (Huzzy) in these hard times, and to get little odds and
ends with in due time. If I were beside you, I should
have to encounter no little molestation, before I could

---

[1] *Dreg*, drain, drop = cup of tea.

prevail upon you to accept this most small matter: but being at the safe distance of seventy miles, I fear it not. You would tell me I am poor and have so few myself of those coins. But I am going to have plenty by and by: and if I had but one, I do not see how I could purchase more enjoyment with it, than if I shared it with you. Be not in want of anything, I entreat you, that I can possibly get for you. It would be hard indeed, if in the autumn of a life, the spring and summer of which you have spent well, in taking care of us, *we* should know what could add to your frugal enjoyments, and not procure it. Ask me, ask me for something.

I am very busy at present, as Alick will tell you; and therefore moderately happy. If health were added.—But there is always some *if*. In fact, I ought not to complain, even on this latter score. I think I am at least *where I was*, when you saw me: perhaps better on the whole; and I hope frosty weather is coming, which will make me better still. The other day I saw one of my constant walks last summer; and I could not help of accusing myself of ingratitude to the Giver of all good for the great recovery I have experienced since then.

I intend to labour as hard as possible throughout the winter, finding nothing to be so useful for me every way. I shall make occasional excursions into the country, by way of relaxation. I think of going to Kirkcaldy (whither I am bidden) for a day or two about Christmas: and I have a standing invitation, from a very excellent Mrs. Welsh, to go to Haddington, often, as if I were going *home*. This is very *plea*sant, as Ha' bank said.

My Father is to write me next time: and what hinders Mag and Mary and James the Ploughman? I shall [be] very angry with them if they keep such silence. Tell them so, one and all. My love to Jean and Jenny: they cannot write, or they would. I long to hear of your own welfare, My dear mother, particularly of your health, which costs me many a thought.—I am always, your affectionate son,

THOMAS CARLYLE.

LXXVIII.—To Alexander Carlyle, Mainhill.

Edinburgh, Cusine's Lodgings,
5 College Street, 19th December 1821.

My dear Alick— . . . Within a few days I have set fairly to work, and am proceeding lustily; not in the whimpering, wavering, feeble, hobbling style I used; but stoutly as a man cutting *rice*[1] would wish to do. I rise between seven and eight; if I have got good sleep—well; if not—well; I then seize my pen and write till the unfortunate people have cooked me a morsel of lukewarm tea for breakfast; and afterwards proceed leisurely to Great King Street in the back of the New Town, where I teach a very sparing portion of Mathematics to two young women and one young man—quiet, stupid people, with whom I spend my time till ten. Next comes a Captain of the Sea, one Anderson in George Street, not rude and boisterous like the Element he has been used to, but shrill and smooth-spoken; who gasps and burrs and repeats Euclid to me till eleven. On returning home I resume the pen and write till after two; then a walk till three; then dinner or dozing or walking or reading silly stuff or scribbling it (as now) till five, when I go to hear Peter Swan overhaul his lessons; and come back after six to write or read or do whatever I incline. This is a laborious life, but such a one as suits me, and I design persisting in it. Nothing in the world gives such scope to discontent as idleness, no matter whether forced or voluntary: a man had better be darning stockings than doing nothing. It is also profitable as well as happy. I calculate on making a small penny this winter; of which my need is not small, as things are, and would have been indispensable, if Thrift had not lent me her aid sometimes. The work at which I am writing is *Legendre*, the Translation I spoke of. It is a *canny* job; I could earn five guineas in the week at it if I were well. I restrict myself to three,—working four hours each day. The evenings I design to devote to original composition, if I could but gather myself. I *must* do something—or die, whichever I like better. As to the latter, I have *nae* *will o't*,[2] as Curly said, at all.

---

[1] *Rice*, rise, brushwood.

[2] No inclination for it.

In this systematic division of my time, I find myself greatly impeded by the want of a proper chronometer: they have no clock in the house; and I often feel the want of one. Is the old watch at home still alive? If so, send it me. Or have you sold her, which were as well? In this case, try if by hook or by crook you can get me any *thing* to measure time with, and send it out by Farries *immediately*. I care not if it were twin brother to a potato-plum in appearance, so it will but wag, and tell me how the hour goes. I beg of you to mind this, for you cannot conceive how I am straitened for the want of the article.

Certainly this sheet has gone away by magic! I had a thousand things to ask about Cobbett, and Mainhill with its ever dear inhabitants, and Annandale, and Farries of Stonylee (*is* the poor man shot?). And see! the game is done! You will write a full sheet next time, will you not?—Your brother, THOMAS CARLYLE.

Give my mother that note carefully. She may send the cheese, when the box goes out, if she like. *Make pens* for my many silent correspondents beside you: surely they have none.

LXXIX.—To JANE CARLYLE, Mainhill.

3 MORAY STREET, *January* [1822].

DEAR LITTLE JANE—Thou never wrotest me any kind of letter, yet I would be glad to see one from thy hand. There is in that little body of thine as much wisdom as ever inhabited so small a space; besides thou art a true character, steel to the back, never told a lie, never flinched from telling truth; and for all these things I love thee, my little Jane, and wish thee many blithe new years from the bottom of my heart.

Does the little creature ever make any rhymes now? Can she write any? Is she at any school? Has she read the book we sent her? Tell me all this—if thou hast power even to form strokes, that is, to go through the first elements of writing. I am living here in a great monster of a place, with towers and steeples, and grand houses all in rows, and coaches and cars and men and women by thousands, all very grand ; but I never forget the good people at Mainhill—nor thee, among the least in stature though not the least in worth. Write then if thou canst. I am very tired, but always thy affectionate Brother,

TH. CARLYLE.

Give my compliments to *Nimble*, that worthiest of curs. Is Jamie Aitken with you still?   I reckon him to be a worthy boy.

LXXX.—From his FATHER.

MAINHILL, *5th January* 1822.

DEAR SIR—I take pen in my hand to write a kind of scrawl to you, to tell you what is going on here. In the first place, I must tell you that I would have written you long before this time to thank you for your kindness manifested to me by the present you sent me. A pair of silver spectacles is a thing I have often looked at and thought of, but never could call any of them my own before. The second reason for my not writing before this is, I have had a very bad cold for three or four weeks back, and I did not wish to write you unless I could tell you that I was in my ordinary state of health, which I can almost say plainly is the case now. Blessed be God for all His mercies towards us ! I need not tell you that times are very bad for farmers just now, for that, I suppose, is known over all the country ; but I can tell you that we hear that Mr. Sharpe is about to give us some down-steep of Rent, but the accounts about it are so variable that we cannot say exactly what it will be, some says twenty per cent, some says more, and others says it will be less, only we will know against Candlemas, but, however that may be, I can tell you that I think we can meet him at Candlemas with our full Rent at least for this year, but how we may come on after that I cannot say. The only thing that is talked about here in Smitheys and Mills for these two or three weeks back is final reduction of the Duke of Queensberry tacks ;[1] they are now broken without peradventure, and Bogside and Bell of Townfoot

[1] The calling-in of the leases which had been granted by the former Duke, "Old Q."

and Bank, who for a long time hath fed on green pastures and beside the still waters, must now look about themselves like other men. I believe they will get their farms again if they will give as much rent as any other men will give. . . . I must now begin with the most interesting thing of all, that is to tell you how glad I am to hear that you enjoy a modest share of health this winter, which is the first of all Earthly Blessings and a blessing that none can give but He who is the Giver of every good and perfect gift. I understand you have been troubled much with flitting from house to house this winter, but never mind that, you will get over these things. You were telling us you were very throng at this time ; that I am very glad to hear, for so far as I know your mind idleness seems to be a trouble to you. You will have a number of scrawls to read this time. We cannot all look for letters from you at this time, but we hope we will hear from you at any rate, and the number of letters will be according to the time you have. My paper is done and I must stop with subscribing myself your loving Father, JAS. CARLYLE.

LXXXI.—To his MOTHER.

3 MORAY STREET, 12th January 1822.

MY DEAR MOTHER—I have not only finished my Father's letter, but also discussed my dinner—of more wholesome materials I trust than the last was ; and I now gladly address myself to you. Few things in the world give me greater pleasure than to hear from you or write to you. . . .

It is needless to say that I participate in the enjoyment you derive from the continuance of health ; a blessing, which, in this singularly unwholesome winter, I am more than usually happy to be assured, continues with you, in some moderate degree. Be thankful ; and to show your thankfulness, *be careful !* For my own share, I ought not to complain much either. This room of mine is very excellent in almost all respects. . . . That unutterable nervousness which I laboured under while at home, and far worse before, is now in a great measure gone. I can think and feel like other people ; my heart is again become a heart of flesh ; and the *grime* is gradually vanishing from the mirror of the mind. By and by, it will be bright as a new-scoured tankard, or as Will Boggs's boots ; and I shall see all things clearly as I was wont. My dear Mother, never be uneasy on my account ! I tell you I am going to become a very 'sponsible character yet, and a credit to the whole parish. Seriously, I have better hopes than ever I had,—considerably better.

I know not whether you have heard of Irving's journey to London. He went thither, about three weeks ago, by special request, to close a bargain with the directors of a Scotch chapel there, as to becoming their minister. I believe he has produced a great impression ; and is likely (if certain legal formalities can be got rid of) to become their pastor under very favourable auspices, and to earn a vast renown for himself, and do much good among the religious inhabitants of the Metropolis. There are not ten men living that deserve it better. His journey is also likely to prove of some consequence to me.[1] A Lady of a great Indian Judge, obliged at present to come home for his health's sake—one Mrs. Buller—heard Irving preach, and without further introduction called upon him next day to talk about the education of her two sons, now at a noted school near London, Harrow-on-the-Hill. It was settled that they were to go to Edinburgh ; and I was proposed as their Tutor with a yearly fee of £200, and good accommodations in the house. The woman, he says, is a gallant accomplished person, and will respect me well. He warned her that I had seen little of life, and was disposed to be rather high in the humour, if not well used. She agreed to send the boys into some family in Town for three months, till her husband and she could themselves come ; and wished me to take charge of them in the meantime any way ;—for altogether, if we should suit each other. I accepted the offer : and shall get fifty pounds for my quarter's work, however it prove. The place, if I like it and be fit for it, will be advantageous for me in many respects. I shall have time for study, and convenience for it, and plenty of cash. At the same time, as it is uncertain, I do not make it my bower-anchor by any means. If it go

[1] See *Reminiscences*, i. 193, *seqq.*

to pot altogether, as it well enough may, I shall snap my finger and thumb in the face of all the Indian judges of the earth, and return to my poor desk and quill, with as hard a heart as ever.[1]   But you see I am over with it for a time, and must withdraw abruptly.   Write whenever you can.— I am ever, my dear Mother's true son,   THOS. CARLYLE.

LXXXII.—To ALEXANDER CARLYLE, Mainhill.

12th January 1822.

I have told my Father and Mother almost all that is worth telling and unknown to you in my situation here.   I was at Kirkcaldy the week before last ; and spent two days *jannering* and eating dinners with the good people.   Mr. Martin the minister offered me the Editorship of a Dundee Newspaper—£100 a-year, and a percentage on the profits ; but my ambition to become a Knight of the Paragraph was very small, and I *had nae wull o't*.   The minister is a kind man, and true stuff to the core.   After returning, I set to on a criticism on *Faust*, which the *Review* people were wanting.   They have now agreed to pass it till the next number, and I go on more leisurely.   I shall send it whenever it is printed ; though it will be very poor, being written on a subject which I have never expressed myself about before, and hence with no small difficulty.   It will be far too good, however, for the place it is going to.   The dogs have paid me nothing yet—nothing but smiles and fair words, which being hollow are worse than none.

While I was busy with this, Irving's letter came ; about the Tutorship—for which see my Father and Mother's letters.   I accepted of it the same night ; I mean the trial of it.   He would get my answer to-day.   I have some hopes from the thing : but we can do either way.   Irving is

---

[1] "I desire you," wrote his Mother to Carlyle in answer to this letter, "not to be anxious about succeeding in your new place, but live in a humble dependence on Providence, and walk in the ways of virtue, and there is no fear.   Perhaps you may be a blessing to the boys.   By all means take care of your health.   You will have a walk every day from Leith to the place you teach at.   Mind not to sit up too late at night ; rise early in the morning.   My own health depends on yours."

to be in Annan, I understand, very shortly. He seems to
have raised the waters yonder ; they like him as well as you
and Ben Nelson do.

.   .   .   .   .   .

LXXXIII.—To John A. Carlyle, Annan.

3 Moray Street, 12*th January* 1822.

My dear Jack—I have been writing very copious letters
to Mainhill all this afternoon ; and as I had no time to get
one ready for you, my heart partly smites me now that I
have come back from the carrier's ; and as at any rate I
feel somewhat indisposed for dipping into the character and
projects of *Faust* to-night, I purpose to solace myself by
holding a little chat with you before I go to bed. It is uncertain when you may see this : for I have nothing to communicate but what you will soon know fully by another
channel ; and therefore I am not going to take your nine-
pence halfpenny out of its dry lodging in Wellington Street
to put it into his Majesty's treasury, on this occasion ; but
to give this letter to the Jurist or some other trustworthy
person, and let it come cost-free though more slowly.

I thank you very kindly for your letter. It is of the
right open-hearted kind, written without reserve from the ful-
ness of your own thoughts ; and that is just the thing I want.
Write to me often in the same style, not waiting for carriers
or the like, but using the convenience of the Post-office
without reserve. I always rejoice to see one of your letters,
because I am sure of its coming from an honest soul that
loves me. I am glad also to find by the epistle in question
that you are so much in the way of improvement, and
making such large advances in the acquisition of knowledge,
—of facts as well as of reflective habits, which are most
valuable of all. Go on, my brave Jack ! and fear no
weather ! We have both a sore fight to wage ; but we
shall conquer at the last. There are many men now lolling
upon the pillow of inglorious sloth, and pitying such
adventurers as we : but this *pity* shall not always endure—
the lazy *haggises ;* they must sink when we shall soar.

Now that you have finished Rollin, I think you ought
to begin some other book on general literature, directed if

possible like it, in some degree to the progress of your classical studies. There is a *Roman History*, by Hooke, if I mistake not, in your catalogue. Concerning its merits I am not entitled to speak,—never having seen it: I suspect they will be small; but it will undoubtedly contain many details of advantage for you to be familiar with; therefore I partly advise you to get hold of it. Failing this, you might commence Smollett's *Continuation of Hume*, or any continuation of him—for a worse one can scarcely be imagined than Smollett's; and endeavour to make yourself acquainted with the outlines of recent English history. There are some "histories of Scotland" which relate to periods with which perhaps you would like to become acquainted. Laing is a sensible, hard-hearted man (*sic*): Pinkerton has the most hateful mind of any living author —but his *House of Stuart* is worth looking into. The *Early History* cannot be read by any thinking creature; it is fit only for antiquarians. At all events, read something. A continual exercise of the memory and judgment alone wears out one's energies, and is unprofitable to the faculties in the long run. You will be abundantly able to hold up your head here in the Classes next winter, without over-straining yourself. So take it leisurely upon you. And count upon it, Jack, as a settled thing that you are to appear here. I expect to be able to set you above all fear, whether you get teaching or not,—which, however, is very probable. They will tell you at home about a projected Tutorship, which is yet uncertain, but which, if I like it,— for the most lies there,—will yield me a nett revenue of £200 a-year. Where is the risk then, my boy Jack? And if this all evaporate, I can still translate and compile and write and do rarely. I think my health *is* improving; and I have often said, that I want nothing more. So be of good cheer, benighted Teanglegg![1] day will dawn upon thee, and a fine country lie disclosed at thy feet, before the year's end.

Parson Sloane must have very peculiar views on the nature of adverbs. "Fence *in* the tender shrubs" is no mysterious phrase; and *in*, if there be any logic upon Earth, is a preposition to all intents and purposes; in

---

[1] *Tang-leg*, one of John Carlyle's nicknames in the family.

composition with "fence" to be sure, and not governing "shrubs," but still a preposition if there ever was one. Does the hysterical pedagogue not know or understand the property of all Saxon languages, and of English among them, which permits the separation of a verb from the preposition in composition with it, and the inversion of their usual arrangement if necessary? Did he never read "I have set-to my seal" in his Bible? Did he never say, "Put to the door"? And is *to* an adverb likewise? After all it is simply a question about terms; and makes no jot of difference, however it be decided. But one does not like to be bravadoed and cowed out of anything. . . .

Now thou must write again, boy, in a few days and tell me all that is in thy liver, both *pro* and *contra*. How does Ben do? Make my best respects to him. I intend writing: but alas! How busy am *not* I? as Potty[1] said —that is Potty of Lauder, who is a good man notwithstanding.

I have written in a strange humour to-night, Jack: melancholickish, ill-naturedish, affectionatish—all in *ish*— for I am very weak and weary, having slept little last night, and sat too much. I am for bed now. Good-night, my Jack! I love thee as well as I can, which is pretty well, considering all things.

If I can rise in time to-morrow morning (which is far from likely) I intend giving this to Dr. Johnston, who has been here witnessing about Armstrong of Glingan's trial. Armstrong is to be quit for a month's imprisonment, as you will hear. Johnston did not give his evidence in full; for they saw, he said to me last night in Waugh's room, he was going to *waken* on them—and so prudently let him travel.

I like my room well—the air is good, the landlady is good, and there is *peace*. Alas! for my poor *Book*. But it *shall* appear yet. When shall I begin? Good-night again! Thy affectionate brother,

THOS. CARLYLE.

---

[1] Annandale name for a pedlar of pottery.

LXXXIV.—To John A. Carlyle, Annan.

3 Moray Street, 30*th January* 1822.

My dear Jack—The Carrier came in to-day, and found me in such a bustle, that though I scrawled off a letter for Home, and delivered it to him, I fear they will be able to make neither "top, tail, nor root out of it:" and I sit down, now more at ease, to give you some regular picture of affairs, in the faith that you will carry it up to Mainhill on Saturday, and so contrive to eke out some tolerable conception of my "whereabout and how" among you. I am going to charge you with postage; but we cannot help it; you must just submit.

In the first place of all, then, you will thank my Mother again and again for her kindness in sending materials out to me in the box, and good wishes in the letter. I will answer, as I may, in due season. Take up some tea and other such traffic with you—for my sake as well as your own. In the second place, I would have you tell Polwarth [Alexander Carlyle] that his epistle (which I have just read over a second time) is very smart, and contains *just* two small errors: "thankful*l*" and "wh*i*ther" in place of "wh*e*ther." I can see that he has studied Cobbett to some purpose: I hope he will reap the full fruit of his diligence in time. The "old watch" I got duly, and find very serviceable: it goes well, though somewhat nimbly. If there is anything to pay Robie or others connected with it, some of you will stand good: the article is worth fifty of the old one, which indeed was worth very little—if anything. . . .

You, of course, know all the outs and ins, up to a certain date, of this tutoring business. . . . The boys arrived about a week ago, and are to continue some six months at board in the house of one Dr. Fleming, a clergyman, till their parents arrive. I have entered upon duty, but in a desultory way, and expecting further advice from London. I have offered to take the matter upon trial for a month or two at any rate; and then, if it answer, to commence business regularly, and with the regular salary —£200, and an allowance in the interim instead of board.

Mr. Buller, the father, wished some abatement in this period of uncertainty. I proffered leaving the payment at his own discretion, *for the two months;* and having *no* further uncertainty at all. The "memorandum" in which I stated this, together with some other considerations necessary to be impressed upon the man, is now in his possession. It was written with as much emphasis as I could contrive to unite with respectfulness; Irving also has spoken magnificently of me; so that if I enter the family at all, I need expect no supercilious or uncomfortable treatment there: and I still consider the office as lying at my own option, that is, depending on the character of the young men themselves and my suitableness to it. This latter point I have naturally been doing my utmost to determine during the last week: and though, of course, I have not quite succeeded in *bodomming*[1] the fellows yet, I am rather inclined to hope they will *do.* Both are of superior talents, and much classical instruction: they have few positively bad qualities that I can see, and considerable good nature. *Levity* and inattention are the prevailing faults; and in the elder boy they will be rather difficult to surmount: however I have no fear that he or any one connected with him will ever get the length of *despising* me, and I imagine that patient management on my part will bring about the desired result. A short time will try, and I will tell you regularly how it goes on. They take up all my day—at least the better part of it—at present: from ten o'clock till about one, and from six till nearly eight. If I undertake finally, I shall need to make a fierce push at Greek. But a man will do much for such advantages.

Now, Jack, I have told you all that can be told about this thing. If it prosper, we may all be the better for it. You, certainly, need be under no apprehensions about your education—there will be cash enough to fit you out royally. Indeed you need not fear though it were again the nothing it was four weeks ago. You will almost for certain get teaching next winter: and if not—I have a pen still, and a stout heart belonging to myself. So be of good cheer, my jolly boy; let not thy *winnow-cloth* picture aught sinister in the future. Mind not the *ineptiæ* of the midge Duncan C.,

---

[1] *Bottoming* = fathoming, testing.

or the down-looks of Biggar and the burghers of Annan.
Stick to Ben (to whom my best compliments), keep working
cannily as "doth the little busy bee"—and let the Earth
wag as it will. Observe I expect a long letter very soon—
by the post; it comes soonest and sureliest. Describe
everything to me—*sans peur et sans souci*. What matters
what you write to me?—I am, your Brother,

THOMAS CARLYLE.

Johnson's *Tour* will do excellently well to read—or
some of Swift's works if you like humour: did you ever see
his *Tale of a Tub* or *Gulliver*? What think you of *Rasselas*
or the *Lives of the Poets*? Do you ever make an onslaught
upon poetry? There is Pope and Dryden and all the
moderns—which people read, independently of their merits,
to talk about them. There are also plays out of number
from Shakespeare, the greatest of geniuses, down to
Cumberland, very far from the greatest. There is much
good to be got of reading such things—they improve the
style, and fill the imagination with fine objects, and the
heart sometimes with bold feelings. Read to amuse yourself as well as to learn; and be not diligent over much.

LXXXV.—To Mr. JAMES JOHNSTONE, Glasgow.

EDINBURGH, *4th February* 1822.

MY DEAR JOHNSTONE—Your letter is dated about three
weeks ago, has been expected about two months, and came
into my hands only this morning. As I do fully intend to
answer it soon, and as there is odds that I shall not find
myself soon in a better mood for answering it than at
present, I have adopted the wise resolution of consecrating
the passing hour to that duty—obedient to the prudent saw,
which assures us that opportunity, hairy in front, is bald
behind: *fronte capillata, post est occasio calva*. I say duty;
but I might have used a kindlier word. In fact there are
few events in my history that yield a more placid enjoyment to my mind, than reading a letter from you or writing
one for your perusal. In such cases the sober certainty
of your many affectionate and faithful feelings towards me
—not altogether unrequited, I hope—mingles itself with

the happy recollection of many virtuous and cheerful hours that we have spent together long ago—before either of us had tasted *how* bitter a thing is worldly life ; and how wofully our young purposes were to be marred by the low impediments of this confused, inane, and noisy vortex into which both of us have been cast, and where we are still toiling and striving and jostling and being jostled, according to the sentence passed on Adam, and fulfilled on all his poor descendants.   The moonshine nights during which we have strolled along the *loanings* of our native Annandale, the sunny days we have spent in basking on our own *braes*,— talking so copiously and heartily of all things that we knew or did not know ; those nights and days are " with the days beyond the Flood," we shall not see them more ; but the memory of them is still bright in the soul, and will make us recollect each other with pleasure even to the end.   It is a rare fortune that gives to the man the friends of the boy, unsullied by unworthy actions, and still maintaining some similarity of tastes : it is a happiness, however, which has been ours, and I trust, will continue so always.   Nor do I in the smallest abandon the hope that future days will be calmer than those that have passed and are passing over us.   Depend upon it, my good friend, there is a time coming, when though we may not be great men, we shall be placid ones ; when, having mended by much toil what is capable of being mended in our condition, and resigned ourselves to endure with much patience what in it is incapable of mending, we shall meet together like toil-worn wayfarers descending the mountain cheerily and smoothly which we climbed with danger and distress.   " We will laugh and sing and tell old tales," and forget that our lot has been hard, when we think that our hearts have been firm and our conduct true and honest to the last.   This should console us whatever weather it is with us : the task is brief ; and great is the reward of doing it well.

But this is not a homily : so I take leave of preaching— for which indeed I have no talent.   You sadden me by the outline which you draw of your actual situation.   A state of health " but indifferent " is signified in one short sentence ; yet comprises within it a catalogue of vexatious discomforts which might furnish matter for many volumes.

I entreat you in the name of common sense to suspend *every* pursuit that interferes with your attention to this first of all concerns. Out, I say, from your confined dwelling-place! Away to the banks of Clyde, to the Green, to the Country, to free air! What is all the Greek in the Universe to this? There is more happiness, nay more philosophy, in a sound nervous system, than in all the systems described by Brucker or Buhle, or conceived by any mortal from Thales down to Mr. Owen of Lanark, who scarcely knew the horn-book but "had *no* nerves." Happy brute! I would give all the world sometimes to have no nerves.

These Irish schemes are not likely to be of service, I fear. You did right to reject at once and totally the "potato-plot" and cabin, as well [as] the "thirty pounds" tutorship: and if I were in your place, I would be well assured that the Newton Barry School was certain of yielding something considerably beyond sixty or seventy Pounds annually, before I thought of encountering the *tristia of the Sod* or the vulgar annoyances of those who tread upon it. Still the place seems worth inquiring after; and I hope you will yet hear more of it. But you must absolutely never say another word about New Holland whatever befalls. This I insist upon. Take my word for it, sir, you are no[t ma]de for emigration. The Colonists may say that Botany Bay is this and that and the other : *n'en croyez rien*. The society will please you infinitely less in the land of Colonists and Kangaroos than it did in Canada or Nova Scotia; and the emoluments of anything in which you could be serviceable must be what they are in all new countries, of a kind quite inadequate to procure you satisfaction of even a tolerable degree. Can you be content with a life in which the stomach shall be filled never so royally, whilst the head and the heart are both left w[aste] and empty? Can you submit to be judged by an ermined sheep-stealer? Can you associate with the half-reformed sweepings of creation, with emeritus felons, with broken agriculturists, ruined projectors, and persons having the bones and sinews of men but nothing more? This is an overcharged picture, I know; but much of it *must* be true : and other pictures look more flattering, chiefly because they embrace the exception, instead of the rule. Consider this, and lay

aside your project *for ever*. Stay at home where your
merits—slow of making themselves known anywhere—are
at least appreciated by many who respect you and are
anxious to patronise you for the sake of them. You can
teach well and honestly ; your present employment will
render you fitter for the task than ever you were ; and
situations are often casting up which may be gained by
honest methods, and made the means of a respectable and
permanent establishment *at home*. I had rather go and set
up teaching—anywhere in Britain, with no introduction but
my staff and scrip, than go to *Australasia* with all the
recommendations that could be given me. Be patient and
diligent, and you *must* ultimately succeed. In the meantime, if nothing better occur, I think you should return to
Bogside in spring for the sake of your health, if it do not
completely recover. Take no desponding view of things,
my friend ; you are young and solidly qualified and true-
minded : you will be happy in the end—happy as any one
Here need care much about being. All that know you like
you ; food and raiment is sure ; what need of more ?

I have prosed and prosed till I have left no room to
tell you of my own affairs, in which I know you feel deep
interest. Write to me immediately, and I will describe
everything. Edward Irving has found me a situation, if it
answer : ask him about it. Adieu !—I am always your
friend,   THOMAS CARLYLE.

LXXXVI.—To his FATHER.

EDINBURGH, *5th February* 1822.

MY DEAR FATHER—I have just received your letter from
the hands of Garthwaite, and delivered the box to him. He
is going away about five o'clock, and it is already near four ;
so I have very little time to write in, and you will therefore
excuse the confusion and meagreness of which it is probable
my letter will exhibit so many proofs. At any rate, I wrote
Jack by the post last week, and on that occasion gave him
a full detail ; and I suppose you have perused it before now.

I am very glad to learn that you are going on still " in
the old way "—which if not the best possible way, certainly
deserves to be reckoned a very fair one, in such times as the

present. Even the trifling reduction of twelve per cent
will be of some service ; and I entertain no doubt that
something permanently beneficial to the farming interests
must be effected soon by the Legislature : the state of the
Country imperiously requires it. You have not surely any
reason to fear for your own part : so long as you and my
Mother and the rest are blessed with moderate health, there
is every reason to be thankful for the actual state of things,
and to hope that the future state of them will have improved.

I feel very sorry to learn that Bogside, so long used to
health and quiet, has been visited at length with such severe
sickness. I trust it will only be for a short time : he is a
worthy person in his way ; and I have often experienced
his kindness. Johnstone wrote to me for the *first* time the
day before yesterday ! He has been rather sickly, and exceedingly busied. His Irish affair is too likely to evaporate ;
and he naturally looks into the coming years with no small
anxiety. I feel much for James : he is an honest kind soul
as lives by bread; and his fluctuating fortunes are to be
imputed less to imprudence or faults on his part, than to
the original circumstances in which he grew up, and to the
undue neglect he has experienced from those who hold the
patronages of this world in their hands. He is irresolute,
because he is at once sharp-tempered and affectionate,
impatient and indolent, vexed with present evil, and not
careful of future good. His mind is not great or strong ;
but it is true as gold. I wrote him encouragingly yesterday.

Another still more unfortunate and far less amiable character than Johnstone, I mean the celebrated Waugh,[1] comes in
contact with me here now and then. Waugh navigates the
stream of life, as an immense Dutch lugger would drift
along a rocky shoaly sea—at the rate of one mile per hour—
the sails and rigging being gone, the compass and chart over-
board, the captain, however, still standing by the helm, and
by his ignorance and blindness making matters only worse
than if he were asleep continually. I know not what is to
become of him. One day I pity his case very deeply ; and
the next some gross imprudence converts my pity into irrita-

[1] "A kind of maternal cousin or half-cousin of my own. Had been
my school comrade (several years older) . . . who, though not without
gifts, proved gradually to be intrinsically a good deal of a fool."—*Reminiscences,* i. 93.

tion. He has no money I doubt, and little rational prospect of getting any. I offered him some teaching, which he was very glad of when I spoke about it first, which he declined when I saw him a second time, wished to consider further of when I saw him a third time, and finally rejected when I saw him a fourth time. He will most likely find some shark ready to seize upon his property for about the fifth part of its value in ready cash—which he at present longs to do; then spend this hundred pounds in half a year; and afterwards become—I wot not what.

But I have dwelt too long on those points: I must turn to myself. Those boys from London I am still attending daily—from ten o'clock to one, and then from six to eight. They improve upon me. The eldest I have talked a good deal with; and brought at last—I hope permanently, but cannot affirm—to a more rational style of feeling. He is no bad-hearted fellow: and I am inclined to think will do pretty well in the end. But we have yet heard no word from the Father, though we expected some two days ago; and no durable arrangement can yet be thought of. I like the business for many reasons, and dislike it chiefly because it will cut up my time so enormously for a while. I designed to set about writing some Book shortly; and this (at which I must ultimately arrive, if I ever arrive at anything) will of necessity require to be postponed greatly. On the whole, however, I am in no bad spirits about myself at present. My health is incomparably better than it was a year ago: by the aid of some simple drugs, I keep things in a kind of passable state, which, though far from a right one, is a state calculated to yield me no small consolation, when I compare it with that which preceded. The air I live in too being very good, I expect to go on improving. I am still much pleased with my lodgings, so that everything, if not exactly as it should be, is at least far better than it might be.

I firmly proposed to write my dear and kind Mother a long letter this opportunity: but five o'clock is already struck; and I must again defer it. Assure her of my continued love—of which indeed she requires no assurance; remember me in brotherly affection to Alick and Jack (from whom I had a letter which went round by Glasgow, and came with Johnstone's), to Mag and Jamie, Mary, Jane

and Jenny; not doubting that I remain, my dear Father,
your dutiful son,

THOMAS CARLYLE.

I read Robt. Carlyle's letter; but unless you are much
better informed about the name of Carlyle than I, the
London Gentleman is likely to receive very little insight
from us into that ancient patronymic. A large bell was
dug up at Dumfries not long ago, of which I suppose
he has heard. There is also some notice of Carlyle in
Murray's *Genealogy of Bruce:* but I am afraid it is a bad
concern,—this " history."

That great-coat will not suit Edinburgh any longer.
Jack may have it if he like—if not, any one. I am done—
for it is quite night.

LXXXVII.—To ALEXANDER CARLYLE, Mainhill.

EDINBURGH, 22*d February* 1822.

. . . It is surely galling to a young active mind to look
forward to such a fate as sometimes overtakes the impro-
vident or unfortunate cultivator of the soil in our days.
To become a Dick of the Grange for example! But
beyond all doubt you have no such thing to fear; you are
at present discharging a sacred duty; and you have every
reason to look forward to a comfortable termination of it.
A hundred or two hundred pounds would stock you a neat,
snug little farm if times were better, and none who knows
your habits and talents would have the smallest doubt
about repayment. Who is to advance me two hundred
pence? you ask. Whoever of us has it, I answer; and
till then we are all alike. Circumstances seem to render
it conceivable that I, your obliged, and not ungrateful
brother, may have such a sum in my own possession, ere
a year or two elapse; and I here make the promise—not
rashly, for I have thought of it fifty times—to let you have
the use of it, whenever you think fit. This is, to be sure,
selling the chickens while the hen is hatching; and in this
light, it looks rather foolish : but you know it is honestly
meant; and the hope it points to is not quite chimerical.
And granting that it should utterly evaporate—are you not
still a hardy free-minded Scotsman, with habits of diligence

and frugality known only to few Scotsmen, ready to front
the world whatever way it offers itself—and to gather an
honest livelihood, from any point of the compass, where a
livelihood is to be found?   I say, therefore, fear nothing !
You or any one of us, will never be a *snool*;[1] we have not
the blood of snools in our bodies.   Nor shall you ever seriously meditate crossing the great Salt Pool to plant yourself
in the Yankee-land.   That is a miserable fate for any one,
at best ; never dream of it.   Could you banish yourself from
all that is interesting to your mind, forget the history, the
glorious institutions, the noble principles of old Scotland,
that you might eat a better dinner perhaps (which you care
little for), or drink more rum (which you care naught for)
as a great pursey Yankee?   Never ! my boy—you will
never think of it.   Scotland has borne us all hitherto ; we
are all Scots to the very heart ; and the same bleak but
free and independent soil will, I hope, receive us all into
its bosom at last.

.   .   .   .   .   .

LXXXVIII.—To John A. Carlyle, Annan.

EDINBURGH, *7th April* 1822.

MY DEAR JACK— . . . Your letter with the enclosed
five pounds came to me in due time : I was much pleased
with your punctuality—though just what I expected.   When
you want the money again, let me know.   I calculate that
I have now as much as will serve me till the Bullers come,
when I shall get more ; and I beg you will not be in any
strait without applying to me—not only for your own (if I
should be so negligent as to need being applied to)—but
for any sum within the extent of my resources.   Waugh,
the bookseller, I caused pay me ; and he has done it like
a scurvy person—with fifteen pounds, where there should
have been five and twenty.   "The *Review*[2] has so limited
a sale ; the, etc., etc."   I design writing no more for him,
unless driven to it by a necessity harder than I like to
anticipate.   Yet I give him no rude words—both because
rude words generally degrade the person who employs them

---

[1] A mean-spirited fellow.

[2] The short-lived *New Edinburgh Review*.

as much as the person who endures them, and because not knowing what may turn out in the future, I consider that "better a wee bush than nae bield,"[1] and even Waugh's *Review* may be of use to me. At any rate I doubt not the "limited sale" is a very sufficient excuse for his parsimony. My own wonder is that there exists any "sale" at all. If it were not that Providence is a rich provider—furnishing nourishment for all the animated tribes of the universe—one could not *à priori* expect a single purchaser far less a reader for this literary moon-calf. Peace be with it! and with all the *hashes* that contribute to create it! They have each a right to a certain portion of the beef slaughtered within this city, and to a certain portion of the oxygen gas that floats around it : far be it from me to wish their privileges curtailed.

The translation of *Legendre* puzzles me a little. I had finished about four or five sheets of it long ago ; but the people are getting clamorous for it now, and I not only find no kind of pleasure in the task, but cannot even perform it at all without sacrificing considerable prospects of a far more alluring kind. I have thoughts of giving it up in favour of John Waugh. Could you do it, Jack? Have you time and spirit for it, I mean? If you think so—I wish you would try a portion and let me see ; the beginning of the fifth book, for example : write it out in a legible hand (no matter how ugly) and send it up by the first opportunity. This idea struck me about a minute ago : consider of it seriously. If the work did not too much destroy your time, it would pay very well, and such things do not always occur when one wants them. I am confident I could make you do it well if I had you here. Say what you think of it—if you think anything. . . .

I want a long letter from you, as soon as possible—including all your experiences, your hopes. Send me large batches of news ; let everything be fish that comes within your net. . . .

I am going to enclose the critique on *Faust*. You may show it to Ben, if he cares for it ; and then let them have it at home. I hope you go often up to Mainhill—and take little nicknacks with you sometimes to our invaluable

---

[1] A Scotch proverb : Better a little bush than no shelter.

Mother.   Carry my love to her and our worthy Father, and all the rest of them.   Remind Polwarth and my other correspondents of their epistolary duties.   Farewell, my good Jack; it is bedtime, and I am tired enough, and feeble, though still your affectionate brother,

THOMAS CARLYLE.

LXXXIX.—To ALEXANDER CARLYLE, Mainhill.

EDINBURGH, *Saturday, 27th April* 1822.

MY DEAR ALICK—I have just read over your very lively, kind, and acceptable letter; which, though the Carrier as usual has left me completely in the dark as to the period of his outgoing or even his personal identity, I proceed to answer as minutely as the various calls upon my time will permit. . . .

I feel very contented in my usual state—full of business even to overflowing, with projects of all sorts before me, and some few rational hopes of executing a definite portion of them.   With regard to the Book, it is true, as you guess, that I have been "riddling Creation" for a subject to dilate upon; and have felt no small disquietude till I could find something suitable.   Within the last month, however, I have well-nigh fixed upon a topic, and I feel considerable alacrity and much more contentment than formerly, in laying in materials for setting it forth.   My purpose (but this only among yourselves!) is to come out with a kind of Essay on the Civil Wars [of] the Commonwealth of England—not to write a history of them—but to exhibit, if I can, some features of the national character as it was then displayed, supporting my remarks by mental portraits, drawn with my best ability, of Cromwell, Laud, George Fox, Milton, Hyde, etc., the most distinguished of the actors in that great scene.   I may, of course, intersperse the work of delineation with all the ideas which I can gather from any point of the universe.   If I live, with even moderate health, I purpose to do this; and if I can but finish it according to my own conception of what it should be, I shall feel much happier than if I had inherited much gold and silver.   The critics, too, may say of it either nothing or anything, according to their own good pleasure;

if it once pleased my own mighty *self*, I do not value them or their opinion a single rush. Long habit has inured me to live with a very limited and therefore a dearer circle of approvers : all I aim at is to convince my own conscience that I have not taken their approbation without some just claims to it.

These are the fairy regions of Hope, from which I am incessantly recalled by multitudes of less glorious but more urgent actual duties. The printing of *Legendre* is fairly begun—and intended to proceed at the rate of two sheets per week. I thought to steer clear of it, and fix it on Waugh, but it would not do : so I am in for it myself, and expect to be kept as busy with it "as a cock on the spit" till after August. I purpose making Jack help me a little : I have indeed need of help ; and my studies, even with it, in so far as *the* Book is concerned, must in the meantime go on rather leisurely. The hours I spend in teaching are by no means uncomfortable—except as they consume my leisure, which I would gladly devote to other objects : the boys are very brave-hearted fellows—particularly the elder, —and respect me sufficiently. I still look upon our final agreement. however, as a thing not to be counted on : but fortunately, like *Cowthat's* weather, " it may be *owther* way," without affecting me immensely. I have plenty of offers from Booksellers. etc. (whose anxiety to employ me naturally increases in the inverse ratio of my want of employment), to undertake editions of works, and so forth, under terms sufficiently liberal : and at the beginning of August I shall have " money in my purse" to set me above the necessity of drudgery for a long while. So I do not feel much apprehension ; none at all, if it were not for the matter of health, which also, as I have said, has a favourable aspect at present.

Thus, my dear fellow, have I prated to you for "a strucken hour" of myself and my doings—sure of an attentive and interested listener, and careless of concealing whatever solicited utterance. I must now draw bridle. There were a thousand questions that I meant to ask you ; but you must endeavour to forestall them next opportunity, and to send me all the details you can collect. . . .

I wish I could get a box home this time ; for I want

some cakes and eggs : I think if you sent about a *quarter* of meal, the landlady here could make me cakes herself. She bakes tolerable ones out even of the sawdust, which they—falsely—call oatmeal in these parts.   But I must off to the Carrier's lodgings, and see what can be done.   Adieu, my dear Alick !—I am always, your affectionate Brother,

THOMAS CARLYLE.

XC.—To Miss WELSH, Haddington.

EDINBURGH, 30*th April* 1822.

MY DEAR MADAM—I address myself with the greatest pleasure to the task you have so kindly imposed on me. I very much approve your resolution to exercise your powers in some sort of literary effort ; and I shall think myself happy, if by any means I can aid you in putting it in practice.   There is nothing more injurious to the faculties than to keep poring over books continually without attempting to exhibit any of our own conceptions.   We amass ideas, it is true ; but at the same time we proportionally weaken our power of expressing them ; a power equally valuable with that of conceiving them, and which, though in some degree like it, the gift of Nature, is in a far higher degree the fruit of art, and so languishes more irretrievably by want of culture.   Besides, our very conceptions, when not taken up with the view of being delineated in writing, are almost sure to become vague and disorganised ; a glimpse of the truth will often satisfy mere curiosity equally with a full view of it ; so hallucinations are apt to be substituted for perceptions : and even if our materials were all individually accurate, yet being gathered together from every quarter, and heaped into one undistinguished mass, they form at last an unmanageable chaos, serving little purpose except to perplex and cumber the mind that lives among them—to make it vacillating, irregular, and very unhappy—at least if it have not the fortune to be a pedant's mind—who, I believe, is generally a very cheerful character.

So that you see it is every way incumbent upon you to commence writing without loss of time ; and to continue it steadily as you proceed in the acquisition of knowledge, thus causing the development of your taste and of your ability to realise its dictates to go forward hand in hand. I do not imagine that you stand in need of all this confused logic to animate you in this undertaking :—inclination, I know well enough, impels you sufficiently at present; but inclination is ofttimes rather an unsteady guide, and at no time the worse for having conviction along with it.

There is not room here for dilating upon the peculiarities of your genius; to which at any rate I have no right to make myself inspector, even if my knowledge of the subject rendered my opinion worth the giving. I cannot help saying, however, that according to my imperfect observations, you seem, with great keenness of intellectual vision generally, to unite a decided tendency to the study of human character both as an object of curiosity and of love or contempt, and to manifest a very striking faculty of expressing its peculiarities, not only by description, but imitation. This is the very essence of dramatic genius; and if I mistake not, the blame will lie elsewhere than with Nature if you fail of producing something worth producing in this department. It depends on other circumstances than your intellectual powers, whether you should adopt the tragic or the comic species of composition : you know whether you feel more disposition to sympathise with the wretched or to laugh at the happy; to admire excellence or to search out defects ; to cherish long, vehement, heartfelt, perhaps extravagant enthusiasm, or to exert the force of your heart in brief, violent sallies, the violence of which a sense of propriety is ever subduing and rendering of short continuance—converting indignation into derision, sympathy into pity, and admiration into respect. The truth is, those two kinds of talent are never so accurately divided in nature, as the two objects of them are in art ; most people who could write a tragedy of merit could write a sort of comedy also, and *vice versa*. It is not indeed necessary to confine your efforts either to the one or the other ; the kind of genius named dramatic may be employed in a thousand ways unconnected with the theatre ; it gives life and splendour to the picturesque novels of Sir Walter Scott ; and forms, in a different shape, the basis of much sublime philosophy in the treatises of Madame de Staël.

It is misemployed only when it is unoccupied; when the understanding, the invention, the fancy which might have given it a local habitation and a name, a shape and vehicle, are devoted to purposes into which it does not enter—to studying abstract sciences or manufacturing smart paragraphs—writing epigrams or reading metaphysics and mathematics—or anything of a similar stamp. I would not have you, therefore, confine yourself too rigidly to mere Plays; it will be enough if you are engaged in the delineation or inspection of Character—without which I imagine you cannot do justice to your powers; but in the investigation of which you are not bound to any particular form of composition, being at liberty to cast your ideas into the shape of a historical description, of a Panegyric, of a novel, quite as much as of a regular drama. For this reason—But the subjects? you say—the subjects—and have done with this prosing! . . . *Cetera desunt.*

T. CARLYLE.

XCI.—To his MOTHER, Mainhill.

3 MORAY STREET, Saturday,
[May 1822?]

MY DEAR MOTHER— . . . You will find here a bonnet of Imperial chip or Simple chip, or Real chip, or whatever it is, which I hope will arrive safely and be found to suit you. I think it looks like your head. I wish it were fifty times better for your sake: it would still be the most feeble testimony of what I owe to your kind affection, which has followed me unweariedly through good and evil fortune, soothing and sweetening all the days of my existence, and which I trust Providence will yet long, long continue for a blessing to us both.

I know you will fret about those things, and talk about expense and so forth. This is quite erroneous doctrine: the few shillings that serve to procure a little enjoyment to your frugal life are as mere *nothing* in the outlay of this luxurious city. If you want any other thing, I do beg you would let me know: there is not any way in which I can spend a portion of my earnings so advantageously. Tell me honestly, Do you get tea and other things comfortably?

I should be very sorry if you restricted yourself for any reason but from choice. It would be a fine thing surely, if you that have toiled for almost half a century in nourishing stalwart sons, should not now by this means have a little ease and comfort, when it lies in their power to gain it for you! I again entreat you, if you wish for anything within the reach of my ability, to let me hear of it.

.   .   .   .   .   .

I entrust you with my affectionate remembrances to my Father, and all the family, every one. They owe me letters now, which they cannot pay a minute too soon. Bid the Carrier be sure to ask for the box next time he comes; it will be in readiness for him. At the present, I do not want anything. I shall give you proper notice when I do.

Farewell, my dear Mother! May all Good be with you always! Your affectionate Son,

TH. CARLYLE.

XCII.—To JOHN A. CARLYLE, Annan.

3 MORAY STREET, 19*th May* 1822.

MY DEAR JACK—I was hindered from writing to you last night by the most ignoble of all causes, the presence of that small pragmatical Jurist, whose visits to me—happily of rare occurrence—seldom yield *the same* degree of satisfaction to both parties concerned. I cannot altogether dislike the poor wight, for he is not without many goodish qualities, and aims after better things than the mere practitioning of Law: I only regret that he should select me for his Mentor, especially when actually enduring the operation of so much speculation upon ephemeralities,—so feeble and so fearfully compensating its shallowness by its breadth. He does not afflict me, however, above once a week or so; being chained to his desk in general, or doing the errands of his pettyfogging Principal in the mighty deep of Attorneyship here; a task of which himself even seems to feel very heartily sick. I wish the boy no harm at all.

Your paper came duly to hand.[1] I thank you for the anxious punctuality you have shown; and I am happy, on

---

[1] The translation of a part of *Legendre*.

looking over the article, to find that you have acquitted yourself so manfully; happy both for your sake, to see you possessed of, and going on to acquire, so steady a knowledge of the English tongue and the art of composition,—and for my own sake, to find the manuscript so well fitted for going directly to the Press. . . .

As for the Trigonometry, begin it when you like; I shall take your assistance joyfully,—though I again insist that you do not let it vex you overmuch, or consume your time too greatly. I am so kept with the thing, that no help will give me the faculty of serious study or any kind of permanent composition, till it be done : therefore it is not fit that you should throw good diligence after bad—in labour which can at best be little more than intermission to me, not rest—if it indeed do anything but encourage my indolence, already more than sufficiently abundant.

You have not written me any long or full account of your walk and conversation, for a long while. See you try this soon. . . .

My own condition is mending very greatly, on the whole : I have not had such a measure of health and spirits for three years as I enjoy at present. It was the very making or rather saving of me that I came down here to live ; no mortal but a nervous dyspeptic wretch can tell what heaven it is to escape from the tumult and stench and smoke and squalor of a city out into the pure ether and the blue sky, with green fields under your very window and bushy trees in the distance, and little noise but the gambols of happy children, the peaceful labours of spadesmen, the voice of singing birds. I sit down to my desk or my book, with the windows pulled down and up—the fresh young air of May around, all Nature seeming to awake like Beauty from her couch ; and my very heart is glad sometimes that I am delivered so as even partially to enjoy this pure and simple pleasure. I go down and bathe every morning before breakfast, when I can effect it ; which has been daily for the last three days, the distance not being above a mile, and the water clear as glass. This I find to be a most excellent practice. Yesterday I fell in with Waugh on the beach, his broad fat face appearing among the Newhaven fishing-craft, just as I emerged. (I should have said I did not get down yesterday till noon.) Waugh had been calling for me, and missing his purpose, had advanced to the far-end. I proposed going home directly, but Waugh fixed his eye on a monstrous *meerswine* (porpoise, or *purpose* as they call it) which some fishers had just flayed; and being smit with the lust of knowledge, he insisted on dissecting the carcass to discover its anatomical structure. It would have made the weeping Philosopher himself smile to see Waugh gutting this monster of the Deep—up to the elbows almost in gore and filth, descrying with a rapturous shout the various midriffs and puddings and cats-collops of its bestial belly—stretching its guts along the gravel and measuring their length with a measuring-reed (made of sea-tangle—one of the small guts of the beast was like a short day's journey in length—somewhere about sixty feet, if I recollect)—the whole of this amid a crowd of brown fishermen, idle serving-maids, and scrubby boys, who eyed Waugh with astonishment and awe, and stood waiting *till* he would extract the oil or ambergris or balm or precious stone, for which they felt sure he must be digging so painfully. I tired of it, or he would have struck upon a young shark also, which attracted his attention by similar allurements. Waugh is the placidest man on Earth for certain: at the instant when he was gutting this shapeless hulk of stinking flesh, I believe he could not have commanded *sixpence* anywhere in Nature. Yet he minds not, living on Hope.

The Bullers and I go on very well together: they are really good creatures and pleasant to be near, though they do not stick to their learning as I could wish. I have never yet calculated on the absolute certainty of my engaging in their family. I can do it, or not do it, as occasion serves; which is the fine way to be in. If this stomach-disorder ("the *baddest* disorder that follows the *kyercage*," as an old blind Irishman called it yesterday) will but be kind enough to take its leave; then *basta !*—I care not for any man or thing !

Send my love to Mainhill, when you have a chance; I long for the Carrier, that I may get eggs and cakes. Tell them to send my jean trousers and as many cotton socks as they can raise—if any. Will you or Alick also write to

Shaw of Dumfries for another pair of shoes exactly like the last pair, or just one hair's breadth longer? He may send them out to Ecclefechan at his leisure ; from whence they may find their way hither. I have detained you long, Jack, and *must* now withdraw. I am glad our mother's bonnet fits, I need not bid you be kind to her by every way you can.—I am always your affectionate Brother,

THOMAS CARLYLE.

XCIII.—From his MOTHER.

MAINHILL, *26th May* 1822.

DEAR SON—I got the bonnet which you sent me. It fits very well ; I am certainly highly pleased with this fresh token of your kindness and attention towards me. Amid all this turmoil it soothes me to think that there is one who can sympathise with me ; who knows all the little inconveniences I have to struggle with ; who is so fond of anticipating all my wants.

I once more remind you to be thankful to the Giver of all good for his kindness in granting you better health. Be careful to preserve your health. I am glad to hear that you bathe every morning before breakfast ; you must take care not to go too deep in. Is the place level? I am anxious to know when you will get home. I long to have a long crack with you and to talk all matters over. Tell me about this next time.

I intend to go to Dumfries on Wednesday to see all my friends. Mary Stewart has been ill ever since you went away. I wish you would write to John Aitken ;[1] he has had a good deal of trouble of late, and it would be some consolation to him.

I have had your socks ready for a long time ; but I have not had an opportunity of sending them : Farries called for the box last time he was out, but he says that he could neither find you nor the landlady. Send it home. And write me fully and tell me about all your affairs. You know none of them can be uninteresting to me.—I am, dear Tom, yours affectionately,   MARGARET CARLYLE.

---

[1] Old Mrs. Carlyle's brother ; Mary Stewart was his wife.

XCIV.—To Miss Welsh, Haddington.

3 Moray Street, *27th May* 1822.

My dear Friend—I kept looking out for you or your Mother almost every day last week ; not once suspecting that you could visit Edinburgh and leave it, without communicating that event to so important a person as myself. It were unprofitable, not to say absurd, to make any kind of outcry about this occurrence now ; and very absurd to charge you with any blame in the matter : another time, however, I hope for better fortune.

I have little leisure for writing to-day ; only I could not defer sending you Sismondi's book, which I hope you will peruse with some profit as well as enjoyment. It is equally remote from the *nonsense* of *Atala*, and from the rude, melancholy vastness of that famous work—otherwise in truth so full of gross deformities. Sismondi is a lively, dapper, elegant little fellow, full of good sense and learning and correct sentiment : he resembles our Jeffrey somewhat —a *clever* man, with rather less of natural talent than Jeffrey has, and about ten times as much knowledge and culture. You must read his Treatise if possible ; were it but for the sake of the Italians, in whose literature he is extremely versant.

It gives me great pleasure to find you so hearty in our poetical project : I trust good will come of it to us both. Hardly any creature is born without some thrills of poetry in his nature, which practice and instruction might enable him to express : and surely it were delightful, if when the mind feels so inflamed or overpowered in the various turns of this its confused and fluctuating existence,—astonished at the stupendous aspect of the universe—charmed, saddened, tortured in the course or in the prospect of its own great and gloomy and mysterious destiny,—it could embody those emotions, which now serve only to encumber and depress it, in music and imagery, in " thoughts that breathe and words that burn "; so gratifying, by employing, its own best faculties ; and brightening its own sensations, by causing all around to share in them. Nature, it is true, makes one right Poet seldom—scarcely in the hundred years ; but she makes a thousand rhymers in the day, with less or more of poetry in each. Our attempt then is not too arduous : I predict, that if we persevere, we shall both succeed in making very tolerable verses, *perhaps* something more than tolerable ; and this itself I reckon a very pleasing and harmless and very ornamental acquirement. Many a time I have wished that, when ruining my health with their poor lean triangles and sines and tangents and fluxions and calculi, I had but been writing any kind of doggerel, however weak : it would have improved the understanding, at least *mine* I am sure, quite as much or more—that is, left it where it was ; and *now*, I might have been inditing odes and dithyrambics by the gross ! The past is gone for aye : but —" better late than never !" as the adage runs. Do not think me altogether crazy : I am no poet, " have no genius," I know it well ; but I *can* learn to make words jingle whenever I think fit ; and by the blessing of Heaven, we two will try it now in concert as long as we like.

I wish, therefore, you would meditate some plan, some terms and conditions for carrying it on. Shall we prescribe the subject alternately ? And should it be a *specific* subject that is prescribed—or merely the *class* of subjects to which it must belong—" a descriptive piece " for instance,—" an incident—pathetic—tragical—ludicrous "—" a character— great—bad," etc.—or *some* descriptive piece—*some* incident —*some* character ? Or shall it merely be that each is to give in a certain quantity of verse within a stated time ? Settle all this to your own satisfaction—or leave it all unsettled if you like better. I have yet had no time to consider the business properly, or even to select a proper topic for our *coup d'essai.* The most plausible task I can hit upon is a little article to be entitled *The Wish,* wherein we are to set forth respectively the kind of fate and condition we most long for—and have some feeble expectation of attaining. Yours will be very different from mine, I know. It will be curious to compare notes, if we both deal honestly—which is not necessary, however. Try this ; and send it along when ready—with another theme, so it be an easy one.

These little *parergies* and recreations will do you no harm, I am persuaded ; yet I cannot help still wishing to see you employed in some more serious composition, while your stock of knowledge from books and other sources must be augmenting so rapidly. Did you think anything about the essay on Madame de Staël? I am still of opinion that it would be a very fine exercise for you ; and one you are well prepared for, having studied all her writings and feeling so deep an interest in all that concerns her. What is to hinder you from delineating your conception of her mind ; saying all you feel about her character as a thinker, as a poet, and still more as a woman ; comparing her in all these respects both with the ordinary throng of mortals, and with all the distinguished females you have heard or formed any idea of? I really wish you would begin in sober prose, and do this for me as honestly and correctly as you possibly can. I inquired after her *Life* for you to-day ; but it could not be had : however, if you engage to execute this undertaking, or otherwise desire to see the book, I will certainly find it. Consider this at any rate, for I am eager about it, being convinced it would prove useful to you.

The interest you take in my unfortunate projects I feel with the gratitude due to your kind treatment of me on all occasions. That historico-biographical one is still in embryo, but not yet abandoned. It seems quite indispensable that I should make an effort soon ; I shall have no settled peace of mind till then. Often it grieves me to be besieged with Printers'-Devils wanting *Copy* (of *Legendre*, a " most scientific " treatise on Geometry which I unhappily engaged to translate long ago)—with small boys studying Greek, and the many cares of life ; when I *might* be, etc. Till August, I cannot even get this *Book* fashioned into any shape, much less actually commenced. Meantime I read by snatches, partly with a view to it. If ever, which is just possible, I get the mastery over these difficulties, which it is hard to strive with but glorious to conquer, I shall experience many an enviable feeling at the thought of having vindicated Jane for the encouragements she gave me. Excuse this silly idea—for it is pleasant to me ; and this dull letter, which I have already spun out too long.—I am, ever yours,

THOMAS CARLYLE.

I am already too late for the Coach ; so I shall take time enough with your translation of " The Fisher." Be sure to send me abundance of such " trash " as your verses on the sunset, and those from *Atala ;* it is of the kind I like.

If Shandy understood articulate speech, I would gladly return his compliments ; for he is a dog of worth undoubtedly.   He would give me welcome whenever he met me, which is all he can do, poor fellow,—and more than every one of our human friends can do.

You should take a long ride, *every* day—your mother should insist on it.

XCV.—To Alexander Carlyle, Mainhill.

3 Moray Street, *2d June* 1822.

.   .   .   .   .   .

You make a great work about the little *Junius,* my brave and proud young man : it cost me nothing, being given me by the fat bookseller Boyd ; it was worth to me nothing ; and I thought it might not be quite useless to you—that is all.   The list of books you send me I shall be most prompt to purchase on the easiest terms possible, and I mean to set about the needful inquiries directly.   Knox you will find in the box.   I bought it many weeks ago.   There is one of the works mentioned in your list, which I cannot make out ; *"Raley's" Shipwreck* it seems to be, and *Raley* is a man I never heard of.[1]   Write it more distinctly next time, or give Jack in charge to transmit the name from Annan if he send me a letter sooner.

I would not have you be in anxiety about the state of your intellectual culture : I assure you it seems to me to proceed at a most respectable rate ; and as to the reading of books, I may remind you how little that of itself will perfect any man ; how much is to be learnt by daily observation, and solitary reflection, which no book can give us ; how much more valuable is the strong good sense of a true man, the minute and ever-present knowledge of his duties in every emergency, and the firm purpose to act accordingly—than all the mere *learning* which School or College ever taught.   I have no doubt you will find

---

[1] His brother doubtless wanted that entertaining and pathetic book, Captain James Riley's *Narrative of the Loss of the American Brig " Commerce " on the West Coast of Africa.*   It was reprinted in London in 1817.

abundant time to read, if you improve it all; you have within a year or two already mastered the elements of correct composition and general knowledge,—can now write a letter *well*, and understand the outlines of history and literature; you have men around you to study, a heart within you and a world without to survey; and your natural talents for doing all this are good. Be of good cheer then, boy; go on discharging your duties in the same diligent manful manner you have done hitherto,—improve your faculties as you have opportunity; and be sure of acting at a future day that honourable part in life which your rational ambition makes you wish to act. But I am preaching, when I should be *telling:* let me cease for once!

I have gone on enjoying very considerable improvement of health since I wrote last. The weather may be called delightful at present; sun shining, small breeze blowing, ground green *as leeks.* My windows "look to the Forth," —which I do not see, however, though I used to hear its hoarse and everlasting voice in winter winds,—and I get a view nightly of the Sunset. It is very grand to witness the great red fiery disc, sinking like a giant to sleep, among his crimson curtains of cloud—with the Fife and Ochil hills for his bedstead! I often look at him till I could almost break forth into tears, if it would serve,—or into some kind of poetical singing, if I could sing. To return to prose, the good weather and the sea-bathing, and the eight miles I have to walk daily are doing my poor shattered carcase no small service : in a year, at this rate, I might be as well as you.

I am also very busy, which is another great thing. That lubber Translation is proceeding at an easy though irregular rate; then I read for the *Civil Wars*—which, alas! are still like birds in the shell—and may be, I dread, for many months. . . .

T. CARLYLE.

XCVI.—To his MOTHER, Mainhill.

3 MORAY STREET, 2d *June* 1822.

MY DEAR MOTHER—I feel I am going to be very hurried, yet I cannot let slip this opportunity of scribbling you a few lines, however brief and insufficient, to let you know the state of my affairs for some time; and to thank you for these new proofs of your constant attention to me. I *hushed* a great many things into the Box, which, however, you need be in no haste to send back, as I am sufficiently provided by the supplies of to-day.   Perhaps it were better to send merely letters by Farries next time; and to bid him call for the little Box to carry home with him, seeing it is of a more reasonable size than the one I sent.   I need no more socks, etc., at present, having purchased three pairs the other night, which together with yours make up a very reasonable stock.   I gave 1s. 4d. a pair for them—dear, I suppose—for they are thin as nets, but cool and agreeable in ˌthis warm weather.   I hope Shaw will not neglect the shoes I wrote to Jack about : I shall soon want them.

These matters of business being adjusted, I proceed to give you some sketch of my way of doing at present, in which I know you ever feel a tender and truly motherly interest.   It will give you pleasure to know that I continue progressively improving in that most important of qualities, good health.   The bathing does me great good ; and you need be under no apprehension of my drowning ; for the bottom is smooth shelving sand or pebbles, I stay but a moment in the water, and never go near the end of my depth : besides, I swim if need were, which is not.   Unfortunately my mode of sleeping is too irregular to admit of my bathing constantly before breakfast ; though I manage this often, and almost always go some time in the day. . . .

You ask about my home-coming ; but this must be a very uncertain story for a while.   I cannot count on any such thing till *Legendre* be done, and the Buller people arrived : and in the event of my engaging with the latter, my period of absence must of course be [brief].   However, there is good and cheap conveyance to Dumfries daily, and it shall go hard if I do not steal a week or so to spend at Home.

I was in Glasgow some time ago, seeing Irving and all the rest of them.   It was during this period that Mr. Lawson called on me, and found me not : present my best thanks and services to him for so doing.   They have been holding their General Assembly here the other week, had Dr. Chalmers among them, etc.: I did not see anything of it, except a few Beef-eaters, pages with cocked hats, etc., dangling after the Commissioner's chair. The Commissioner himself I understand to be one of the meanest knaves north of the Tweed. But *there* is six o'clock, my hour of marching. Farewell, my dear Mother! It is the dearest blessing of my lot that I have you to write to, and to care for me. Send me a long account of all you do and feel. My Father has not written to me for a long time : give my love to him and to all the rest, Mag, Jamie, Mary, Jane, and Jenny. I suppose they are busy planting potatoes or hoeing turnips, or they would write to me.—I am ever, my dear Mother, your affectionate Son,

THOMAS CARLYLE.

XCVII.—To John A. Carlyle, Annan.

3 MORAY STREET, 23*d June* 1822.

MY DEAR JACK—I must either borrow a few minutes from the Sunday, in order to send you my news, or I am like to find no other time for doing it. And after all I am not sure that this employment is much worse than the one I was last engaged in. Physically speaking, at least, it is much better; and morally, if we only view the life that now is. Three-quarters of an hour ago I was mewed up in Lady Yester's Church, frying with heat, and subject to the genial influence of fifteen hundred pairs of Lungs all exhaling their invigorating products against me ; while for compensation I had the intellectual refreshment of hearing a black lean scarecrow of a Probationer illustrate and prove like Euclid himself " that all conditions of life have their own peculiar sorrows," a truth which most likely none of his audience ever dreamt of before. And here—I am sitting under the shadow of my own roof, with the windows all up, a calm shower pattering around me ; my dinner swallowed, and the pen in my hand to scribble whatsoever comes uppermost, for the behoof of one who cares for all that concerns me. " Judge ye !" . . .

You do well to read Gillies, but as for Hallam, you may safely let him rest, he is heavy as clay, and you would relish him little or profit by him little till after reading Gibbon and various others. Washington Irving has a new

Book, *Bracebridge Hall*, which is very good. You ought
to read *all* Scott's Novels at odd hours—and Byron's poetry
—and Shakespeare—and Pope—and the like. These
things are of the very highest value.

You ask about my coming home in August: but this
must depend on other wills than mine. The Bullers are
not arrived yet, though soon expected; and if we engage
with each other, I fear I shall hardly get down. . . . Of
course you will make all arrangements in due time for
leaving Annan. I anticipate great pleasure from having
you beside me next winter. Even living with the Bullers,
I may see you daily. Write soon; and tell me everything
about the Mainhill friends—to whom my warmest Love.—
I am always your affectionate brother,   TH. CARLYLE.

XCVIII.—To his MOTHER, Mainhill.

EDINBURGH, *29th June* 1822.

MY DEAR MOTHER—Contrary to expectation I have
still a few minutes before me, in which I can scribble a
line or two for your perusal; and as I know you are always
pleased at hearing from me, I gladly devote them to that
purpose. There are two letters here which have lain for
you and Alick many weeks; they are now out of date to
all intents and purposes, but I send them as proofs that if
I disappointed you last time there was a box here, the
blame was not mine.

I have got none but the most scanty notices from
Mainhill, for a long while; and I am very anxious, as is
natural, to have more particular information. I can only
trust in the meantime that Providence still favours you with
a moderate degree of health and comfort; and I entertain
the hope that in spite of all obstacles I shall see you ere
long—to have a cup of tea and a whiff together, and talk
over all our mutual concerns. In reckoning over my
blessings, and balancing them against my woes, one of the
largest articles in the former side of the account is the
happiness of having you to share so deeply as I know you
do in all that affects my interests. I should be worse than
a dog, if I could ever forget the kind treatment I ex-

perienced at Mainhill, when it was so difficult, though at the same time so needful to treat me kindly. . . .

I am in very fair health considering everything; about a hundred times as well as I was last year this time, and as happy as you ever saw me. In fact I want nothing but steady health of body (which I shall get in time) to be one of the comfortablest persons of my acquaintance. I have also books to write, and things to say and do in this world, which few wot of. This has the air of vanity, but it is not altogether so: I consider that my Almighty Author has given me some glimmerings of superior understanding and mental gifts; and I should reckon it the worst treason against Him to neglect improving and using to the very utmost of my power these His bountiful mercies. At some future day, it shall go hard, but I will stand *above* these mean men, whom I have never yet stood *with*. But we need not prate of this.

I am very much satisfied with my teaching: in fact it is a pleasure rather than a task. The Bullers are quite another sort of boys than I have been used to, and treat me in another sort of manner than tutors are used to. When I think of General Dirom's brats, and how they used to vex me, I often wonder that I had not broken their backs at once, and left them. This would not have done, to be sure; but the temptation was considerable. The eldest Buller is one of the cleverest boys I have ever seen: he delights to inquire—and argue and—be demolished; he follows me nigh home almost every night. Very likely I may bargain finally with the people: but I have had no certain intimation on the subject; and in fact I do not care immensely whether or not. There is bread for the diligent to be gained in a thousand ways.

I am very sorry to learn that my aunt Mary Stewart has been so long poorly. I will certainly write to my uncle John some time very soon. My Father has not written to me for a long series of weeks.[1] I would have sent him

---

[1] On the 21st of July his Father wrote: "I must declare that my communication with you this season has been very limited . . . but writing letters is a strange work to me now, and I do not come well at the work. . . . You will be thinking I should tell you all the news in this place, but as it is the Sabbath morning and I am going to hear sermon, it will not answer to dwell on that subject. I will only tell you that we are

a letter to-day, if I had not been hurried beyond expression.
Write to me yourself or by proxy if you can manage it the
first opportunity.—I am ever, my dear Mother, your
affectionate son,

TH. CARLYLE.

XCIX.—To JOHN A. CARLYLE, Annan.

3 MORAY STREET, *5th July* 1822.

MY DEAR JACK— . . . Your parcel arrived by the
Penny-post on Monday night : and gratified I was to see
the pains you had been at in serving me.   The manuscript
was all made right, with great ease, before bedtime ; and is
at this instant in the act of being *set up*, as they call it ; so
that you may look for a printed copy by almost the first
opportunity.   It was all very good and serviceable : it does
you credit in my eyes, as a proof of your diligent and
successful attention to the art of composition ; and gains
you favour in another even more gratifying respect, as a
proof of your readiness to engage in any task likely to ease
or benefit your much-obliged Brother.   I am now within
forty pages of the end, and expect soon to relinquish and
have concluded the long labour, which has occupied me
much, though not unprofitably or disagreeably.

Edward Irving and W. Graham came in upon me last
night, while sipping my tea with Dr. Fleming and the rest.
Edward is gone out to Haddington to-day, and proposes
setting off towards London on Wednesday next.   He told
me of some conversation he had had with you, touching
your embracing some profession ; and also of his having
recommended Medicine as the most promising line of life
on which you could enter.   I have frequently meditated
on this subject myself ; and certainly it is of vital importance for you to consider it deeply, now that you are
about to quit your pedagogic situation at Annan, and to
enter upon the acquisition of those accomplishments which
are to gain a livelihood and respectability for you during
the rest of your days.   I can tell you from experience that

all well, and just fighting on in the old way ; the weather is good and
hath been so for a long time, and the crop looks well, and we are as
independent as ever."

it is a sad thing for a man to have his bread to gain in the
miscellaneous fashion which circumstances have in some
degree forced me into ; and I cannot help seeing that with
half the expense, and one-tenth of the labour which I have
incurred, I might at this time have been enjoying the
comforts of some solid and fixed establishment in one of
the regular departments of exertion, had I been lucky
enough to have entered upon any one of them.   It is true,
no doubt, that by diligence and good talents a man may
pick out a kind of peculiar path by his own ingenuity in
this world ; but still this is so precarious an enterprise that
I would counsel no one to embark in it without a strict
necessity compelling him.   If you think you could relish
the study and practice of Medicine, I make no doubt of
your ability to excel in it ; and for the necessary qualifica-
tion—I bid you be in no pain whatever.   It shall go
harder with me than it looks to do, if you be not made
fully able to attend all their classes here, without interruption
on any pecuniary score ; and for the diligence and intellect
required in the business—you have already shown all these
qualities in sufficient abundance to put me to peace on
that head.   Upon the whole, I wish you would turn this
matter calmly over in your mind with all due attention,
and write to me about it as soon as you can come—not to
any conclusion—but simply to any tangible deliverance on
it.   If your mind leads you to relish the project, you can
partly be putting it in execution the first winter you come
hither ; you might attend to Anatomy and Chemistry at
the same time that you were perfecting your Greek and
Natural Philosophy : for observe, if you shall undertake
the project, it is not a common Tom Bogs [1] or Parliament [2]
that I will have you become, but a medical *savant* at
length, bringing to bear upon his own science the mind of
a man improved by literature and science in general, and
looking forward to respectability in life, not merely because
of a mechanical skill in his own particular trade, but also
because of a general refinement of character, and a superiority both of intellectual and moral deportment.   I beg
you will think of this, with all solidity, as soon as possible.

[1] *i.e.* Tom of Bogside.
[2] Dr. Little, nicknamed Parliament and Parliament Geordie.

If you go to Mainhill to-morrow, you will get large news of me, arrived two days before, by way of Farries : you will also find your Book V. of *Legendre*, which I took care to enclose among the letters for home. There is no change in my situation since that period. I am going along in the old style, my life marked by no incident worth remembering, but happy on the whole, and peaceful and diligent in one way or another. . . . Give my kindest affection to our Father and Mother and all of them at Mainhill.—I am, always yours,

THOMAS CARLYLE.

C.—TO JOHN A. CARLYLE, Annan.

3 MORAY STREET, 25*th July* 1822.

MY DEAR JACK— . . . Since I wrote to you last, and even since I wrote to my Father not many hours ago, there is a kind of change in my situation, which may be worth communicating. I am now engaged with the Bullers, whom I conversed with for a long time yesternight ; and I expect, in two weeks at farthest, to have commenced my regular line of proceeding in their family, and so to continue it for one twelvemonth at least. I like the people much ; Mrs. B. in particular seems one of the most fascinating refined women I have ever seen ; nor is the Goodman far behind her in his own particular walk—that of an honest, worthy, straightforward English Gentleman, —which, however, is a character that one naturally feels more disposed to value than admire. The terms are the same as were first talked of—or rather nothing at all was said on that subject ; with this single difference, that as they have found it quite impossible to get a house large enough for their establishment, it was agreed upon between us, that I should have a lodging of my own to sleep in in the neighbourhood, to which I might retire at nights after passing the day with them. By this arrangement, you see, —in which I found quite as much to attract as repel—you and I shall have the pleasure of living together next winter —which I know will be far from a slight pleasure to either of us. We shall thus enjoy all the benefits of mutual intercourse and fraternal sympathy ; we may advise together, learn together, rejoice together, condole together, or do whatever we choose, in honesty.

Things being so ordered, I can take up the subject of your medical enterprise with a freer hand and clearer vision. Considering your alacrity in the prospective study of this science, there is hardly anything but the pressing danger of your being stopped by the *res angusta domi*, which could have made me hesitate in advising you to set your mind towards it forthwith. That danger is now in a great degree withdrawn. Knowing your qualities natural and acquired, I can have no doubt about your ability to conquer all the intellectual difficulties of the business, when you have no other to strive with; and therefore I give it as my frank opinion that this profession is the best channel of exertion I can see for you. The question, where you shall turn this knowledge when acquired to account—is no doubt a natural subject of anxiety; but it ought not by any means to operate as a bar to your attempt. Every department of human life is crowded with aspirants at present—and has always been so, I suppose; the medical department is not less crowded than others; but no other that I know of presents so fair a field for adventure. The Physician's scene of action is not confined (like the Lawyer's or the Clergyman's) to this country or to that: it extends over all the inhabited globe; wherever men exist, they are liable to diseases; and ready to reward the person who is able to alleviate them. In Britain at present there are many modes of turning such knowledge to account besides practising it in a country town: there is the Navy, the Army, India, and a thousand other channels. Nor is it correct to take the riotous apothecaries of Annandale as a specimen of the medical profession in our country towns. I cordially agree with you in utterly rejecting and despising such a life as theirs generally is: I had rather be at once and honestly a genuine unpretending cobbler or street-porter, than combine the character and intellect of a cobbler with the dress and title of a man of science; to which they generally add the morals and manners of a Bawdy-house bully. This will never do; nor need it. There has been a Sydenham, a Mead, a Darwin, a Gregory in Medicine; there still are a Baillie, a Moore, and many other persons whose names would do honour to any class of intellectual and moral men : several of these have spent their lives in provincial towns ; and depend upon it, there is still enough of good feeling and taste left in the land to secure even in country towns a proper degree of reverence for depth of understanding and nobleness of conduct whenever they are visibly and habitually displayed. In Medicine, too, the fair objects of intellectual competition—which I love to see you aiming at—are more thickly scattered than in almost any other branch of science. The number of living Physicians who display anything like cultivated or powerful understandings is the most limited imaginable, and the number of objects in their science which calls for investigation about the most numerous. So that if a man is ambitious of scientific distinction—here, if he has any claim to seize it, it hangs in larger clusters than almost anywhere else.

All which reasons, my beloved Jack, I would have thee to study and con over and over ; and if they weigh in thy immense Tron-beam [1] of an understanding,—to determine on combining, this very winter, the study of Anatomy and Chemistry, at all events the latter, with the pursuit of Greek, Latin, and Natural Philosophy. Write to me forthwith what is thy opinion. For the present, I leave it.

I am just in the act of getting done with that thrice wearisome *Legendre*. Brewster talks of settling with me for it ; otherwise I should very gladly have asked for money, and the more so as I have actually been destitute of that needful commodity for many weeks. The Landlady thinks I am so idle I will not settle with her ; she is in easy circumstances, and cares not. I hoped to get home almost directly, yesterday : but I find it cannot be for several weeks at any rate, and then only during a short space. Tell our good Mother that I am going to send her all the linens home for bleaching. The new shirts I would have made with very fine *linen* necks, if convenient—if not, not. I also want a few neckcloths (like the last double ones) ; for which I desire you to give our Mother whatever money she wants, in my name. . . .

---

[1] Scales. (The ancient weighing-machine at the Trongate of Edinburgh was so named.)

They need not send me any more boxes at present ; but
if you can find Schiller's Tragedy of *Wilhelm Tell*, I wish
you would send it up, in the next bundle of clothes.   Perhaps it will surprise you to learn that Oliver and Boyd have
agreed to go half with me in printing a poetical Translation
of this work !   I have sometimes tried a little jingle last
winter, and found it do me no hurt at all.   *Tell*, however,
is still *in dubio*.   Write to me very soon.   Where is the
Targer ? [1]   Good-night !—Yours always,

THOMAS CARLYLE.

CI.—To Miss WELSH, Haddington.

3 MORAY STREET, *Monday night*
[*July* 1822].

MY DEAR FRIEND—After a very admirable display of
patience, I was rewarded one evening, while I thought of
no such thing, by the sight of your much-valued packet.
"That Ass" I never liked ; but then I absolutely hated
her, and wished fervently that she had either delivered you
from her inane presence altogether, or at least timed her
visit better.   As it is, I give you thanks from the heart for
your letter.   It is quite delightful, in its way, for me to
enjoy those little peeps you afford me here and there into
your domestic doings.   I see the " feathers " overshadowing
your hat ; I tremble at the " four angry notes " inflicted on
your dressmaker ; imagine the " nose and ear " of the
conqueror of the Goths ; and think what I would give to
hear you practising never so " badly " the Themas of
Mozart and Beethoven.   It is when letters are thrown off
in that gay cheerful social way, that one has some pleasure
in them.

I viewed your poetical despatches with a feeling made
up of pleasure and surprise.   This is greatly the best
collection you have ever shown me : if you go on at anything like the same rate, I indeed may wish you " a good
journey "—but I shall not the less rejoice at your reaching
the promised land—though myself still lingering in the
wilderness.   In fact I am quite ashamed, on considering
your verses, to compare them, either in quantity or quality,

---

[1] James Johnstone's nickname (meaning a tall sweeping figure).

with my own performance in the same period. I am certainly an idle knave; and shall never rhyme, or do anything else, to right purpose. Your "Wish" is quite an emblem of your usual treacherous disposition. There you go on persuading us that you are growing a delightful romantic character—alive to all the simple enjoyments of existence—and prizing them above all others as they ought to be; and when you have fairly *led us in*, and we are beginning to admire you in good earnest,—we hear a suppressed titter, which dissipates the whole illusion, and tells us that we are—poor fools! I like the accompanying pieces better; the lines beginning with "I love" the best of all. In these the ideas are brilliant, the language emphatic and sonorous, the rhythm very musical and appropriate. The little epigram from the Provençal Satyrist is also a favourite with me: it seems to be rendered with great spirit and liveliness. Ferdusi and the hesitating lover are subjects which interest me less; but you have succeeded in translating both extremely well.

It is truly gratifying to me to contemplate you advancing so rapidly in the path of mental culture. Proceed as you have begun; and I shall yet see the day, when I may ask with pride: Did not I predict this? There are a thousand peculiar obstacles—a thousand peculiar miseries that attend upon a life devoted to the task of observing and feeling, and recording its observations and feelings—but any ray of genius, however feeble, is the "inspired gift of God;" and woe to him or her that hides the talent in a napkin! that allows indolence or sordid aims to prevent the exercise of it, in the way designed by our all-bountiful Parent—the elevation of our own nature, and the delight or instruction of our fellow-mortals—on a scale proportioned to our power! And look to the reward, even in the life that now is! Kings and Potentates are a gaudy folk that flaunt about with plumes and ribbons to decorate them, and catch the coarse admiration of the many-headed monster, for a brief season—then sink into forgetfulness or often to a remembrance even worse: but the Miltons, the de Staëls —these *are* the very salt of the Earth; they derive their "patents of nobility direct from Almighty God," and live in the bosoms of all true men to all ages.

Alas! that it is so much easier to talk thus than to act in conformity to such rational maxims! I verily believe you are quite right in your estimate of me: I seem indeed to be a mere talker—a *vox et preterea nihil.* Look at these most unspeakable jingles that I have sent you; and see the whole fruit of my labours since I wrote last. I declare it is shameful in myself; and barbarous in those stupid louts that waste my time away in their drivelling. Here was the best-natured and opaquest of Glasgow merchants with me for a whole week! He talked and—— But why should I trouble you with it? Simply, I say this must not last. In a few weeks I shall be done with that blessed treatise on Geometry; and then, if I do not *attempt* at least, I deserve to die as a fool dieth.

These are shadows: let us turn to the sunshine. The *Siege of Carcassonne* will hardly do, I fear; though you show a right spirit in aiming at it. The persecution of the Albigenses has little to distinguish it from other persecutions more connected with our sympathies, except a darker tinge of bloody-mindedness, and a degree of callous ferocity which would tend rather to disgust the mind, than to inflame or exalt it. Simon de Montfort and Fouquet are horrible rather more than tragical. To be sure the Count is a fine subject: but there are no peculiar incidents to work upon, and to paint the manners and feelings of those people, even if they were worth painting, would involve you in long laborious researches which would yield no fruit proportionate to the toil of gathering it. I rather advise you, therefore, to dismiss the subject altogether. Yet if you feel any deep emotions, see any magnificence of accompaniment which you could combine with it,—tell me, and I will search you out all the information possible. So much depends on the natural bent of your own inclination—it is so important to have this along with you in whatever you undertake. that a suggestion of your own should be preferred under many disadvantages to one from any other. A subject from our own history would answer best—if we must have a historical subject. But why not one of pure invention? or why not try a comedy, originating wholly incidents and characters from yourself?

You do not mention what Play of Schiller's you are

reading, or whether I can help you in it at all. You also forget to select any theme for our next poetical effort; a speculation, in which, though as I have said, you are going to leave me entirely behind, I feel determined to go on. What if we trust to Fortune next time, and engage only to write *something*—name not given? I hope you will not keep me long: it was very kind in you to think of my wishes, and send the *first* volume the moment it was finished. I would not harass you or burden you, however, with my impatience, write to me when you *can ;* only think, if I were an absolute Monarch, *how* often I would have you write. . . .

But surely I must conclude this most ugly and absurd of letters. I beg you to believe that I have not been so stupid for six months—sore throat, etc. etc., have quite undone me for some days. You will write when you have done with *Bracebridge Hall,* and send me your verses. The rest of Sismondi I shall transmit forthwith. If you cannot conveniently read Washington [Irving] without farther cutting the leaves—do it without scruple.

Farewell! I am half asleep—so excuse my blunders and miserable penmanship.—I am always yours,

THOMAS CARLYLE.

CII.—To Miss WELSH, Haddington.

3 MORAY STREET, *Thursday* [1822].

MY DEAR FRIEND—Unless some one has anticipated me in regard to this *Voice from St. Helena,* I calculate on furnishing you with some amusement, by introducing you to the sound of it. O'Meara's work presents your favourite under somewhat of a new aspect: it has increased my respect for Napoleon, and my indignation against his *Boje.* Since the days of Prometheus Vinctus, I recollect of no spectacle more moving and sublime, than that of this great man in his dreary prison-house; given over to the very scum of the species to be tormented by every sort of indignity, which the heart most revolts against :—captive, sick, despised, forsaken ;—yet rising above it all, by the stern force of his own unconquerable spirit, and hurling back on his mean oppressors the ignominy they strove to load him with. I declare I could almost love the man. His native sense of honesty, the rude genuine strength of his intellect, his lively fancy, his sardonic humour, must have rendered him a most original and interesting companion; he might have been among the first writers of his age, if he had not chosen to be the very first conqueror of any age. Nor is this gigantic character without his touches of human affection—his simple attachments, his little tastes and kindly predilections—which enhance the respect of meaner mortals by uniting it with their love. I do not even believe him to have been a very wicked man; I rather ——But it is needless to keep you from the book itself with this *palabra*. Send me word if you would like to see the second volume; which in the affirmative case you shall have, so soon as Mrs. Buller has done with it. This lady likes Napoleon even better than you do; made a pilgrimage to his grave, stole sprigs of willow from it, etc.; and called him the greatest of men in the presence of Mr. Croker himself. I am sorry, however, that I cannot bring her to a right sense of Byron's merit; she affirms that none admire that nobleman, so much as boarding-school girls and young men under twenty—which she reckons as a sure sign of his being partly a *charlatan*. . . .

I have some doggerel translations, etc., which I meant to send; but they are not fit to be seen by you—perhaps never will. When shall I get your productions? I have no right to be impatient, but these two weeks have seemed very long.

I am not happy at present; and for the best of all reasons, I stand very low in my own esteem. Something must be done, if I would not sink into a mere driveller. For the last three years I have lived as under an accursed spell—how wretched, how vainly so, I need not say.[1] If nothing even now is to come of it, then I had better have

---

[1] "Other things," wrote Carlyle, in recalling in late years this period, "with one precious thing, clearly in my favour, might have made me hopeful and cheerful as beseemed my years,—had not *Dyspepsia*, with its base and unspeakable miseries, kept such fatal hold of me. Which perhaps needed only a *wise* Doctor, too, as I found afterwards, when too late! Heavy, grinding, and continual has that burden lain on me ever since to this hour, and will lie; but I must not complain of it, either; it was not wholly a *curse*, as I can sometimes recognise, but perhaps a thing needed, and partly a *blessing*, though a stern one, and bitter to flesh and blood."

been anything than what I am.   But talking is superfluous:
I only beg for a little respite, before you mark me down
for ever as an unhappy dunce, distinguished from other
dunces only by the height of my aims and the clamour of
my pretensions.

Will you not write to me soon?   It were a kind act.—
I am always your affectionate friend,

THOMAS CARLYLE.

CIII.—To his FATHER, Mainhill.

3 MORAY STREET, 16*th October* 1822.

MY DEAR FATHER—On coming out of my temporary
abode in India Street, I was met to-day about noon by the
good Jack, holding in his hands a letter, on which I was
happy to recognise your well-known handwriting.   By the
aid of my "learning" and other faculties, I succeeded
without difficulty not only in "making out" the epistle,
but also in deriving great pleasure from the task of doing
so.   We next proceeded to a Book-shop, and procured the
work you asked for,—along with some Bibles for the other
branches of the family, and two small memorials, the one
for Jane, the other for Jenny.   I am now down writing
with all the speed I can, hoping to make out a letter for
you before the hour of my departure arrive ; and careful
rather of the quantity than the quality of what I say—
which I know is your principle also.

I am very sorry to hear of Alick's bad success in the
matter of horse-buying—the more so, as I conceived that
a long experience in the dishonesties of Jockies had fortified
him against imposition from that knavish set of people.   I
trust, however, that before this time he is returned with a
satisfactory adjustment of all difficulties ; and enriched in
caution far beyond what he is impoverished in money.
After all, to mistake at times is the common lot of mankind ; and Alick has committed fewer errors than most
people so circumstanced would have done. . . .

But I am fast filling up my allotted space with reflections
which you yourself have made a hundred times ; instead of
giving you some details about myself, which I know you
greatly prefer.   Happily my duty on this head may be soon

discharged. I am still in the same state of comfort which I described myself to be enjoying last time I wrote. The people are very agreeable and kind to me ; the pupils go on at a reasonable rate in their studies : in short all is very nearly as it should be. I have sometimes a day of languor and bilious disquietude ; but in that respect also I am improving ; and a strict attention to the results of former experience is generally sufficient to guard against any considerable inconvenience. I have not lost half a night's sleep since I returned to Edinburgh.

All this is very pleasant in the meantime ; and may continue to be so for a good while to come : yet I should be a very stupid person if I set my ultimate hopes upon it, and did not look beyond the period of its termination to a fresh scene of exertions and wants, which it behoves me at present to be making every effort to provide against. Accordingly, my chief desire now is that I were fairly engaged in the execution of some enterprise which might present a likelihood of being permanently and substantially useful to me. I am trying all that in me lies to fix upon some literary undertaking of the sort referred to ; and I expect to find no complete rest—indeed I wish to find none —until I am fairly overhead in the composition of some *valuable* Book ; a project which I have talked about till I am ashamed, and shall therefore say no more concerning it at this time.

Jack's presence here I find to be very agreeable to me. He is a quiet, diligent, friendly soul as ever broke bread : it is pleasant to me to find his broad placid face looking forth goodwill to me, when I return from the day's exertions. I think he has a good chance to fall into teaching in Edinburgh ; and get himself qualified for earning his bread in some independent and respectable station ; a purpose which he himself is anxious even more than enough to accomplish. Of his final success I have no doubt.

There is nothing in the shape of news that I can send you from our City at present : the place seems very quiet, and what little stir there does exist in it very rarely comes the length of my abode. In Edinburgh, properly so called, I do not appear once in the fortnight. My path from India Street and to it supplies me with bodily exercise sufficient ;

and it leads me away by a succession of clean, well-paved streets up the very back of the New Town, where I feel too happy to escape the noise and smoke of the old black Harlot, ever to give myself much trouble about what is passing within her precincts.

While I was writing—about five minutes ago, the Carrier Geordie came to say or rather to try to say that he could not take up the box to-day. I sent my Mother's spectacles along with him, and a pair of shoes which must be returned to Shaw at Dumfries, being uselessly little. If he can make a bigger pair and stronger he may send them. Jack is going up with the books—which you will distribute according to the addresses with my most affectionate compliments to the several owners, all of whom I would gladly have written to had my time in any measure allowed me. I must now conclude my scrawling, with the hope to hear from you soon and more at large—having no subject nearer my heart than the welfare of one and all of you.—I am ever, my dear Father, your affectionate son,

THOMAS CARLYLE.

CIV.—To his MOTHER, Mainhill.

EDINBURGH, *Wednesday night*
[*October* 1822].

MY DEAR MOTHER—I have literally only ten minutes to write you in ; but knowing your mind in that respect, I think it better to send you the smallest note in the world rather than none at all ; and accordingly I am at work, writing with as much spirit as if I had an hour before me.

One reason that impels me is the wish I feel to have more precise and certain information about the state of your health and spirits than I have obtained for some weeks : and next time the Carrier comes out, I expect to hear a minute account of the condition in which you find yourself, now that the hurly-burly of harvest is over, and you have leisure to collect yourself so far as to consider and say how it actually fares with you. I will hope that you study by all means to make yourself comfortable, and keep the measure of health that is allowed you ; and which you cannot doubt is a greater blessing to all of us than we have in the world besides. I give you the most strict injunction to be no moment in want of anything which I can procure for you. I should think it the worst usage you could give me, if you yielded to the voice of any foolish scruple in such a case, and held your peace when any effort of mine might help you. What is there in this world that is half so valuable to us as to love one another, and to live in the hope of loving one another for ever? I do entreat of you to let me know whenever I can serve you in the smallest matter. The spectacles we have sent down : they seem not a jot the worse; and having two pairs, you will now be enabled to sew, etc., with the inferior pair, keeping the *bettermost* for Church and other such occasions.

Tell me truly, do you get tea every day? If you do not, I *command* you (being a man skilful in such matters, and therefore entitled to command) to get into the practice of habitually taking it, without delay. I know it is useful to you ; and it would spoil the taste of my own to think that you were unserved.

But my time is elapsed, and I must run. It is half-past five, and I have not dined yet! I designed to send you a long discussion about these *greet folk* some day soon. They do not seem a whit happier than you—not a single whit.

Give my respects and love to all the people about Main-hill. We have a hope to see you here in winter! Adieu, my dear Mother!—I am ever yours,

TH.　CARLYLE.

CV.—To his FATHER, Mainhill.

3 MORAY STREET, 4*th December* 1822.

MY DEAR FATHER—I know not whether strictly speaking I owe you a letter in the fair way of one for one, as traders count ; but certainly in every other way of reckoning I should have written to you long ago. . . .

We have heard so scantily from home that we can only form an imperfect guess at what is going on there. The most important thing, however, the fact of your continued health and general welfare, we have learned ; and that is everything. In other respects I suppose you to be struggling away making what head you can against these meagre times, the pressure of which all men are feeling. How it will end I cannot see or form any conjecture. I observe they are making movements in the South ; but showing thereby only that they feel the evil, not that they know how to remedy it. Meanwhile industry and thrift, the only shield and sword by which the tyrant Necessity can be met and vanquished, are not wanting on your part ; you have only to await the issue patiently, happy that you are so little involved in it. There will be many a ruined man before twelve months go round again.

You have not told me whether you liked the sermons. If there is any other book you stand in want of, or at all care about having, it will be a pleasure for me to get it for you. I think you do very well to read in the winter nights ; they are tedious otherwise ; and of all states for a mortal man, the unhappiest is where his mind, requiring constant employment and a continuous flow of ideas, can find nothing to employ it. There are some good books in the Ecclefechan Library, which I think you would like if you tried them.

Having written so largely and frequently of late, little remains for me at present to communicate in the shape of news about my situation or proceedings. I find my health slowly but gradually improving ; the duties I have to go through are of an easy sort ; the people are on the whole very agreeable : so that I am as happy and contented as I could expect to be. The old squire Buller is a great favourite with me ; a downright, true, unaffected, honest Englishman as I would wish to see. We meet not above once or twice a week ; but we are always very blithe when we do meet, we talk and speculate about politics and learned men and morals and letters and things in general ; we are very comfortable in spite of his deafness, which disturbs the pleasure of conversation somewhat, particularly at first. . . .

A while ago, one Galloway whom I knew here invited me to become a candidate for a vacant Professorship in the Royal Military College at Sandhurst away beyond London, where he now is. It is to teach Mathematics ; the salary is about £200 a year with house and garden ; the labour is not great : the whole establishment is under Government.

I wrote to inquire farther about it ; but have not yet received any answer. I do not think I shall mind it much ; though it is good to have such a thing before one. . . .

But I must conclude this scrawl, with a petition for a letter from you the first time you can prevail upon yourself to write. If you knew how much pleasure we take in your letters you would send us more of them. Jack would have written to you by this opportunity, but he has no moment of time left now. He will mend the matter next chance.— I remain, my dear Father, your affectionate son,

THOMAS CARLYLE.

CVI.—To his MOTHER, Mainhill.

3 MORAY STREET, *4th December* [1822].

MY DEAR MOTHER—It is already past twelve o'clock, and I am tired and sleepy ; but I cannot go to rest without answering the kind little note which you sent me, and acknowledging these new instances of your unwearied attention to my interests and comfort. I rejoice to be assured that you still retain a moderate share of health : watch over it, my dear Mother, as the first of earthly blessings. It will give you a genuine satisfaction to know in return that I am daily improving in that point myself. In another twelvemonth, I expect to be completely whole. Disorders which have been accumulating long must be long in curing : but to be assured that one is recovering is almost as good as to be recovered.

I am almost vexed at these shirts and stockings : I had already as many as I could set my face to. My dear Mother, why will you expend in these superfluities the pittance I intended for very different ends ? I again assure you, and would swear it if needful, that you cannot get me such enjoyment with it in any way as by convincing me that it is adding to your own. Do not therefore frustrate my purposes : when I want any more shirts, etc., I will not be slack in letting you know.

I send you a small *screed* of verses, which I made some time ago : I fear you will not care a doit for them, though the subject is good—the deliverance of Switzerland from tyranny by the hardy mountaineers at the battle of Morgarten some five hundred years ago.

This is my birthday : I am now seven and twenty years of age ! What an unprofitable lout I am ! What have I done in this world to make good my place in it, or reward those that had the trouble of my upbringing ? Great part of an ordinary lifetime is gone by : and here am I, poor trifler, still sojourning in Meshech, still dwelling among the tents of Kedar ! May the great Father of all give me strength to do better in time remaining, to be of service in the good cause in my day and generation, and " having finished the work which was given me to do," to lie down and sleep in peace and purity in the hope of a happy rising ! Amen !

But I have done. Good-night, my dear Mother ! I wish you sweet sleep and all blessings.—Your affectionate son,   TH. CARLYLE.

Give my affectionate respects to all the brothers and sisters ; and tell them sharply to write to me. What are they dallying about ?

CVII.—To Miss WELSH, Haddington.

3 MORAY STREET, 16th December 1822.

MY DEAR FRIEND—I am doubly vexed at the large mass of soiled paper which you receive along with this ;—both because of its natural qualities,.and because it has detained me a whole week from writing to you. I have need of motives for exertion ; and I wished to keep this prospect before me throughout my stupid task. It is at last accomplished, and I am now to reap my reward.

My dear Friend, if you do not grow more cross with me soon, I shall become an entire fool. When I get one of those charming kind letters it puts me into such a humour as you cannot conceive : I read it over till I can almost say it by heart ; then sit brooding in a delicious idleness, or go wandering about in solitary places, dreaming over things— which never can be more than dreams. May Heaven reward you for the beautiful little jewel you have sent me ! How demurely it was lying in its place, when I opened the letter,—bright and pure and sparkling as its mistress ! I design to keep it as long as I live ; to look on it after many years, when we perhaps are far asunder,—that I may enjoy the delights of memory when those of hope are passed away. You are indeed very kind to me : would it were in my power to repay you, as I ought !

I thank you for the clear outline you have traced to me of your daily life : it gratifies me by the persuasion of your diligence, and enables me to conceive your employment at any hour I like. Even now I can see you—time of "playing with Shandy or your reticule" being past, bending over your Rollin with lexicons and maps and all your apparatus lying round—toiling, striving, subduing the repugnances within, resisting the allurements to dissipation from without—vehemently, steadfastly intent on scaling the rocky steep "where Fame's proud temple shines afar." It is well done, my dear and honoured Jane ! Go on in this noble undertaking; it is worthy of your efforts : persevere in it, and your success is certain.

I always knew you to be a deceitful person, full of devices and inexplicable turns : but who could have thought you would show so much contrivance in the plain process of getting on with your studies? To " sew skirts and waists together," to discard and combine, so that you accomplish in ten minutes what to an ordinary *belle* is the great business of her day ! And then how convenient to have letters to write (bless you for being so good a correspondent to me, *in truth .*)—to take cold so exactly in the nick of time ! I believe I ought to send you out Andrew Thomson's Sermon on the gross sinfulness of bidding your servant say *not at home*, or give you a lecture on that solemn point myself; but so it is, you have such a way of setting things forth, that do what you will I cannot get angry at you—I must just submit. Still, however, I must seriously protest against the over-labour which you describe : it is greatly more than you are fit for ; and I heartily pray that some interruption may occur every second evening, to drive you away from books and papers, to make you talk and laugh and enjoy yourself, though it were but with the " *imbecilles*" who drink tea and play whist in such a place as Haddington. You ought to thank your stars that you are so circumstanced : if left to yourself with that fervent temper and that delicate frame, you would be ruined by excessive exertion in twelve months. This to an absolute certainty. For the rest, I rejoice that you are proceeding so rapidly with M. Rollin, and gathering so many ideas even from that slender source. I love you for admiring Socrates, and determining to be a philosopher like him; though I do wish that your nascent purposes may sustain no more shocks so rude as the one you mention. Have you found the amethyst? I question if there are a dozen philosophers in this country that could bear such a trial much better than you bore it. After all, it is a fine thing to be a *lover of wisdom :* yet there was also a good deal of justness in your version of the *quantis non egeo,* which I once got from you as we walked along Princes Street, and which has often brought a smile across me since. " How many things are here which I do not want," said I, affecting to be a philosopher; " How many things are here which I cannot get," said Jane, speaking the honest language of nature, and slyly unmasking my philosophy. The truth is, everything has two faces : both these sentiments are correct in their proper season, both erroneous out of it.

It is certainly a pity that M. Rollin should be so very weak a man. He moralises to the end of the chapter, and all his morality is not worth a doit. Yet you will [get] many useful thoughts from him, many splendid pictures of men and things,—of a mode of life which was not only highly interesting in itself, but also which has formed the basis of many principles that still give a deep colour to the speculations and literature of all civilised nations, and which is therefore worthy of your study in a double point of view. You must continue in him to the conclusion ; you will get better guides through other portions of your pilgrimage. In the meantime, as I am anxious to reward the industry you have already shown, I propose that by way of vacation you shall suspend the perusal of M. Rollin, whenever you are through the seventh volume, which most likely you now are—for the period of three days, till you examine this Novel which I have sent you. Three days will do the whole business, and you will go on with greater spirit afterwards. You see I am not absolutely without mercy in my nature; I would not kill you all at once. In this *Anastasius* I hope you will find something to amuse you, perhaps to instruct; it will at least give you the picture of a robust and vigorous mind, that has seen much, and that wants not some touches of poetry to describe it eloquently, or some powers of intellect to reflect well upon it. I enjoyed *Anastasius* the "Oriental *Gil Blas*" very much. Let no man despair that has read this book! In the year 1810 Mr. Thomas Hope brought forth a large publication upon fire-screens and fenders and tapestry and tea-urns and other upholstery matters which seemed to be the very acme of dulness and affectation; ten years afterwards he named himself the author of a book which few living writers would be ashamed to own. Let us persist, my friend, without weariness or wavering! Perseverance will conquer *every* obstacle.—It is right in you to employ some portion of your time in light reading: this too you may turn to advantage as well as pleasure. Have you read all Pope's works? Swift's? Dryden's, and the other classics of that age? Tell me, and I shall know better what to send you out. There is no way of acquiring a proper mastery of the resources contained in our English language, without studying these and the older writers in it. Many of them also are exceedingly amusing and instructive. What are you doing with *Wallenstein?* I will send you *Faust* whenever you have finished: I fear you will not like it so well as you expect—or will think I have misled you: but you shall try. I admire your inflexibility in the reading of *Tacitus;* it is a hard effort, one which few in your circumstances would be capable of making. Do not toil too much over it.

But I must not trifle away your paper and time in this manner: I promised to send you some intelligence about our *opus magnum*, an enterprise which, too like the *great work* of the Alchemist, appears to be attended with unspeakable preparation and discussion, and with no result at all. I must now tell you what I can say on the subject. You will be very angry at me; but nevertheless I must go through with my detail. One virtue at least I may lay some claim to, the virtue of candour; since to you, whose good opinion it is about my very highest ambition to acquire, I am brave enough to disclose myself as the most feeble and vacillating mortal in existence. Perhaps you will impute this practice less to the absence of hypocrisy than to the presence of a strong wish to talk ; perhaps with reason. *On veut mieux dire du mal de soi-même que de n'en point parler.* So says La Rochefoucault. Be as merciful to me as you can ; and you shall hear.

After writing the last long letter to you, I seriously inclined myself to the concoction of some project in the execution of which we two should go hand in hand. I formed a kind of plan, and actually commenced the filling of it up. We were to write a most eminent novel in concert : it was to proceed by way of letters ; I to take the gentleman, you the lady. The poor fellow was to be a very excellent character of course ; a man in the middle ranks of life, gifted with good talents and a fervid enthusiastic turn of mind, learned in all sciences, practised in many virtues,—but tired out, at the time I took him up, with the impediments of a world by much too prosaic for him, entirely sick of struggling along the sordid bustle of existence, where he could glean so little enjoyment but found so much acute suffering. He had, in fact, met with no object worthy of all his admiration, the bloom of novelty was worn off, and no more substantial charm of solid usefulness had called on him to mingle in the business of life : he was very wretched and very ill-natured ; had determined at last to bid adieu to the hollow and contemptible progeny of Adam as far as possible—to immure himself in rustic solitude, with a family of simple unaffected but polished and religious people who (by some means) were bound in gratitude to cherish him affectionately, and who like him had bid farewell to the world. Here the hypochondriac was to wander about for a time over the hill-country, to muse and meditate upon the aspects of nature and his own soul, to meet with persons and incidents which should call upon him to deliver his views upon many points of science, literature, and morals. At length he must grow tired of science, and nature, and simplicity, just as he had of towns ; sickening by degrees till his heart is full of bitterness and ennui, he speaks forth his sufferings—

not in the puling Lake-style—but with a tongue of fire—sharp, sarcastic, apparently unfeeling, yet all the while betokening to the quick-sighted a mind of lofty thoughts and generous affections smarting under the torment of its own over-nobleness, and ready to break in pieces by the force of its own energies. Already all seems over with him, he has hinted about suicide, and rejected it scornfully—but it is evident he cannot long exist in this, to him, most blasted, waste and lonely world,—when *you*—that is, the heroine—come skipping in before him with your *espiègleries* and fervency, your "becks and wreathed smiles," and all your native loveliness. Why should I talk? The man immediately turns crazy about you. The sole being he has ever truly loved, the sole being he can ever love; the epitome to him of all celestial things, the shining jewel in which he sees reflected all the pleasures of the universe, the sun that has risen to illuminate his world when it seemed to be overshadowed in darkness for ever! The earth again grows green beneath his feet, his soul recovers all its fiery energies, he is prepared to front death and danger, to wrestle with devils and men, that he may gain your favour. For a while you laugh at him, and torment him, but at length take pity on the poor fellow, and grow as serious as he is. Then, oh then! what a more than elysian prospect! But alas! Fate, etc., obstacles, etc. etc. You are both broken-hearted, and die; and the whole closes with a mortcloth, and Mr. Trotter and a company of undertakers.

I had fairly begun this thing, written two first letters; and got the man set down in a very delightful part of the country. But I could not get along: I found that we should require to see one another and consult together every day; I grew affrighted and chilled at the aspect of the Public; I wrote with no *verve:* I threw it all into the fire. Yet I am almost persuaded that we might accomplish such a thing; nay I often vow that we *will* accomplish it yet, before all is done: but first we must have better auspices, we must be more near each other, we must learn to write more flowingly. What then was to be tried? I thought of a series of short tales, essays, sketches, miscellanies. You are to record your thoughts and observations

and experience in this way, I mine. Begin, therefore ;
and let me have a little story with descriptions of manners
and scenery and passion and character in the Highlands or
Lowlands, or wherever you like best and feel yourself most
at home. Do not say you cannot : write as you are used
to write in those delightful cunning little lively epistles
you send me, and the thing we want is found. I too will
write in my own poor vein, neither fast nor well, but sted-
fastly and stubbornly : in time we shall both improve : and
when we have enough accumulated for a volume, then we
shall sift the wheat from the chaff, arrange it in concert
sitting side by side, and give it to the world fearlessly,
secure of *two* suffrages at least, and prepared to let the
others come or stay as they like best. Now will you do
this ? Think of it well, then give me your approval ; you
shall be my task-mistress, and I promise to obey you as a
most faithful vassal. Consider it ; and tell me next time
that you have *begun* to work.

The stupid farrago which you receive along with this is
the first of the series ! Do not absolutely condemn me for
that lumbering piebald composition. A man must write a
cartload of trash before he can produce a handful of excellence. This story might have been mended in the names
and many of the incidents, but it was not worth the labour :
I gave it as I heard it. It is a *sooterkin*, and must remain
so. I scarcely expect you will read it through.

Now, my dear Friend, my time is done and I must leave
you. I could sit and talk with you here for ever ; but the
world has other humbler tasks in it. I had many things
more to tell you, had not my irregular confused mode of
writing exhausted all my room. There is not a word more
of Sandhurst : I understand the man is to be here at Christmas, and tell me all verbatim. You would not have me go ?
Jack is delighted with your compliments—delighted that you
should know such a being as he exists in the world. He
bids me return his kind and humble services, and hopes to
know more of you before the end. He is a good soul,
and affords me some enjoyment here—a well-formed mind
too, but *rudis indigesta*—much more placid and contented
and well-conditioned than the unfortunate person you have
made a friend of.

Now *do* not be long in writing to me. If you knew how much your letters charm me, you would not grudge your labour. Write to me without reserve—about *all* that you care for—not minding what you say or how you say it. Related as we are, dulness itself is often best of all, for it shows that we are friends and put confidence in one another. What an impudent knave I am to ask this of you, to affect to be on such terms with you! It is your own kind way of treating me that causes it. I have often upbraided fortune; but here I ought to call her the best of patronesses. How many men, the latchet of whose shoes I am not worthy to unbind, have travelled through the world and found no noble soul to care for them! while I —God bless you, my dear Jane!—if I could deserve to be so treated by you I should be happy. Now you *must* not grow angry at me. Write, write!—I am "hungering and thirsting" to hear of you and all connected with you.—I am ever yours,

THOMAS CARLYLE.

CVIII.—To ALEXANDER CARLYLE, Mainhill.

EDINBURGH, 18*th December* 1822.

MY DEAR ALICK—We got your parcel a few hours ago; and all within it was safe—money and all. I am obliged by your punctuality in that matter. Your letter also, though it was brief, conveyed to us the most important intelligence, in assuring us that you were all in the "usual way" of health and spirits. I am now to scribble you a few hurried lines by way of reply.

. . . . . .

We live in a very retired manner here, and so, very little of what is called news reaches us at any time. Perhaps about once in the fortnight some student or preacher strays down to see us,—and then goes his way after chatting an hour: but we seldom repay such visits, privacy being the arrangement we prefer on all accounts. They lead a very melancholy life, these poor preachers and teachers; waiting for a quarter of a century in the city before any provision is made for them, struggling all the while to keep soul and body together, and perhaps destined in the long run to see all their expectations of preferment dashed away. There was one Craig, a little withered man, whom I saw once or twice, a teacher of Greek here, that waited long for some kirk or other establishment, was frequently disappointed, and lately having been more grievously disappointed than ever, took it to heart, and grew low-spirited about it, and is now gone home in a state little if at all short of derangement! I pity the poor body sincerely. Few conditions of life are more oppressive than such a one as this.

Now, my dear Alick, the new year is coming on, and the "storms of winter;" can you or Father or Mother, or any or all of you say anything definite about the visit you half-promised us? We can get you accommodations here, such as they are, without inconvenience in any shape, the warmest welcome you count upon at all times, and we will not let you want a *hurl* up and down in the coach, whenever you like to fix upon a time. I really think you should take the *good-wife* and the *good-man* to task on this matter, and try to persuade them. They *must* see Edinburgh some time ; that is flat : why not now as well as afterwards? Write us about this.

Also you must send me word about your readings and studies and all your news and undertakings. Poor Gullen! To be so nearly eaten up of the Foul Thief, in so ugly a shape! Have they found none of the sacrilegious Kirk-robbers? Write me about all and sundry.—I am ever, my dear Alick, your affectionate brother,

TH. CARLYLE.

CIX.—To his MOTHER, Mainhill.

MY DEAR MOTHER—I have still a few minutes' time, and I cannot let the Carrier go without writing you a line or two which, however dull or barren, may at least gratify you by the conviction that I *would* amuse and interest you, if I *could*. . . .

I wish you had learned to write as you proposed last harvest : we should in that case hear more precisely and fully of your situation than we usually do ; a circumstance which would greatly enhance the pleasure we always feel at the sight of a packet from home. As it is, I must content myself with general conjectures—trusting that you go on as happily as could be expected, bustling and fighting away as usual, having many things to suffer and do, but also possessing many resources for suffering them and doing them with courage and equanimity. My dear Mother, I am vexed that you never tell me of anything I can do for you : always doing for *me*, busying yourself for my sake, never showing me the means to add in any respect to *your* happiness. This is not fair : I am sure you know me well enough to be assured that you could not promote my comfort, in the truest sense of the word, more effectually, than putting it within my power to serve you in some shape. Do think, and *tell* me what you want. Are you in the habit of taking tea yet? I fear it [*sic*] : and I again charge you to *begin forthwith*, and I will be answerable for the result. Now mind these are not words, but real injunctions, which you must not disregard. It would be *such* a thing, if you, who have toiled among us so long and faithfully, were restricted from any comfort— become a necessary to one in your situation—which we could procure for you. My dear Mother, this thought would be gall and wormwood to me long afterwards : no sum of hundreds would make me amends for the presence of it. *Do not* heap it upon my head ! consider what I am telling you, and do as I bid you—for it comes earnestly from the heart. Tell me next time that you have begun the tea-system —if you do not wish me to send you *half a stone* of the article down by the first opportunity.

But I am wasting away the paper in this lecture ; my time too is all but run, Jack being nearly finished and just on the wing for Candlemaker Row. I wish you would try to write me yourself—however indifferently : you can never learn younger ; and I rejoice to see your hand, however rude and crabbed.

What ails all the young people that no soul of them thinks of writing? We might suppose they had all got Palsy or some such distemper. Have they a fear of touching goose-feathers, or are they careless about their Brothers? No! I feel that they are not, but they want some motive to rouse them from their slumber. Tell Mag and Jamie and Mary that I expect to hear from them next time—if it were but with the "compliments of the season." Are Jane and Jenny at any school? Give my love to all the honest little creatures : I know that all of them like me, though they have not tongues to say it. When is my Father going to write? We half expected to hear from him by this opportunity. But Jack is grunting !—I must bid my dear Mother farewell !

THOMAS CARLYLE.

CX.—To ALEXANDER CARLYLE, Mainhill.

EDINBURGH, 20th December 1822.

. . . You ask me after Edward Irving; but I have nothing to say about him, or little, except what you know already. Like another Boanerges he is cleaving the hearts of the Londoners in twain, attending Bible Societies, Presbyterian dinners, Religious conventions of all kinds; preaching and speculating and acting so as to gain universal notoriety and very general approbation. Long may he enjoy it ! There are few men living that deserve it better. He has written to me only once since he went away, and has been a letter in my debt for some time ; I am expecting payment very soon.

That is a kind of life, which, though prized by many, would not by any means suit my perverted tastes. Popularity is sweet in all cases : but if I were aiming for it in the Pulpit, the idea that a thousand drivellers had gained it more lavishly, that even John Whitfield used to rouse the Londoners from their warm beds, and make them stand in rows, with lanthorns in their hands, crowding the streets that led to his chapel, early in raw wet November mornings—would come withering over my imagination like the mortifying wind of Africa, and as Thomas Bell said in his bold metaphorical way, would "dash the *cup* of fame from my brow." It is happier for me therefore that I live in still shades—shunning the clamorous approval of the many-headed monster as well as avoiding its censure, and determined if ever I be marked out never so slightly from the common herd, to be so by another set of judges. After all it is a blessing little worth coveting ; the best and richest part of the most famous man's renown is the esteem he is

held in by those who see him daily in his goings out and
comings in, by his friends and relations and those that love
himself more than his qualities; and this every one of us
may gain, without straying into the thorny paths which
guide to glory, either in the region of arts or of arms.

But see where my digressive temper is leading me!
The sheet is done, and I have yet said nothing! I had
much to ask about yourself and Home—about your employ-
ments, studies, thoughts: but I have no room to form my
longings into thoughts—far less to *back-spier*[1] you sufficiently
on these to me most interesting topics. I wish you would
sit down some night when you feel "i' the vein," and give
me a full disclosure; describe to me all that is going on
in the shape of sentiment or action about Mainhill or the
environs, never minding in what order or how, so it be but
there. . . . Give my affectionate remembrances to all the
true-hearted though too silent population of Mainhill; and
wish them in my name a brave new year better than all
that are gone, worse than all that are to follow. They will
surely write to me on that stirring occasion.—I am ever
your affectionate Brother,

TH. CARLYLE.

CXI.—To Mr. R. MITCHELL, Kirkcudbright.

3 MORAY STREET, LEITH WALK,
23d December 1822.

MY DEAR MITCHELL—It is many a day since I wrote
to you or heard from you; yet there are few of my early
friends whom I have more cause to feel an interest in, few
periods of my life that I look back to with more pleasure
than the period when our pursuits were more similar, our
places of abode more adjacent than they are at present. It
is in the hope of recalling old times and thoughts to your
memory that I have taken up the pen on this occasion: I
am still ambitious for a place in your esteem, still anxious
to hear of your welfare.

It is so long since you have been in Edinburgh, that
all except the general interests connected with the place

<hr>

[1] Cross-question.

must have become indifferent to you. I know few people here myself, you I suppose still fewer ; and of these even only a very small portion seems to merit much attention. They are getting into Kirks gradually, or lingering on the muddy shore of *Private teaching*, to see if any Charon will waft them across the Styx of Patronage into the Elysium of teinds and glebe. Success attend them all, poor fellows ! they are cruising in one small sound, as it were, of the great ocean of life ; their trade is harmless, their vessels leaky ; it will be hard if they altogether fail.

James Johnstone is gone to Broughty Ferry (Dundee) some weeks ago. He seems to aim at being a Scottish Teacher for life : I think if he stick to it, he must ultimately prosper. In the meantime, however, things wear a very surly aspect with him. He has got planted among a very melancholy race of people—Psalm-singing Captains, devout old women, Tabernacle shoemakers, etc. etc., who wish him to engage in exposition of the Scripture, and various other plans, for the *spread* not of grammar and accounts, but of the doctrines of Theosophy and Thaumaturgy. It is galling and provoking ! You must write to console and encourage poor James : he is a true man as breathes ; has no natural friends, and feels at present, I can easily conceive, very lonely and dejected.

For myself, I lead a very quiet life here. The Bullers are exceedingly good people, and what is more comfortable, having still a home of my own, I depend less on their good qualities. I am with them only four hours a day : and I find the task of superintending the studies of my two pupils more pleasing than I had reason to expect. I sit here and read all the morning—or write, regularly burning everything I write. It is a hard matter that one's thoughts should be so poor and scanty, and at the same time the power of uttering them so difficult to acquire. I should be happy, if I were in health—which in about a twelvemonth or so I keep hoping I shall be. I am greatly better than I was, though yet ill enough to break the heart of any but a very obstinate person.

Have you seen the *Liberal?* It is a most happy performance ; Byron has a " Vision of Judgment " there, and a letter to the Editor of " My Grandmother's Review," of the wickedest and cleverest turn you could imagine. The Vice Society, or Constitutional Association, are going to prosecute. This is a wild, fighting, loving, praying, blaspheming, weeping, laughing sort of world ! The *literati* and *literatuli* with us are wrangling and scribbling ; but effecting nothing, except to "make the day and way alike long." At present, however, it is mine to make the sheet and story alike long ; a duty I seem in danger of forgetting. Write to me whenever you can spare an hour : I want to have all your news, your difficulties and successes, your hopes and fears, a picture of your whole *manière d'être.* Salute Mr. Low in my name.—I am always, my dear Mitchell, your sincere friend,

Thomas Carlyle.

CXII.—To Miss Welsh, Haddington.

3 Moray Street, *25th December* 1822.

My dear Friend—I got your parcel about two hours ago. I had been living for the last week in the dread of a lecture ; I now think it happy that I am quit so easily. It is very true I am a kind of *ineptus ;* and when I sit down to write letters to people that I care anything for, I am too apt to get into a certain ebullient humour, and so to indite great quantities of nonsense, which even my own judgment condemns—when too late for being mended. The longer I live, the more clearly do I see that Corporal Nym's maxim is the great elixir of Philosophy, the quintessence of all moral doctrine. *Pauca verba, pauca verba* is the only remedy we can apply to all the excesses and irregularities of the head and heart. *Pauca verba,* then !

You are too late by a day in asking for *Faust.* It is not to be got in the bookshops here, and the College library is shut for the Christmas holidays. You shall have the volume on the 2d or 3d of January. In the meantime, I have sent you *Tell* and the *Bride of Messina,* the former of which Schiller's critics have praised greatly ; generally condemning the latter as written upon a false system, though with immense care and labour. I was disappointed in *Tell ;* it struck me as too disjointed and heterogeneous, though there are excellent views of Swiss life in it, and Tell himself is a fine patriot-peasant. I want your criticism on it. You did well to cry so heartily over *Wallenstein :* I like it best of any in the series. Is it not strange that they cannot for their hearts get up a decent play in our own country? All try it, and all fail. Lord John Russell has sent us down what he calls a "tragedy" the other day— and upon a subject no less dangerous than the fate of Don Carlos. Schiller and Alfieri yet live. The Newspapers say Lord Byron is greatly obliged to his brother lord, the latter having even surpassed *Werner* in tameness and insipidity; so that Byron is no longer Author of the dullest tragedy ever printed by a lord. This is very foul to Byron; for though I fear he will never write a good play, it is impossible he can ever write anything so truly innocent as this *Don Carlos.* I would have sent it to you; but it seemed superfluous. There is great regularity in the speeches, the lines have all ten syllables exactly—and precisely the same smooth ding-dong rhythm from the first page to the last; there are also little bits of metaphors scattered up and down at convenient intervals, and very fair whig sentiments here and there; but the whole is cold, flat, stale, and unprofitable, to a degree that "neither gods nor men nor columns can endure." You and I could write a better thing in two weeks, and then burn it. Yet he dedicates to Lord Holland, and seems to say like Correggio in the Vatican, *ed io anche son pittore.* Let us be of courage! we shall not be hindmost any way.

I am really sorry to see you in such a coil about your writing. What use is there in so perplexing and over-tasking yourself with what should be the ornament and solace of your life, not its chief vexation? I take blame to myself in the business; and pray you to be moderate. One thing ought to afford you some consolation : "Genius," said Sir Joshua Reynolds, and he never spoke more truly, "is nothing but the intense direction of a mind to some intellectual object—that consecration of all our powers to it, which leads to disregard all toils and obstacles in the attainment of it, and if strong enough will ultimately bring success."[1] Some such thought as this was Sir Joshua's;

---

[1] The words of Sir Joshua which were in Carlyle's mind were probably the following from his *Second Discourse :* "Nothing is denied to well-

and truly it contains nine-tenths of the whole doctrine : it should lead every one that feels this inspiration and unrest within to be proud of feeling it, and also to adopt the only means of turning it to good account—the sedulous cultivation of the faculties—by patiently amassing knowledge and studying by every method to digest it well. This, my dear pupil, is the great deficiency with you at present ; this I would have you to regard as your chief object for a considerable time to come. Be diligent with your historical and other studies ; and consider that every new step you make in this direction *is* infallibly, however circuitously, leading you nearer to the goal at which you are aiming. For composition, the art of expressing the thoughts and emotions you are thus daily acquiring, do not by any means neglect it ; but at the same time feel no surprise at the disproportion of your wishes to your execution in regard to it. How long did it take you to learn playing on the Piano? and what execrable jingling did you make when you first tried it ? But what are all the stringed instruments of the Earth in point of complicacy compared to one immortal mind ? Is it strange that you should feel a difficulty in managing the rich melodies that " slumber in the chords " of your Imagination, your Understanding, and your Heart ? Long years of patient industry, many trials, many failures must be gone through, before you can even begin to satisfy yourself. And do not let this dishearten you—for if rightly gone about, the task is pleasant as well as necessary. I have promised that if you will but take hold of my hand, I—dim-sighted guide as I am—will lead you along pleasant paths up even to the summit. I am still confident in my predictions, still zealous to perform : my only stipulation is that we go on constantly and regularly ; you shall neither stop to trifle by the way, nor run till you are out of breath—as you are now doing, and must soon cease to do in disgust and exhaustion—or else break your heart in vain striving.

I partly guess what hinders you from beginning your directed labour : nothing is to be obtained without it. Not to enter into metaphysical discussions on the nature or essence of genius, I will venture to assert, that assiduity unabated by difficulty, and a disposition eagerly directed to the object of its pursuit, will produce effects similar to those which some call the result of *natural powers.*"

"story:" it is the excess of that noble quality in you, which I have preached against so vigorously, and still love for all my preaching—the excess of your *Ambition*, the too high ideas you have formed of excellence, and your vexation at not realising them. It is safe to err on this side so far as feeling is concerned; but wrong to let your action be so much cramped by these considerations. Cannot you do as others do? Sit down and write—something short—but write and write, though you could swear it was the most stupid stuff in nature, till you fairly get to the end. A week after it is finished it will look far better than you expected. The next you write will go on more smoothly and look better still. So likewise with the third and fourth,—in regular progression,—till you will wonder how such difficulties could ever stop you for a moment. Be not too careful for a subject; take the one you feel most interest in and understand best—some description of manners or passions—some picture of a kind of life you are familiar with, and which looks lovely in your eyes: and for a commencement, why should it give you pause? Take the precept of Horace,—*proripe in medias res ;* rush forward and fear nothing. You really magnify the matter too much: never think of the press or public when you are writing: remember that it is only a *secondary matter* at present, to be taken up as a light task, and laid down again whenever it interferes with your regular studies. If you cannot think of any proper theme, cannot get in motion for whatever cause; then let the business rest for a week; cease to vex yourself about it, in time materials will come unsought. Finally, my dear Friend, possess your mind in patience, follow your laborious but noble task with peaceful diligence ; study, read, accumulate ideas, and try to give them utterance in all ways ; and look upon it as a cardinal truth that there is *no* obstacle before you which calm perseverance will not enable you to surmount.

Now, I am sure, you cannot say I have tried to flatter you on this occasion. My speech has been at once dull and honest ; I have preached till we are both grown stupid, you observe ; and I leave you undeceived at any rate if uninstructed. The sum of my doctrine is : Begin to write something, if you can, without delay, never minding *how* shallow and poor it may seem; if you cannot, drive it altogether out of your thoughts, till we meet. I entertain no fear whatever of the result: I know well you *will* write better than you yet dream of, and look back on these sage prescriptions of mine with an indulgent pity. Shall we not also write together when times are better? Yes we shall —in spite of your good-natured sarcasms at my "wit and genius," and the lubberly productions I send you at present —we *shall* write in concert—if Fortune does not mean to vex me more than she has ever done. This Hope is a fine creature after all! I owe her more than the whole posse of saints and angels put together.

By the Belfast Town and Country Almanack, Spring will be here in a month. Perhaps you think to steal away again without seeing me: but try it—! To be sure, it is only the brief space of a year, since we met, for about five minutes; and we have so many hundred centuries to live on Earth together—I confess I am very unreasonable.

But why should I keep prating? The night is run, my pen is worn to the stump; and certain male and female Milliners in this street are regaling themselves with *Auld Langsyne*, and punch and other viler liquors, and calling back my thoughts too fast from those elysian flights to the vulgar prose of this poor world. May Heaven be the comforter of these poor Milliners! Their noise and jollity might call forth anathemas from a cynic: my prayer for them is that they may never want a sausage or two and a goose better or worse and a drop of "blue ruin" to keep their Christmas with; and whatever quantities of tape and beeswax and diluted tea their several necessities require.

I will write again with Faust—briefly, I promise—and tell you all that I am doing and mean to do. Good-night! my dear Friend.—I am always yours in sincerity,

THOMAS CARLYLE.

CXIII.—To his MOTHER, Mainhill.

3 MORAY STREET, *4th January* 1823.

MY DEAR MOTHER—I see there is a long letter lying for you already, and seasoned by a fortnight's keeping; yet I have begun another sheet which I have spread out before me, and am determined to fill before quitting. I do not think ever people had so voluminous a correspondent : it matters not whether you write or keep silence, you are loaded with epistles every fortnight, enough to break the back of *Robby* himself, if he were not rather lightly freighted in this dull season. How you will get them all read I know not—or care not, for that is your concern, mine is only to write as long as the pen will move.

I hear no particular tidings of my Mother ; only I am inclined to include her under the general head of "all going on as usual," and to hope that her health and spirits do not altogether fail her, but continue to afford strength to discharge her many duties and make head against her many difficulties. I hope to live beside you yet a long time, though we see one another too rarely of late. You must know I am to have a pleasant dwelling-place in the course of years ; and there you and I shall reserve a place for colleaguing together, and what talking and smoking and gossiping and tea-*shines* we shall have ! All this is coming yet. In the meantime, I am going on quite well in all respects—except for some noises which have disturbed me at nights a little, concerning which Alick will instruct you, and from which we are now sure one way or another soon to be completely delivered.

It is a pitiful thing to be so touchy ; but one good effect of it is that it may teach one the utility of Patience. There is no other remedy in fact but this universal one ; if you would tear the very liver out of yourself, you cannot mend the matter, you must *just submit.* However, I am getting stronger and stronger every month : I now reckon myself in quite a tolerable state ; and you may be sure I shall neglect no precaution for improving and confirming these favourable symptoms. Heaven be praised that I am so well ! If you would offer me health in the one hand and the sceptre of Europe in the other—I should hesitate few moments which to choose.

Poor Jenny Crone is gone at last ! She was a good woman : seemed to keep "the noiseless tenor of her way" through the wilderness of life in peace and blamelessness ; that now is more for her than if she had been Empress of all the Earth. Well was it said, " Let me die the death of

the Righteous, and let my last end be like his!" It is a
wish which all of us should be busied in seeking the means
to get accomplished. Strange that the shallow pageant of
this transitory being should have power so far to draw us
from the "vast concerns of an Eternal scene"!

I know not what books you have to read, or which of
them you are most in favour with at present. Cannot you
tell me some which I can get you? Or if not, cannot you
point out some other thing which I can do for you?
"Dear! Bairn, I want for nothing," I hear you reply. Now
I know you do want for many things, and I am often really
vexed that you do not mention them. Will you never
understand that you cannot gratify me so much, by any
plan you can take, as by enabling me to promote your
comfort in any way within my power? Speak, then!
Speak, I tell you! . . .

Jack is busy writing to my Father, or he would have
sent you a line. He is doing well here, enjoys good health,
and follows out his studies without flinching. His old propensity to logic or the "use of reason" he still retains in
considerable preservation. Often in our arguments I am
tempted to employ my Father's finisher "*thou Natural,
thou*"—but poor Jack looks out with his broad face so
honestly and good-naturedly that I have not the heart.
He is a very good soul, and comforts me greatly when I
am out of sorts.

Now surely, my good Mother, you must confess yourself to be a letter in my debt: you ought to pay it with the
earliest time you have. I do wish you would learn to write,
and send me letters by the quire. It only wants a beginning. My best love to all the *childer*. I am ever your
affectionate son,   TH. CARLYLE.

CXIV.—To Miss WELSH, Haddington.

3 MORAY STREET, 12*th January* 1823.

. . . What a wicked creature you are to make me laugh
so at poor Irving! Do I not know him for one of the best
men breathing, and that he loves us both as if he were our
brother? Yet it must be owned there is something quite
unique in his style of thought and language. Conceive

the chords of sensibility awakened by the sound of *Caller herring!* It is little better than the pathos of a great fat greasy Butcher whimpering and blubbering over the calf he has just run his knife into. The truth is, our friend has a radically dull organ of taste ; he does everything in a floundering awkward ostentatious way. I have advised him a thousand times to give up all attempts at superfineness and be a son of Anak honestly at once, in mind as in body : but he will not see it thus. Occasionally, I confess, I have envied him this want of tact, or rather the contented dimness of perception from which it partly proceeds : it contributes largely to the affectionateness and placidity of his general character ; he loves everything, because he sees nothing in its severe reality ; hence his enthusiastic devotion, his fervour on topics adapted to the general comprehension, his eloquence, and the favour he gives to all and so gets from all. I still hope he will improve considerably, but not that he will ever entirely get free of these absurdities. And what if he should not ? He has merit to balance ten times as many, and make him still one of the worthiest persons we shall ever meet with. Let us like him the better, the more freely we laugh. . . . .

CXV.—To Miss WELSH, Haddington.

3 MORAY STREET, *Monday*
[*January* 1823].

. . . . Four months ago I had a splendid plan of treating the history of England during the Commonwealth in a new style—not by way of regular narrative—for which I felt too well my inequality, but by grouping together the most singular manifestations of mind that occurred then under distinct heads—selecting some remarkable person as the representative of each class, and trying to explain and illustrate their excellences and defects, all that was curious in their fortune as individuals, or in their formation as members of the human family, by the most striking methods I could devise. Already my characters were fixed upon —Laud, Fox, Clarendon, Cromwell, Milton, Hampden ; already I was busied in the study of their works ; when that wretched Philomath with his sines and tangents came to put me in mind of a prior engagement,—to obstruct my efforts in this undertaking, and at length to drive them totally away. Next I thought of some work of imagination: I would paint, in a brief but vivid manner, the old story of a noble mind struggling against an ignoble fate ; some fiery yet benignant spirit reaching forth to catch the bright creations of his own fancy, and breaking his head against the vulgar obstacles of this lower world. But then what knew I of this lower world ? The man must be a hero, and I could only draw the materials of him from myself. Rich source of such materials ! Besides, it were well that he died of love ; and your novel-love is become a perfect drug ; and of the genuine sort I could not undertake to say a word. I once thought of calling in your assistance, that we might work in concert, and make a new hero and heroine such as the world never saw. Could I have obtained your concurrence ? Would to Heaven we could make such a thing ! Finally I abandoned the project.—I have since tried to resume the Commonwealth ; but the charm of it is gone : I contemplate with terror the long train of preparation, and the poorness of the result. . . .

CXVI.—To Miss Welsh, Haddington.

3 Moray Street, 20*th January* 1823.

. . . I wish I had not sent you this great blubbering numskull D'Israeli : his " Calamities " have sunk upon your spirits, and tinged the whole world of intellect with the hue of mourning and despair. The paths of learning seem, in your present mood of mind, to lead but through regions of woe and lamentation and darkness and dead men's bones. Hang the ass !—it is all false, if you take it up in this light. Do you not see that his observations can apply only to men in whom genius was more the want of common qualities than the possession of uncommon ones ; whose life was embittered not so much because they had imagination and sensibility, as because they had not prudence and true moral principles ? If one chose to investigate the history of the first twenty tattered blackguards to be found lying on the benches of the watch-house, or stewing in drunkenness and squalor in the Jerusalem Taproom, it would not be difficult to write a much more moving book on the "calamities of shoemakers" or street-porters, or any other class of handicraftsmen, than this of D'Israeli's on Authors. It is the few ill-starred wretches, and the multitude of ill-behaved, that are miserable, in all ranks,—and among writers just as elsewhere. Literature, I do believe, has keener pains connected with it than almost any other pursuit; but then it has also far livelier and nobler pleasures, and if you shudder at engaging in it on those terms, you ought also to envy the stupidity of other people, their insensibility, the meanness of their circumstances, whatever narrows their sphere of action, and adds more stagnation to the current of their feelings. The dangers with which intellectual enterprises are encompassed should awake us to vigilance, to unwearied circumspection, to gain the absolute dominion of ourselves : they should not dishearten but instruct. You say rightly that you would not quit this way of life although you could : no one that has once tasted the nectar of science or literature, that will not thirst for it thenceforth to the end. Nor shall my own scholar repent this her noble determination. Dangers beset her, neither few nor small ; but her steadfastness and prudence will conquer them ; she will yet be happy and famous beyond her hopes.

"Oh! if this were true!" you exclaim, "but—" Nay, I will have no buts : it depends entirely upon yourself. I have no more hesitation in affirming that Nature has given you qualities enough to satisfy any reasonable am-bition—to secure you the much longed-for elevation you pant after—than I have to believe my own existence. It is no doubt in your own power to frustrate all these hopes, to ruin the fairest promises it has been my chance to witness in any one, and to make your life as wretched as it will be useless. But I trust in God you will be better guided ; you will learn in time to moderate your ardour, to cultivate the virtues of patience and self-command, to believe that the sole though certain road to excellence is through long tracts of calm exertion and quiet study. Do think of this, my dear Jane, both for my sake and your own. Why will you vex and torment yourself so, for a precocious fruit, which Time itself would bring to a much happier and more glorious maturity? You must absolutely acquire far more knowledge before your faculties can have anything like fair play : in your actual condition, I confess they often amaze me. When I was of your age, I had not half the skill. And what haste is there? Rousseau was above thirty before he suspected himself to be anything but a thievish apprentice, and a vagabond littleworth : Cowper became a poet at fifty, and found he was still in time enough. Will you also let me say that I continue to lament this inordinate *love of Fame* which agitates you so ; and which, as I believe, lies at the root of all this mischief? I think this feeling unworthy of you : it is far too shallow a principle for a mind like yours. Do not imagine that I make no account of a glorious name : I think it the best of *external* rewards, but never to be set in competition with those that lie *within*. To depend for our highest happiness on the popular breath, to lie at the mercy of every scribbler for our daily meed of enjoyment—does seem to me a very helpless state. It is the means of fame not the end that chiefly delights me ; if I believed that I had done the very uttermost that I could for myself, had cultivated my soul to the very highest pitch that Nature meant it to reach, I think I could be happy though no suffrages at all were given me ; my conscience would be at rest, I should actually *be* a worthy man, whatever I might *seem*. You may also take it as an indubitable truth that there is nothing lasting or satisfying in these applauses of others ; the only gratification, worth calling by that name, arises from the approval of the *man within*. I may also state my firm conviction, that no man ever became *famous*, entirely or even chiefly from the *love of fame*. It is the interior fire, the solitary delight which our own hearts experience in these things, and the misery we feel in vacancy, that must urge us, or we shall never reach the goal. The love of Fame will make a Percival Stockdale,[1] but not a Milton or a Schiller. Do you believe in this doctrine? Then study to keep down this strong desire of notoriety ; give scope

[1] A forgotten writer, "voluminous, egotistical, and shallow," commemorated in D'Israeli's *Calamities of Authors*. He published his *Memoirs* in 1809 ; "I know," he declares, "that this book will live and escape the havoc that has been made of my literary fame." There are notices of him in Croker's *Boswell*, chaps. xxiii., xxv., lxxx.

rather to your feeling of the Beautiful and the Great within
yourself, conceive that every new idea you get does actually
exalt you as a thinking being, every new branch of knowledge you master does in very truth make you richer and
more enviable though there were no other being but
yourself in the Universe to judge you.   There is an
independence, a grandeur of solitary power and strong
self-help in this, which attracts one greatly.   It makes us
the arbiters of our own destiny: it is the surest method
of getting glory,' and the best means of setting us above
the want of it.   I do beg of you with all my heart to consider these things well; my own opinion seems to me true
as the truest sentence in the Gospel; and if you could
adopt it, how much happier would it make you !

I am sorry for you with your Highland Cousin and the
gallant Captain Spalding.   But it is wrong in you to take
these things so much to heart.   A little interruption does
no harm at all, and these visits, as they bring you more in
contact with the common world, are in your case absolutely
beneficial.   Therefore do not cloud your countenance when
Spalding enters; do not [flash] those bright eyes of yours
with indignation when he lingers.   Study rather to make
the man happy, and to be happy with him : throw by your
books and papers, and be again a lively, thoughtless,
racketing girl, as you were before.   There is much improvement to be got in such things; they give an exercise to the
mind as difficult and valuable as any literary study can.
Be happy, I tell you; diligent in moderation when the
time bids, and idle and gay as willingly.   For your Mother,
I do entreat you to continue to love her and honour her
and prefer her company to that of any other.   The exercise
of these placid affections is the truest happiness to be got
in this world, and the best nourishment for all that is
worthiest in our nature.   I dare not promise that you will
ever find so true a friend as your Mother.   Some love us
for our qualities—for what we are or what we do; but a
Mother's bosom is ever the home of her *child* independent
of all concomitants; ever warm to welcome us in good and
bad report, a kindly hiding-place which neither misfortune
nor misconduct, woe, want, or infamy, or guilt itself, can
shut against us.

.   .   .   .   .   .

You cannot speak too much to me of your difficulties in any point. God knows there are few sacrifices I would not make to help you. For your writing, I do not wonder in the least that it agitates and embarrasses you. There never was a human being in your state that did not a thousand times look on himself just as you do, as the stupidest creature in the whole Universe. Nor was there ever a human being more mistaken than you are, this time; or more sure of seeing his mistake.—But hark! Two o'clock is striking and still here! . . .

CXVII.—To Miss WELSH, Haddington.

3 MORAY STREET, *Wednesday night*
[*February* 1823].

. . . You are right to keep by Gibbon, since you have begun it : there is no other tolerable history of those times and nations within the reach of such readers as we are; it is a kind of bridge that connects the antique with the modern ages. And how gorgeously does it swing across the gloomy and tumultuous chasm of those barbarous centuries: Gibbon is a man whom one never forgets—unless oneself deserving to be forgotten; the perusal of his work forms an epoch in the history of one's mind. I know you will admire Gibbon, yet I do not expect or wish that you should love him. He has but a coarse and vulgar heart, with all his keen logic, and glowing imagination, and lordly irony : he worships power and splendour; and suffering virtue, the most heroic devotedness if unsuccessful, un-arrayed in the pomp and circumstance of outward glory, has little of his sympathy. To the Christians he is frequently very unfair : if he had lived now, he would have written differently on these points. I would not have you love him; I am sure you will not. Have you any notion what an *ugly* thief he was? Jack brought down his *Life* to-day, and it has a profile of his whole person—alas for Mlle. Curchod! Alas for her daughter, Wilhelmina Necker, who wished to marry him when she was thirteen—not out of love to him but to her Mother! I would have sent you this *Life*, but it is a large quarto—and I knew not if you would receive it patiently. Should you wish it, write to me to-morrow and I will send it out. There is some amusement in it, but you will relish it more when you know more fully and think more highly of the studied labours of the mind which it shows you in deshabille.

.   .   .   .

Now have I not tired you enough for once? There is poor Schiller lying too, at whom I must have a hit or two before I sleep. It will be an invaluable life this of Schiller's, were it once completed: so splendid and profound and full of *unction*—Oh! I could beat my brains out when I think what a miserable, pithless ninny I am! Would it were in my power either to write like a man or honestly to give up the attempt for ever. Chained to the earth by native gravitation and a thousand wretched fetters, I am miserable unless I be soaring in the empyrean; and thus between the lofty will and the powerless deed, I have no peace, no peace. Sometimes I could almost run distracted; my wearied soul seems as if it were hunted round within its narrow enclosure by a whole legion of the dogs of Tartarus, which sleep not, night or day. In fact I am never happy except when *full* of business and *nothing more*. The secret of all is, " I have no genius," and like Andrew Irving's horse, I *have* "a *dibbil* of a temper." We must just submit!

Boyd the pursy Bookseller wishes me to translate Goethe's *Wilhelm Meister*, which I have told him is very clever. It will not be determined for some weeks—not till I see where I am to be and how, during summer. . . .

CXVIII.—To Miss WELSH, Haddington.

EDINBURGH, 4th March 1823.

. . . I am really vexed that you are not going forward with any composition: the art of giving out ideas is about as essential and certainly more laborious than that of gathering them in. We must really make an effort to remedy this deficiency, and that as early as possible. In the meantime do not disturb yourself about it; go on with your Gibbon and your other studies calmly and diligently, and assure yourself that if not in the best of all modes, your employment is in the next to the best. I do trust you will not grow idle or irregular again; there is nothing satisfactory to be accomplished by you if you do; everything if you avoid doing it. You must make another effort upon *Götz*: it is hardest at the first. This Goethe has as much in him as any ten of them: he is not a mere bacchanalian rhymester, cursing and foaming and laying about him as if he had breathed a gallon of nitrous oxide, or pouring forth his most inane philosophy and most maudlin sorrow in strains that "split the ears of the groundlings;" but a man of true culture and universal genius, not less distinguished for the extent of his knowledge and the profoundness of his ideas and the variety of his feelings, than for the vivid and graceful energy, the inventive and deeply meditative sagacity, the skill to temper enthusiasm with judgment, which he shows in exhibiting them. Wordsworth and Byron! They are as the Christian Ensign and Captain Bobadil before the Duke of Marlborough. You must go on with *Götz*: it will serve you to read while *here*, if it do no better. I wish it would. . . .

CXIX.—To his MOTHER, Mainhill.

3 MORAY STREET, 22d March 1823.

MY DEAR MOTHER—It appears that Farries is here to-day, and as I am got down from India Street in time for writing you a few words, I cannot omit this opportunity of doing so. We have not got a syllable of intelligence from Mainhill; but this we impute solely to Geordie's having set out without giving you proper warning, and we force ourselves to believe that you are all in your usual health and circumstances,—a blessing which it has pleased Providence long to continue with us, and which we shall never prize sufficiently till it is taken away. For you, my dear Mother, we are seldom without anxieties; your infirm state and many cares but too well justify them. I can only entreat you again more earnestly than ever to take every possible care of yourself—to watch over your health as the greatest treasure to all your children, and to none more than me. I still hope to find you whole and well when we meet, and to have our tea and smoke and small talk together *down the house*, many, many happy times, as heretofore. There are no moments when I can forget all my cares, as in these. I seem to lose twenty of my years, when we are chatting together, and to be a happy, thoughtless urchin of a boy once more. Amid all my sorrows (of which I often think I have had my share first and last), there is nothing which has yielded me so constant a gratification as your affection and welfare, nothing that I ought to [be] so thankful for enjoying,—or that I should pray more earnestly for having still vouchsafed to me.

There is nothing in this sort of prating I am going on with ; but [it] is about as good as anything I have got to tell you. When I have said that Jack and I are still in our common state of health and going forward with our customary occupations, I have as good as finished my tale. There is no change in our individual conditions, and the changes which pass in the world around us are things in which we have little part or lot, and so take little note of. Life to both of us is still very much *in prospect :* we are not yet what we hope to be. Jack is going to become a large gawsie,[1] broadfaced Practiser of Physic—to ride his horse in time, and give aloes by rule, and make money, and be a large man ; while I—in spite of all my dyspepsias and nervousness and hypochondrias—am still bent on being a very meritorious sort of character—rather noted in the world of letters, if it so please Providence—and useful, I hope, whithersoever I go, in *the good old cause*, for which I beg you to believe that I cordially agree with you in feeling my chief interest, however we may differ in our modes of expressing it. For attaining this mighty object, I have need of many things—which I fear I shall never get ; but if my health were once sound again, I should feel such an inextinguishable diligence within me that my own exertions might supply almost every want. This greatest of blessings is yet but partially restored to me : however, I do verily believe that it is coming back by degrees,—so I live as patiently as I can and fear nothing.

The next summer I hope will do great things for me— almost set me on my feet again. . . .

But I am at the bottom of my sheet, and must conclude

---

[1] Jolly.

this palaver. There are many debts lying against me to my worthy correspondents at Mainhill—which lie heavy on my conscience and must in due time be discharged. I beg you will try to keep the creatures quiet in the meanwhile, and advise them to send me another file of epistles. Is Jane going on to rhyme? I showed her "meanest of the letter kind" to several judges, and they declared she must be a very singular *crow*.[1]—This is a real truth.

You must give my love to my Father and all the rest *conjunctly and severally*. Tell Sandy and my Father to write next time, if they can snatch as many moments from the sowing. Write to me yourself the very first spare hour you have. Good-night, my dear Mother—it is dark, and I must cease.—I am ever yours,

T. CARLYLE.

CXX.—To Miss WELSH, Haddington.

EDINBURGH, *6th April* 1823.

. . . As to your literary hopes, entertain them confidently! There is to me no better symptom of what is in you than your despair of getting it expressed. Cannot write! My dear Pupil, you have no idea of what a task it is to every one, when it is taken up in that solemn way. Did you never hear of Rousseau lying in his bed and painfully wrenching every syllable of his *Nouvelle Heloise* from the obscure complexities of his imagination? He composed every sentence of it, on an average, *five times over;* and often when he took up the pen, the whole concern was vanished quite away! John James is my only comfort when I sit down to write. I could frequently swear that I am the greatest dunce in creation : the cooking of a paragraph is little better than the labour of the Goldmaker; I sweat and toil and keep tedious vigil, and at last there runs out from the tortured melting-pot an ingot—of solid pewter. There is no help but patient diligence, and *that will conquer everything.* Never waver, my own Jane! I shall yet "stand a-tiptoe" at your name. Not write! I declare if I had known nothing of you but your letters, I should have pronounced you to be already an excellent writer. Depend upon it,

---

[1] His little sister "Craw Jean," so nicknamed because of her black hair.

this is nothing but your taste outgrowing your practice. Had you been a peer's daughter, and lived among literary men, and seen things to exercise your powers of observation, the world would ere this have been admiring the sagacious humour of your remarks and the graceful vigour of your descriptions.   As it is, you have only to begin and to go on : time will make all possible, all easy.   Why did you give up that Essay on Friendship? *For my sake,* resume it and finish it !   Never mind how bad, how execrable it may seem, go through with it.   The next will be better, and the next, and the next ; you will approach at each trial nearer the Perfection which no one ever reached.   If I knew you fairly on the way, I should feel quite easy : your reading is going on as it ought ; there wants only that you should write also.   Begin this Essay again, if you love me !

Goethe lies waiting for your arrival.   You make a right distinction about Goethe : he is a great genius and *does not make you cry*.   His feelings are various as the hues of Earth and Sky, but his intellect is the Sun which illuminates and overrules them all.   He does not yield himself to his emotions, but uses them rather as things for his judgment to scrutinise and apply to purpose.   I think Goethe the only living model of a great writer.   The Germans say there have been *three* geniuses in the world since it began —Homer, Shakespeare, and Goethe !   This of course is shooting on the wing : but after all abatements, their countryman is a glorious fellow.   It is one of my finest day-dreams to see him ere I die.

As you are fond of tears, I have sent you a fresh supply of Schiller.   His *Kabale und Liebe* will make you cry your fill.   That Ferdinand with his *Du Louise und ich und die Liebe* is a fine youth ; I liked him well—though his age is some five years less than mine.   You will also read Schiller's life : it is written by a sensible and well-informed but very dull man.   I forget his name—but Schiller once lived in his house—near Leipzig, I think.

That miserable farrago of mine on the same subject goes on as ill as anything can go.   I have been thrice on the point of burning it, and giving up the task in despair. Interruption upon interruption, so that I have scarcely an hour in the day at my disposal; and dulness thickening round me till all is black as Egypt when the darkness might be felt! There is nothing for it but the old song Patience! Patience! I *will* finish it. By the way, I wish you would think of the most striking passages you can recollect of in *Karlos, Wallenstein, Tell*, etc.: I design to give extracts and translations. Have them at your finger ends when you *come*.

CXXI.—From his MOTHER.

MAINHILL, 13*th April* 1823.

DEAR SON—I take the pen in my hand, however roughly I may handle it, for I am greatly in debt in this respect, but cannot pay off as I would; you will, I hope, take the will for the deed. I hope and look forward when we shall meet, if it please Providence, then I will thank you for all your kind letters and presents. I like to hear of your going to the bathing, I hope it will do you good if you do not go too deep. Will you be home, think you, before you go? Sandy has a sprightly little horse,—come home and get him, I think it would fit nicely. Tell me truly, are you stout, and is the book begun yet? I suppose you have little time for it at present. Dear me! what's Jack about? tell him to write me all his news, good or bad. I fear if you go to the country we will not get so many of your good epistles; they do me a great deal of good in comforting me in my old age; it is like reaping my harvest. May you be long in health and prosperity, a blessing to me and the rest of your friends. I believe if we would weigh our mercies with our crosses it would help to content us in our wilderness journey, for a wilderness this world is, though it is full of mercies from our kind Father.

We have fine weather, and are very throng[1] managing and getting in our crop. I need not tell you of the stormy winter; you would feel it; notwithstanding we are all alive and well, thank God! We have been rather uncommonly quiet this winter, and in general happy. We had no Servant but Jamie Aitken, till now we have got a man. Have you heard anything about Johnstone and Irving, how are they

---

[1] Busy.

coming on? tell us.   Tell Jack we advise him to come home; I think it will be better for his health; he can learn well enough here and get the country air, and we will be glad to see him to spend the Summer with us.   But it is growing dark, and I rather fear you scarce can read this scrawl.

So I add no more, but still remain your affectionate Mother,   MARGRET CARLYLE.

O could I but write!

CXXII.—To JOHN A. CARLYLE, Mainhill.

3 MORAY STREET, *9th May* 1823.

MY DEAR JACK—I had given up hopes of your letter for Wednesday night, when the Postman knocked his heavy knock, and sent me the wished-for tidings, a little after dusk.   I was heartily glad to learn that you had reached home so snugly, and found all our kind friends there in such a case.   Long, long may they be so!   We poor fellows have much to strive with; but there is always some sweetness mingled in our cup, while we have parents and brethren to befriend us and give us welcome with true right hands.

In pursuance of your order, as well as to gratify my individual inclinations, I have selected one of those long sheets, and placed myself down at the desk to tell you my news, or rather having so few to tell, to scribble for an hour to you, as if you were still sitting by me at tea in the gloaming, and I only obliged to talk with the pen instead of that more unruly member, which in sulky nights used to utter so many hard sayings.   I am better humoured this evening; and besides, Jack, we are sundered now by moors and mountains many a weary league, so that chatting together is a more moving business than it lately was.   We shall write *very* often during summer, and to some purpose I doubt not.

Having found such a reception at home, I have no doubt that you will feel reasonably happy during summer, will make no small progress in various useful studies, and what is still better, completely recover your goodly corporeal fabric, which under the sinister influences of this miserable place had certainly begun to suffer somewhat.   The only thing, as you well know, which can make and keep a rational creature happy is abundant employment; and this I feel certain, your sedulous and rather anxious disposition will not let you want. By the time I reach Mainhill, you will read me a leash of German, give me your opinion of Buffon, talk confidently about Anatomy and Chemistry, and know all *the doses* as well as Lavement himself did.

This is what may well be called "reading Gregory's *Conspectus:*" there is, you mind, another branch of study, that of "English Composition;" and for this also I have cared. Listen to me. Boyd and I have talked repeatedly about the French Novels *Elisabeth* and *Paul et Virginie:* we have at length come to a bargain. I have engaged that you, "the Universal Pan," shall translate them both in your best style (I overlooking the manuscript, and correcting the Press), and receive for so doing the sum of £20 : the whole to be ready about August next. You will get the French copies and the existing translations, by Farries ; and then, I read you, betake yourself to the duty with might and main. I have no doubt you will do it in a sufficient manner. You have only to consult the old copy at any dubious point, and never to be squeamish in imitating it. All that Boyd wants is a reasonable translation, which no one can prosecute him for printing. Those already before the public are very good, I understand, particularly that of *Elisabeth* by Bowles, and I need not advise you to read it over carefully before commencing, and study as much as may be not to fall below it. I was happy in getting this task for you, on various accounts. In the first place, it is a very favourable method of training yourself in the art of composition ; secondly, it will serve to put some " money in your purse ;" and thirdly, it will vastly increase your comfort and *respectability* at Mainhill during Summer. This last is what I chiefly look to : a young man of any spirit is apt to vex himself with many groundless imaginations while in such circumstances as yours, to think he is useless and burdensome and what not ; for all which, there is no remedy equal to giving him some work *to keep his hand in use*, and tie the limbs of Fancy, while those of real industry are kept in motion. In this respect I trust the task will not be without its use to you. For the rest, never trouble your heart about the difficulties of it. I saw by your operations last year on *Legendre*, and I judge by the improvement you have since made, that you are quite equal to such a thing: and at the very worst, I can brush away all the impurities of your work with my critical besom in less than no time. So be content, my good Jack, with this " day of small things," go through it calmly and diligently, looking on it as the earnest of better and more weighty enterprises that are to follow. I expect that you and I are yet to write mighty tomes in concert.

There never was such a *blethering bitch* as I. There is the end of my sheet, and not one word said about my news or anything I meant to write about. Tell my ever-kind and dear Mother, that I am in very truth all but quite healthy. There is next to no disease about me, only vexed nerves, which the multiplied irritations of this city vex still further. I have not tasted drugs since you left me. With quiet usage in the country for six months, I feel confident, I should be completely well. And thither we are going soon! The Buller family set out on Thursday first, and I follow them at my leisure a few days after. Since you went off I have been unusually well. The first day or so I was rather surly; but I took to reading vehemently, and the evil spirit left me. I am now quite contented, as I used to be last year. At any rate I have no time to be otherwise: there is such regulating and arranging as you never knew, I am kept busy from morn to night. *Wilhelm Meister* I have almost engaged to translate: Schiller also is to go on: what scribbling I shall have! I have grown better ever since we parted—to-day and yesterday I bathed: it was very fine.

But I must close this despicable rag of a letter, and engage to send you another before I leave Town. How I long to see all the world at Mainhill! Give my heartfelt love to every one of them young and old. I expect to hear from Alick by Farries, and constantly throughout the season: his late silence I excuse for the sake of his seed-time labours, and well I may. Tell my Mother she must take tea every night. I do not think I shall want any socks; but she shall hear in time if I do. Tell my Father that it is *his* time to write, he is in my debt and

cannot pay me a minute *o'er soon*.   Remember me kindly
to Graham : give my services to the poetess and all our
beloved sisters and brothers *nominatim*.   Excuse this
miserable scrawl : I am hurried to death, but always yours,

TH. CARLYLE.

Get blacker ink next time, and be a *canny bairn*.   Tell
Sandy to write and *not* to send the pony till he hear.

CXXIII.—To Rev. THOMAS MURRAY, Edinburgh.

KINNAIRD HOUSE,[1] 17*th June* 1823.

My DEAR MURRAY—In due time I was favoured with
your letter, the first I had received since my arrival ; the first
tangible proof, that in removing from the country of all my
friends, I had not also removed from their recollections.
Finding the commissions you had undertaken all discharged
with your accustomed kindness and fidelity, I had nothing
further to do but abandon myself to the cheerful feelings
with which your articles of news and speculation and other
curious and pleasant matter naturally enough inspired me.
Your letters have a charm to me independently of their
intrinsic merit ; they are letters of my first and oldest correspondent ; they carry back the mind to old days—days in
themselves perhaps not greatly better than those now passing
over us—but invested by the kind treachery of Imagination
with hues which nothing present can equal.   If I have any
fault to find with you, it is in the very excess of what renders
any correspondence agreeable ; the excess of your com-
plaisance, the too liberal oblations which you offer at the

---

[1] In a bit of unprinted reminiscences Carlyle thus describes Kinnaird
House and his life there ;—" In Perthshire, about a mile below the junction
of Tay and Tummel, not far below the mouth of Killiecrankie Pass. . . .
I lodged and slept in the *old* mansion, a queer, old-fashioned, snug enough,
entirely secluded edifice, sunk among trees, about a gunshot from the new
big House ; hither I came to smoke about twice or thrice in the daytime ;
had a good oak-wood fire at night, and sat in a seclusion, in a silence not
to be surpassed above ground.   I was writing *Schiller*, translating *Meister* ;
my health, in spite of my diligent riding, grew worse and worse ; thoughts
all wrapt in gloom, in weak dispiritment and discontent, wandering mourn-
fully to my loved ones far away ; *letters* to and from, it may well be
supposed, were my most genial solacement.   At times, too, there was
something of noble in my sorrow, in the great solitude among the rocking
winds ; but not often."

shrine of other people's vanity. I might object to this with more asperity, did I not consider that flattery is in truth the sovereign emollient, the true oil of life, by which the joints of the great social machine, often stiff and rusty enough, are kept from grating and made to play sweetly to and fro ; hence that if you pour it on a thought too lavishly, it is an error on the safe side, an error which proceeds from the native warmness of your heart, and ought not to be quarrelled with too sharply, not at least by one who profits though unduly by the commission of it. So I will submit to be treated as a kind of slender genius, since my friend will have it so : our intercourse will fare but little worse on that account. We have now, as you say, known each other long, and never, I trust, seen aught to make us feel ashamed of that relation : I calculate that succeeding years will but more firmly establish our connection, strengthening with the force of habit and the memory of new kind offices what has a right to subsist without these aids. Some time hence, when you are seated in your peaceful manse, you at one side of the parlour fire, Mrs. M. at the other, and two or three little M.'s, fine chubby urchins, hopping about the carpet, you will suddenly observe the door fly open, and a tall meagre care-worn figure stalk forward, his grim countenance lightened by unusual smiles, in the certainty of meeting with a cordial welcome. This knight of the rueful visage will in fact mingle with the group for a season ; and be merry as the merriest, though his looks are sinister. I warn you to make provision for such emergencies. In process of time, I too must have my own peculiar hearth ; wayward as my destiny has hitherto been, perplexed and solitary as my path of life still is, I never cease to reckon on yet paying scot and lot on my own footing. Like the men of Glasgow I shall have " a house *within myself*" (what tremendous *abdomina* we householders have !) with every suitable appurtenance, before all is done ; and when friends are met, there is little chance that Murray will be forgotten. We shall talk over old times, compare old hopes with new fortune ; and secure comfort by Sir John Sinclair's celebrated recipe, by *being comfortable.* These are certainly brave times : would they could only be persuaded to come on a little faster.

But I must quit empty imagining, and set before you

some specific "facts." You want to be informed how I spend my time here, and what novelties I have discovered in the country of the Celts. As to my time, it passes in the most jocund and unprofitable manner you can figure. I have no professional labour to encounter that deserves being named; I am excellently lodged, and experience nothing but suitable treatment in all points. There are plenty of books too, and paper and geese; there are mountains of mica-slate, and woods and green pastures and clear waters and azure skies to look at : I read, or write and burn, at rare intervals; I go scampering about on horseback, or lie down by the grassy slopes of the Tay, and look at Schiehallion and Bengloe with their caps of snow, and all the ragged monsters that keep watch around them, since the creation never stirring from their post; I dream all kinds of empyrean dreams, and live as idly as if I were a considerable proprietor of land. Such work, of course, will never do at the long run, and pity that it will not, for it passes very smoothly : but I strive to still my conscience when it murmurs by persuading it that "the poor man is getting back his health." An arrant lie ! for I am not getting back my health ; I do not think I shall ever more be healthy, nor does it matter greatly. By and by I shall have learned to go on very quietly without that convenience : I am fast training to it. . . .

You must come and see this country the first month you have at your own disposal. Dunkeld is about the prettiest village I ever beheld. I shall not soon forget the bright sunset, when skirting the base of " Birnam Wood " (there is no wood now), and asking for " Dunsinane's high hill," which lies far to the eastward, and thinking of the immortal link-boy who has consecrated these two spots which he never saw, with a glory that is bright, peculiar, and for ever,— I first came in sight of the ancient capital of Caledonia standing in the lap of the mountains, with its quick broad river rushing by, its old gray cathedral, and its peak-roofed white houses peering through massy groves and stately trees, all gilded from the glowing west. The whole so clear and pure and gorgeous as if it had been a city of fairy-land, not a vulgar *dachan* where men sell stots,[1] and women buy eggs

----

[1] Steers.

by the dozen.   I wandered round and round it till late, the evening I left you.   You must come and see this spot, if you should go no farther.

My paper is done, or I was going to have told you multitudes of things besides.   I beg you will write me soon, some leisure hour, and let me have another chance at talking.   I have still some hopes of seeing you in Edinburgh before you leave it—perhaps before the end of July.   Meantime I long for news of you and it and everything.   Nothing but dumb silence here, and the chicking is heard no more.[1] What are you doing or about to do?   What writing, or what studying?   How is it with the Earl of Stair, and with the world in general?   Except for a *Dumfries Courier* and a *Daily Times*, I might as well be living in the fifth Belt of Jupiter.   Adieu !—Truly yours,

TH. CARLYLE.

CXXIV.—To Miss WELSH, Haddington.

KINNAIRD HOUSE, 1st July 1823.

. . . There is in fact, I see it more clearly every day, nothing but literature that will serve to make your life agreeable or useful.   In your actual situation you have two things to choose between : you may be a fashionable lady, the ornament of drawing-rooms and festive parties in your native district, the wife of some prosperous man who will love you well and provide for you all that is choicest in the entertainment of common minds ; or you may take the pursuit of truth and mental beauty for your highest good, and trust to fortune, be it good or bad, for the rest.   The choice is important, and requires your most calm and serious reflection.   Nevertheless, I think you have decided like a prudent woman no less than like a heroine.   I dare not promise that your life will be free from sorrows ; for minds like yours deep sorrows are reserved, take the world as you will : but you will also have noble pleasures, and the great intention of your being will be accomplished.   As a fashionable fine lady, on the other hand, I do not see how you

---

[1] Carlyle used to tell of a preacher who compared death to the breaking of the main-spring of a watch, " and the chicking (*Anglice*, ticking) is heard no more."

could get through the world on even moderate terms : a few
years at most would quite sicken you of such a life; you
would begin by becoming wretched, and end by ceasing to
be amiable.

.   .   .   .   .   .

I am fast losing any little health I was possessed of :
some days I suffer as much pain as would drive about three
Lake poets down to Tartarus; but I have long been trained
in a sterner school; besides by nature I am of the *cat* genus,
and like every cat, I have nine lives.   I shall not die therefore, but unless I take some prudent resolution, I shall do
worse. . . .

Never mind me, my good Jane : allow me to fight with
the paltry evils of my lot as best I may; and if I cannot
beat them down, let me go to the Devil as in right I should.

.   .   .   .   .   .

CXXV.—To Rev. Thomas Murray, Wigton,
Galloway.

MAINHILL, *8th August* 1823.

My DEAR MURRAY—I received your two letters in due
succession, and great cause I had to commend your friendly
activity in my behalf.   The virtue of punctuality makes
little figure in treatises of Ethics, but it is of essential importance in the conduct of life; like common kitchen-salt,
scarce heeded by cooks and purveyors, though without it
their wares would soon run to rottenness and ruin.   You
have managed these Book-concerns admirably; it is very
probable that *in return* for your diligence in that matter I
may ere long trouble again.

A more suitable *return* would have been to comply with
your friendly wish to see me in Galloway during this your
holiday excursion.   I have thought of it frequently since
my arrival here; at one time I had well-nigh determined
on treating myself with that delicacy; but the wet weather
made my resolutions waver, and the lateness of your visit has
at length forced them to settle on the other side.   I must be
at Kinnaird on this day se'ennight; I have yet seen no
friend in Annandale, except those under my Father's roof :
judge then if *I can* set out for your native district when so

circumstanced.   I have still about fifty ways to go, and having a horse to take with me to the North, I am compelled to set out about Wednesday next, that I may not break down the "gallant gray" before seeing Perthshire. Therefore you must excuse me for this once.   Next year, unless the fates have written it otherwise, I intend that we shall ride in company through the whole length and breadth of Brave Galloway, and spend ten days together in seeing all manner of sights and talking all manner of talk.   Meanwhile I can only wish you may have better luck than I have had ; may find fair skies and pleasant faces everywhere to welcome you, that so you may refresh your faculties of head and heart for another and a busy winter in the city of stench and science (the *focush*[1] of both), where I hope to see you many a, many a merry time.

This last month has been among the idlest and barrenest of my existence.   My chief pleasure and employment has been galloping, nowhither, amid wind and rain, for the mere sake of galloping.   The weather !   The weather ! If it were not that all men, women, and children in the British Islands have exclaimed ten times a-day for the last six weeks : " Bless me ! *such* weather !" I too would say something very pithy on the subject.   But what would it avail ?   Let it rain guns and bayonets if it like ; the less I say of it the better.

See that you get along with Stair and these worthies without delay.   There is nothing in this world that will keep the Devil out of one but hard labour.   Of *my* devils at least I may say : this kind goeth *not* out by fasting and prayer.   I will get the weather-gage of him yet. . . .

Jack and I are for Annan spite of the clouds and glar ;[2] he is fidgeting like some hen in an interesting condition.   So I must leave you for the present.

.   .   .   .   .   .

I am, always most faithfully yours,

THOMAS CARLYLE.

---

[1] " An old bankrupt minister had, while staying with Murray, always referred to Edinburgh as the ' focus (which he pronounced *focush*) of Society.' "
[2] Mud.

CXXVI.—To Miss Welsh, Haddington.[1]

Mainhill, 10th August 1823.

. . . Have you actually "admonished" the great Centre of Attraction? If not, wait for two months, and you will see his "raven locks and eagle eye" as you have done of old, and may admonish him by word of mouth. I was at Annan; and found *the* Argument for Judgment to Come, in a clear type, just arrived, and news that Irving himself was returning soon to the North—to be married! The lady is Miss Martin of Kirkcaldy—so said his Mother. On the whole I am sorry that Irving's preaching has taken such a turn. It had been much better, if without the gross[2] pleasure of being a newspaper Lion and a season's wonder, he had gradually become, what he must ultimately pass for, a preacher of first-rate abilities, of great eloquence and great absurdity,[3] with a head fertile above all others in sense and nonsense, and a heart of the most honest and kindly sort. As it is, our friend incurs the risk of many vagaries and disasters, and at best the certainty of much disquietude. His path is steadfast and manly, in general only when he has to encounter opposition and misfortune; when fed with flatteries and prosperity, his progress soon changes into "ground and lofty tumbling," accompanied with all the hazards and confusion that usually attend this species of movement.[4] With three newspapers to praise him and three to blame, with about six peers and six dozen Right Honourables introduced to him every Sunday, tickets issuing for his church as if it were a theatre, and all the devout old women of the Capital treating him with comfits and adulation, I know that ere now he is "striking the stars with his sublime head:" well if he do not break his shins among the rough places of the ground! I wish we saw him safely down again, and walking as other men walk. The comfort is he has a true heart and genuine talents: so I conclude that after infinite flounderings and pitchings in the mud he will at last settle much about his true place,

---

[1] The greater part of the following extract is printed by Mr. Froude.

[2] "Gross" omitted by Mr. Froude.

[3] "And great absurdity" omitted by Mr. Froude.

[4] "Movement" appears as "condiment" in Mr. Froude's copy.

just as if this uproar had never taken place. For the rest, if he does not write to his friends, the reason is, not that he has ceased to love them, but that his mind is full of tangible interests continually before his face. With him at any time the present is worth twenty times the past and the future; and such a present as this he never witnessed before. I could wager any money that he thinks of you and me very often, though he never writes to either; and that he longs above all to know what we do think of this monstrous flourishing of drums and trumpets in which he lives and moves.[1] I have meant to write to him very frequently for almost three months; but I know not well how to effect it. He will be talking about "the Lord" and twenty other things, which he himself only wishes to believe, and which to one that knows and loves him are truly painful to hear. See that you do not think unkindly of him; for except myself, there is scarcely a man in the world that feels more true concern for you.[2]

Happy Irving[3] that is fitted with a task which he loves and is equal to! He entertains no doubt that he is battering to its base the fortress of the Alien, and lies down every night to dream of planting the old true blue Presbyterian flag upon the summit of the ruins.

.   .   .   .   .   .

CXXVII.—To his MOTHER, Mainhill.

EDINBURGH, 19th August 1823.

MY DEAR MOTHER—Before leaving this miserable city, in which I have been destined to experience so many vexations first and last, I determined in packing up my great-coat to enclose a piece of tartan in it to make you a cloak of. It was the best I could find; but surely the knaves have made me take nearly twice as much as was required. You can make yourself a substantial covering from the winter wind out of it in the first [place], and turn the rest into a scarf or whatsoever you think fittest. Wear it when you go to Church or Market, in bad weather, and

---

[1] From "The comfort is" to "and moves" omitted by Mr. Froude.
[2] This sentence is omitted by Mr. Froude.
[3] The words "after all" are inserted here by Mr. Froude.

think with yourself that never mortal was more welcome to all the accommodation such a thing can afford, or more deserving of it at my hands. These little things are of no importance in themselves; but as pledges of mindfulness and affection, they become more valuable than aught else. Wear this, then, for my sake.

I purposed sending down a great-coat for my father; but none could I find of a suitable sort, under about three pounds price; and I doubted if some other more suitable gift could not be got for such a sum. I have therefore postponed the purchase of this, till I hear from home. I wish you would endeavour in a *clandestick* way to ascertain what had best be done. I am *determined* to send my worthy Father a gift of some kind: the only thing now is to decide what would be of most service to him. Tell me about it, or make Jack tell me: but mention no syllable of it to the goodman.

I have the worst of pens, and my hand is very unsteady; besides I am just about to set forth on my journey. I have been lucky in the weather; but as usual very much disturbed in my sleep. I wish I were at Kinnaird, since I have left Mainhill. Farewell, my dear Mother; you shall come and order my *cottage* for me yet. Sick or whole, I am ever your affectionate son,

TH. CARLYLE.

CXXVIII.—To Miss WELSH, Haddington.

KINNAIRD HOUSE, 18*th September* 1823.

. . . I was looking out, while there, in the valley of Milk, for some cottage among trees, beside the still waters; some bright little place, with a stable behind it, a garden, and a rood of green—where I might fairly commence housekeeping, and the writing of books! They laughed at me, and said it was a joke. Well! I swear it is a lovely world this, after all. What a pity that we had not *five* score years and ten of it!

Meanwhile I go on with Goethe's *Wilhelm Meister*: a book which I love not, which I am sure will never sell, but which I am determined to print and finish. There are touches of the very highest most ethereal genius in it; but diluted

with floods of insipidity, which even *I* would not have
written for the world.   I sit down to it every night at six,
with the ferocity of a hyæna ; and in spite of all obstructions
my keep-lesson is more than half through the first volume,
and travelling over poetry and prose, slowly but surely to
the end.   Some of the poetry is very bad, some of it rather
good.   The following is mediocre—the worst kind.

> " Who never ate his bread in sorrow,
>   Who never spent the darksome hours
>   Weeping, and watching for the morrow,
>   He knows you not, ye gloomy Powers.
>
> " To Earth, this weary Earth, ye bring us,
>   To guilt ye let us heedless go,
>   Then leave repentance fierce to wring us ;
>   A moment's guilt, an age of woe !"

.   .   .   .   .   .

CXXIX.—To Mr. James Johnstone, Broughty Ferry, Dundee.

Kinnaird House, 21st September 1823.

My dear Johnstone—I have already been guilty of a
sin of omission in neglecting so long to send you a letter ;
I fear I shall now only change it into one of commission by
writing to you in the dullest style that ever man used to
man.   The weather is as delightfully dripping to-day as it
has been constantly for the last ten weeks ; I am solitary,
idle, or disgusted with my work ; and cheerful, warm, and
inspiriting as the Greenland Moon.   Nevertheless, being
very anxious to learn how it fares with you, and finding
that you will not write till I set you the example, I attack
you in spite of all disadvantages.

How *has* that Cupar concern been finally decided—for
decided it must needs be ere this?   Are you to go thither,
or to Dundee, or Annandale, or whither?   Is your health
good?   Your spirits?   How is the world wagging with you
in all its various departments?   Such are the questions
which I wish to be resolved about, with all the speed
imaginable.   I beg you will tell me ; it will do us both
good.   It is a mournful thing to sit solitary even in joys :

how much more when our lot is deeply tinged with woes and difficulties and distresses which often render life a very sorry piece of business. Be assured, my old friend, this case can never be yours while I live, and retain my right judgment about me. Few scenes of my life are more innocently pleasing than those I have passed with you; and the world abounds not so plentifully with deserving people, that I should forget the earliest, almost the only early friend I have. Oh! why cannot I cut out eight years from the past and return to A.D. 1815! We were so cheery then, so busy, so strong of heart, and full of hope! You observe I am verging to the Lake School in sentiment? I will leave it then.

My journey to Annandale, and stay there, offered nothing in the least surprising. It rained *every* day while I was at home; so I could stir nowhither from Mainhill. My only excursions were two to Annan, in the last of which I returned by Ruthwell. The fashion of this world passeth away! All seemed changed at Ruthwell; Mitchell was not there; Mrs. D. was absent; his reverence and myself were the only interlocutors; and before we got over the threshold of our conversation, it was time for me to rise and ride. I was twice at Bogside, and had many kind inquiries to answer about you, there as well as elsewhere. They wanted to know if you were coming; if you were going, if, etc. etc. Did you get the letter left for you at the Post-office of Dunkeld? I forgot to leave it at Perth. You should write to them without loss of time.

On returning hither I brought out an *elegant* gray pony with me, intending to drive indigestion out of me by dint of riding on it. While at home, I recovered very fast. On the road I was annoyed to the verge of death, by blackguards and whiteguards, noises, slutteries, and all kinds of devilry. Here I am not improving, let me ride as I will. If Satan would be kind enough to carry all the *billusness* of this planet down with him to Tophet, and keep it there for the use of his boarders, it would be a great improvement in this best of all possible worlds. Patience! Patience! that is the eternal song. I wish only that Disease were a *living thing*, with a tangible carcase, though hideous as the Hyrcanean tiger, that I might grapple with it face to face, and trample it and tread it into atoms, and cast it on the waters and make all the people drink of them ! ! !

In the meantime I am busily engaged every night in translating Goethe's *Wilhelm Meister :* a task which I have undertaken formally and must proceed with, though it suits me little. There is poetry in the book, and prose, prose for ever. When I read of players and libidinous actresses and their sorry pasteboard apparatus for beautifying and enlivening the " Moral world," I render it into grammatical English—with a feeling mild and charitable as that of a starving hyæna. The book is to be printed in Winter or Spring. No mortal will ever buy a copy of it. *N'importe !* I have engaged with it to keep the fiend from preying on my vitals, and with that sole view I go along with it. Goethe is the greatest genius that has lived for a century, and the greatest ass that has lived for three. I could sometimes fall down and worship him ; at other times I could kick him out of the room. . . .

The people talk of staying here all winter ; an arrangement which I by no means like : it is solitary and very dull. They then wish me to go with them to Cornwall in the month of May. If they were not civil, nay kind to me beyond measure, I should have left them ere now. As it is, I am in doubts what should be done. The Post is here ! Adieu, my dear friend ! Write me instantly and tell me *every*thing—everything !—I am, always your true and old friend,

TH. CARLYLE.

Write instanter !

CXXX.—To his MOTHER, Mainhill.

KINNAIRD HOUSE, 28th September 1823.

. . . We are a most fluctuating people, we of Kinnaird. At the beginning of autumn, it was settled that the juniors of us should go to Edinburgh in winter, the others remaining here ; after which one youth was to go to Germany, the other to Oxford, and I to take my leave I supposed for ever and a day. It now appears that we are not to go to Edinburgh, that Arthur need not go to Germany unless perfectly convenient, and that Charlie is learning far better with me than he would have any chance to do at the "southern seat of the Muses." So they have formally asked me if I am willing to accompany them in spring down into Cornwall, where they mean to settle till their sons are educated! I said that but on the score of health I had no manner of objection. This they professed their extreme readiness to do all in their power towards remedying. It appears probable, therefore, that after Whitsunday I may take a farther jaunt to the southward. One thing I am determined on: to have my *own house* if I go thither. I mean to take lodgings if any are to be had near—if not I will almost venture to furnish *the* Cottage I have been speaking of so often. For a man of my habits and health, it is very sweet to sit by his own hearth—or some friend's which he may call his own. . . .

Thus I am to spend the winter among the highland hills. I shall finish my translation (with which I go on as regularly as clockwork) about February or so; in March or April I must solicit leave of absence for a couple of months to get it printed in Edinburgh; then I shall come galloping down to see you all for three or four weeks; and then dispose of myself according to circumstances. . . .

To-day there came no paper; an omission which in this your most busy season I can very easily excuse. I spent the day in reading part of Irving's *Sermons*, which I have not finished. On the whole he should not have published it—till after a considerable time. There is strong talent in it, true eloquence, and vigorous thought: but the foundation is rotten, and the building itself is a kind of monster in architecture—beautiful in parts—vast in dimensions—but on the whole decidedly a monster. Buller has stuck in the middle of it—"can't fall in with your friend at all, Mr. Carlyle"—Mrs. Buller is very near sticking. Sometimes I burst right out a-laughing, when reading it; at other times I admired it sincerely. Irving himself I expect to see ere long, though at present I suspect I am a little in disfavour with him. On arriving here I found a letter from him, written (as I found only a little while ago) just two days after the date of mine; to which at first I took it for an answer. On this hypothesis, the thing had rather a cold look; there was very little in it, and that little taken up with assurances to his "Scottish friends" that he *had* not forgot them, the whole carrying an air of *Protection* with it, which rather amused me.   So one day when very bilious I wrote a reply of a rather *bilious* character, giving him to know by various indirect and pleasant methods that to certain of his "Scottish friends," his forgetting or remembrance was not a thing that would kill or keep alive.   I also told him my *true* opinion of his Book—a favourable one, but some thousand degrees below his own.   We have had no further communication.   I love Irving, and am his debtor for many kind feelings and acts.   He is one of the best men breathing : but I will not give his vanity one inch of swing in my company; he may get the fashionable women and the multitude of young men whom no one knoweth, to praise and flatter—not I one iota beyond his genuine merits. . . .

CXXXI.—To John A. Carlyle, Edinburgh.

KINNAIRD HOUSE, *20th October* 1823.

. . . I staid from Monday night till Thursday morning last with Johnstone.   I had gone thither to meet Edward Irving and his spouse, though I did not effect this object till I returned to Dunkeld. . . . He himself is the same man as ever, only his mind seems churned into a foam by the late agitations, and is yielding a plentiful scum of vanities and harmless affectations.   The hair of his head is like Nebuchadnezzar's when taken in from grass : he puckers up his face into various seamy peaks, rolls his eyes, and puffs like a blast-furnace ; talking abundantly a flood of things, the body of which is nonsense, but intermingled with sparkles of curious thinking, and tinctured with his usual flow of warm-hearted generosity and honest affection. We talked and debated, and the time went pleasantly along. He was for me up to London with him, for three months in summer, to see the world, that so I might begin writing in good earnest.   I said nay—the offer being incompatible at present with my other engagements, and at any rate savouring too much of patronage to suit my taste.   He is a kind, good man, with many great qualities, but with absurdities of almost equal magnitude.   He meditates things in which he must evidently fail ; but being what he is, he must always retain a high place in the estimation of a certain portion of the public. He and his beloved are returning to Annan in a week or two, where they purpose to make some stay. I shall always wish him well : as men go, I know of no one like him.

"Schiller's Life and Writings" is printed in the last number of the *London Magazine*. The Editor sent me a letter full of that "essential oil "—flattery, and desiring to have the remainder of the piece without delay. Goethe is in consequence suspended. I begin "Schiller," Part II., to-morrow, if I can. Whenever I am done with it, I will be down with you in Edinburgh to settle about many things which you have to do for me in winter, and see how you are coming on. This, I take it, will be about the middle of November. . . .

CXXXII.—To Miss WELSH, Haddington.

KINNAIRD HOUSE, *22d October* 1823.

. . . He [Irving] figured out purposes of unspeakable profit to me, which when strictly examined all melted into empty air. He seemed to think that if set down on London streets some strange development of genius would take place in me, that by conversing with Coleridge and the Opium-eater, I should find out new channels for speculation, and soon learn to speak with tongues. There is but very small degree of truth in all this. Of genius (bless the mark !) I never imagined in the most lofty humours that I possessed beyond the smallest perceptible fraction ; and this fraction be it little or less can only be turned to account by rigid and stern perseverance through long years of labour, in London or any other spot in the Universe. With a scanty modicum of health, a little freedom from the low perplexities of vulgar life, with friends and peace, I might do better ; but these are not to be found by travelling towards any quarter of the compass that I know of ; so we must try what can be done with our present very short allowance of them. Untiring perseverance, stubborn effort is the remedy : help cometh not from the hills or valleys.

On the whole our friend's mind seems to have improved but little since he left us.   He is as full as ever of a certain hearty unrefined goodwill, for which I honour him as I have always done : his faculties also have been quickened in the hot-bed of Hatton Garden, but affectation and vanity have grown up as rankly as other worthier products.   It does me ill to see a strong and generous spirit distorting itself into a thousand foolish shapes ; putting wilfully on the fetters of a thousand prejudices, very weak though very sanctified ; dwindling with its own consent from a true and manly figure into something far too like a canting preacher of powerful sermons.   He mistakes too : this popularity is different from fame.   The fame of a genuine man of letters is like the radiance of another star added to the galaxy of intellect to shine there for many ages ; the popularity of a pulpit orator is like a tar-barrel set up in the middle of the street to blaze with a fierce but very tarnished flame for a few hours, and then go out in a cloud of sparkles and thick smoke offensive to the lungs and noses of the whole neighbourhood.   Our friend must order matters otherwise. Unless he look to it, he bids fair for becoming a turgid rather than a grand character ; a kind of theological braggadocio, an enlarged edition of the Rev. Rowland Hill, but no great man, more than I or any other of the King's liege subjects.   However, as the preachers say, " I hope better things, though I thus speak."   I expect something from the prudence of his wife ; more from the changes of fortune that await him.   There is a strong current of honest manly affection and wholesome feeling running beneath all this sorry scum ; perhaps a clearance will take place in due time.   I love the man with all his nonsense, I was *wae* to part with him. . . .

CXXXIII.—To ALEXANDER CARLYLE, Mainhill.

KINNAIRD HOUSE, *2d November* 1823.

MY DEAR ALICK—Having an hour and a half at my disposal to-day, and an opportunity of conveyance, I hesitate not, though rather stupid, to sit down and send you some inkling of my news.   This is the more necessary, as it seems possible enough that ere long some change may take place in my situation ; of which I would not have you altogether unapprised.

Your little fragment of a letter was gratifying by the news it brought me that you are busy in your speculations, lucky hitherto, and bent on persevering. I cannot but commend your purpose. There is not on the earth so horrible a malady as idleness, voluntary or constrained. Well said Byron : " Quiet to quick bosoms is a hell." So long as you are conscious of adding to your stock of knowledge· or other useful qualities, and feel that your faculties are fitly occupied, the mind is active and contented. As to the issue of these traffickings, I pray you. my good boy, not at all to mind it. Care not one rush about that silly cash, which to me has no value whatever, except for its use to you. Pride may say several things to you ; but do you tell her she has nothing to meddle or make in the case : I am as proud in my own way as you ; but what any brethren of our Father's house [may possess] I look on as a common stock, mine as much as theirs, from which all are entitled to draw, whenever their convenience requires it. Feelings far nobler than pride are . my guides in such matters. Are we not all friends by habit and by nature ? If it were not for Mainhill, I should still find myself in some degree *alone* in this weary world.

Jack's German "all goes well" appeared on the newspaper last but one : I have vainly sought for it on the last. I suppose he is gone to Edinburgh, or just going ; and I hope ere long to have that solacing announcement repeated more in detail. I understand the crop is now in the yard ; I trust that it bids fair to produce as it ought ; that you have now got in the potatoes also, and made your arrangements for passing the winter as snugly as honest hearts and active hands may enable you. Above all, I trust that our dear Mother and the rest are enjoying that first of blessings, bodily health, without which spiritual contentment is a thing not once to be dreamed of. As for us of Kinnaird, we are plodding forward in the old inconstant and not too comfortable style. The winter is setting in upon us ; these old black ragged ridges to the west have put on their frozen caps, and the sharp breezes that come sweeping across them are loaded with cold. I cannot say that I delight in this.   My " Bower " is the most polite of bowers, refusing admittance to no wind that blows from any quarter of the ship-man's card.   It is scarcely larger than your room at Mainhill, yet has three windows and of course a door ; all shrunk and crazy : the walls too are pierced with many crevices ; for the mansion has been built by Highland masons, apparently in a remote century.   Nevertheless I put on my gray duffle sitting *jupe ;* I bullyrag the sluttish harlots of the place, and cause them make fires that would melt a stithy.   Against this evil, therefore, I contrive to make a formidable front. . . .

I believe I mentioned to Jack that they had printed a pitiful performance of mine, Schiller's " Life," Part I., in the *London Magazine ;* and sent very pressingly for the continuation of it.   In consequence, I threw by my translation, and betook me to preparing this notable piece of Biography.   But such a humour as I write it in ! . . . What my next movements may be, I am unable to say positively.   I must have my Book (the translation) printed in Edinburgh, but first it must be ready.   It is not impossible that I may come down to Mainhill for a couple of months till I finish it.   Perhaps after all I may give up my resolution and continue where I am, though on the most solemn deliberation, I do not think such a determination can come to good.   Next time I write you will hear more.   Anyway you are likely to see me ere long : I must be in Edinburgh shortly, to arrange with Brewster and others.   Whether I leave this place finally or not, I have settled that poor Bardolph must winter at Mainhill.   A better pony never munched oats than that stubborn Galloway.   But they are hungering him here ; he gets no meat but musty hay and a mere memorial of corn every day ; so he is very faint and chastened in spirit compared with what he was.   Out upon it ! the spendthrift *is* better than the miser ; anything is better. . . .

I meant to write to my Father ; but this stomach has prevented me.   Give my kindest love to him and our good Mother, and all the souls about home.   Tell my Mother to take no anxiety on herself about me, lest anything serious happen to me : at present, two weeks of Annandale air would make me as well as she has seen me for many years.

Good-night, my dear Alick! My candle is lit, yet I have not dined, the copper captain being out riding. Write to me the first moment you have, and advise Jack to do it if with you still.—I am, always your faithful Brother,

T. CARLYLE.

CXXXIV.—To JOHN A. CARLYLE, Edinburgh.

KINNAIRD HOUSE, 11*th November* 1823.

. . . You inquire about your general reading; concerning which I regret that I have so little space here for discussing it. There can be no objection to your reading Gibbon, provided you feel spirit enough in you for undertaking at leisure hours so heavy a task as twelve volumes of substantial reading. It is likely to awaken you, read it when you will. History, you have heard me say a thousand times, is the basis of all true general knowledge; and Gibbon is the most strong-minded of all historians. Perhaps, however, you had better let him be till summer; for he will require all your thought, and at present you have it not all to spare. General literature, as it is called, seems the best thing for you in winter—amusing, instructive, easy. You know the English classics by name : it is little matter in what order you begin them. Johnson's *Life of Boerhaave* you may get; it is, as well as several other lives, the production of his first literary years, therefore slight and trivial compared with his later performances. But nothing that Samuel wrote is unworthy of perusal : I recommend his works especially to your notice ; they are full of *wisdom*, which is quite a different thing and a far better one than mere knowledge. You will like him better the older you grow. Swift is also a first-rate fellow : his *Gulliver*, and *Tale of a Tub*, and many of his smaller pieces, are inimitable in their way. Have you read all Shakespeare? Have you read Fielding's novels? they are genuine things ; though if you were not a decent fellow, I should pause before recommending them, their morality is so loose. Smollett's too are good and bad in a similar style and degree. One of your first leisure afternoons should be devoted to *Don Quixote :* it is a classic of Europe, one of the finest books in nature. Did you ever see Boswell's *Life of Johnson?*

There is a "British Theatre," of which you may read a play or two whenever you feel in the vein. Peter's *Letters to his Kinsfolk*, a worthless book, will give you some idea of the state of literature in Edinburgh at this time : it was in great vogue three years ago, but is now dead as mutton. Then there are poets new and old; Mason's Gray (very good and diverting), Prior (not amiss), Pope (eminently good), in short Campbell's *Specimens of the British Poets* (which you should read immediately—at least vol. i.) will give you names enough of this kind : the living names are Byron, Scott (nearly done), Southey, Coleridge (very great but rather mystical, sometimes absurd), Wordsworth (much talked of), Moore's *Lalla Rookh*, Rogers, Milman, etc. etc. In prose we have Hazlitt (worth little, though clever), Southey (for history), Washington Irving, etc. etc. Poor Washington is dead three months ago ![1] I almost shed a tear when I heard it : it was a dream of mine that we two should be friends ! On the subject of these studies I will tell you more when we meet. . . .

When I may see you cannot yet be settled to a day or a week. I shall not start till I am done *at least* with Part II. of "Schiller." I get on with it dreadfully slow : I am now almost half-done with writing it the second time— often harder than the first ; some nights I am fitter for the hospital than the writing-desk ; all nights (and I never get it touched till then) I am sick and stupid and done, as never man was that persisted in such a task. Nevertheless I do persist, and will do while I live. . . .

CXXXV.—From his MOTHER.

MAINHILL, 15th November 1823.

MY DEAR SON—It is a long time since I wrote you. I am deeply in arrears, nor do I hope to get clear at this time, but I hope you will take the will for the deed. I can tell you, however feebly, that I am in my ordinary way of health—much about as when you left us : which I ought to be thankful for, but cannot as I ought, yet I am still spared a monument of mercy. I am just come from sermon, and am thinking where Jack and you have been

---

[1] A false report.

attending, or whether attending at all, you are much in my thoughts, particularly on the Sabbath mornings. This scene shall soon pass ; it becomes us to think, and think seriously, how it will stand with us at last, for surely there is an end of all things. I am glad to hear that your health is improving, though slowly, yet I hope you will be a stout lad yet ; may your soul also prosper and be in health. O dear bairn, read the Bible and study it, and pray for a blessing on it. Dear me, what's John about ? he promised to write me often when he went away. I miss him on the Sabbath days ; is he very throng ? it looks like it, but he must write good or bad. Tell me truly how you have stood the storm, and all your news *much* and little, and I desire you to take no thought about me. I want for nothing, only if you have any pills about hand you may send me a few down with the box, and be sure to write me as you have dutifully done. I look forward when we shall have a smoke and a cup of tea together, but let us both hope and quietly wait.

I will write you largely next time.—Your affectionate Mother,

MARGARET CARLYLE.

This letter is endorsed : "Old letter of my Mother's,—strangely found this day,—after forty-five years !—T. C., 12*th March* 1868."

CXXXVI.—To ALEXANDER CARLYLE, Mainhill.

KINNAIRD HOUSE, 25*th November* 1823.

. . . The Bullers and I have had some further conversation on the subject of my going or staying : they are to give me a letter to George Bell, the celebrated surgeon in Edinburgh, who is maturely to investigate the state of my unfortunate carcase, and see if nothing can be done to aid me. By his advice I must in some degree be guided in my future movements. They are anxious of course that I should return ; but fully prepared for my quitting them should that seem necessary. . . . They are all very kind to me here, and would do anything to make me comfortable, and take me back on almost any terms.

I confess I am greatly at a loss what to do ; and for that cause, if there were no other, I am ill at ease. That some change *must* be made in my arrangements is clear enough : at present, I am bowed down to the earth with such a load of woes as keeps me in continual darkness. I seem as it were *dying by inches ;* if I have one good day, it is sure to be followed by three or four ill ones. For the last week, I have not had any one sufficient sleep ; even porridge has lost its effect on me. I need not say that I am far from happy. On the other hand, I have many comforts here ; indeed I might live as snugly as possible, if it were not for this one solitary but all-sufficient cause. I know also and shudder at the miseries of living in Edinburgh, as I did before ; this I will not do. "On the whole," as Jack says, it is become indispensable that I get back some shadow of health. My soul is crippled and smothered under a load of misery and disease, from which till I get partly relieved, life is burdensome and useless to me. We must all consult together, after I have heard the opinion of the "cunning Leech," who I suppose will put me upon mercury ; and *see what is* to be done. If I were well, I fear nothing ; if not, everything. You need not think from all this that I am dying ; there does not seem to be the slightest danger of that : I am only suffering daily as much bodily pain as I can well suffer without running *wud.*[1] So having finished this "Life of Schiller," Part II., and sent it off to London yesterday, I determine to set off for Edinburgh on Thursday morning ; I shall be there on Friday.

.   .   .   .   .   .

CXXXVII.—To John A. Carlyle, Edinburgh.

Kinnaird House, 25th November 1823.

I shall be with you on Friday night. . . . It seems very possible that the day after to-morrow, I may take my *final* leave of Kinnaird. In fact I am to consult George Bell, surgeon, and shape my course accordingly. I suppose he will " throw mercury into the system."[2] I fear the system will not care a doit about all his mercury. At all events,

---

[1] Wild, mad.

[2] An incipient physician in Edinburgh had, as reported to Carlyle by Frank Dixon, ordered a patient to " throw vegetable into the system."

I *must* be rid of this horrible condition of body : it absolutely torments me till my soul is dark as the pit of Tophet. I have had no good sleep for above a week. Judge ye in what a pleasing frame of mind I am !

.   .   .   .   .   .

CXXXVIII.—To John A. Carlyle, Edinburgh.

KINNAIRD HOUSE, 16*th December* 1823.

. . . Since my return nothing singular has happened : I go croaking about with about the usual quantity of sickness to suffer, and the usual quantity of impatience to endure it with. . . . Would to God I might never more have to tell any man whether I am well or ill. . . .

To-day the Proof-sheet of "Schiller" came to hand : the thing fills above two and twenty pages, and seems very weak. If Providence ever give me back my health I shall write very greatly better; if not, not. To-morrow I correct the thing, and send it down again. The third Part is *not begun yet !* I have only been reading Wallenstein ; I mean to begin it in two days positively. If it were done, I shall have nothing to mind but Goethe, which is easy.

.   .   .   .   .   .

CXXXIX.—To Mr. James Johnstone, Broughty Ferry, Dundee.

KINNAIRD HOUSE, 20*th December* 1823.

MY DEAR JOHNSTONE— . . . I need not say that I felt gratified at hearing of your settlement, so respectable and so opportune : I trust it more than realises all your hopes. These I can gather from your letter were not of the most sanguine kind ; indeed it is easy to perceive that such a place is not formed to content you : nevertheless it is a city of refuge in the meanwhile ; you may save a few pounds in it ; and be constantly on the outlook for some better and more permanent engagement, which you will then be in a case to undertake under far better auspices. I have no shadow of doubt that you will ultimately, and that ere long, be provided for according to your wish. The proportion between your qualities and your hopes assures me of this. You are gathering experience and getting knowledge and making friends. Did Irving ever write to you? He had some notable project in his head about setting you into some school at Haddington; which I had little faith in. Of course he will *not* have written : he writes none. Tell me by the first opportunity, how all things are going with you at the General's.[1] Stupid boys are a dreadful curse ; and foolish mothers often make it worse : there is no remedy but *patience ;* let things take their train without struggling too fiercely against them ; you will find it best. There is a text, not quite scriptural, but which suits you exactly in its purport. A minister in the Middlebie pulpit was attempting to preach upon these words : " He that is unholy, let him be unholy still." The poor man, as you know perhaps, could do nothing but repeat and re-repeat the verse, *He that is un, etc.,* having totally forgotten the beginning of his sermon. An upland Proprietor listened to him with increasing impatience, reiterating the words ; till at length another *he that is unholy* drove the worthy Laird out of all composure ; he started up, squeezed on his hat, and stalked gruffly along the passage muttering : " He that is a confounded Jackass, let him be a Jackass still !" There is much truth in that prayer, much good sense.

I have been in Edinburgh since I saw you. I returned from it only ten days ago. The increasing pressure of Dyspepsia and discontent were afflicting to such a degree that I came to the resolution of giving up my situation here, of retiring into Annandale and trying for six months by all means under heaven if health of body could not be regained : in the affirmative case, I should be the happiest man alive ; in the negative, it was but to go distracted, and take a dose of arsenic and so be done with it. The people of the house advised me that it would be better to consult a Doctor ; they seemed also to think it would be using them rather scurvily if I went away at this season. I accordingly delivered my introductory letter to George Bell, who examined me and prescribed to me *secundum artem.* He has given me mercury, and solemnly commanded me to abstain from tobacco in all its shapes. Snuff he says is

---

[1] Johnstone had entered as tutor into the family of a General M'Kenzie, on a salary at the rate of £60 per annum.

as pernicious as any other way of it. Do you mark that, Master Brook? I have tasted no morsel of the weed for nearly three weeks. On the whole I cannot say that I am perceptibly better; I have returned hither, to stay with the worthy people till the end of February, when they leave the place for Edinburgh, and thence for London. Whether I shall accompany them must depend on the state of my "outward fellow," and several other circumstances. In the meantime, I exercise no small philosophy. The aspect of things is dreary and dull; it is all one can do at present to keep from dying of the spleen. These wild moors are white as millers; the roads are ankle-deep with half-melted snow; the very Celts are going about with livid noses and a drop at the end—the picture of cold and destitution. I read nonsensical books and talk insipidities, and walk to and fro with a greatcoat, galoches, and a huge hairy cap. I ought likewise to be busy; but Satan is in me; I cannot work a stroke. The *second* Part of "Schiller" is printed, yet I cannot for my heart begin the third. This will never do.

.   .   .   .   .   .

The "literary news" of Edinburgh were of very small account. *Blackwood's Magazine* is said to be going down; the sale is lessening I hear, and certainly the contents are growing more and more insipid. I hope yet to see it dead: it is a disgrace to the age and country. Talent joined with moral baseness is at all times painful to contemplate. The *New Edinburgh Review*, Waugh's, is with the spirits of its Fathers! They gave it up last number: so perish all Queen Common-sense's enemies! There is a phrenological journal—a journal of Spurzheim's skull doctrine: Error and stupidity are infinite in their varieties, eternal in duration.

I wish you would write to me as soon as possible, and try to predict where we shall meet. It is mournful to think how few friends one has.—I am always yours,

THOMAS CARLYLE.

CXL.—To his MOTHER, Mainhill.

KINNAIRD HOUSE, 23*d December* 1823.

. . . I am waiting for February, when I go to Edinburgh to get the German book printed.   The third Part of "Schiller" is yet to *begin :* but I am so *feckless*[1] at present that I have never yet had the heart to commence it.   It *must* be done ere long.   I spend my evenings mostly in reading, and always about eight o'clock I go in to the good people and have one cup of tea with them, and an hour or more of small talk, which lightens the tedium of solitude and makes the night go faster away.   It is a sad thing to have to study how to *drive the night away ;* a thing which till now I never had occasion to practise : but at present I am reduced to it; it is the best thing I can do.   This medicine is a searching business : it leaves me often almost free of pain, but very, very weak.   I still have not tasted tobacco in any shape for three weeks : but whether this abstinence does me any good or not I cannot undertake to say.   I do not find that it is difficult to give up the practice : never seeing a glimpse of it from week to week, it seldom comes into my head.   If I could be sure that it was for my health I would never taste it again while I lived. . . . .

CXLI.—From his FATHER and MOTHER.

MAINHILL, 28*th December* 1823.

DEAR SON—I have taken the pen in my hand to write a few lines to you to tell you how I come on, but indeed I, for some years, have written so little that I have almost forgotten it altogether, so I think you will scarce can read it, but some says that anything can be read at Edinburgh,[2] so I will try you with a few lines as is, and if it is not readable I will try to do better next time.

I begin then with telling you the state of my own health, which I am glad to say is just as good as I could wish for at my time of life, though frailty and weakness which goeth along with old age is clearly felt to increase ; but what can I say? that is natural for all mankind.   But I must not leave this subject that way, but tell you that I have not as yet taken the cold that I was troubled with in some former winters ; and that I can sleep sound at night

---

[1] Spiritless.

[2] A neighbour's remark, after being unable to decipher what he himself had written, " Let it go ; they can read anything at Edinburgh."

and eat my meat and go about the town,[1] and go to the meeting house on the Sabbath Day, so that I have no reason for complaint. I go on next to tell you about our Crop, which doth not turn well out, but our Cattle is doing very well as yet, and we do not fear to meet the Landlord against the rent day. I was down at Ecclefechan this day, and was very glad to find a letter in the office from you, as we were beginning to look for one, and Sandy was preparing a letter for you, and we thought best to join our scrawls together. If there is any news, I leave that for Sandy to tell you all these things, and I will say no more at this time, but tell you that I remain, dear son, your loving Father,

JAS. CARLYLE.

DEAR TOM—I need not tell you how glad I was to receive your kind letter, for I began to be uneasy. . . . O my dear Son, I have many mercies to be thankful for, and not the least of these is your affection. We are all longing for February, when we hope to see you here, if God will. Do spare us as much time as possible when you come down; in the meantime let us be hearing from you often. —Your affectionate Mother,

MARGARET CARLYLE.

CXLII.—To ALEXANDER CARLYLE, Mainhill.

KINNAIRD HOUSE, 13*th January* 1824.

MY DEAR ALICK— . . . "Time and hours wear out the roughest day;" this dreary period of pain and idleness and depression and discomfort is now near a close. The old people go down to Edinburgh this day week, and we younger ones follow in about ten days. I am not to revisit Kinnaird. The printing of *Meister* commences immediately on my arrival, and is to be concluded in about two months. About three-fourths of it are yet to translate; for the writing of this weary *Schiller* has occupied me to the exclusion of everything beside. Nor is it finished yet! The *third* and last Part is not above half done, though it will be wanted in a few days. Till within the last week, I could not for my heart begin it handsomely and honestly. The mercury

---

[1] Farm boundary, farm.

has made me weak as any sparrow; and besides I was very idly-inclined. So I am now obliged to write like a Turk, and vex myself day and night that the thing is not done faster and better. It certainly satisfies me very little.

Yet the writing of it has done me good. It has yielded myself along with all the trouble considerable pleasure : it is also an improving task, and brings in money. The amount of the whole will be about sixty guineas. Oh ! if I were well, I could soon make rich and bid defiance to fortune. The publication of this very mean performance has further raised me considerably in the estimation of these worthy people. About ten days ago the Introduction to Part II., which you have never seen, appeared quoted in the *Times* newspaper ; an honour, very slender in itself, but sufficient to astonish the natives in this Gothic district. They begin to look upon me as a youth of parts superior to what they had suspected. The glory of being approved by " Bloody old Walter," as Cobbett calls the Editor of the *Times*, is no doubt very very small : yet his approval was, so far as I can recollect, almost the *first* testimony to merit on my part which *could* not be warped by partiality, my very name and existence being totally unknown to " Bloody old." Therefore I read it with pleasure : it made me happy for ten minutes ; cheerful for a whole afternoon : even yet I sometimes think of it. If I told all this to any other, I might justly be accused of weak and immeasurable vanity : but to you, I know it will give pleasure, as every pleasant thing that happens to me does. Jack and you are the only two to whom I should think of mentioning it. Let us not despise the day of small things ! Better times are coming.

Have they sent you Irving's *Orations?* And how are they relished at Mainhill ? I still think it was a very considerable pity that he had published them. It is not with books as with other things : *quantity* is nothing, *quality* is all in all. There is stuff in that book of Irving's to have made a first-rate work of the kind out of. But it is not dressed, it is not polished. We have not the *bottle* of heart-piercing " mountain-dew," but the *tub* of uncleanly *mash*, or at best of ill-fermented ale, yeasty, muddy, full of hops and sediment, so that no man can drink of it with comfort. There is a sturdy lashing of it in the last *Quarterly Review* (which makes me notice it), apparently by the pen of Southey. It will be well for Irving to attend to these advices of Southey's; for though excessively severe they are all to a certain extent grounded upon truth. Tell me about those "Arguments" and Cobbett, etc. etc., when you next write.

As to this project of the farm, which we were speaking of, I of course cannot, more than you, say anything definite. I do not think my proper place is in the country, but in London or amid some great collection of men. Did my state of health permit it, I think I should go southward without delay. But unfortunately *that* in the present state of matters cannot once be thought of; and a year's residence in the country would, if convenient, be by far the most profitable speculation I could think of. Nor, for your part of it, am I surprised that you are wearied of Mainhill: it is a place of horrid drudgery, and must always be so. Surely our father and you, by laying heads together, might manage to find out a better. And as to the want of money, I do not think it should be made an obstacle. I have at this time between three and four hundred pounds, for which I have not the smallest use; and certainly, independently of all regard to you, I should like better to see the whole or any part of that sum invested in a good farm under your superintendence than lying dormant in the bank. Of this I positively assure you. Except for the education of Jack, this money is of no avail to me: to see it serving any brother that I have is by far the most profitable use I can put it to. I should therefore wish that you would still keep this scheme in your eye; and be ready to give me some more precise account of it against my home-coming. The Bullers are to stay about three weeks in Edinburgh, after which I partly purpose to come down to Mainhill, and print the Book in Edinburgh—correcting the press by aid of the post. If not comfortably lodged in Edinburgh, I surely shall. I wish I were there even now, riding upon the outside of Dolph, getting back my health and fearing nothing! I am glad to hear that the poor beast is getting up its heart again. Take it forth sometimes and give it a sharp race, observing to keep it at the "high trot." I learned the use of this pace while here: it trains the horse to lift up its feet freely and avoid stumbling. You should also make him carry my Mother down to Sermon on the Sabbath days.

If postage were free I would surely answer at very great length the estimable epistles that accompanied your last. Tell my Father that when I get to Edinburgh I will show him that I have "read" his letter. As for my Mother, she *must write more frequently :* there is nothing to hinder her from writing a sheet full whenever she pleases. No piece of penmanship that I have seen for many a day touched me as hers did : I will write to her *next* time, that is, whenever I get to Edinburgh—about a fortnight hence or rather more. Do you mind to write *within* that period ; my answer will not be long in following. Commend me to the love of all my loved kinsmen and kinswomen. I think of them *all*, but have not room for names. Adieu, my dear Boy !—I am, ever your affectionate Brother,

T. CARLYLE.

CXLIII.—To Miss WELSH, Haddington.

KINNAIRD HOUSE, 25*th January* 1824.

. . . Never let the slowness of your intellectual faculties disturb you. Life is short, but not nearly so short as your fancy paints it : there is time in it for many long achievements, many changes of object, many failures both of our hopes and fears. *Festina lente* is the motto : you make the greatest speed that way ; if anything can be attained, you attain it ; if nothing, nature did not mean it ; she has had fair play, and wherefore should we fret ? That you write so slow and can still fix on nothing, I do not value a rush ; in your circumstances, secluded and solitary as you have always been, it is of no account whatever. See ! I am half a dozen years older than you ; have done nothing else but study all my days, yet I write slow as a snail, and have no project before me more distinct than morning clouds. And do you think, my dear, that I have given up hopes of writing well, as well as nine-tenths of "the mob of gentlemen that write with ease"—far better than almost any of them, when in my vain key ? By no manner of means, I assure you : my hopes are as good at this time as they ever were.

Faith ! and Patience !   These are literary as well as religious virtues.   Let us fear nothing.

.   .   .   .   .

"Schiller" will be done at last in about a week, God be thanked ! for I am very sick of him.   It is not in my right vein, though nearer it than anything I have yet done. In due time I shall find what I am seeking. . . .

.

CXLIV.—To Alexander Carlyle, Mainhill.

Edinburgh, 1 Moray Street,
10th February 1824.

. . . I have got leave of the Bullers for three months, two of which, it was understood, I should devote to translating and printing of the German Novel, and the third to seeing you all at Mainhill, instead of August, after which I was to join them in London, thenceforth proceeding to the burgh of Looe in Cornwall, and establishing myself permanently there as the Tutor of their eldest son. . . . The people have behaved well to me : they have all along treated me with the greatest consideration ; of late, they even seem to have some glimmer of affection for me.   My small *authorial* labours have elevated me in their esteem ; and it says not a little for people such as they are to value intellectual worth at a higher rate than any other.   If Mrs. Buller to her other gifts added the indispensable one of being a good housewife, one might live very happily beside her.   Buller I have all along esteemed a very unadulterated specimen of an English gentleman : he is truly honest to the very heart.   If I have recovered, as I expect to do at Mainhill, I shall feel no objection to go forth and see them and London both at once.   Tell my dear and over-anxious Mother, that going to Cornwall is as easy as going to Waterbeck, for any danger there is in it : the people also are good sober Christians and will use me no way but well. . . .

CXLV.—To Alexander Carlyle, Mainhill.

Edinburgh, 1 Moray Street,
2d March 1824.

. . . With regard to my home-coming, I have been of

X

various minds. . . . I at last hit on this expedient. I am
to translate and print the first two volumes of the book ;
and whenever these are finished, I set off for home ; there
to translate the third, and not to trouble Edinburgh with my
presence till this is ready for the press. It can after that
be printed in ten days ; and I get it managed as I pass
through the place here, on my way to London. This at
last has been agreed to by all parties. I am accordingly,
very busy getting my part of it done : I translate ten pages
daily ; at which rate, I shall be through my allotted task
and ready to start for the country somewhat less than three
weeks after the present date. Whether or not the Printers
will be ready then is another question : but on the whole,
you may count on seeing me come down before the beginning of April, to stay about a month. I am as anxious on
the subject as any one of you ; Mainhill is associated in my
mind with ideas of peace and kindness and health of body
and mind, such as I do not elsewhere enjoy.

Beyond the circle of my books and papers, I have
nothing to do with this heartless and conceited place : I
have called on no man since I came within the walls of it ;
and I care no jot if on turning my back on it three weeks
hence, I should never see the vain and hungry visage of it
any more. I must call on Brewster to settle accounts ; old
Dr. Fleming I ought also to see, for the sake of some emblem of kindness I experienced from him ; Dr. Gordon
also, if I have time ; and then my circle of visits will be
concluded. There is one Pearse Gillies,[1] an advocate here,
who knows of me, and whom I am to see on the subject of
this book ; he being a great German Scholar, and having
a fine library of books, one or two of which I wish to examine. . . .

CXLVI.—To Miss WELSH, Haddington.

1 MORAY STREET, 7th March 1824.

　　. . . It is a pity on the whole that you have abandoned

---

[1] The name of Mr. Robert Pearse Gillies is unfamiliar to most readers,
but he was a man of much culture who had resided in Germany, and seen
Goethe and other celebrities. He had a large acquaintance with literary
people in England and Scotland, and his *Memoirs of a Literary Veteran,*

Gibbon ; but it is of no use to struggle against the stream. Dr. Johnson said with considerable justice, that it was hardly ever advisable to read any book against your inclination. Where the inclination is averse, the attention will wander, do as you will. I recollect reading Harte's *Gustavus Adolphus* with an immense sacrifice of feeling to will ; and I remembered less of it than of any book I ever perused. I trust by and by you will resume Gibbon, and finish both him and Hume. Do you like Robertson ? I used to find in him a shrewd, a systematic, but not a great understanding ; and no more heart than in my boot. He was a kind of deist in the guise of a Calvinistic priest ; a portentous combination ! But if you are for fiery-spirited men, I recommend you to the Abbé Raynal, whose *History*, at least the edition of 1781, is, to use the words of my tailor respecting Africa, " wan coll (one coal) of burning sulphur."

   .   .   .   .   .   .

Monday morning.—They have sent me down the remaining sheets of *Meister*, which I must now wrap up and send to you. " Out of economical motives " do not send me back *any* of them. Keep them all lying together in some of your desks or drawers ; and when the number is complete we will have them bound together by way of curiosity, and keep them as a monument of pleasant times. In other respects they are worth nothing : so if you happen to lose one or two of them, do not fret about it : you are to have another copy the moment the book is finished. I fear, however, you will never read it : the romance, you see, is still dull as ever. There is not, properly speaking, the smallest particle of *historical* interest in it, except what is connected with Mignon ; and her you cannot see fully till near the very end. Meister himself is perhaps one of the greatest *ganaches* that ever was created by quill and ink. I am going to write a fierce preface, disclaiming all concern with the literary or the moral merit of the work ; grounding my claims to recompense or toleration on the fact that I

published in three volumes in 1851, contains many entertaining sketches and anecdotes of distinguished people. Their most permanent interest, however, lies in some admirable critical letters of Wordsworth's, which are printed in the second volume.

have accurately copied a striking portrait of Goethe's mind, the strangest and in many points the greatest now extant. What a work! Bushels of dust and straws and feathers, with here and there a diamond of the purest water. . . .

CXLVII.—To ALEXANDER CARLYLE, Mainhill.

EDINBURGH, 1 MORAY STREET,
16th March 1824.

. . . Since I wrote last I have proceeded pretty regularly with my translation, at the rate of ten pages daily, correcting the proof-sheets as we go along. . . .

One material part of the affair I have already satisfactorily concluded ; I mean the bargain with the Bookseller. . . . He is to pay me down £180 on the day of publication, and to make what hand he pleases of the 1000 copies he is printing. This is very handsome payment for my labour, however it may turn ; and what I like best of all, it is dry hard cash, totally independent of risks. If the book sell the man will repay himself royally : and he deserves it for his risks. I too shall gain in that case, for after these 1000 copies are sold I am to have £250 for every further 1000 he chances to print. So that it does not by any means seem improbable that within a year I may make £500 more of it ; but anyway I have the £180, fair recompense for my labour, and I am satisfied. . . .

I will likely be with you some time next week. . . . Tell Mother that she must get the teapot overhauled and all the tackle put in order : I am going to stay a month, and mean to drink tea with her very diligently. . . .

CXLVIII.—To Mr. JAMES JOHNSTONE, Broughty Ferry.

HADDINGTON, *Saturday night*
[*29th May* 1824].

MY DEAR JOHNSTONE—Your letter was lying for me at the office of Messrs. Oliver and Boyd when I returned from Annandale, last Tuesday night. The newspapers, you must understand, for which you thanked me so cordially, were all transmitted from Mainhill, where I resided from the beginning of April till the day above mentioned. Had my occupation been less incessant, I should undoubtedly have broken your repose, and assisted by my suggestions the " compunctious visitings " of your own not yet altogether seared conscience. But alas! Goethe and *Meister* kept me busy as a cock upon the spit : it was not till yesterday that I got liberty to leave Edinburgh, and throw that wretched novel off my hands for ever and a day. I am here, spending with a kind and worthy family a brief space of rest before setting off for London and Cornwall. You too are going to Vannes in Brittany ! What strange shiftings to and fro in the monstrous whirligig of life ! And are we to go without once having met ? Old friends to part for we know not how long, and take no farewell ? My dear James, I cannot bear to think of it : and I write at present for the purpose of preventing it. This letter reaches you on Monday morning ; I sail next Saturday by the steamboat. Could not you contrive to make a start for Edinburgh, and meet me there about Wednesday night, and stay with me the next two days ? Or, which would be better, could not you come out hither ? I would show you Gilbert Burns, little Brown (now married to Margaret Farries), and the people I am staying with, who could not fail to please you. Whichever way you like, only do if possible do one of them. Consider how often I have been at Broughty Ferry ! I would have gone again in all probability had I had time. Besides, you will see the General Assembly in Edinburgh, and Murray, etc. etc. ; and I will give you a copy of *Meister* with you in your pocket, if you have a pocket large enough to hold three volumes 8vo.

In short you must really make an effort : tell the General you have not been a day from home since your arrival ; and that in very truth he must give you leave. Write at any rate on Monday night, the letter will not fail to find me here on Wednesday morning ; on which morning if you also should embark from Dundee, we might meet in Edinburgh at night. . . .

I write this in the hurry of an hour after dinner, in momentary expectation of the post. You see the purport of it, and will pardon blunders. My address here is : To the care of Mrs. Welsh, Haddington. Write, and come quickly, and believe me always, my dear Johnstone, your sincere old friend,

THOMAS CARLYLE.

CXLIX.—To his MOTHER, Mainhill.

EDINBURGH, *5th June* 1824.

MY DEAR MOTHER—I am within an hour of sailing for London, and as it is likely to be longer than I anticipated before you hear of me, I scribble you a few lines in the greatest possible hurry, to let you know that it is well with me, and that you must not be uneasy till you hear from me.

I was not more hurt by my journey hither than I expected: I went out to Haddington, and they nursed me with the greatest care till I was completely recovered. . . . The worthy people would not let me leave Haddington; or by dint of making great efforts I might have been in London to-day by the steamboat of Wednesday. To-night I sail in a handsome smack with only four fellow-passengers, Sir Something and two ladies and Mr. Something. The wind is pretty good. We expect to be there in a week. About ten or twelve days after this, the Coach will bring you a letter from me. . . .

Here in Edinburgh I have managed all things quite well. I have just accompanied to Farries' lodgings a packet for home, containing two copies of the Novel for the Boys, some odds and ends for my father, and a small cheap shawl for you. This was selected and cheapened for you at Haddington by my good Jane; a circumstance which I assured her would not diminish its value in your eyes. I saw the Targer[1] for two days; he left me this morning; we are to meet again in London. He goes to France about July; is well enough, I think, but as full of whims as possible. He thought I had poisoned him by pouring *two* not *one* spoonful of milk into his tea this very morning. At least so I declared to him, with much laughter. He is as affectionate and honest as ever. I have got a letter to Thomas Campbell the Poet from Brewster, and one to Telford (for whom I care not two doits): the Doctor promises me a multitude of others, as soon as he can get

---

[1] James Johnstone.

them written.   With Boyd I settled finally, and yesterday
converted his bill into a check for £180 payable at sight
in London.   I rejoice that such was my bargain : I should
have been very unhappy else at present.   I have also sent
off all my copies—8 to London, 2 home, 1 Targer, 1
Murray, 1 Mrs. Brewster, Mrs. Johnstone, Ben Nelson,
Waugh, etc. etc.   George Bell the surgeon would take
nothing for his advising and drugs : I gave him a copy
also.   So that now they are all disposed of together.

Tell Jack that *Wilhelm Tell* is coming for him by Farries :
I would have sent the shoes, but could not possibly get
them packed.   Bid the good Logician, but most faithful
brother, write as soon as ever he gets my address.   Great
things are expected of him by various people.   Tell him
Boyd will send two *Pauls*[1] down whenever they are ready.
I also make him heir to my seal-skin cap : I missed it
three minutes after he was gone,—just three minutes too
late.

But now my dear Mother I am going.   The people are
bringing me tea ; after which Murray is to come and accompany me down to Leith.   I will write directly.   There
is no danger at all : the weather is beautiful as summer
should be : and is not God the ruler of water as of land?
May His blessing be upon you all for ever ! Give my kindest
love to all the posse of brothers and sisters, beginning with
Alick and ending with Jenny.   Their names and interests
are all present with me at this moment.   My best affection
to my Father.   I am always, my dear Mother, your true
son,

T. CARLYLE.

CL.—To ALEXANDER CARLYLE, Mainhill.[2]

KEW GREEN, 25*th June* 1824.

. . . When I see you I will tell you of Westminster
Abbey ; and St. Paul's, the only edifice that ever struck
me with a proper sense of grandeur.   I was hurrying along
Cheapside into Newgate Street among a thousand bustling

---

[1] John Carlyle's translation of *Paul and Virginia*, published by Boyd.
[2] The most interesting of the letters written by Carlyle during his stay
in England and his visit to France are printed in Mr. Froude's *Life* of him.

pigmies and the innumerable jinglings and rollings and crashings of many-coloured Labour, when all at once in passing from the abode of John Gilpin, stunned by the tumult of his restless compeers, I looked up from the boiling throng through a little opening at the corner of the street—and there stood St. Paul's—with its columns and friezes, and massy wings of bleached yet unworn stone; with its statues and its graves around it; with its solemn dome four hundred feet above me, and its gilded ball and cross gleaming in the evening sun, piercing up into the heaven through the vapours of our earthly home! It was silent as Tadmor of the Wilderness; gigantic, beautiful, enduring; it seemed to frown with a rebuking pity on the vain scramble which it overlooked: at its feet were tomb-stones, above it was the everlasting sky, within priests perhaps were chanting hymns; it seemed to transmit with a stern voice the sounds of Death, Judgment, and Eternity through all the frivolous and fluctuating city. I saw it oft and from various points, and never without new admiration.

.   .   .   .   .   .

Did you get *Meister*, and how do you *dis*like it? For really it is a most mixed performance, and though intellect-ually good, much of it is morally bad. It is making way here perhaps—but slowly: a second edition seems a dubious matter. No difference! I have the produce of the first lying here beside me in hard notes of the Bank of England, and fear no weather. I bought myself a suit of fine clothes for six pounds; a good watch for six; and these were nearly all my purchases. . . .

CLI.—To Alexander Carlyle, Mainhill.

BIRMINGHAM, 11*th August* 1824.

. . . I was one day through the iron and coal works of this neighbourhood,—a half-frightful scene! A space perhaps of thirty square miles, to the north of us, covered over with furnaces, rolling-mills, steam-engines, and sooty men. A dense cloud of pestilential smoke hangs over it for ever, blackening even the grain that grows upon it; and at night the whole region burns like a volcano spitting fire from a thousand tubes of brick. But oh the wretched

hundred and fifty thousand mortals that grind out their
destiny there!   In the coal-mines they were literally naked,
many of them, all but trousers; black as ravens; plashing
about among dripping caverns, or scrambling amid heaps
of broken mineral; and thirsting unquenchably for beer.
In the iron-mills it was little better: blast-furnaces were
roaring like the voice of many whirlwinds all around; the
fiery metal was hissing through its moulds, or sparkling
and spitting under hammers of a monstrous size, which fell
like so many little earthquakes.   Here they were wheeling
charred coals, breaking their ironstone, and tumbling all
into their fiery pit; there they were turning and boring
cannon with a hideous shrieking noise such as the earth
could hardly parallel; and through the whole, half-naked
demons pouring with sweat and besmeared with soot were
hurrying to and fro in their red nightcaps and sheet-iron
breeches rolling or hammering or squeezing their glowing
metal as if it had been wax or dough.   They also had a
thirst for ale.   Yet on the whole I am told they are very
happy: they make forty shillings or more per week, and few
of them will work on Mondays.   It is in a spot like this
that one sees the sources of British power. . . .

CLII.—To Miss WELSH, Haddington.

PARIS, HÔTEL DE WAGRAM,
28th October 1824.

. . . France has been so betravelled and beridden and
betrodden by all manner of vulgar people that any romance
connected with it is entirely gone off ten years ago; the
idea of *studying* it is for me at present altogether out of the
question; so I quietly surrender myself to the direction of
guide books and *laquais de place*, and stroll about from sight
to sight, as if I were assisting at a huge Bartholomew fair,
only that the booths are the Palais Royal or the Boulevards,
and the Shows, the Theatre Français instead of Punch, and
the Jardin des Plantes instead of the Irish giant or Polito's
menagerie. . . .

Yesterday I walked along the *Pont Neuf*; jugglers and
quacks and cooks and barbers and dandies and gulls and
sharpers were racketing away with a deafening hum at their

manifold pursuits; I turned aside into a small mansion
with the name of *Morgue* upon it; there lay the naked
body of an old gray-headed artisan whom misery had
driven to drown himself in the river! His face wore the
grim fixed scowl of despair; his lean horny hands with
their long ragged nails were lying by his sides; his patched
and soiled apparel with his apron and *sabots* were hanging
at his head; and there fixed in his iron slumber, heedless
of the vain din that rolled around him on every side, was
this poor outcast stretched in silence and darkness for
ever. I gazed upon the wretch for a quarter of an hour;
I think I never felt more shocked in my life. To live in
Paris for a fortnight is a treat; to live in it continually
would be a martyrdom. . . .

CLIII.—To Alexander Carlyle, Mainhill.

23 Southampton Street,
Pentonville, 14th December 1824.

My dear Alick— . . . Your letter found me in due
season; and a welcome visitant it was. I had not got the
Courier that preceded it, and the intelligence of your proceedings and welfare was no small relief to me. You
must thank our Mother in my name in the warmest terms
for her kind note, which I have read again and again with
an attention rarely given to more polished compositions.
The sight of her rough true-hearted writing is more to me
than the finest penmanship and the choicest rhetoric. It
takes me home to honest kindness, and affection that will
never fail me. You also I must thank for your graphic
picture of Mainhill and its neighbourhood. How many
changes happen in this restless roundabout of life within a
little space! . . .

In London, or rather in my own small sphere of it,
there has nothing sinister occurred since I wrote last.
After abundant scolding, which sometimes rose to the very
borders of bullying, these unhappy people [the publishers]
are proceeding pretty regularly with *the* Book; a fifth part
of it is already printed; they are also getting a portrait of
Schiller engraved for it; and I hope in about six weeks the
thing will be off my hands. It will make a reasonable-

looking book; somewhat larger than a volume of *Meister*, and done in somewhat of the same style. In the course of printing I have various matters to attend to; proofs to read; additions, alterations to make; which furnishes me with a very *canny* occupation for the portion of the day I can devote to labour. I work some three or four hours; read, for amusement chiefly, about as long; walk about these dingy streets, and talk with originals for the rest of the day. On the whole I have not been happier for many a long month: I feel content to let things take their turn till I am free of my engagements; and then—for a stern and serious *tuffle* with my Fate, which I have vowed and determined to alter from the very bottom, health and all! This *will not* be impossible, or even I think extremely difficult. Far beyond a million of " weaker vessels " than I are sailing very comfortably along the tide of life just here. What good is it to whine and whimper? Let every man that has an ounce of strength in him get up and put it forth in Heaven's name, and labour that his " soul may live."

Of this enormous Babel of a place I can give you no account in writing: it is like the heart of all the universe; and the flood of human effort rolls out of it and into it with a violence that almost appals one's very sense. Paris scarcely occupies a quarter of the ground, and does not seem to have the twentieth part of the business. O that our father saw Holborn in a fog! with the black vapour brooding over it, absolutely like fluid ink; and coaches and wains and sheep and oxen and wild people rushing on with bellowings and shrieks and thundering din, as if the earth in general were gone distracted. To-day I chanced to pass through Smithfield, when the market was three-fourths over. I mounted the steps of a door, and looked abroad upon the area, an irregular space of perhaps thirty acres in extent, encircled with old dingy brick-built houses, and intersected with wooden pens for the cattle. What a scene! Innumerable herds of fat oxen, tied in long rows, or passing at a trot to their several shambles; and thousands of graziers, drovers, butchers, cattle-brokers with their quilted frocks and long goads pushing on the hapless beasts; hurrying to and fro in confused parties, shouting, jostling, cursing, in the midst of rain and *shairn*,[1] and braying discord such as the imagination cannot figure.   Then there are stately streets and squares, and calm green recesses to which nothing of this abomination is permitted to enter.   No wonder Cobbett calls the place a Wen.   It is a monstrous Wen !   The thick smoke of it beclouds a space of thirty square miles ; and a million of vehicles, from the dog or cuddy-barrow to the giant waggon, grind along its streets for ever.   I saw a six-horse wain the other day with, I think, Number 200,000 and odds upon it !

There is an excitement in all this, which is pleasant as a transitory feeling, but much against my taste as a permanent one.   I had much rather visit London from time to time, than live in it.   There is in fact no *right* life in it that I can find : the people are situated here like plants in a hot-house, to which the quiet influences of sky and earth are never in their unadulterated state admitted.   It is the case with all ranks : the carman with his huge slouch-hat hanging half-way down his back, consumes his breakfast of bread and tallow or hog's lard, sometimes as he swags along the streets, always in a hurried and precarious fashion, and supplies the deficit by continual pipes, and pots of beer.   The fashionable lady rises at three in the afternoon, and begins to live towards midnight.   Between these two extremes, the same false and tumultuous manner of existence more or less infests all ranks.   It seems as if you were for ever in "an inn," the feeling of *home* in our acceptation of the term is not known to one of a thousand. You are packed into paltry shells of brick-houses (calculated to endure for forty years, and then fall); every door that slams to in the street is audible in your most secret chamber ; the necessaries of life are hawked about through multitudes of hands, and reach you, frequently adulterated, always at rather more than *twice* their cost elsewhere ; people's friends must visit them by rule and measure ; and when you issue from your door, you are assailed by vast shoals of quacks, and showmen, and street sweepers, and pickpockets, and mendicants of every degree and shape, all plying in noise or silent craft their several vocations, all in their hearts like "lions ravening for their prey."   The

<hr>

[1] The dung of cattle.

blackguard population of the place is the most consummately blackguard of anything I ever saw.

Yet the people are in general a frank, jolly, *well-living*, kindly people. You get a certain way in their good graces with great ease : they want little more with you than now and then a piece of recreating conversation, and you are quickly on terms for giving and receiving it. Farther, I suspect, their nature or their habits seldom carry or admit them. I have found one or two strange mortals, whom I sometimes stare to see myself beside. There is Crabbe Robinson, an old Templar (Advocate dwelling in the Temple), who gives me coffee and *Sally-Lunns* (a sort of buttered roll), and German books, and talk by the gallon in a minute. His windows look into—Alsatia ! With the Montagus I, once a week or so, step in and chat away a friendly hour : they are good clever people, though their goodness and cleverness are strangely mingled with absurdity in word and deed. They like me very well : I saw Badams there last night ; I am to see him more at large to-morrow or soon after. Mrs. Strachey has twice been here to see me—in her carriage, a circumstance of strange omen to our worthy [friend]. . . . Among the Poets I see Procter and Allan Cunningham as often as I like : the other night I had a second and much longer talk with Campbell. I went over with one Macbeth, not the "Usurper," but a hapless Preacher from Scotland, whose gifts, coupled with their drawbacks, cannot earn him bread in London, though Campbell and Irving and many more are doing all they can for him. Thomas is a clever man, and we had a much more pleasant conversation than our first : but I do not think my view of him was materially altered. He is vain and dry in heart ; the brilliancy of his mind (which will not dazzle you to death after all) is like the glitter of an iceberg in the Greenland seas ; parts of it are beautiful, but it is cold, cold, and you would rather look at it than touch it. I partly feel for Campbell: his early life was a tissue of wretchedness (here in London he has lived upon a pennyworth of milk and a penny roll per day); and at length his soul has got encrusted as with a case of iron ; and he has betaken himself to sneering and selfishness—a common issue !

Irving I see as frequently and kindly as ever. His church and boy occupy him much. The *madness* of his popularity is altogether over; and he must content himself with playing a much lower game than he once anticipated; nevertheless I imagine he will do much good in London, where many men like him are greatly wanted. His wife and he are always good to me.

Respecting my future movements I can predict nothing certain yet. It is not improbable, I think, that I may see you all in Scotland before many weeks are come and gone. Here at any rate, in my present circumstances, I do not mean to stay: it is expensive beyond measure (two guineas a week or thereby for the mere items of bed and board); and I must have a *permanent* abode of some kind devised for myself, if I mean to do any good. Within reach of Edinburgh or London, it matters little which. You have not yet determined upon leaving or retaining Mainhill? I think it is a pity that you had not some more kindly spot: at all events a better house I *would* have. Is Mainholm let? By clubbing our capitals together we might make something of it. A house in the country, and a horse to ride on, I must and will have if it be possible. Tell me all your views on these things when you write.

. . . Good night! my dear Alick!—I am, ever your affectionate Brother,

T. CARLYLE.

CLIV.—To Miss WELSH, Haddington.

PENTONVILLE, 20*th December* 1824.

. . . But I must not kill you with my talk, one little piece of news, and thou shalt have a respite. The other twilight, the lackey of one Lord Bentinck came with a lackey's knock to the door, and delivered me a little blue parcel, requiring for it a receipt under my hand. I opened it somewhat eagerly, and found two small pamphlets with ornamental covers, and—a letter from—Goethe! Conceive my satisfaction: it was almost like a message from Fairy Land; I could scarcely think that *this was* the real hand and signature of that mysterious personage, whose name had floated through my fancy, like a sort of spell, since boyhood; whose thoughts had come to me in maturer years with almost the impressiveness of revelations. But what says the letter? Kind nothings, in a simple patriarchal style, extremely to my taste. I will copy it, for it is in a character that you cannot read; and send it to you with the original, which you are to keep as the most precious of your literary relics. Only the last line and the signature are in Goethe's hand: I understand he *constantly* employs an amanuensis. Do you transcribe my copy, and your own translation of it, into the blank leaf of that German paper, before you lay it by; that the same sheet may contain some traces of him whom I most venerate and her whom I most love in this strangest of all possible worlds. . . .

CLV.—To Alexander Carlyle, Mainhill.

LONDON, *8th January* 1825.

MY DEAR ALICK—Your letter came to me the day before Christmas; it is time that it were answered. I am much obliged to you for your punctuality; a virtue which in my situation I am called upon to rival or even to surpass. I have no news for you; only harmless chat; but that and the assurance that there is no *bad* news will repay you for the charge of postage. . . .

Everything goes on with me here very much as it was doing when I wrote last. . . . I think I have well-nigh decided on returning to Scotland, when this Book is off my hands. This tumultuous capital is not the place for one like me. The very expense of it were almost enough to drive me out of it: I cannot live in the simplest style under about two guineas a week; a sum that would suffice to keep a decent roof of my own above me in my Fatherland. Besides I ought to settle somewhere, and get a home and neighbourhood among my fellow-creatures. Now this London, to my mind, is not a flattering scene for such an enterprise. One hates, for one thing, to be a *foreigner* anywhere; and this, after all that can be said about it, is the case with *every* Scotchman in this city. They live as aliens here, unrooted in the soil; without political, religious, or even much social, interest in the community, distinctly feeling every day that with them it is money only that can "make the mare to go." Hence cash! cash! cash! is the everlasting cry of their souls. They are consequently very "hard characters;" they believe in nothing but their ledgers; their precept is like that of Iago, "Put money in your purse;" or as he of Burnfoot more emphatically expressed it, "Now, Jock! get siller; honestly, if thou can; but ony way *get* it!" I should like but indifferently to be ranked among them; for my sentiments and theirs are not at all germane. The first *improvement* they make upon themselves in the South is to acquire the habit of sneering at their honest old country; vending many stale jokes about its poverty, and the happiness of travelling with one's face *towards* the sun. This is a "damnable heresy," as honest Allan Cunningham called it. I have no patience with the leaden-hearted dogs. Often when appealed to that I might confirm such shallow sarcasms, I have risen in my wrath, and branded them with my bitterest contempt. But here they are staple speculation with our degenerate compatriots. BULL himself, again, though a frank, beef-loving, joyous kind of person, *is* excessively stupid : take him out of the sphere of the *five senses*, and he gazes with a vacant astonishment, wondering "what the devil the fellow *can* mean." This is comparatively the state of all ranks, so far as I have seen them, from the highest to the lowest; but especially of the latter. Of these it is unspeakably so! Yesterday I went to see Newgate, under the auspices of the benevolent Mrs. Fry, a Quaker lady who every Friday goes on her errand of mercy to inspect the condition of the female prisoners. She, this good Quakeress, is as much like an angel of Peace as any person I ever saw : she read a chapter, and *expounded* it, to the most degraded audience of the universe, in a style of beautiful simplicity which I shall not soon forget. But oh! the male felons! the two hundred polluted wretches, through whose stalls and yards I was next carried! There were they of all climates and kinds, the Jew, the Turk, the "Christian"; from the gray villain of sixty to the black-guard boy of *eight!* Nor was it their depravity that struck me, so much as their debasement. Most of them actually looked like *animals*; you could see no traces of a *soul* (not even of a bad one) in their gloating, callous, sensual countenances; they had never *thought* at all, they had only eaten and drunk and made merry. I have seen as wicked people in the north; but it was another and far less abominable sort of wickedness. A Scotch blackguard is very generally a thinking reasoning person; some theory and principle of life, a satanical philosophy, beams from every feature of his rugged scowling countenance. Not so here. The sharpness of these people was the cunning of a fox, their stubbornness was the sullen gloom of a mastiff. Newgate holds, I believe, within its walls more human baseness than any other spot in the Creation.

But why do I write of it or aught connected with it, since in a few weeks I hope to tell you everything by word of mouth? We are on the fifteenth sheet of *Schiller; six* more will set us through it. The moment it is finished, I purpose to decamp. I have given the creatures *four* weeks (they engage for three) to settle everything: I should not be surprised if you met me at the Candlemas Fair on the Plainstones of Dumfries! Soon after the beginning of February I do expect to see old, meagre, but true-hearted Annandale again. No doubt, you will have the *wark-gear afoot*, that is, the pony in riding order, and everything in readiness for me. When arrived, my purposes are various, and inviting though unsettled. I have written to Edinburgh about a projected translation of *Schiller's Works;* Brewster sends me word that Blackwood (the Bookseller) "has no doubt he will be able to engage with me, in *Schiller* (which, however, he does not seem to relish), or in some other literary object." Blackwood, I believe, is but a knave; and I put no faith in him. Nay, since I began to write this sentence, I have a letter from the scoundrel Boyd "respectfully declining" to engage in that speculation of *Schiller !* So that I rather suppose *it* must be renounced. No matter! There are plenty more where it came from! I am bent on *farming*, for the recovery of my health; nay "marriage" itself is sometimes not out of my ulterior contemplations! But I will explain all things when we meet.

     .   .   .   .   .   .

But the day is breaking up into fair sunshine; and I

must out to take the benefit of it.   Let me have a letter from you, a long one, and a good one like the last, by the very earliest opportunity.   Thank my kind true Mother for her note: tell her it will not be long till I answer all her queries by word of mouth.   In the meantime, I have a message for her, which I know will please her well, because it is to *do something for me.*   Badams prescribes *warmth* above all things: he made me wear close stockings (flannel or rather woollen) drawers even in summer.   My Mother once offered to get Peter Little to work me such a pair: tell her that now if she has any wool, I will take them.   If she has not, she need never mind in the least: we can settle it,—when—we meet!   Do you regularly hear of Jack?   He is a letter in my debt for ten days.   But I hope the good soul is well.   Does he send you the *Examiner?*   Has he written you a translation of Goethe's letter to me?   I was very glad to hear from the old blade, in so kind though so brief a fashion.   I mean to send him a copy of *Schiller's Life,* so soon as it is ready.

Now, my dear Boy, I must take my flight.   I have purchased me a small seal and the Carlyles' crest with *Humilitate* and all the rest of it engraven on it.   The thing lies at present in Oxford Street, and was to be ready about this time to-day.   I am going thither: if I get it, I will seal this letter with it, for your edification.   Write directly, and tell me all; the progress of the *Gheen* [1] and everything notable, in and about Mainhill.   The smallest incident from that quarter recorded in your pithy style is valuable to me.

Irving and I are as friendly as ever.   He is toiling in the midst of many difficulties and tasks, internal and external, domestic and ecclesiastic.   I wish him well through them!   He is the best man I have met in England.   But here, as I told him lately, he has no home; he is a "missionary" rather than a pastor.—My Father has never written to me: I should like much to see his hand in London.   Give my warmest love to him and Mother, and all the *brethren* and sisters, beginning with Mag and ending with Jenny.   Write soon, good Alick!—I am, ever your true Brother,

T. CARLYLE.

---

[1] Wild cherry.   The phrase here means trivial news.

My dear Jack—In a paper which would reach thee yesterday, I promised to write, whenever that *Life of Schiller* was off my hands; an event which I expected would take place this present Saturday. A man may speculate about his own capacities of action; but woe to him if his calculations include the indolence and capricious mischances of others. Two sheets of this poor book are still to print; and I do not hope to be rid of it for another week. On the whole, it is going to be a very pitiful but yet not utterly worthless thing; a volume of three hundred and fifty pages, with portrait, extracts, etc.; not well printed, worse written, yet on the whole containing nothing that I did not reckon true, and wanting nothing which my scanty and forlorn circumstances allowed me to give it. So I "commit it silently" either to "everlasting Time," or everlasting oblivion; caring no jot about what the despicable gang of newspaper and magazine critics say of it, or whether they speak of it at all. I do find there is nothing but this for it: Convince yourself that your work *is* what you call it, as nearly as your honest powers could make it; and the man who censures it either tells you nothing that you did not know before, or tells you lies; both of which sorts of intelligence you will find it a very simple matter to light your pipe with. There was a luckless wight of an *opium-eater* here, one De Quincey, for instance, who wrote a very vulgar and brutish Review of "Meister" in the *London Magazine.* I read three pages of it one *sick* day at Birmingham; and said: "Here is a man who writes of things which he does not rightly understand; I see clean over the top of *him*, and his vulgar spite, and his commonplace philosophy; and I will away and have a ride on (Badams') Taffy, and leave *him* to cry in the ears of the simple." So I went out, and had my ride accordingly; and if De Quincey, poor little fellow, *made* anything of his review, he can put it in his waistcoat pocket, and thank the god Mercurius. A *counter*-criticism of *Meister* (or something like one) is to appear in the February number,

I believe: to this also I hope I shall present the same tolerant spirit. The "reviews" of that book *Meister* must not go without their effect on me: I know it and believe it, and feel it to be a book containing traces of a higher, far higher, spirit, altogether more *genius*, than any book published in my day: and yet to see the Cockney animalcules rendering an account of it! praising it, or blaming it! Sitting in judgment on Goethe with the light tolerance of a country Justice towards a suspected Poacher! As the child says: " It was *grend !*" [1] . . .

CLVII.—To his MOTHER, Mainhill.

23 SOUTHAMPTON STREET, PENTONVILLE,
31st January 1825.

. . . The *Life of Schiller* is now fairly out of *my* hands; the Booksellers engage to show it on their counters on Wednesday; they send a parcel of copies off to Edinburgh forthwith; then they must pay me my £90; after which I care not if they let the thing lie and rot beside them till the day of Doom. On the whole, it will make a reputable sort of book; somewhat larger than a volume of *Meister*, with a portrait, etc.: I have not put my name to it, not feeling anxious to have the syllables of my poor *name* pass through the mouths of Cockneys on so slender an occasion; though, if any one lay it to my charge, I shall see no reason to blush for the hand I had in it. Sometimes of late I have bethought me of some of your old maxims about pride and self-conceit: I do see this same vanity to be the root of half the evil men are subject to in life. Examples of it stare me in the face every day: the pitiful passion, under any of the thousand forms which it assumes, never fails to wither out the good and worthy parts of a man's character; and leave him poor and spiteful, an enemy to his own peace and that of all about him. There never was a wiser doctrine than that of *Christian humility*, considered as a corrective for the coarse unruly selfishness of men's nature.

I will send *you* a copy of this *Schiller;* and I know you will read it with attention and pleasure. It contains nothing

---

[1] Part of the rest of this letter is in Froude's *Life*, i. 292.

that I know of but *truth* of fact and sentiment ; and I have always found that the honest truth of one mind had a certain attraction in it for every other mind that loved truth honestly. Various quacks, for instance, have exclaimed against the *immorality* of *Meister ;* and the person whom it delighted above all others of my acquaintance was Mrs. Strachey, exactly the most religious, pure, and true-minded person among the whole number. A still more convincing proof of my doctrine was the satisfaction *you* took in it. *Schiller*, though it flies with a low, low wing, compared with *Meister*, will have less in it to offend you. What is it, in fact, but your own sentiments, the sentiments of my good true-hearted mother, expressed in the language and similitudes that *my* situation suggests ? So you *must* like it.[1]

.   .   .   .   .   .

CLVIII.—To Alexander Carlyle, Mainhill.

Pentonville, 14*th February* 1825.

My dear Brother—I expected by this time almost to have been at Mainhill ; and the date of my departure even from London is still in some degree uncertain. I am afraid our Mother will be getting anxious about me ; so I sit down in the midst of bustle and hurry to assure you all that I am quite well, and prevented from coming home by no cause productive of any evil to me.

I expected that this weary *Life of Schiller* would have been published a fortnight ago ; and just when everything was ready on my part, the engraver discovered that the portrait was not right, and would require at least two weeks before it could be put properly in order ! Of course I felt terribly enraged at this new delay ; but what, alas, would rage do for me ?

.   .   .   .   .   .

Meanwhile, except perhaps for the loss of time, I feel perfectly comfortable here. Irving and I talk of all things under the sun, in the friendliest and most *edifying* manner ; and all my friends vie with one another in kindness to the departing dyspeptic. Several of them would fain retain me ;

---

[1] The greater part of the rest of this letter is printed (incorrectly as usual) by Froude, *Life*, i. 294.

and had I not vowed inflexibly to recover health of body in preference to all things, I should be strongly tempted to listen to their solicitations. But I feel that I *may* grow completely well again ; and seven years of perpetual pain have taught me sharply that to this consideration *everything* should give way. I hope, however, not to leave England for good and all at present ; I have got real friends here, whom I should be sorry to quit for ever. Mrs. Strachey and I are to correspond by letters ; so also are Mrs. Montagu and I : the former has presented me with a beautiful gold pencil ; the latter with a seal bearing Schiller's dying words, " *Calmer and Calmer*," for an inscription ; both of which pledges I design to keep with great fidelity as memorials of worthy and kind people.

For my future occupation, I have settled nothing yet definitely. The Booksellers Taylor and Hessey have offered me £100 for a *Life of Voltaire*, to be composed like this of *Schiller*.

.   .   .   .   .   .

A copy of *Schiller* will reach you through Edinburgh, ere long. It is a very reasonable-looking book ; and promises to act its part in society very fairly. If I can find nothing better to do, I will write a whole string of such books. Literary fame is a thing which I covet little ; but I desire to be *working* honestly in my day and generation in this business, which has now become my trade. I make no grain of doubt that in time I shall penetrate the fence that keeps me back, and find the place which is due to me among my fellow-men. Some hundreds of stupider people are at this very time doing duty with acceptance in the literature of the time. We shall see : I am not at all in a hurry ; the time will come. . . .

THOMAS CARLYLE.

CLIX.—To Miss Welsh, Haddington.

BIRMINGHAM, 28th *February* 1825.

. . . My projected movements, you perceive, have been altogether overturned ; far from the danger of surprising you by my presence, I am yet a week from Annandale, and perhaps three weeks from you. The poor Book was ready

on my part at the time predicted; but just two days before
the appointed time of publication, our Engraver discovered
that the plate was incomplete, and could not be *properly*
rectified in less than a fortnight. As I had myself recommended this man to the job, on the faith of Irving's testimony that he was an indigent *genius*, I had nothing for it
but to digest my spleen in silence, and to tell the *feckless
speldring*[1] of a creature, that, as his future reputation de-
pended on the work, he was at liberty to do his best and
take what time he needed for so doing. I settled with
Hessey for my labour; had ten copies done up in their
actual state for distribution in London; and so washed my
hands of the concern, after exacting a solemn promise that
they would lose *no* time in forwarding the rest to Edinburgh.
The fortnight is already past and another fortnight to keep
it company; yet I left Bull[2] still picking and scraping at
his copper, still " three days " from the end of his labour !
So much for the patronage of genius ! Yet I suffer willingly; for my purpose was good, and this poor Cockney
has actually a meritorious heart ; and a meagre, patient
though dejected wife depends upon the scanty produce of
his burin. In two weeks from the present date, I calculate
that you *will* see *Schiller ;* sooner I dare not promise. It
will do little, I conjecture, to justify your impatience ; yet
as the first fruit of a mind that is one with yours forever, I
know that it will meet a kind reception from you ; and with
your approbation and my own, the chief part of my wishes
in the way of *fame* are satisfied. I have not put my name
to it ; for I desire no place among " the mob of gentlemen
that write with ease ;" and if mere selfish ambition *were* my
motive, I had rather not be named at all, than named
among that slender crew, as the author of a lank octavo
with so few pretensions. I seem to see the secret of these
things. Let a man be *true* in his intentions and his efforts
to fulfil them ; and the point is gained, whether he succeed
or not ! I smile when I hear of people dying of Reviews.
What is a reviewer sitting in his critical majesty, but *one*
man, with the usual modicum of brain, who thinks ill of us
or well of us, and tells the Earth that *he* thinks so, at the

---

[1] Feeble sprat.
[2] The engraver of the portrait of Schiller.

rate of fifteen guineas a sheet? The vain pretender, who
lives on the breath of others, he may hurt; but to the
honest workman who understands the worth and worthless-
ness of his own performance, he tells nothing that was not
far better understood already, or else he tells weak *lies;* in
both of which cases his intelligence is one of the simplest
things in Nature.   Let us always be true ! Truth may be
mistaken and rejected and trodden down; but like pure
gold it cannot be destroyed: after they have crushed it and
burnt it and cast it on the waters, they cry out that it is
lost, but the imperishable metal remains in its native purity,
no particle of it has been changed, and in due time it *will*
be prized and made to bless mankind to all ages.   If literature had no evils but false critics, it would be a very
manageable thing.   By the way, have you seen the last
number of the *London Magazine?*   Taylor told me it had a
"*letter to the Reviewer of Meister*" by some man from Cambridge.   I suppose it may be very stupid: but I have not
read it, or the criticism it is meant to impugn.   Goethe is
the Moon and these are penny-dogs; their barking *pro* or
con is chiefly their own concern.   I mean to send the
venerable Sage a copy of this *Schiller:* I like him better
than any living "man of letters," for he is a *man,* not a
dwarf of letters. . . .

CLX.—To Alexander Carlyle, Mainhill.

Birmingham, *4th March* 1825.

My dear Alick—No piece of news that I have heard for
a long time has given me more satisfaction than the intelligence contained in your letter of yesterday.   For several
weeks I have lived in a total dearth of tidings from you;
and both on account of your welfare, and of our mutual
projects in the farming line, I had begun to get into the
fidgets, and was ready to hasten homewards with many unpleasant imaginations to damp the expected joy of again
beholding friends so dear to me.   It now appears that all
is exactly as it should be : you are proceeding in your usual
style at Mainhill; and a dwelling-place upon the summit of

Repentance-height has already been provided for me.[1] This latter incident, I confess, was beyond my hopes. I feared we should be obliged, so soon as I arrived, to commence the weary task of farm-hunting ; in which, as the season was already far spent, it seemed likely enough that we should fail this year as we had done last, and the date of my establishment might be postponed for another twelvemonth. Happily all this is obviated. I make no doubt that Blackadder's place will fit us perfectly : the house, I conjecture, and partly recollect, is one of the best of its kind in the district ; and as for the management of the land, knowing your industry and our general resources, I am under no apprehension. Once fairly settled in that elevated position, we shall go on with the greatest *birr*.[2] . . .

I expect to see you all in a few days ; but in the meantime let not my absence in the least impede your movements. It is only in the furnishing of two apartments in the *house* that I can give you any useful counsel. Proceed, therefore, in laying in your necessary stock and implements as if you had my express and particular sanction. Get the *tack*[3] or minute of tack drawn out in *your own name*, for I am but as a lodger, and should make no figure in the character of one of Hoddam's tenants. The *entry*, I suppose, will not take place till Whitsunday ; but you will need to commence your ploughings and other preparations without delay. Let not my absence cause you to lose a moment. Take money from the Bank, and transact with it as you see proper. I think two such philosophers should show an *example* to the rude boors of Annandale : without " farming by the book," I hope we shall make a different

---

[1] For a description of Hoddam Hill, see *Reminiscences*, i. 285, and *Life*, by Froude, i. 298.

During the year spent at Hoddam Hill Carlyle was busy with the translation of *Specimens of German Romance*, which appeared in 1827 in four volumes.

" With all its manifold petty troubles, this year at Hoddam Hill has a rustic beauty and dignity to me ; and lies now (1867) like a not ignoble russet-coated Idyll in my memory ; one of the quietest, on the whole, and perhaps the most triumphantly important of my life." See the remainder of the striking passage, of which this is the first sentence, in the *Reminiscences*.

[2] Force (*literally*, the whirring of a pheasant on rising).

[3] Lease.

thing of it than a routine clodhopper who thinks the world is bounded by "the five parishes," would make of it.

My Mother need not be assured of the pleasure I feel in having this prospect of being once more under her superintendence. . . . She speaks of knives being cheap in Birmingham ; but I fear I am a bad merchant anywhere. The people seem to read in my face that I cannot higgle or beat down their prices ; so they almost always overcharge me. Nevertheless I mean to try. But we shall need many things of that domestic sort ; and our good Mother shall take a journey to Dumfries and buy them according to her own sagacity by the lump. It is like a sort of marriage ; at least, it is a house-heating ! Let us be thankful that we are all to be together : all still spared to be a blessing to each other. . . .

It is not without regret that I leave England ; and I cling to the hope of often seeing it again. I have found more kindness in it than I ever found in any other district of the Earth, except the one that holds my Father's house. If stony Edinburgh be no better to me than it was, I will shake the dust off my feet against it, and abide in it no more. My health will return, and then I shall be ready for any scene. There are warm hearts everywhere, but they seem to meet one with greater frankness here. Yesterday I had a letter from Mrs. Strachey, which was soon followed by a box containing a *new* present of the most superb writing-desk I have ever seen ! I should think, with its accompaniments, it cannot have cost much less than twenty guineas. I am writing on it at this moment, and design to keep it as a precious memorial all my days. These are things that make me wonder.

. . . The sheet is done. Adieu, my dear Brother.—I am, always yours,

TH. CARLYLE.

I hope my Father approves of all these farming schemes, and will not think of burthening himself further with Mainhill and its plashy soil when the lease has expired. If I write again it will be to him. Meanwhile give my warmest love to every mortal about home, beginning with my trusty Mag and ending with the youngest stay of the house, little Jenny. Tell my Mother I have a book for her, a present from Irving, which he hopes she will like. The time is done; I must be gone.

CLXI.—To Miss Welsh, Haddington.

Mainhill, *22d May* 1825.

. . . I am living here in the middle of confusion worse confounded : the cares that occupy me are not those of the philosopher on paper, but of the philosopher *in foro ;* it is not the talents of the *bel esprit* but those of the upholsterer that will stead me. There is no syllable of translation, far less of composition (save of bed-hangings, and green or yellow washes), nor will there be for two good weeks at least; nothing but cheapening and computation, and fighting with the pitiful details of Whitsunday,[1] and future housekeeping. I have read nothing, but half of one German novel, last Sunday! Not long ago, all this would have made me miserable; but at present I submit to it with equanimity, and even find enjoyment in the thought that in this humblest of the spheres of existence I am *doing* all I can to save my spirit and my fortunes from the shipwreck which threatened them, and to fit me for discharging to myself and others whatever duties my natural or accidental capabilities, slender but actually existing as they are, point out and impose upon me. Alas, Jane! there is *no* Bird of Paradise; nothing that can live upon the odour of flowers, and hover among pure ether, without ever lighting on the clay of Earth! The eagle itself must gather sticks to build its nest, and in its highest soarings keep an eye upon its creeping prey. Once I thought this a sad arrangement; now I do not think so. "The mind of man" is a machine considerably more complex than a pepper or even coffee mill; there is a strength and beauty where at first there seemed only weakness and deformity; our highest happiness is connected with our meanest wants. I begin to approve of this. At any rate *wir sind nun einmal so gemacht,* and there is an end of it.

---

[1] Scotch Term-day, on which Carlyle entered upon his tenancy of Hoddam Hill.

One thing that pleases and consoles me at present is my increased and increasing faith in the return of health, the goal of all these efforts. I am already *wonderfully* better than when you saw me : I am a driveller if, in spite of all impediments from others and myself, I do not grow completely well. The thought of this is like a second boyhood to me : glimpses of old purposes and feelings dawn on my horizon with an aspect more earnest but not less lovely; I swear that I will be a *wise man.* . . .

I more and more applaud myself for having fled from towns, and chosen this simple scene for the commencement of my operations. Heaven pity those that are sweltering to-day along the fiery pavements of London, begirt with smoke and putrefaction and the boundless tumults and distractions of that huge treadmill! Here I can see from Hartfell to Helvellyn, from Criffel to the Crags of Christenberry; a green unmanufactured carpet covers all the circle of my vision, fleecy clouds and the azure vault are above me, and the pure breath of my native Solway blows wooingly through all my haunts. Internally and morally, the difference is not less important in my favour. Stupidity and selfishness make up the general character of men in the country as they do in towns; but here one has the privilege of freedom from the sight of it ; all dunces and Turks in grain, one transacts his painful hour of business with and packs away, with an implied injunction, peremptory though unpronounced, not again to trouble one till another hour of business shall arrive. "But then society?"—There is little of it on Earth, very little : and unhappy is the man whose own door does not enclose what is worth all the rest of it ten times told. . . . .

On Thursday we split up our establishment here, and one division of us files away to Hoddam Hill. What a hurly-burly, what an anarchy and chaos! In less than forty days, the deluge will abate, however ; and the first olive branch (of peace and health) will show itself above the mud. My literary projects are till then stationary, but not unfit for moving in a calmer time. Crabbe Robinson has written to me ; I saw Sir W. Hamilton (apparently among the best men I have ever met in Edinburgh), and Dr. Irving introduced me to Dr. Julius (Yooliooss) of Hamburg,[1] who almost embraced me as a father, because I had written a Life of Schiller and translated a novel of Goethe's. Julius is a man of letters, as well as a Doctor, and a person of official dignity, being sent by his government to investigate the laws of quarantine, which our parliament now meditates altering. I regretted that my previous arrangements hindered me from seeing him above an hour; but I liked him much, and he promised to write me his advice regarding these German books some time in Summer. So far all is well.

I had left my trunks at Moffat, and they did not come till two days after my arrival. Your little box I opened in the presence of many eager faces; your gifts were snatched with *lauter Jubelgeschrei;* I question if ever gifts were welcomed with truer thanks or gave more happiness to the receivers. All stood amazed at the elegance of their "very grand" acquisitions, some praised in words the generous young *leddy* who had sent them, little Jenny flourished her green bag "like an antique Maenad," and for the whole evening was observed to be *a wee carried*, even when the first blush of the business was over. My Mother was as proud (*purse*-proud) as any. . . .

Can you execute a commission for me, and will you? James Johnstone, the meek pedagogue of whom you have héard me speak, is returned from France, and wishes to exchange his present place of Tutor in a family at Broughty Ferry for some permanent appointment in a school. Will you walk over any day to Grant's Braes, and ask Gilbert Burns if there *is* to be a parish-school in Haddington, and when and how, and send me word minutely when you write? I love this good simple man, and would gladly see him settled in a station which he could fill with such profit to himself and others. This is a prosaic charge I give you: but for my sake and your love of goodness you will accomplish it. . . .

---

[1] A widely-travelled scholar and philanthropist. He was in the United States in 1834-35, studying systems of prison discipline, to report on them to his government. His name occurs in the *Life of Ticknor*, whose *History of Spanish Literature* he translated into German.

CLXII.—To Miss WELSH, Haddington.

HODDAM HILL, August [?] 1825.

. . . Poor miserable sons of Adam! There is a spark of heavenly fire within us, an ethereal glow of Love and Wisdom, for it was the breath of God that made us living souls; but we are formed of the dust of the ground, and our lot is cast on Earth, and the fire lies hid among the ashes of our fortune, or burns with a fitful twinkle, which Chance, not we, can foster. It makes me sad to think how very small a part we are of what we might be; how men struggle with the great trade-winds of Life, and are borne below the haven by squalls and currents which they knew not of; how they toil and strain, and are again deceived; and how at last tired nature casts away the helm, and leaves her bark to float at random, careless to what unknown rock or shore the gloomy tide may bear it. Will affection also die at last in that inhospitable scene? Will the excellent become to us no better than the common, and the Spirit of the Universe with his thousand voices speak to us in vain? Alas! must the heart itself grow dull and callous, as its hopes one after the other shrink and wither? "*Armseliger Faust, ich kenne dich nicht mehr!*"

You perceive my preaching faculty is not a whit diminished, had I opportunity to give it scope. This place in fact is favourable for it. . . . My Mother does not know that I am writing to you, or her "kindest compliments" would form a portion of my letter. She is far from well in health, and has not like me the hope of ever recovering it. *Her* country is on the other side of the Stars! I were a Turk if I did not love her.—Jane was here the other night; she is sewing *Samplers*, stitching-in names and robin-redbreasts and all sorts of mosaic needlework. Among a crowd of vulgar initials, I asked her what the "J. W." meant? who was he? She paused; then with a look of timorous archness, answered: "It's no a *he* ava'!" . . .

CLXIII.—To Mr. James Johnstone, Broughty Ferry.

Hoddam Hill, *26th October* 1825.

My dear Johnstone—I was last night assisting at the late but jovial celebration of the Mainhilll *Kirn*,[1] and happened among other members of the party to meet with honest Gavin of Bogside, one of whose first announcements was that he had a few days ago had a letter from you, containing compliments to me, and a memento that in the article of correspondence I was your debtor. This I had for some time known, and felt with proper repentance, and purposes of alteration; Gavin's hint falls in timefully with a slight interval in my occupation; and to-day I mean to clear scores.

Your last letter with the news of your Haddington journey found me in a season of busy dissipation, but was cordially welcomed, and afforded true satisfaction, I may say, to every individual of the family. We all rejoice in your prospects of a settlement, and feel great confidence that you will succeed both in obtaining and happily conducting the employment.[2] In Haddington and its neighbourhood you will find many worthy persons of the stamp you like; among whom you will be able to fix down, as in a home, and feel yourself "a man among your fellow-men." Gilbert Burns I regard as a most estimable character; and I think you may now count on his forwarding your object by all means in his power, as well as rendering it agreeable to you should you attain it. I am told that he has far more to say in the affair than any other. I will give you more introductions should you go to settle there; and in a short

---

[1] Harvest home festival.

[2] Johnstone "heard of Haddington Parish School, applied to me; I sent him with his testimonials, etc., to *her :* she, generous heroine, adopted his cause as if it had been mine and her own; convinced Gilbert Burns (a main card in such things), convinced etc. etc.; and, ere long, sees him *admitted*, as fairly the fittest man! He started, prospered, took an Annandale wife; 'fortunate at last!'—but, alas, his poor agues, etc. (contracted in Nova Scotia), still hung about him, and in five or six years he died. I think I saw him only *twice* after [1826], once at Haddington, in his own house with wife and little daughter; once at Comley Bank on a Saturday till Monday: rather dreary both times; and I had, and again have, to say, Adieu, my poor good James!"— T. C., 1869.

time you will need none.   Brown the late Burgher Preacher
has left that quarter, and come to settle at Moffat ; so that
the coast is now clear.   Let us rejoice in the prospect of
any luck at all, in this most magnificent earth ; and "be
thankful," as the late Mr. M'Leod of Brownknowe was wont
to say, "that we are not in Purgatory"!

Of my own history since you left these parts, I need
say but little.   Few persons in the British Isles have spent
an idler summer than I, and it is long since I spent one as
happy.   Basil Montagu of London wishes it to be written
on his tombstone that he was "a lover of all quiet things ;"
but in my own opinion I (and several snails) may with
justice dispute him the pre-eminence in this distinction.   I
have done, thought, felt, or spoken very little since I saw
you.   At times I get into a Highland anger at this arrangement ; and of late I have begun to change it a little ; but
on the whole I think it prudent to content myself with my
present modicum of even negative good fortune, and like a
prudent Christian to *jook* [duck] *and let the jaw* [gush] *gae
by*, however hard my stance may be, so it but even moderately shelter me.   I believe myself to be improving in
point of health ; and with health I calculate that many
other blessings will be restored to me.   I have been at
school for many years under the tuition of a pedagogue
called Fate ; he is an excellent teacher, but his fees are
very high, and his *tawse*[1] are rather heavy.   By and by I
shall become a good child, and the old knave will cease to
flog me.

We live here on our hill-top enjoying a degree of solitude
that might content the great Zimmermann himself.   Few
mortals come to visit us, I go to visit none ; I have not
even once been down at Ruthwell since my return to
Scotland !   No news, literary, political, or economical, get
at us ; except perhaps a transient hint of the Stagshaw or
Falkirk Tryst, or a note of jubilee at the present *fairish*
prices of oats and barley.   Like Gallio of old I care for
none of these things.   My heart is weary of the inane toils
of mortal men ; I have gladly given them up the world for
a season "to make a kirk and a mill of,"[2] if it please
them ; all I require is that they would be so good as "leave

---

[1] Lashes.   [2] Scotch proverb = in fee simple.

me, leave me to repose." Perhaps a better day is coming; if not, *qu'importe?* "The mind of man," it appears from Mr. Smith, late cordwainer in Ecclefechan, "can accommodate itself to circumstances." Let it do so, and be hanged to it ! . . .

Edward Irving was in Annan last week for a little while; and I passed half a day with him. He is of a green hue, solemn, sad, and in bad bodily condition. The worthy man (for so he is, when every say is said) has lost his boy at Kirkcaldy, and left his wife there, who had brought him a daughter only ten days before that event. He bears it well; for his heart is full of other wondrous things, from which he draws peculiar consolation. He seems, as his enemies would say, still madder than before. But it is not madness : would to Heaven we were all thus mad ! He is about publishing another Book, or Prophecy. Irving is actually one of the memorabilia of this century.

In the last *Edinburgh Review* you would find a critique of *Wilhelm Meister*, apparently by Jeffrey himself. It amused me not a little ; and, I may say, gratified me too. I think the critic very honest, and very seldom unjust in his feeling of individual passages ; but for the general whole, which constitutes the essence of a work like this, he seems to have no manner of idea of it, except as a heap of beautiful and ugly fragments. True criticism, thanks to our Reviews and Magazines, bids fair to become one of the *artes perditæ* ere long : And then—"then joy old England raise," for thy mob of gentlemen will have halcyon times, goose feathers will rise in value, and paper will again be manufactured from straw ! Jeffrey's little theory of Goethe is an exquisite affair. Yet Jeffrey is an honest and clever man, and by far the best of them all.

Gavin tells us you are coming down to Annandale this winter ; my only prayer is, come soon. John, who is sitting by me, hopes to see you as you pass through Edinburgh, and sends you his best regards. All the rest salute you kindly. John has been very busy all summer, and is to leave us in a week or two. Write when you have any time, at large and at length.—I am, ever your affectionate friend,

THOMAS CARLYLE.

CLXIV.—To Miss Welsh, Templand, Thornhill.

Hoddam Hill, 4th November 1825.

. . . During my half-week's repose I was busily meditating some scheme of a *Kunstwerk* of my own ! There are pictures and thoughts and feelings in me, which *shall* come out, though the Devil himself withstood it ! For this time, it was Larry, not the Devil. That ungrateful untoward nag has used me like a knave. He had taken cold, and staid unmolested in his shop for three days ; on the fourth I took him out to *walk* round by *the* Smithy and Hoddam Kirk. I was thinking of you and my *Kunstwerk*, when I met a carrier's cart, and my cursed beast, knowing that I was studying and had nothing but a snaffle bridle, got the bit in his teeth, whirled round at full gallop down a steep place, and had my fair person dislodged from his back and trailed some yards upon the base highway in the twinkling of an eye ! *Proh pudor !* I was stunned and scratched and thoroughly bemired ; I have scarcely got quit of my headache, and the tailor is mending my coat even now. Larry's friendship and mine is at an end ! . . .

CLXV.—To John A. Carlyle, Edinburgh.

Hoddam Hill, 1st December 1825.

. . . For some days after you left me I felt quite *harried*[1] and disconsolate ; a dreary loneliness took possession of me go where I would. Time and diligence in business have now somewhat reconciled me ; and I look upon your absence with a mild regret, and the hope of soon meeting you again. These separations, though painful, are not useless : they teach us to prize duly what the daily presence of makes trivial in our eyes ; if we had our friends always we should never know how much we loved them. Continue to trust me, my good Jack, as of old ; for though distempers and the most despicable distresses make me choleric and frequently unreasonable, I love you truly, and have no dearer wish than to see you prospering beside me. I lament to think that my power of aiding you should be so limited. . . .

---

[1] Despoiled.

Of our proceedings here since your departure the history may soon be told. Conceive the three most quiescent weeks of your experience in Hoddam Hill, and write *ditto ditto* as the account of these. At my return from convoying you, I found Mrs. Irving and Gavin of Bogside waiting here; they had come to take farewell of you, and missed their purpose by a few minutes. Since that night we have had no visitor, or event worth notice even here. Alick feeds his stall-cattle and pokes about doing odd jobs throughout the day, and at night comes and reads beside me. My Mother and I have our private cup of tea as usual: she spins and fights about. . . .

For myself I have gone along with exemplary industry for several weeks; translating daily my appointed task; walking and smoking at intervals, and turning neither to the right hand nor the left, as if I were a scribbling, smoking, sleeping, and dyspeptical automaton. I am through *Mute Love* and *Libussa* in Musäus: yesterday morning I began *Melechsala*, which will conclude my doings with that scornful gentleman; unless I think of adding the *Treasure-digger* to my list. . . .

CLXVI.—To Miss Welsh, Haddington.

Hoddam Hill, 11*th December* 1825.

. . . On computing manuscripts last night, I was surprised to find that *two* of my three volumes are almost wholly in black and white; that is, the translation part of them. I wish the thing were off my hands, that I might make an effort after some undertaking of more pith and moment. Alas! The matter lies deep and crude, if it lies at all, within my soul; and much unwearied study will be called for before I can shape it into form. Yet out it shall come, by all the powers of Dulness! And thou, my fair Guardian Saint, my kind hot-tempered Angel, my beloved scolding Wife, thou shalt help me with it, and rejoice with me in success or comfort me in failure! I do rejoice to hear you talk as you do, and as I always hoped you would, about the vulgar bubble Fame. My experience more and more confirms me in my reprobation of it as a principle of conduct; in myself it never leads to aught but selfish discontent, and distraction of the mind from the true aims of a literary aspirant. " Fame !" says my old Goethe; "as if a man had nothing else to strive for but fame ! As if the attainment of harmony in his own spirit, and the right employment of his faculties, required to be varnished over by its influences on others before it could be precious to himself !" This Goethe is a wise man. These are not his words; but they express his opinion, which I joyed to find so similar to my anticipation. You are right now, and you were wrong then : therefore love me with your whole soul ; and if fame come to us, it shall be welcome ; if not, we care not for it, having something far more precious than it can either give or take away. . . .

CLXVII.—To John A. Carlyle, Edinburgh.

Hoddam Hill, 15th December 1825.

. . . Your letter came about eight days ago, to satisfy us touching your welfare, and found us all pretty much as you represent yourself, " in the old way," each minding his several duties, and struggling on through this rough pilgrimage of life with the usual proportion of *glar* and *Macadam* on our path, and the usual mixture of vapour and sunshine in our sky. It was very mindful in you to write so punctually ; the more so as our Mother says that negligence in that social duty is a sin which easily besets you. There is still a kind of *vaakum* here in your absence ; and many times at night when I lie down to bed, I think that poor Jack is sheltering himself beneath the roof of the stranger : but what can we do ? One must follow the ball just where that slippery jade Fortune chooses to trundle it; and even if we could continue in a place, the place itself would crumble away from beneath us, and we should find that, take it as we may, we are foreigners and wayfarers in this Earth, and have no continuing city within its limits. *Ach, Du guter Gott, erbarme Dich unser !*

I am happy that you have betaken yourself to earnest business, the blessing, disguised as a curse, of sublunary beings ; and are diligently meditating to do quickly whatsoever your hand findeth to do. I think this *Thesis* [1] ought

---

[1] For his Doctorate.

to answer well, and profit you both in the composition of it, and perhaps also in the foundation of a character which you may lay with it. No doubt you are thinking of it often: the more maturely the better. And be not discouraged, though at first your pen be restive, and the sheet remain white after many hours of brain-beating. It is never too good a symptom of a man that he composes easily at first. "In a crowded church," says Swift in some such words, "the doors get jammed as the audience disperses, and the outcome is slow and irregular; when there is none but the parson and the clerk, they come out rapidly and without disorder." Thus likewise it is with ideas in issuing from the secret dormitories of the mind. Æneas Rait could write a poem sooner than Virgilius Maro did.

Last time I wrote, I talked rather distantly about my journey northward: I now find that adventure lying much closer at my door than I expected. *Musäus* is done off, three nights ago; and I find myself within a cat's leap of the end of my existing materials. . . .

CLXVIII.—To JOHN A. CARLYLE, Edinburgh.

HODDAM HILL, 24*th December* 1825.

. . . For the last two weeks I have been very idle again, having done nothing that I can recollect save writing this very pitiful *Life of Musäus*. I have been out of books, indeed; for I cannot resolve upon this *Undine* of Fouqué's, till after I have seen the *Todtenbund* in the Advocates' Library. . . .

The principal public news of this quarter is touching a sort of silver tray or epergne or waiter or some commodity of that sort which certain of the natives, instigated by "Sandy Corrie," have been presenting to Mr. Yorstoun, our venerable parson. The value of the plate is seventy guineas of gold. Nine and thirty men sat down to dinner in the Grapes Inn yesterday, at what hour I know not, His Honour in the chair; and after a due consumpt of tough beef with wine and British spirits the tray, or whatever it is, was laid upon the genial board, and presented by *the* General,[1] with an appropriate speech, which he regretted that a day's hard

[1] General Sharpe of Hoddam.

hunting had prevented him from rendering more appropriate by previous meditation.   Dr. Simpson also sang a bawdy song.   Orations (not for the oracles) were delivered by various hands ; and after protracting the feast of reason and the flow of soul till the keystone of the night had mounted over their heads, the meeting with extreme hilarity and glee, etc. etc.   Will Brand, stinking with whisky like the mash-tub of the Celt, told me this to-day, while I was searching for a book in his Press and finding none.

Of domestic news, more interesting to you, I must not forget to mention the speculation for Shawbrae.[1]   They have offered for the farm together with Hab Hunter's "lower Bogside" a rent of £230, by the hands of Alick last Wednesday.   Miss Welsh has also written a strong letter to Major Creighton in their favour ; so that they have considerable hope of prospering, though several others have offered and are offering.   It will be decided in three weeks ; till which time, for this and similar concerns, there will be nothing but unbounded conjecture and reports assuming new forms daily, and not worth listening to in any form. Our Father is in high spirits about the matter ; our Mother's wishes are still keener though she is "ready to submit to His disposal ; " in fact every one (not even excepting me) is anxious for an affirmative answer. . . .

CLXIX.—To his MOTHER, Hoddam Hill

21 SALISBURY STREET, EDINBURGH
(6th January), Friday night, 1826.

. . . . The first and most important piece of intelligence I have to communicate is the assurance that I am arrived in perfect safety, and proceeding in my affairs with all imaginable prosperity.   Many a time yesterday, as the wild blasts came howling round me, I thought of your dismal imaginings, and wished that you could have known how snug I was, and how little I cared about the tempest.   From the road on this side of Ae-Bridge[2] I looked over my *right* shoulder, and saw Barhill and Burnswark, and the Tower

---

[1] "A 'Duke's farm' fallen vacant ; which my Brother Alick pressingly wanted, but (happily) did not get."—T. C.

[2] On the coach road between Dumfries and Moffat.

of Repentance (no bigger than a moderate pepper-box) all glancing in the clear frosty breeze ; and figured you out as smoking diligently and wondering *" how that poor habbletree was fenning ava ;"* [1] while the "poor habbletree" was fenning as well as any one of you.

Sandy would bring up my history to the date of my parting from the hospitable home of John Greer ; [2] a parting so hurried that I had not time to bid a syllable of farewell even to my Brother.   I buckled up my dreadnought, and thought that a better hour would come.   On the whole that dreadnought did essential service throughout the day : cased in it, I turned my back to the breeze, lit my pipe as occasion served, and sat whiffing in the most composed frame of mind, defying all the war of the elements, and knowing chiefly by report that it was "a very rough day." The poor "mason lad," who sat beside me, suffered most : the rest left us at Moffat ; so that he was exposed on all sides ; and being very insufficiently wrapped, he grew exceedingly cold.   I pitied the poor youth, and thought of the small vein of enterprise which he was pursuing through such hardship, and of his parting from his mother, and the sorry welcome that his light purse would procure him at his journey's end.   Twice I revived his fainting soul with a touch of tobacco-reek, which he inhaled with rapture from my instrument ; I also now and then lent him a lap of my cloak, for which he repaid me gratefully with a bit of gingerbread ; and the result was that when we reached Edinburgh about half-past four, he was *not* either dead or speechless.

.   .   .   .   .   .

CLXX.—To Miss WELSH, Haddington.

EDINBURGH, 21*st January* 1826.

. . . Of late I have been meditating more intently than ever the project of that Literary Newspaper.   Brewster is still full of it, so is the Bookseller Tait : I myself think it would pay well, but the labour is tremendous.   Brewster, it seems, had engaged Lockhart to take a third share in it

---

[1] How that poor lank one was making shift at all.

[2] Carlyle's uncle by marriage, who lived near Dumfries.

along with him and me ; in which case I should have closed
with the proposal without hesitation. Now Lockhart's preferment has overturned all that, and the matter rests where
it was. I view it with wavering feelings, in which on the
whole hope and desire predominate. As to the nature of
the business, it may be honourable or base according
to the nature of its accomplishment. Did not the great
Schlegel edit a literary newspaper at Jena? Did not
Wieland and Schiller at Weimar? By and by the business
would get lighter, and I should get help in carrying it on,
and find leisure for more permanent and weighty undertakings. Brewster would have it begun at Whitsunday or
next November : in either case I should have to live in
this vicinity, in my own hired house. Twice have I actually
been out spying the aspects of the country; it is not an
hour since I returned from Morningside, where there are
houses in plenty of every quality. My plan would be to
take a small one ; bring in Mary and Jane to keep it for
me, till I saw the promise of our enterprise, and then
bring in——If she would come ! would she ? How do
you like this form of action ? Give me all your criticisms
without stint or reservation. It is right that we should
both be satisfied, for it is strictly an affair of the *common-
weal*. Poor old common-weal ! It is pity that it should
not flourish better : but we will manage it and force it to
flourish.

.   .   .   .   .   .

My sheet is done, and the hour of four is just at hand.
To-night I have to write to Goethe, and send him the copy
of *Schiller* by a person that is going to London. Therefore
I must on all accounts have done. There is nothing but
bankruptcy going on here. Constable the huge bookseller
has failed ; then Ballantyne (my present printer); and to-
day Sir Walter Scott. Sir Walter was deeply involved with
both : his debt is said to be £60,000 ; and it seems he
takes it heavily to heart ; is fallen sick and gone to bed,
and refuses to be comforted. *O curas hominum ! O
quantum est in rebus inane !* . . .

CLXXI.—To John A. Carlyle, Edinburgh.

Hoddam Hill, Monday (March 1826).

. . . You are quite correct in your inference about Scotsbrig. Our Father returned, Thursday week, "on his fir deal," at the hind foot of Larry and Alick; after doing great business in the mighty waters. By dint of unbounded higgling, and the most consummate diplomacy, the point was achieved to complete satisfaction of the two husband-men; and Scotsbrig, free of various "clags [1] and claims," which they had argued away, obtained for a rent of £190 (cheap, as they reckon it), in the face of many competitors. A solemn ploughing-day was held last week; and by the aid of ale and stingo, much work was effected. I rode over and saw them; a truly spirit-stirring sight. The people also are to repair the house effectually; to floor it anew, put *bun*-doors [2] on it, new windows, and so forth; and it seems "it is an excellent *shell* of a house already." Alick is ploughing at Mainhill, with two new horses; our Father is looking out for a sedate-minded Galloway to carry him "between toon and toon," [3] and so all is running on cart-wheels with us here. Our Mother declares that there is "plenty of both *peats* and *water ;*" others think "the farm is the best in Middlebie parish*in ;*" our Father seems to have renewed his youth even as the eagle's age.

So, my good Jack, there will still be a home for thee here; with as true a welcome, and I hope better accommodation than ever. Therefore get thy Thesis printed, and thy graduation effected; and come home to us, with the speed of light, in the Dumfries Diligence; and look about thee, and take breath a little, till we see what more is to be done. Tell me in the meantime when thy money is wearing scant, and we will get some more. . . .

CLXXII.—To John A. Carlyle, Edinburgh.

Scotsbrig, [1] *May 1826, Tuesday night.*

My dear Jack—I got your letter on Monday; and I

---

[1] Clogs, incumbrances.
[2] *Bound* or panelled doors.
[3] Between farm and farm.
[4] In May 1826 Carlyle's father had left Mainhill, and got "on another

need not tell you that the contents of it gratified me not a little. You must have had a busy time of it lately ; taking houses and getting degrees ! Let us be thankful that things wear so fair an aspect and have hitherto turned out so well : I doubt not but we shall all by and by be wonderfully comfortable.

I gratified all hands here, as I myself had been, by informing them of your first step towards graduation. "Not of works, lest we should boast !" the Apostle says ; but really it is fair enough to go through so handsomely, without aid from any grinder or *honer* whatever, but purely by one's own resources. For the rest, doubt not that your moodiness was temporary ; the slackening of the long-stretched cord, when the arrow was shot away : in a day or two the yew will tighten it again. The world is but beginning for you yet ; and it is wide and broad, far beyond what you conjecture. It really is, Jack ; though in hypochondriacal moments you will not believe a word of it. Come to me wherever I be, when you have finished ; and take plenty of time to consider what your next step must be. While either of us has a home, the other cannot want one.

We are all got over with whole bones to this new country ; and every soul of us, our Mother to begin with, much in love with it. The house is in bad order ; but we hope to have it soon repaired ; and for farming purposes it is an excellent " shell of a house." Then we have a *linn* with crags and bushes, and a " fairy knowe," though no fairies that I have seen yet ; and, cries our Mother, abundance of grand thready peats, and water from the brook, and no reek and no Honour [1] to pester us ! To say nothing, cries our Father, of the eighteen *yeacre* of the best barley in the county ; and bog-hay, adds Alick, to fatten scores of young beasts !

estate near by, the farm of Scotsbrig, a far better farm, where (1868) our people still are . . . where, if anywhere in the country, I from and after May 1826 must make up my mind to live. To stay there till *German Romance* was done,—clear as to that—went accordingly, and after a week of joinering resumed my stint of ten daily pages, steady as the town clock, no interruption dreaded or occurring. Had a pleasant, diligent, and interesting summer."—*Life*, i. 331.

[1] " His Honour," General Sharpe.

In fact, making all allowance for newfangledness, it is a *much* better place, so far as I can judge, than any our people have yet been in; and among a far better and kindlier sort of people. I believe of a truth they will find themselves much obliged to his Honour for persecuting them away. Long life to his Honour! I myself like the place considerably better, though I have slept but ill yet, and am bilious enough. But I have mounted your old straw-hat again; and fairly betaken me to work; and should, as we say Aberdeen-awa, " be bauld to compleen." . . .

I have had a bout with this *Life of Hoffmann :* it is far the worst, and has been far the most troublesome of them all. Henceforth I hope to supply M'Cork [1] regularly. Write more at large if you can next time. Alick goes to Whitsuntide fair at Dumfries to-morrow, and this should go with him; and all hands are already sound asleep. I have still another *notule* to write, which you will not fail to deliver. Good night!—I am, ever your affectionate Brother,   THOMAS CARLYLE.

Is Johnstone gone? My best wishes to him, if not.

CLXXIII.—To Miss WELSH, Haddington.

SCOTSBRIG, 18*th June* 1826.

. . . How many thousand thoughts might your last letter give rise to! We *are* it seems to begin this wonderful married life; a scene so strange to both of us, so full of hazards, and it may be of highest happiness! May the Fates award the latter; as they will, if we deserve it. . . .

I have called my task an Egyptian bondage, but that was a splenetic word, and came not from the heart but from the sore throat, for I have not been so happy for many a year as since I began this undertaking on my own strength, and in my own home: and is it not to have a *termination* which scarcely an Epic Poem could deserve? . . . The next Book I write, *another* shall help me to correct and arrange! And my fairest recompense will be the glad look of two kind black eyes through which a soul is looking that belongs to my soul for ever and ever! Let

[1] The printer.

us not despond in the life of honourable toil that lies before
us. . . . In labour lies health of body and of mind ; in
suffering and difficulty is the soil of all virtue and all
wisdom. . . . Let us but be true and good, and we have
nothing earthly to dread. . . .

I come to Edinburgh and to you when once this Book
is done. I am about fifth way gone in the last volume ;
the printers are nearly done with the preceding one. It is
very full of small cares, the process of manufacturing it ;
but I go along contentedly : for I reckon it though a poor
enough affair, yet an innocent, even a laudable one ; and
considerably the best sample of German genius that has
yet been presented to the English. And who can blame
me for a little satisfaction in the thought, that even I, poor
I, here in the wolds of Annandale, am doing somewhat to
instruct the thinkers of my own Country to do justice to
those of another? Well, I calculate that this Book, if I
am diligent, which I have cause enough to be, will be over
in about five or six weeks. I come to Edinburgh then, to
devise some other enterprise, to see you, and settle with
you once for all the preliminaries and paraphernalia of this
our magnificent Enterprise ! Till then I despair of thinking
any reasonable thought about this or any other matter :
what with " estimates of genius," what with estimates of
housekeeping, and dreams of· a wicked little gypsy that
haunts me, and solemn hopes and fears, and magnificent
and unfathomable anticipations, — I declare my head is
entirely overset, and has for the time being given up the
reins of management into other hands—those of Habit, I
suppose, and Imagination. . . .

[The following letter is in reply to a friendly and cordial letter from
Murray proposing to Carlyle to endeavour to secure the control and
editorship of the *Scots Magazine*, and offering to assist him with " a
hundred pounds or so " toward the purchase.

Constable, whose disastrous failure at the beginning of this year
had brought ruin to Sir Walter Scott, had been the publisher of this
venerable Magazine, which had now existed for ninety years, and his
creditors had resolved to give it up, as it scarcely did more than pay
for itself. Murray, with his far-sighted confidence in Carlyle's abilities,
felt convinced that if he would undertake to carry it on he could not
fail to make it successful. But nothing came of his suggestion and
friendly urgency in the matter.]

CLXXIV.—To Rev. Thomas Murray, Edinburgh
(care of Mr. Carlyle, 28 Broughton Street).

My dear Murray—I fear I must have seemed very ungrateful; for it is too true that your most friendly and acceptable letter has never yet been answered, though, if I mistake not, I had even in words engaged to repay that act of kindness without delay. You may believe me, want of will was not the *sole* cause. I feel as well as any one how good and helpful you are; nor is it among the least pleasing of my reflections to think that I still hold a place in your regard; that the friend of my boyhood (how rarely can this be told!) is still the friend of my riper years.

The truth of the matter is, I have been unusually busy of late months; not so busy indeed that I had not vacant minutes and even hours; but still so jostled to and fro by my avocations and immersed in the cares of them, as to be peculiarly *inept* for letter-writing, which accordingly (if this is any palliation), except in the most pressing cases, I have altogether forborne. I calculated on writing to you when this *Book* was done: but a new act of your attention forces me to take the pen sooner, if it were but to thank you for your readiness and eagerness at all times, as at this time, to do me service.

As to the practical part of the Speculation, I am wonderfully in the dark and the distance: the business of magazine-writing and the profits and disprofits of magazine-conducting are utterly alien to my thoughts, and still more to my experience; and your project, here in my rustic solitude, stands dim, vague, and unseizable before me, think of it as I may. One thing I know well: some *periodical task* would be peculiarly useful to me in all points of view. Another thing I am not half so sure of, but yet in a case of extremity it might be esteemed as possible: that the duties of periodical Editorship, as they are discharged to various degrees of perfection, by many mortals in these Islands, might also be by dint of great effort discharged by me, inexperienced in the world, unconnected with it, and in many other respects very unfit for such an undertaking as I cannot but feel myself to be. With these two propositions, however, I can say that my convictions on this individual matter are at an end ; and what steps, if any, to take in it is by no means clear to me. The purchase of the copyright, which you suggest, and with a true spirit, which I hope I shall not forget, offer to assist in, is a thing I must not think of. I have laid out nearly all my disposable capital here in the purchase of farm and house ware ; and to strip myself of daily ways and means, for an uncertain and probably distant future, were no wise policy. That therefore I must not do.

On the other hand, if in the vicissitudes of this ancient Periodical such a thing were possible, I think that on fair terms I could actually resolve to undertake the management of it. This is saying much, if you knew all my circumstances ; yet such is my present view of it. It would be particularly suitable, and I would make an effort : for be it known to you (under the rose, somewhat) I actually purpose taking up my abode in Edinburgh next winter, and starting as housekeeper by my present craft.

Now the question is : Can such a project as this same Editorship be in any wise feasible ? I know not, but rather think *nay*. One faint gleam of probability I see in the midst of my utter ignorance of the whole business : you speak of Black as likely to become proprietor ; now Black and Tait I believe are relations, and on a cordial footing ; both honest men, also, and Tait I understand in some little flow of spirits with me at present about his *German Novelists ;* from all which it strikes me as barely possible that the scheme might be worth asking one question about,—the question : Will Tait and Black, or one or other of them, purchase this Magazine, and make me the Editor thereof ? If so, I shall be ready and happy to give the matter a most profound deliberation ; and should their highest estimate of Editorial dues and my lowest be found capable of stretching till they meet,—to close a bargain with them, and start full speed and very shortly in my editorial career.

With you, therefore, my good Friend, I must leave the decision. If you think it worth while, all things considered, to speak with Tait or Black (in case you know him) on the subject, do so, and let me know the result. If you think it not worth while, then there is nothing more that I see for us to do in the matter, but to let it drop into deepest silence—till we meet in Ambrose's, whither I will venture for your sake, and drink one potion of whisky punch to the better luck of this old Scottish herring-boat, be it under the orders of Donald or the Son of Donald, or sunk in shoal water, and not sailing at all. Except Black and Tait, I recollect no bibliopolical person in Edinburgh, whom I should care for engaging with; and except on this principle, I see not that I could prudently take any hand in the concern even with them. Some hour when you have leisure, you will throw me a word on the subject; not forgetting other news of a kindred nature, of which for a great while I have been wonderfully short.

I cannot regret your stay in Edinburgh, though in the meanwhile it must be a sacrifice, for Edinburgh at this moment cannot fail to be a lively type of Purgatory. We have the heat here; but the dust and perfumes are wanting. To-day I bathed in the Solway flood, and actually my bath was tepid. Return thanks to Heaven that you are healthy, and can front all cities and countries with impunity.

What are you busy with since you relinquished the Church History scheme? Is *Samuel Rutherford* advancing?[1] I think you have little cause to regret the failure of that other project, at least its present failure: the great labour was certain, the hope of profit with the Taits inconsiderable; and for the honour of the business, there are fifty ways as open to you for gaining it. The Cameronian subject is too much betrodden at present, and the interest of it, in its present degree, can be but transient, fading away with the first new gloss of Mr. Cleishbotham's *Tales*: but even in your present walk, there are surely ample materials to furnish you with occupation of a far more specific and original sort; occupation too, which you are happy enough not to need except for its own sake. I have often wondered at the meagreness and scantiness of Scottish

---

[1] Murray was busy with a *Life of Rutherford*, a noted Presbyterian divine and professor in the seventeenth century, who became Rector of the University of St. Andrews. Some of his writings have been reprinted, and perhaps read, within late years in America as well as in Scotland.

Biography, especially that of Scottish literary men. Except Buchanan (a heavy enough gentleman, he seemed to me), we have *no* account that I could ever find of any of our ancient worthies. Who was Gawin Douglas? Who was Sir David Lindsay? Who was Baron Napier? These questions we must answer in a half-sentence. Did it never come into your head to start a regular series of Scottish (purely *Scottish*) Literary Biography? A thousand interesting things might be brought to light; touches of old manners, illustrations of history, bright sayings and doings; and no one that I know of is so fairly on the track as you for digging up these ancient treasures. Begin such a thing, and mark me down for your first subscriber. But I am babbling of things of which I know very little.

You mentioned nothing of the Newlands business to me when I saw you, nor in any of your letters. Be in no haste for a Church; and feel happy that you can do very comfortably without one, till the time come, whenever that be. I begin to see, one is fifty times better for being heartily drilled in the school of Experience, though beaten daily for years with forty stripes save one. I used to reckon myself very wretched, and now find that no jot of my castigation could have been spared. My last year, ungainly and isolated as it was, has been the happiest of my last half-score. I am getting healthier, nay more careless of health, more conscious that if the Devil do still please to torment me, I shall have *nous* enough in me to get the weather-gage of him, and snap my fingers in his face. I have thousands of things to say, but you see——!
—I am, truly yours,   T. C.

It is likely I may be in Edinburgh when this Book is published; some six weeks hence. I am in the last volume, but not far in it. The contents are of a strange enough sort, and motley as you could expect: four-fifths respectable *manufacture*, the rest perhaps *creation*. I here sign myself in full.—Your old and true friend,

THOMAS CARLYLE.

You can talk to John about this matter, if you like, for he knows all my secrets.

CLXXV.—To Miss Welsh, Templand.

Scotsbrig, Monday night
[9th October 1826].

"The Last Speech and *marrying* words of that unfortunate young woman Jane Baillie *Welsh*," I received on Friday morning; and truly a most delightful and swan-like melody was in them; a tenderness and warm devoted trust, worthy of such a maiden bidding farewell to the (unmarried) Earth, of which she was the fairest ornament. Dear little child! How is it that I have deserved thee; deserved a purer and nobler heart than falls to the lot of millions? I swear I will love thee with *my* whole heart, and think my life well spent if it can make thine happy.

In fine, these preliminaries are in the way towards adjustment. After some vain galloping and consultation, I have at length got that certificate which the Closeburn Session in their sapience deem necessary; I have ordered the Proclaiming of Banns in this parish of Middlebie, and written out a note giving order for it in your parish of Closeburn. Pity, by the way, that there is no man in the Closeburn Church possessed of any little fraction of vulgar earthly logic! It might have saved me a ride to Hoddam Manse this morning (the good Yorstoun, my native parson, was away), and a most absurd application to the "glass minister" my neighbour. One would think that after fair *crying* three times through the organs of Archibald Blacklock, this certificate of celibacy would be like gilding refined gold, or adding a perfume to the violet: for would not my existing wife, in case I had one, forthwith, at the first hum from Archibald's windpipe, start up in her place, and state aloud that *she* had "objections"? But I will not quarrel with these reverend men; *laissez les faire*, they will buckle us fast enough at length, and for the *How* I care not.

Your own day, Tuesday, as was fitting, I have made mine. Jack and I will surely call on Monday evening at Templand, most likely *after* tea; but I think it will be more commodious for all parties that we sleep at the Inn. You will not see me on Monday night? I bet two to one you will !   At all events I hope you will on Tuesday ; so, as Jack says, " it is much the same." . . .

Your mother will take down this note to the minister, and appoint the hour ?   I think it should be an early one, for we have far to go.   Perhaps also she might do something towards engaging post-horses at the Inn ; but I suppose there is little fear of failure in that point.

Do you know aught of wedding-gloves ?   I must leave all that to you ; for except a vague tradition of some such thing I am profoundly ignorant concerning the whole matter.   Or will you give *any ?   Ach du guter Gott !* Would we were off and away, three months before all these observances of the Ceremonial Law !

. . . I could say much ; and what were words to the sea of thoughts that rolls through my heart, when I feel that thou art mine, that I am thine, that henceforth we live not for ourselves but for each other !   Let us pray to God that our holy purposes be not frustrated ; let us trust in Him and in each other, and fear no evil that can befall us.   My last blessing as a Lover is with you ; this is my last letter to Jane Welsh. . . .

Good night, then, for the last time we have to part.   In a week I see you, in a week you are my own. . . .

Carlyle and Miss Welsh were married, according to the practice of the Scotch Church, in the Bride's home, her grandfather's house at Templand, on the 17th October 1826.

APPENDIX

THE letters that passed between Carlyle and Miss Welsh from
their first acquaintance in 1821 till their marriage in 1826
afford a view of their characters and their relations to each
other, different both in particulars and in general effect from
that given by Mr. Froude. His narrative is a story "founded
on fact," elaborated with the art of a practised romancer, in
which assertion and inference, unsupported by evidence or
contradictory to it, often take the place of correct statement.
Even if the form of truth be preserved, a colour not its own is
given to it by the imagination of the writer.

To exhibit completely the extent and quality of the diver-
gence of Mr. Froude's narrative from the truth, the whole
story would have to be rewritten, and letters would have to be
printed which, in my judgment, are too sacred for publication.
But I believe that, consistently with a due regard to the nature
of the source from which they are drawn, some illustrations
may be given of Mr. Froude's method that will suffice to show
the real character of his work, and the amount of trust that is
to be reposed in it.

Near the outset of his account of the first acquaintance of
Carlyle and Miss Welsh, Mr. Froude tells the story, which
will be remembered by all readers of his book, of the relations
between Edward Irving and Miss Welsh, of his falling in love
with her after his engagement to his future wife, of her recipro-
cation of his feeling, of her refusal to encourage him because
of the bonds by which he was held, and of the conclusion of
the affair by his marriage to Miss Martin. It was an affair
discreditable to Irving, and for a time it brought much suffering to Miss Welsh. Mr. Froude is aware that the telling of
such a private experience requires excuse, and he justifies it

by the following plea :—" I should not unveil a story so sacred in itself, and in which the public have no concern, merely to amuse their curiosity ; but Mrs. Carlyle's character was profoundly affected by this early disappointment, and cannot be understood without a knowledge of it. Carlyle himself, though acquainted generally with the circumstances, never realised completely the intensity of the feeling which had been crushed." —*Life*, i. 156.

Both of these alleged grounds of excuse are contradicted by the evidence of the letters of Miss Welsh and of Carlyle. Her letters show that her feelings for Irving, first controlled by principle and honour, soon underwent a very natural change. Her love for him was the passion of an ardent and inexperienced girl, twenty or twenty-one years old, whose character was undeveloped, and who had but an imperfect understanding of the capacities and demands of her own nature. In the years that followed upon this incident she made rapid progress in self-knowledge and in the knowledge of others, chiefly through Carlyle's influence, and she came to a more just estimate of Irving's character than she originally had formed. Irving's letters to her, his career in London, his published writings, revealed to her clear discernment his essential weakness,—his vanity, his mawkish sentimentality, his self-deception, his extravagance verging to cant in matters of religion. The contrast between his nature and Carlyle's did "affect her profoundly," and her temporary passion for Irving was succeeded by a far deeper and healthier love. "What an idiot I was for ever thinking that man so estimable," she wrote in May 1824. "My standard of men is immensely improved," she said in a letter in September of the same year.

Mr. Froude asserts, later on in his well-worked-up narration, "that an accident precipitated the relations between himself [Carlyle] and Miss Welsh, which had seemed likely to be long protracted, and after threatening to separate them for ever, threw them more completely one upon the other" (i. 303). He then gives an account of certain somewhat officious letters written by Mrs. Montagu to Miss Welsh, concerning her feelings for Irving and her engagement to Carlyle, and of the effect produced by them. He says that he alludes to the subject only because Mrs. Carlyle "said afterwards that but for the unconscious action of a comparative stranger her engagement with Carlyle would probably never have been carried out" (i. 304, *note*). If Mrs. Carlyle ever used these words, her fancy, her memory, or her temper would seem at the

moment to have played her false.   The evidence afforded by
her letters is ample, is convincing, that Mrs. Montagu's action
did not affect the result.

Mr. Froude gives a long abstract of a letter of Mrs.
Montagu's, the date of which, omitted by him, was 3d July
1825, urging Miss Welsh not to marry Carlyle if she retained
her old feeling for Irving, now married for some years, and he
says : " With characteristic integrity, Miss Welsh on receiving
this letter instantly enclosed it to Carlyle " (i. 306).   This is
an error.   Writing to Carlyle some days after receiving it,
Miss Welsh says : " I had two sheets from Mrs. Montagu the
other day, trying to prove to me that I knew nothing at all of
my own heart.   Mercy, how romantic she is ! "   In a later
letter (undated, but post-marked 20th July), Mrs. Montagu
urged her not to conceal from Carlyle the feeling she had
once had for Irving, and this letter Miss Welsh instantly sent
him, accompanying it with the declaration that she had " once
passionately loved Irving," and that she had no excuse, " none
at least that would bear a moment's scrutiny," for having con-
cealed the truth.   " Woe to me then, if your reason be my
judge and not your love !"   " Never were you so dear as at
this moment when I am in danger of losing your affection, or
what is still more precious to me, your respect."   In his
abstract of this letter Mr. Froude inserts the following sentence as if it represented words of Miss Welsh's, but there is
nothing like it in what she wrote, " She who had felt herself
Carlyle's superior in their late controversy, and had been able
to rebuke him for selfishness, felt herself degraded and humbled
in his eyes."   By " their late controversy " Mr. Froude probably
intends the letters that had passed between them in the preceding winter in regard to their relations to each other, but if
so, and there seems to be nothing else to which he can refer,
these letters do not deserve the term, and there is nothing in
them to justify the statement that Miss Welsh " had been able
to rebuke Carlyle for selfishness."   Carlyle's reply was the
natural one : " You exaggerate this matter greatly."   " Let it
go to strengthen the schoolings of Experience."   " You ask
me to *forgive* you."   " Forgiveness ?   Where is the living
man that dare look steadfastly into his ' painted sepulchre '
of a heart, and say, ' I have lived one year without committing
fifty faults of a deeper dye than this ' ? "   But he would imitate
her sincerity and say to her that she did not know him, that
she could not save him, that she must not let her love for him
deceive her.   " Come and see and determine.   Let me hear

you, and do you hear me. As I am, take me or refuse me : but not as I am *not*, for *this* will not and cannot come to good. God help us both, and show us both the way we ought to walk in."

Mr. Froude's remark, after giving an abstract of a part of this letter, is, "It was not in nature—it was not at least in Miss Welsh's nature—that at such a time and under such circumstances she should reconsider her resolution" (i. 308). Before she had received Carlyle's reply to her contrite confession she had written again to him, "You may be no longer mine, but I will be yours in life, in death, through all eternity." It was not necessary, she said, for her "to come and see and determine ;" but she came, and after her visit at Hoddam Hill she wrote : "When shall I be so happy again as I have been in these last weeks ? " "Alas, alas, the Sabbath weeks are past and gone !" "I am yours, oh that you knew how wholly yours."

In speaking of Miss Welsh's feelings for Carlyle at an earlier period of their acquaintance, Mr. Froude says : " It amused her to see the most remarkable person that she had ever met with at her feet. His birth and position seemed to secure her against the possibility of any closer connection between them" (i. 181). The letters of Miss Welsh, which are, of course, the only source of direct information concerning her feelings toward Carlyle, afford no ground for a statement so disparaging to her sense and character as that "she was amused at seeing him at her feet." Her letters from the beginning of their correspondence are like her letters in later life, full of unique charm from their freedom, humour, and originality. She had one of the rarest of epistolary gifts, that of genuine and graceful liveliness. Her letters are instinct with her life, are the easy expressions of her moods and tempers. She does not spare Carlyle in them, she shows him her ill-humour as well as her good, but she does not wantonly trifle with him, and in the lightest of them is a quality of regard for him that indicates her admiration and respect. But few of her letters during the first eighteen months of their acquaintance remain, and among these few is a note repressing "those importunities of which I have so often had cause to complain ;" but in May 1823 she signs herself, "Your affectionate friend at all times and everywhere ;" and two months later she writes, "It is a pity there is no other language of gratitude than what is in everybody's mouth. I am sure the gratitude I feel towards you is not in everybody's heart." Again, a month later, on the 19th of August, in a letter written at Templand, her grandfather's house, but emphatically dated from *Hell*, she says, "I owe you much; feelings and sentiments that ennoble my character, that give dignity, interest, and enjoyment to my life—in return I can only love you, and *that* I do from the bottom of my heart."

Of Miss Welsh's feeling as shown in this letter, Mr. Froude, not citing its words, says, "she expressed a gratitude for Carlyle's affection for her more warm than she had ever expressed before. He believed her serious, and supposed that she had promised to be his wife. She hastened to tell him, as explicitly as she could, that he had entirely mistaken her" (i. 181, 182). Miss Welsh's words surely express something more than gratitude, and Carlyle was surely not wrong to believe her serious, if mistaken in supposing she had promised to be his wife. In what sense he so supposed appears from his reply, on 31st August, which Mr. Froude does not quote. "I often ask myself," Carlyle wrote, "'Is not all this a dream? No, thank God, it is not a dream. . . . She shall yet be mine as I am hers.' . . . In more reasonable moments, I perceive that I am very selfish and almost mad. Alas! my fate is dreary and obscure and perilous: is it fit that you whom I honour as among the fairest of God's works, whom I love more dearly than my own soul, should partake in it? No, my own best of maidens, I will not deceive you. Think of me as one that will live and die to do you service; whose good-will, if his good deeds cannot, may perhaps deserve some gratitude, but whom it is dangerous and useless to love."

Mr. Froude cites imperfectly (i. 182) a passage from Miss Welsh's answer, 16th September, in which she says that Carlyle must not mistake her, that she loves him, but will never be his wife. And citing, imperfectly also, a passage from Carlyle's reply, 18th September, Mr. Froude declares he "took his rebuke manfully." It would have been well to cite a sentence or two more, which indicate that Carlyle at least did not feel that he had received a rebuke. "I honour your wisdom and decision: you have put our concerns *on the very footing where I wished them to stand.*" The italics are his own. "Thus, then," he adds, "it stands: you love me as a sister, and will not wed; I love you in all possible senses of the word, and will not wed any more than you. Does this reassure you?"

They neither of them recognised whither such feelings as they cherished toward one another must inevitably bring them, if the fates did not interfere. In her very next letter Miss Welsh wrote, " My happiness is incomplete while you do not share it." " Stripped of the veil of poetry which your imagination spreads around me, I am so undeserving of your love ! But I *shall* deserve it—*shall* be a noble woman if efforts of mine can make me so."

The nineteenth chapter of the first volume of Mr. Froude's *Life* is in great part occupied with an account of various projects considered by Carlyle and Miss Welsh, after their engagement, in regard to a place of residence, and other necessary arrangements preliminary to marriage. Mr. Froude paints Carlyle as throughout selfish, and inconsiderate of the interests of Miss Welsh and her Mother. But the letters which he prints complete or in part,[1] as well as those which he does not print, do not seem to me to support this view. " However deeply," he says, " she honoured her chosen husband, she could not hide from herself that he was selfish,—extremely selfish " (p. 337). This charge Miss Welsh may be allowed to deny for herself. " I think you nothing but what is noble and wise." " At the bottom of my heart, far from censuring, I approve of your whole conduct " (4th March 1826). " It is now five years since we first met,—five blessed years ! During that period my opinion of you has never *wavered*, but gone on deliberately rising to a higher and higher degree of *regard* " (28th June 1826).

The apparent disposition to represent in an unpleasant light the character and conduct of Carlyle, as well as of Miss Welsh and her Mother, which marks Mr. Froude's narrative, is displayed in many minor disparaging statements, so made as to avoid arousing suspicion of their having little or no foundation, and arranged so as to contribute artfully to the general effect of depreciation. A single instance will suffice for illustration. On p. 337 Mr. Froude says, " For her daughter's sake she [Mrs. Welsh] was willing to make an effort to like him, and, since the marriage was to be, either to live with him, or to accept him as her son-in-law in her own house and in her own circle. . . . Mrs. Welsh had a large acquaintance. He liked none of them, and 'her visitors would neither be diminished in numbers, nor bettered in quality.' No ! he must have the small house in Edinburgh ;

---

[1] These letters as printed by Mr. Froude abound in errors and in unmarked omissions of words, clauses, and sentences, by which their tone is sometimes greatly altered. Almost every letter in the Life which I have collated with the original is incorrectly printed, some of them grossly so.

and 'the moment he was master of a house the first use he would turn it to would be to slam the door against nauseous intruders.'" The fact is that no such plan as would appear from Mr. Froude's statement was in question. The plan was, as Miss Welsh sets it forth in a letter of 1st February 1826, that Carlyle was to hire a little house in Edinburgh, "and next November we are to—hire one within some dozen yards of it !! so that we may all live together like one family until such time as we are married, and after. I had infinite trouble in bringing my mother to give ear to this magnificent project. She was clear for giving up fortune, house-gear, everything to you and I [*sic*], and going to live with my poor old grandfather at Templand. . . . But how do you relish my plan? Should you not like to have such agreeable neighbours? We would walk together every day, and you would come and take tea with us at night. To me it seems as if the Kingdom of Heaven were at hand." To this Carlyle replied, 9th February, "What a bright project you have formed! Matured in a single night, like Jack's Bean in the Nursery Tale, and with houses in it too. Ah Jane, Jane! I fear it will never answer half so well in practice as [it] does on paper. It is impossible for two households to live as if they were one ; doubly impossible (if there were degrees of impossibility) in the present circumstances. I shall never get any enjoyment of your company till you are all my own. How often have you seen me with pleasure in the presence of others? How often with positive dissatisfaction? For your own sake I should rejoice to learn that you were settled in Edinburgh ; a scene much fitter for you than your present one : but I had rather that it were with *me* than with any other. Are you sure that the number of *parties* and formal visitors would be diminished in number or bettered in quality, according to the present scheme?" [This refers to Miss Welsh's frequent complaint on this score. In one of her last letters, 8th December 1825, she had spoken of recent visitors at Haddington, and declared, "This has been a more terrible infliction than anything that befell our friend Job." Carlyle goes on] "My very heart also sickens at these things: the moment I am master of a house the first use I turn it to will be to slam the door of it on the face of nauseous intrusions [not 'intruders,' as Mr. Froude prints] of all sorts which it can exclude."

On p. 342 Mr. Froude says, "When it had been proposed that he should live with Mrs. Welsh at Haddington, he would by consenting have spared the separation of a mother from an only child, and would not perhaps have hurt his own intellect by an effort of self-denial."

No proposal to live with Mrs. Welsh at Haddington was ever made. In a letter of 16th March 1826, a part of which, including the following sentences, is printed by Mr. Froude himself (p. 343), Miss Welsh says, " My mother, like myself, has ceased to feel any contentment in this pitiful [not ' hateful,' as printed] Haddington, and is bent on disposing of our house here as soon as may be, and hiring one elsewhere. Why should it not be in the vicinity of Edinburgh after all ? and why should not you live with your wife in her [not ' your,' as printed] mother's house ?"

There is no foundation whatever for the statements (p. 336) that " all difficulties might be got over . . . if the family could be kept together," and that " this arrangement occurred to every one who was interested in the Welshes' welfare as the most obviously desirable." Mrs. Welsh's " consent to take Carlyle into the family . . . made Miss Welsh perfectly happy." Mrs. Welsh's consent does not appear to have ever been asked, much less to have been given to any such arrangement. In a part of Miss Welsh's letter of 16th March, not quoted by Mr. Froude, she says, " I will propose the thing to my Mother," that is, the project that they should all live together, in case Carlyle should approve it. He wisely did not approve it. Mr. Froude's account of the whole matter is a tissue of confusion and misrepresentation.

One more example of Mr. Froude's method, and I have done. The following passage is from p. 358. It refers to arrangements for the journey to Edinburgh after the wedding. " Carlyle, thrifty always, considered it might be expedient to ' take seats in the coach from Dumfries.' The coach would be safer than a carriage, more certain of arriving, etc. So nervous was he, too, that he wished his brother John to accompany them on their journey—at least part of the way."

What foundation this insinuation of mean and tasteless thrift on Carlyle's part, and of silly nervousness, possesses, may be seen from the following extracts from a letter of Carlyle's of 19th September. " One other most humble care is whether we can calculate on getting post horses and chaises all the way to Edinburgh without danger of let, or [if] it would not be better to take seats in the coach for some part of it ? In this matter I suppose you can give me no light : perhaps your mother might. At all events tell me your *taste* in the business, for the coach *is* sure if the other is not." . . . " John and I will come up to Glendinning's Inn the night before ; he may ride with us the first stage if you like ; then come back with the chaise, and return home on the back of Larry, richer by one *sister* (in relations) than he ever was. Poor Jack !"

Such is the treatment that the most sacred parts of the lives of Carlyle and his wife receive at the hands of his trusted biographer ! There is no need, I believe, to speak of it in the terms it deserves.

The lives of Carlyle and his wife are not represented as they were, in this book of Mr. Froude's. There was much that was sorrowful in their experience ; much that was sad in their relations to each other. Their mutual love did not make them happy, did not supply them with the self-control required for happiness. Their faults often prevailed against their love, and yet " with a thousand faults they were both," as Carlyle said to Miss Welsh (25th May 1823), "true-hearted people." And through all the dark vicissitudes of life love did not desert them. Blame each of them as one may for carelessness, hardness, bitterness, in the course of the years, one reads their lives wholly wrong unless he read in them that the love that had united them was beyond the power of fate and fault to ruin utterly, that more permanent than aught else it abided in the heart of each, and that in what they were to each other it remained the unalterable element.

THE END

Printed by R. & R. Clark, *Edinburgh.*